Christmas Joy

Christmas Joy

Nancy Naigle

St. Martin's Paperbacks

This is a work of fiction. All of the characters, organizations, and events portrayed in this novel are either products of the author's imagination or are used fictitiously.

CHRISTMAS JOY

Copyright © 2016 by Nancy Lee Naigle.
Excerpt from *Hope at Christmas* copyright © 2018 by Nancy Lee Naigle.

For information address St. Martin's Press, 175 Fifth Avenue, New York, NY 10010.

Library of Congress Catalog Card Number: 2016020659

ISBN: 978-1-250-19020-8

Our books may be purchased in bulk for promotional, educational, or business use. Please contact your local bookseller or the Macmillan Corporate and Premium Sales Department at 1-800-221-7945, ext. 5442, or by e-mail at MacmillanSpecialMarkets@macmillan.com.

Printed in the United States of America

St. Martin's Griffin edition / October 2016
St. Martin's Paperbacks edition / October 2018

St. Martin's Paperbacks are published by St. Martin's Press, 175 Fifth Avenue, New York, NY 10010.

10 9 8 7 6 5 4 3 2 1

To my mom for being the best role model, consistently instilling the priorities and values of what is truly important about Christmas—not the gifts and toys. Thanks, Mom, for the years of family gatherings, handmade gifts, traditions, and doing for others to refill the well during this season of joy, hope, and love.

Merry Christmas.

Acknowledgments

Hugs and high fives to the incredible team of people that helped bring this Christmas story to life: My agent, Kevan Lyon, for believing in me and opening doors faster than a team of SWAT guys with a battering ram, only in a lady-like way. My editor, Eileen Rothschild, for her ideas and partnership, because let's be real . . . two girls who love romance and happy endings as much as the two of us can't be beat. And to the whole marketing and publicity team at St. Martin's Press . . . thank you for the beautiful cover, and the innovation and creative efforts to help bring *Christmas Joy* to the masses.

Thank you to Daniel's Tree Farm in Dunn, NC, for the lovely inspiration their farm brought to this story. There's nothing like a family business to make things extra special. Goats help, too.

And to those who helped me daily behind the scenes: Mom, *aka Miss Bettie to my friends;* Pam Murray; Stephanie Brittain; Kelsey Browning; Tracy Mastaler; Dad and Greta and my best dog, Dakota—thanks for the beta reads, the cheerleading, the sounding board, boosting me up when things went sideways, snuggles, giggles, and celebrations. Writing this novel would not have been nearly as satisfying without your help and fellowship.

**AND TO ALL OF YOU READING
THIS—THANK YOU!**

Chapter One

How could two pint-sized kids whip my well-controlled focus group into a frenzy in a matter of mere seconds?

"Let's all be quiet and settle down." Joy Holbrook kept her voice steady, but her stomach was knotted. She felt more like a teacher than a market research executive this morning. And the fact that MacDonald-Webber gave every job a cutesy name didn't help. Her executive position over "all things Christmas" had been tagged Red Suit Blitzen Bunch Lead. She was darned if she'd ever put that on her résumé, but despite the ridiculous title, this job was a step up from and a pay increase over her position at the stuffy old-school competitor she used to work for.

Silly title aside, life always came down to trade-offs, and this session was beginning to rank near the top of the list of challenging ones. Hopefully her last trade-off if she landed that promotion to Director of Focus Groups. The misbehaving little girl did a pirouette and tapped her chubby hand on one of the other children's heads as if she were playing a *Swan Lake* version of Duck, Duck, Goose. Her brother swiped a candy bar off the table, then raced around the room so fast that his sneakers squeaked against the floor.

"Now," Joy said, leveling her gaze on the two towheaded terrors. "Please. Take a seat." If the Weather Channel was looking for tropical storm names, Joy had two to recommend.

Lola and Richard.

Otherwise known as the boss's kids.

Lola rolled her eyes as her brother skidded across the floor and into one of the chairs with a *thunk*. She hesitated, but finally followed Richard's lead and sat down in a huff.

Joy's insides vibrated as if a thousand angry bees had taken up residence within her. She was running important focus groups, not the corporate babysitting service.

How could Margie do this to me again? Breathe. Smile. Just a few more questions and we're done. Joy powered through the final points, not allowing a single second's pause for the children to deviate from the plan. With one last count of raised hands, she was done.

"You did great!" She applauded the children and they joined in, smiling. "Thank you for sharing with me today." Joy lifted the top from a silver foil-wrapped box that had served as the centerpiece on the table, revealing a cache of candy bars. Squeals of delight filled the room as most of the kids reached into the box. No surprise, Richard grabbed another candy bar in each hand and even stuffed one into his pocket.

"My mom says candy bars make you fat," said a tiny redheaded girl.

Of all the kids at the table, she looked like she needed a candy bar the most. The little girl with the strawberry curls that tumbled wildly across her forehead, much like Joy's, had been the best-behaved child in the group. "Maybe your daddy would like one," Joy whispered quietly.

The little girl's bright blue eyes danced. "Thank you!" She pressed her finger to her lips, carefully deciding which one to select.

Most of the children had already unwrapped and begun to chomp on their treats.

Joy transferred the last data to her moderator's guide, then signaled for Renee to herd the little ones back out to their parents.

"You can come with me now," Renee said from the doorway. Chairs slid across the tile floor, sounding like an out-of-tune tuba followed by the crinkling of candy bar wrappers as the kids scampered toward the door on a sugar high.

Renee tipped her head toward Lola and Richard. "Sorry," she mouthed to Joy as she led the kids out of the room.

Joy shook her head. Poor Renee. Her chestnut hair, usually hanging long down her back, had been pulled into a knot with her pencil stuck through it—a sign that Renee was stressed, and, boy, did Joy know how that felt.

Joy's jaw ached from clenching her teeth so tightly. She stacked her things, trying not to lose her composure in front of whoever might be lingering in the observation room, where her team had been collecting data from the session. Her reflection in the two-way glass revealed a composed professional woman wearing a suit and heels, but underneath that guise, she felt ready to put a blitz on her own boss for another near mishap that had almost ruined her research. Was Margie that clueless, or was she out to sabotage her? Joy was really beginning to wonder.

A few moments later, Renee rushed back into the room. "I tried to tell Margie that we'd already checked everyone in. She just wouldn't take no for an answer." She spoke in a hushed whisper, glancing toward the mirrored wall, then grabbed a roll of paper towels and a spray bottle from a cabinet next to the table. "When I didn't get out of my chair, she just took them into the focus group herself!"

Testing holiday packaging for the nation's leading candy

manufacturer, and one of MacDonald-Webber's biggest
clients, was usually a quick process, but Joy's team had run
into a few challenges. Not because there was a problem
with the packaging. This time it was more of an *internal*
problem. A Margie problem.

"It's not your fault." Joy turned her back to the mirrored
glass. "I know how pushy Margie can be. And her kids are
out of control. I'm just not used to that. It's days like this
that make me thank goodness I never had children." She
grimaced at how harshly that had come out. "No offense."

"None taken. My girls would never carry on like that.
In public, anyway." Renee laughed. "All kids get a little
wild now and then, but even at their worst, they are the
best thing in life."

"I'm going to have to just take your word for that," Joy
said, because after the past year of leading all the market
research analytics completed by the Red Suit Blitzen
Bunch for the under-twelve demographic, parenting wasn't
something she could see herself signing up for.

Renee blasted a stream of cleaner across the surface of
the chocolate-smudged table.

The smell of bleach replaced the sugary scent in the air.
Joy pulled an arm's length of paper towels off the roll. With
all the vigor of a gambler with a scratch-off ticket, Joy
scrubbed away the last remains of the rough morning.

"At least it's done. Come on. Let's get out of here." Joy
picked up her paperwork from the session and headed out
the door with Renee right behind her.

Joy held her temper until she and Renee got into the
elevator and the doors slid shut. "Margie has got some
nerve." Joy hugged her paperwork to her chest. "If she hadn't
done the same thing last week, we'd already have been finished. What is wrong with her?"

"She's clueless. Rumor has it she's the sister-in-law of

one of the Webbers," Renee said, leaning against the wall of the elevator.

At least that would make sense. "I tried to politely explain that she was compromising the research the last time this happened. She either doesn't understand, or doesn't care. I'm not sure which is worse."

Joy wouldn't vent like this to just anyone, but she and Renee had become close over the past year. "We've finally got all the demographics covered for this test now. We'll deliver on time and on budget, despite Margie's interference."

"I was so worried her brats were going to ruin it."

Joy had been too. "We deserve a long lunch after that. Let's make it an early one. What do you say?"

"I'm so in." Renee tugged the pencil from her hair and let out a sigh.

The elevator doors opened on the eleventh floor. From here you could see the heart of D.C. MacDonald-Webber held office and meeting space on three floors of this building in the business district of the capital city. When Joy left Sonic Group in beautiful Northern Virginia to come to MacDonald-Webber, giving up her office with the view had been the hardest part.

Renee followed Joy through the maze of tall-walled cubes.

Joy placed her paperwork on the desk in her cubicle. The Christmas shopping list she'd started just yesterday during the back-to-back conference calls was covered in red and green Christmas doodles. She ripped the list from the notepad and showed it to Renee.

"At least my holiday list looks festive, even if I don't feel that way," Joy said. "We're down to just weeks before Christmas, and I haven't even begun to shop."

"An occupational hazard," Renee said. "A person can look at wrapped presents, new holiday products, and Santas dressed in every color of the rainbow for only so long and stay in the spirit."

Joy tucked the list in her purse. Her spirit had definitely dwindled. "I've been focused on this red and green holiday for the sake of market research for nearly sixteen months straight." She dropped into her chair, trying to push aside the aftermath of Lola and Richard's surprise appearance. "About six months too long to stay sane," she responded with a sigh. "We'd better change the subject."

"Fair enough. A friend of mine just took a job over at Sonic Group. Isn't that where you used to work?"

"Yes. For five years." Joy still missed her office with the view of lush, green Northern Virginia.

"She loves it there. Their offices sound amazing," Renee said with a lift of her brow.

"True, but they don't get the high-visibility work we get here. It's a trade-off." *Hopefully a good one.* Joy had nailed the interviews for the new director position at MacDonald-Webber. She envisioned a big red bow on the door of the vacant office across the way—the one with the street view and access to the private outdoor terrace. She could totally see it. . . .

JOY HOLBROOK
Director of Focus Groups

Her name in block print letters on the frosted glass door. And the best part—her calendar filled with a nice balance of campaigns to manage, not just holiday-focused assignments, and she could get that stupid "Red Suit Blitzen Bunch" off her business cards. *That would make for a Merry Christmas, indeed.*

"Guess we have to take the good with the bad. Walls

would be nice, though," Renee said, leaning on the edge of Joy's desk.

"Knock, knock." Margie Stokes's voice was a little too loud under regular circumstances, but for some reason when she did that singsongy "knock, knock," it made Joy grind her teeth.

Joy and Renee exchanged a subtle knowing glance.

"What brings you by?" Joy forced a smile, camouflaging her anger until she could find a polite way to address the sore subject of Margie dropping off her kids in Joy's focus group *again*.

"That little focus group this morning was over in a jiffy. Richard and Lola had so much fun. Didn't it work out perfectly that I happened to have them here with me?"

No time like the present. "Well, actually, Margie, we'd already recruited for that session. It was a bit of a problem."

There was a momentary flash of annoyance in Margie's expression. "What's a couple extra opinions? It's fine."

Joy held her tongue. If she let loose now, it wouldn't be good for anyone. Maybe the best part about the possible promotion wasn't the office with the view after all, but that she wouldn't report to Margie any longer.

Margie tugged on her bright pink suit jacket. The Chanel-like chains and pearls embellishing the pockets might look cute on a twentysomething girl, but on middle-aged Margie, they came across as a failed attempt to keep up with the younger crowd.

Margie fanned out a handful of glossy red and green tickets. "I knew you wouldn't want to miss out on Richard and Lola's Christmas pageant the week after next. I saved you the best tickets in the house—right next to me."

Margie was nearly sharkish about her approach to these things. Swimming in quietly. Cornering her prey. And with the seats right next to her, you couldn't even not show up. All she lacked was the ominous musical accompaniment.

Renee's lips pulled into a tight line. "I'm going to go get those reports."

"But don't you want—?" Margie spun and wedged herself between Renee and the opening to the cubicle.

"Oh no. I've got a family commitment. This time of year is so busy," Renee said, squeezing between Margie and the cubicle wall. "I'll check back later, Joy."

And there Joy sat. Captive.

"My Lola is the lead." Margie waved the tickets around like they'd grant admission to the National Symphony Orchestra at the Kennedy Center. But they were for her kids' Christmas pageant, and Joy wasn't interested. She'd seen enough of Margie's wicked little wackadoodles this morning to last her a year.

"You must be so proud." Visions of Richard with chocolate smeared across his cheeks like a sugar-crazed Rambo flashed in Joy's mind.

Margie rattled on. "I had to practically force that new teacher to cast Lola in the lead. For heaven's sake, that woman was going to put her in the role of a tree. Can you imagine? My Lola. Standing there wrapped in burlap like a wooden trunk, holding felt leaves. No, ma'am." She rolled her eyes and blew out a breath that had her hair-sprayed-stiff bangs flying up, then settling all catawampus.

Margie's irritating eye roll—similar to Lola's—stabbed at Joy's sanity.

"There's so much going on—"

Margie narrowed her eyes. "It's a fund-raiser." Her words were clipped, almost curt; then Margie plastered a too-white smile on her face. "'Tis the season, and all that. I'll put you down to buy two. They're only a hundred apiece. I knew I could count on you."

Lucky me. "Great." Joy regretted ever pretending to be impressed by Margie's kids to establish common ground with her boss. It wasn't that Joy disliked children, but she was an only child herself and she'd known little to nothing about the under-twelve demographic before getting the dreaded Red Suit Blitzen Bunch assignment. Mom had always said that lies never paid off, and, boy, did Margie's Richard and Lola plucking Joy's every last nerve prove Mom right.

Margie counted out two tickets, but just before handing them over, she snapped her fingers. "I almost forgot. I need you to cover my meeting at Wetherton's this afternoon."

Joy's throat went dry. "*At* Wetherton's? The executive offices?" She'd led the Santa @ W event last year and had been invited to only one meeting at the flagship store. This was a big deal—her chance to really shine in front of MacDonald-Webber's biggest client. Hope filled her hammering heart.

"Yes. Just a quick update. Nothing fancy. I can't go. I have to take Lola to rehearsal."

Maybe good karma is making up for the debacle this morning. "Of course, I'll be happy to cover for you. What time?"

"You'll have to get a move on. They wanted me there around one o'clock." She twisted her wrist and checked her watch. "I meant to mention it earlier."

Joy could probably get there in a single bound on the energy coursing through her right now. *Is it possible this is some kind of test before the final decision on the promotion?* "I'm on it. I've got everything right here."

"Great. I knew you could handle it." Margie handed the tickets to Joy.

The purchase of the tickets was a little easier to bear now. "Wouldn't miss it." *Another lie. Wonder what the penance for that one will be?*

Chapter Two

Ben Andrews parked his dark blue 4WD pickup in front of Mars Hardware on Main Street. Snippets of Christmas carols collided in an offbeat but beautiful noise from the neighboring stores as customers opened and closed their doors. From the looks of the hustle and bustle, business was booming in Crystal Falls.

Ben dropped the tailgate of his truck and dragged the scaffold ladder from the bed. He hoisted it over his shoulder, taking the time to check out the front window of Mars Hardware, which had been empty just yesterday.

Jason, the owner of the hardware store, had already been hard at work this morning. A wintry scene showcased a Mr. Snowman made from five-gallon paint buckets with blue spigot handles for eyes, holding the gloved hand of a snow kid who'd been fashioned out of regular paint cans with a red bucket turned upside down as a hat. Mrs. Snowman stood next to a Christmas tree as if decorating it while she watched the boys play nearby in the snowy backdrop. The tree was the same one Jason had created last year—made from hand-tied nuts, bolts, and all kinds of shiny gadgets into twenty-four six-foot lengths of hardware garland swept out to form the shape of a shiny metallic tree. A huge bow made of drywall tape spray-painted Carolina chrome graced the top.

Ben edged closer to the window, trying to figure out what Jason had used to create the snowy substrate beneath the snowman.

Popcorn? Well, not edible popcorn. Ceiling spray texture used to touch up those old popcorn ceilings. Genius. It really does look like snow, and it probably didn't take two bags to fill the whole window. A twenty-buck solution.

It wasn't quite so original as Jason's Halloween display—an array of different types of brooms hung from wire with WITCH BROOM? spelled out in an assortment of nails and tacks hammered into a length of one-by-eight wood—but pretty cool just the same.

The bells on the front door jingled as Ben walked inside.

Jason pushed his long hair behind his ear and gave Ben a chin-nod as he cut a key for an old man in an Elmer Fudd earflap hat. "Hey, bro, be right with you."

"Take your time." Ben headed toward the counter, the ladder clanking against the floor with each step he took. They weren't related, but there'd been a time when the two of them hung out so much that people thought the two tall, dark-haired, blue-eyed guys were brothers.

Ben inhaled the familiar smell of bagged fertilizer left over from the summer. That, mixed with the oily metallic scent from the key-cutting machine and the woodsy, sweet scent of sap of fresh lumber, teased his senses. This hardware store always brought back good memories. He and Jason had racked up hours of hard work there as teens, learning skills that you just didn't get in school.

"Nice job on the window," Ben said.

"Thanks. You done decorating already?" Jason lowered

a pair of clear safety glasses and put the final cuts on the key.

"Hospital? Pretty much. Haven't started at my house, but don't need this scaffold for that." Ben slid the ladder back into the bin from which Jason had removed it yesterday, then meandered over to the counter. Once the customer left with his keys, Ben said, "But that scaffold worked like a charm putting up the tree at the hospital. Thanks, man."

"No problem."

"The girls had a system going, one up on the scaffold stringing lights as the other pushed her around the tree. Saved a ton of time. Then they repeated the process with the bucket of ornaments. Have to admit it looked like they were having fun. I was a little envious."

"Well, putting up Christmas decorations isn't the worst thing you can ask people to do. Has to be better than desk work."

"True. They got the tree done so quickly that we were able to get the live pine roping up too. Thanks for ordering that with your discount. The lobby smells great."

Jason rang up another customer, then leaned on the counter. "No problem. Since I couldn't be there to help this year, I'm glad I could at least give you a hand with supplies. That rolling scaffold was the best twenty bucks I ever spent at an auction."

Friends since junior high, he and Jason had been to more than their fair share of farm and equipment auctions with the older men from Mars Hardware. Once Ben had scratched his head and ended up buying a stack of oak rough-cut lumber. Getting splinters in both hands, and sweating it out in the Carolina humidity, had taught Ben a hard lesson about the art of conduct at an auction.

Unlike Ben's dad, who had crunched numbers his whole

life and wasn't much of an outdoorsman, Jason's dad farmed, and his grandfather owned the hardware store. They'd treated Ben like another son, and taught him every handy skill he had.

"Need any help from me decorating the hospital this weekend?"

Ben shook his head. "Nope. Everything's been delegated. The guys from Fire Station Nine offered to hang the building lights with the new ladder truck. Mom wrangled donations of foil to wrap all the doors in the pediatric wing, and her friends from the Senior Circle are doing that on Monday. And Ashley is handling the judging of the annual Carolina's Best Flour Extreme Gingerbread Bakeoff this year."

"I saw the article in the *Crystal Falls Courier* this morning announcing all the entrants. I bet your mom was glad you weren't judging it this year, so you could help her again."

"Yeah, well, she did win last time I helped."

"No surprise. That extreme gingerbread mansion with Santa and his reindeer flying over those three-story houses was mind-boggling. Never forget when you came in here to buy a new drill and dowels because you were making a cake. I was going to take your man card."

"That was a cool cake. Wait until you see this year's creation. I found an old record player at an estate sale last month. I plan to put that turntable to good use on our part of our entry. On a timer. Top of the hour, every hour. Like feeding time at the zoo."

"You're crazy, but I have no doubt it will be amazing. I'll have to take the kids over to see it and cast my vote for you," Jason said.

"Don't promise your votes until you've seen them all. The theme is 'Country Christmas.' It just might be the best year yet."

Jason shrugged. "I honestly don't know where you find the time."

"Being single doesn't hurt." Jason had his hands full with a wife, and three kids all under the age of six. Then again, having someone to help wouldn't be bad now and then either. When those kids were older, Ben would be the one wishing he had all those handy helpers. "I'm almost afraid to admit it, but my life is going amazingly smooth."

"Don't say that out loud. You'll jinx your good luck and everything will crash and burn."

Ben knocked twice on the solid wood counter, just in case. "I take it back."

"You putting the lights up at your house this weekend?"

"I could use a hand with that. It's a two-person job, that's for sure." Ben's historic three-story home boasted fine trim work that he had spent over two years repairing, even having new pieces recast to match the original. His house had once been known as one of the most palatial homes in three counties. One day she'd shine like that again. Unfortunately, the house had lost most of her charm sitting empty for years, deteriorating.

"It'll take all day to get that many lights up. It's a ton of work to do just for less than a month of dazzling display."

"And bragging rights."

"Well, there is that." Seeing families cruise by all month, knowing the kids had their faces pressed against the car windows in awe, made the effort totally worth it. "I'm not really complaining. You know how much I love Christmas."

"More than anyone I know. If we get an early start, maybe we can get it knocked out tomorrow and then you can help me drywall Ol' Lady Watson's house on Sunday."

"Sure thing." Ben had almost forgotten that the poor

widow had accidentally burned down half her kitchen in a chicken-frying incident last month. She couldn't afford to repair it, so the locals pulled together to raise the money for the supplies. Jason and Ben had offered their labor for free to get her place back in shipshape before Christmas.

"If we start at seven on Sunday, then we can be done before the football game starts. I've got some guys ready to come do the mudding on Monday," Jason said.

"Like you're going to be up at seven on a weekend? Who are you fooling, but the Panthers play the Steelers, so let's put the stuff in my truck while I'm here. That way I can guarantee at least one of us will have an early start."

"You insinuating something?"

"Early to you and early to me are like two different time zones." Ben followed Jason to the back of the store. Jason already had a pushcart full of supplies marked for the Watson project.

"So I'm a night owl. That's why I open the store at nine thirty instead of seven like Gramps used to," Jason said. "I stay open later when more people have time to stop in." He lifted a finger to his temple. "Got to work smarter these days."

"Or you just didn't want to get up early."

"True. Especially when Gramps quit coming in and I couldn't afford to replace him. Seems like every year I have to figure out new ways to do more with less."

"Who are you telling? My staff at the hospital is half what it was last year. I mean, it made sense—administration isn't nearly so important in a hospital in the scheme of things—but it sure hasn't been easy. I thought we could get a lot of the same things done with the help of volunteers, but everybody is stretched everywhere. It's an ongoing challenge."

"At least you found a way to keep the hospital here in

Crystal Falls. The way they were talking there for a while, I was afraid they were going to close it down for good. Driving sixty miles just to get stitches would've been crazy."

"I was worried about that too." Ben still felt the churn from that ordeal. It had been no easy task to find a way to make things work for everyone.

"Then again, if that had happened, you and I could be flipping houses together for a living, and taking three months off a year." Before Jason inherited the hardware store from his grandfather five years earlier, he and Ben had flipped a half dozen houses in their spare time. They'd each made enough profit to purchase homes and renovate them themselves with hardly any mortgage.

Those house-flipping days were over. Dad had been adamant that Ben go away to college, and since he'd inherited Dad's head for numbers, the accounting and business degree was a natural path. He'd been at the right place with the right degree when the accounting position became open at Bridgewater Regional, and he stepped into that job and moved up quickly.

Jason pushed a cart toward the front of the store, one wheel wobbling and clanking like an old freight train.

Ben held the door and then helped Jason unload an air compressor, drills, boxes of drywall screws, a pair of drywall stilts, and other materials into the back of his truck.

Ben climbed into his truck, then pulled away from the curb. In the short time he'd been in the store, the barbershop had wrapped the blue stripe of its spinning barber pole in red and green, and a Christmas tree sparkled with scissors and silver combs hanging from the branches in the front window.

The town's cherry picker was parked on the side of the

street. Two men dressed in hard hats and blaze orange safety vests hung a MERRY CHRISTMAS flag from a lamppost. Giant lighted snowflake sculptures were being strung between every other pole down the street. If snowflakes that big ever fell in Crystal Falls, the town would surely shut down. There wasn't much chance of that today, though, not with it being an unseasonably warm sixty degrees.

Then again, this town had a way of building things up. Even the town name was an exaggeration, the "falls" being no more than slightly unimpressive rapids at the river.

Being the first Thursday in December, it was no surprise to see every merchant in the five-block town square busy decorating for Christmas. It wasn't an official law, but one that everyone abided by. He didn't mind helping enforce it, Christmas being his favorite holiday and all. Ever since the year he'd played one of the Three Wise Men in the church play on Christmas Eve, only to be rewarded with the clear-as-a-bell sound of hooves on the roof. He'd lain there, afraid to open his eyes. Wanting so badly to see Santa himself.

Even right now, he could feel that rush of excitement he'd felt as a boy that night. Lying as still as he could, hoping Santa wouldn't realize he was awake, and his heart pounding so fast and hard that he was certain the jolly old man was going to know.

Years later, Dad had held the ladder as Ben climbed to the roof, clomping a hiking boot just above the gutter to give the kids who lived next door a magical night even though their own father, who was in the military, had been shipped out to a country they'd never heard of.

If there was one thing that could be said for Crystal Falls, it was that the town had a firm grasp on tradition. A local could guess the date by the activities and events going on. Each holiday throughout the year was clearly defined. No overlap. No siree. Halloween wouldn't overlap Thanksgiving, and nary a speck of red and green would appear until those leftovers were pretty well gone on the first of December.

Only once did anyone break that tradition. A new merchant. Two years ago. The locals had quickly schooled him, though. In a nice way, of course, helping him take down the decorations, but also helping him put them up again in December.

Old-fashioned? Maybe. But the traditions were what made Crystal Falls special. There'd never been a doubt in Ben's mind that he'd live and raise his family here in this town someday.

Chapter Three

Joy tossed the tickets to Margie's children's Christmas pageant on her desk. Two hundred was a small price to pay if it helped her land her dream job. Margie notwithstanding, MacDonald-Webber was a great place to work, and Joy loved being responsible for the data that allowed her to follow and forecast marketplace and sales trends.

A tingle of excitement coursed through her as she pulled her things together. She couldn't wait to give that update at Wetherton's this afternoon. It was true those corporate bigwigs couldn't care less about the R-value and other statistics, but, boy, did they love it when she broke down what all that meant into simple English. And that put a smile on her face.

With her attitude readjusted, she focused on her customer. Wetherton's deserved her best, and it would get her best.

With the latest stats from its project plan tucked inside her leather tote along with her laptop, she was ready to leave when Renee poked her head in Joy's cube.

"I see the coast is clear," Renee said.

"No thanks to you," Joy said with a playful glare.

"Ready for that early lunch?" Renee hugged her purse to her side.

"Change of plans."

Renee slumped.

"Just a detour, though. First stop, Wetherton's, to cover a meeting for Margie."

Renee's face lit up. "That's great!"

"I know." Joy patted her briefcase. This kind of last-minute opportunity was exactly why she was so crazy about making sure all the data and analyses were always in ready-to-report shape. "Plus, the alterations are finished on my dress for the gala. I can pick it up while I'm there. The timing really couldn't have been more perfect."

Renee straightened to her full five-seven in flats. "You bought a dress at Wetherton's and didn't tell me?"

Joy almost regretted mentioning it. "I hope the Christmas bonus covers the splurge. It's my present to myself. The meeting shouldn't take long. Then we can do lunch like we'd planned."

"Please tell me we have time to try on dresses while we're there."

Joy stood, always feeling short next to Renee, even in her high heels. "You will have plenty of time while I'm in the meeting."

"Perfect. If only I could afford something from there. Even window-shopping is a treat at Wetherton's. I wouldn't miss this for anything," Renee said.

"Let's go, then," Joy said. "When I'm done with the executives, I'll meet you on the fourth floor."

Joy pulled her red Prius right up to the curb to drop Renee off in front of the grand entrance of Wetherton's. The stately limestone architecture of the eight-story building had taken up the high-traffic corner since the 1940s, and it was still stunning in contrast with the modern buildings in the surrounding area. "I'll meet you as soon as I'm done."

"Seriously, take all the time you want. I'll be in heaven." Renee stepped out of the car and headed inside.

Joy pulled away from the curb and drove around to the east side of the building. Using her temporary parking pass, she swiped it at the gate and then parked near the private elevator to the administrative floors of the building. There were no longer many stand-alone stores of this size, but then Wetherton's wasn't just any store. It advertised and delivered a high-end shopping experience. From the doorman to the elevator assistants and the high-fashion salespeople who greeted every customer by name if they'd ever shopped there before, Wetherton's delivered a one-of-a-kind experience.

Joy took the elevator up, then stepped through the ornate wooden double doors onto the executive floor. The opulent surroundings of Wetherton's flagship store always gave her goose bumps. It was like stepping into another time, and today was beyond important.

Carols filled the air, and a decked-out tree, complete with an angel on top, filled an entire corner of the waiting area. Wetherton's proudly displayed decorations throughout all its stores. No amount of outside pressure had changed its Christmas traditions. *Poppy Wetherton's touch for sure.* Under her leadership, the upscale retailer had become known as the elite place to shop soon after Poppy had taken the reins from her father, the business's founder. She didn't care if she offended anyone with her Christian beliefs or traditions. And somehow her making no apologies seemed to make it more acceptable. Joy admired the fearless businesswoman for her tremendous accomplishments.

Joy rubbed her hands together, trying to expend some nervous energy. She'd made presentations like this hundreds of times, but now she was among the best of the best at Wetherton's. Customer-facing opportunities like this were her chance to shine. She'd worked hard to ensure this project was perfect. Her heart raced just thinking about the possibility of presenting to Poppy Wetherton.

The VP of Marketing met Joy at the front desk and escorted her to the meeting room. He was on the tall side of six feet, and his tan skin, even in December, told of weekends spent doing other things aside from being hunched over a laptop. Probably sailing, or some other luxury pastime.

Joy yearned for the day she'd be in a position that would give her a little more work-life balance, but for now her focus was on her career.

The marketing VP opened and held the door to the conference room for her. They took their seats, and he got right down to business. "Our second annual Santa at W event has been sold out for over a month. Leveraging what we learned from the market research conducted by MacDonald-Webber last year, we are positioned for an even bigger success this year. Joy Holbrook is here to give us an update."

Joy noted the faces of the executives at the table, then sucked in a breath when she made eye contact with the petite woman sitting at the end. *Poppy Wetherton*. "Thank you." Joy ignored her twirling tummy, diving straight into the data points. All those butterflies began to settle as she outlined the next key milestones of the plan. "My team has completed the calls to generate the right representative sample for our post-event focus group."

She glanced toward Poppy Wetherton. Her upswept white hair might look severe on anyone else, but she appeared youthful and vibrant despite her years. No one seemed to know exactly how old Poppy was, and even standing this close to the woman, Joy couldn't guess with any confidence. "Ms. Wetherton's generosity certainly made it easier for us this year. It's a difficult time to recruit, but parents were delighted at the chance to earn the exclusive twenty-percent discount in exchange for their child's participation in the study."

Poppy gave Joy a nod.

Joy paused, not for effect, although it would certainly appear so, but because a nod from Poppy was like an all-out gale of wind in Joy's sails. *This might be the best day of my career.*

Joy continued with the update, making eye contact with each person in the room. *This. This is what I want to be doing, impacting big business and interacting with senior leaders. Not dangling candy bars in front of children.*

"We've refined the questions and we'll be working diligently to keep the focus group session to a maximum of fifteen minutes, start to finish. My experience has been that if it goes any longer than twenty-two minutes, the data becomes a bit unreliable because we start losing the children's attention. We'll get the information you need while making it a fun and exciting session for your customers."

"Maybe we should try keeping our staff meetings to twenty-two minutes," the marketing VP joked.

Polite laughter filled the room.

The executives appeared pleased with the progress report, and those who hadn't been around last year seemed eager to see the event unfold.

Hoping she'd nailed her presentation, Joy shook hands with the team, then headed for the door.

"Joy?" Poppy Wetherton said with a lift of her chin.

"Yes, ma'am." Joy's stomach sank. *Maybe I didn't nail*

it. Why would Poppy call me aside? She ran through a mental checklist, hoping she hadn't forgotten an important detail. "What can I do for you?"

"May I have just a moment with you?"

Joy's hands trembled. "Yes, ma'am." She gripped her tote bag to steady herself. "Of course." She followed Poppy to the edge of the conference room as the others cleared out.

"I've been watching you." Poppy tilted her head slightly. "You did a wonderful job on our Santa at W event last year, and I admire your dedication to this project. I'm very impressed by what you've done for us over the past year. Your ideas and innovation have pushed my team to work even harder. You've exceeded all my expectations to make this year's event even brighter. I like that."

Was there a "but" coming? She held silent for a two-count, but no. *She's impressed!* "Thank you." Joy hoped the words actually came out. She was so overcome by the compliment that she glanced away to be sure she was really still in Wetherton's executive meeting room. *This is really happening.*

Poppy extended a shiny gold envelope with a swirly silver *W* on it. "From me, but don't open it until Christmas." The old woman gave her a mischievous wink.

Joy hesitated, worried about the rigid guidelines that restricted MacDonald-Webber employees from accepting gifts from clients. Even so, she was dying to know what was inside the envelope. "What is—?"

"I know what you're thinking. Don't. It's not business. It's personal. Just say thank you, dear."

"Thank you." If it had been anyone else, Joy would feel obligated to refuse. But this was Poppy Wetherton! And she'd said it was personal. Even making the Christmas-card list of someone like Poppy was a gift in itself.

"Good. Now, you keep infusing energy and ideas into my team." Poppy placed a gentle hand on Joy's arm. "If you ever want a position here at Wetherton's, you come talk to me personally."

Poppy's vote of confidence was better than anything that could possibly be in the pretty envelope Joy had just tucked into her bag. She tried to swallow past the lump in her throat. "You can't begin to imagine how much that means coming from you."

"You remind me of myself about a hundred years ago." Poppy smiled and, without so much as a wobble, walked away in heels higher than Joy's.

Rather than take the elevator, Joy headed for the stairs. For one hot second, she wished she were brave enough to set her butt on the shiny brass railing and slide down with a whoop. She was that exhilarated!

As soon as she stepped out of the stairwell and into the store, the melody of "Silver Bells" filled the air. The Bing Crosby version had always been Mom's favorite. An overwhelming feeling of pride mixed with nostalgia filled Joy.

She blinked back tears as she whisked through the racks of gem-colored gowns to a beautiful off-white desk that appeared to be a turn-of-the-century antique, empty except for the simple tablet register, which took up very little space. A sales associate appeared out of nowhere, as they always seemed to, and said, "How can I help you today?"

"I'm here to try on my dress," Joy said. "The last name is Holbrook."

Without having to check a log or look up anything, the tall, model-like platinum blonde responded, "Yes, ma'am. We have it ready for you to try on. Right this way."

Joy followed her. "Oh, and I'm meeting a colleague. Her name is Renee. If she comes looking for me, would you let her know how to find me?"

"She's actually in the Cameo Dressing Room now, trying on some dresses."

The sales associate led Joy through the spacious salon area furnished with upholstered couches with white-on-white swirly Wetherton *W*s woven into the fabric, flanked by silver side tables. Champagne buckets were placed like sculptures throughout the room.

"Champagne?" the associate offered.

Joy almost declined. It was barely afternoon after all, but this was a good day to celebrate, so she answered with a simple "Thank you."

With a crystal flute of champagne in hand, Joy was led to the Fleur-de-Lis Dressing Room, where her gown hung from a dazzling hanger that looked as if it were studded with Swarovski crystals. Her heart fluttered just as it had the day she'd spotted the dress for the first time. She'd been killing time before a meeting, wandering through Wetherton's with no intention of buying a thing, when she'd laid eyes on the emerald green dress. The color was rich, the lines elegant and simple. And seeing it again today, she had that same awestruck feeling, like this was the most beautiful dress she'd ever seen.

Joy stepped out of her heels, then her deep teal blue pantsuit, and draped the slacks over a padded hanger. She scratched her manicured nail over a smudge on the hip of her pants. "Chocolate?" She stepped to the mirror. Thank goodness there wasn't anything on her face. *How many people in that meeting noticed I had something on my slacks?*

Even if they had, it didn't stop the most important person in the room from complimenting her. A flurry of excitement zipped through her again as Poppy's words replayed in her head. Turning her back on the pants, she marveled at the dress hanging there.

Joy reached for the exquisite fabric. The airy fabric slipped between her fingers, light as snow. And the translucent beading shimmered under the dressing room's bright lights. It wasn't often that she splurged on something so frivolous, but she hadn't been able to resist this dress. The shoes she'd purchased were placed neatly on the floor beneath the gown—barely there strappy sandals that looked as if they'd been made to match her dress. They were as comfortable as they were expensive, and that was *very*.

Joy stepped gingerly into the dress, then pulled up the zipper. Her heart danced as she gazed at herself in the mirror. The dress's simple neckline didn't reveal a thing, but was still alluring in a sophisticated way.

A light tap sounded at the door. "How are we doing in there?"

"You can come in."

The sales associate walked in and helped Joy zip the back. "Beautiful. The color accents your green eyes. Not just anyone can pull off that color green." She linked the tiny hook at the top of the zipper for Joy, then tugged in a few places. "It hangs nicely. What do you think?"

Joy smoothed her fingers along the fabric. She'd been worried that too many junk food lunches on the run might have compromised the fitting she'd had two weeks ago. "Even prettier than I remembered."

She turned and looked at her reflection in the wall of angled mirrors. "I love the way the top is embellished like fine jewelry." She lifted the skirt, liking the way it fell ever-so-softly. "But the rest is so simple."

The saleswoman stepped out of the dressing room and motioned to Joy. "Come on out here."

Joy stepped out into the main salon. Renee stood on a platform in the center of the room in a short, shimmery black dress that showed off her never-ending legs.

Renee's expression in the mirror made Joy blush.

"You look breathtaking," Renee said, then turned and faced her. "I think I need to go back and find something more like that." She stepped down from the platform, looking a little deflated. "You look beautiful and smart and capable, and you even look sexy with just about every inch of you covered."

"Don't be silly, that dress is great on you," said Joy. "You look amazing. I could never pull it off."

"We have different styles, but your dress is perfect for the gala. I'm so glad you get to go this year."

Joy couldn't wait to attend the MacDonald-Webber holiday gala, to which old, new, and prospective clients were invited. The event had such a reputation that it was often the differentiator that had caused some of the company's most impressive accounts to choose MacDonald-Webber over the competition.

"I set the research schedule this year, and I made sure it didn't conflict with the gala," Joy said. "Last year, while everyone else was enjoying a swanky evening rubbing elbows with clients and celebrating, I was gathering data from dozens of sugar-buzzed children while they waited for Santa. Talk about a bum deal."

"I remember." Renee shook her head. "I was so glad my job with you didn't start until the next week. If I'd had to miss the gala, I would have been crushed. It's one of the best perks of working there."

Joy lightly twisted a loose tendril of hair that had fallen across her shoulder. Renee's choice of a short, flirty number made Joy feel almost overdressed. "You don't think this dress is too fancy for the gala, do you?"

"No. It's elegant and feminine," Renee said. "It's absolutely you."

Joy barely recognized herself in the mirror. "The bodice reminds me of my favorite Christmas ornament when I was a kid." *That's what drew me to this dress in the first place.* "A delicate, sphere-shaped glass ornament with finely etched details that seemed to change color from every angle—from turquoise to deep emerald green." The fabric felt smooth against her skin. "Just like this."

"That sounds pretty," Renee said. "We always had a theme tree. One color. Lots of ribbons, and I wasn't allowed to help. Christmas was just one more business party for my mother."

"I can't imagine not getting to help with the tree. When I was a kid, it was almost as fun as Christmas morning. I'm sure your Christmas tree was picture-perfect, though."

"Like in-a-magazine perfect in that living room look-don't-touch kind of way. Trust me. It was no fun."

"Our tree was probably a hot mess in comparison, but we loved decorating it together. Mom loved the holidays." Joy's throat felt dry. She missed her mom more than anything. "Picking the right spot for that special ornament on the Christmas tree with her is one of my favorite memories." Joy wasn't sure what had happened to all the boxes of family decorations after her mom died, but it didn't really matter. She hadn't bothered to have a tree since then. Christmas just wasn't the same without Mom.

The sales associate poured more champagne for Joy and Renee.

"Are you bringing Todd to the gala?" Renee asked.

"Todd?" Joy was surprised to hear his name. "No, he's pretty much in the ex category these days."

"I hadn't heard you mention him in a while, but I didn't know it was over between you two. Sorry."

"No, it's okay. That relationship never really went anywhere. He's more into his work than I am. Who knew that was possible?" But she'd be lying if she didn't admit that she still missed having him around for those late-night ten-minute chats. Feeling connected to someone—heck, anyone—meant more to her than she'd realized. But if Joy wanted to meet her thirty-year goals by her next birthday, her job had to be her top priority. "Hard to be over, when it never really got started."

"He never really seemed like your type anyway. He always seemed just a little too slick to me." Renee finished her glass of champagne.

"Why didn't you say anything?"

"I would've if I ever thought you might get serious about him, but I figured you saw him for what he was. Anyway, that's not important now. Tell me! How'd the meeting go?"

"Amazing."

"I knew it would, and when you get that promotion to director, Margie won't be able to drop her kids off on you anymore." Renee cut her eyes. "And when you're choosing your new team, please think of me being stuck with that crazy woman." Renee pressed her hands together. "You wouldn't do that to me, would you?"

"You mean like how you left me earlier today when Margie was shoving tickets to her kids' Christmas pageant down my throat?"

Renee raised her hand to her mouth. "I did leave you hanging, didn't I? I had to. There was no way I was letting her guilt me into buying tickets. Besides, I'm not as nice as you. I'd have ended up fired for sassing her about that mess with her kids."

"Cost me two hundred dollars," Joy said.

"You'll make more than that with the raise that comes with the promotion."

"That promotion is not mine yet."

"Everyone says you're the best candidate. I think the interview was just a formality." Renee placed her empty glass on a nearby side table.

"I hope you're right. My fingers are crossed. Well, I better change out of this so we can get back to work. Now's not the time to look like I'm slacking off." Joy headed to the Fleur-de-Lis Dressing Room to change.

Back in their business attire, Renee stood looking through a display of holiday scarves while Joy settled her alterations bill.

Joy's phone rang. She glanced at the unfamiliar number and quickly silenced the incoming call as she signed the receipt. Just as Joy took the clear plastic dress bag from the sales associate, that musical tone letting her know someone was calling sounded again. "Someone is being persistent. I better take this. Thank you for your help."

"You're welcome, Ms. Holbrook."

Joy answered the call.

"Joy, honey, it's your aunt Ruby's friend. Shirley."

Her mind spun as she imagined a hundred dreadful situations. "Yes. Is everything okay?" Joy hugged the dress.

"Ruby took a fall and broke her foot. Her ankle—well, I'm not sure what all, but it didn't sound good. They just took your aunt into surgery. I thought I better call and let you know." Shirley's words were rushed and hushed. Joy could picture her in the hospital waiting room.

As the news sank in, Joy's body felt weak. She walked over to an upholstered bench and sat down.

"Is everything okay?" Renee whispered, looking concerned.

Joy held up a finger. "Do they know how she fell? Was it an accident or did something else cause her to lose her balance?"

"I'm not sure. Ruby was fussy and kind of out of it. I'm

not entirely sure what happened or how long she'd been lying out there hurt when I found her. She told me not to bother you, but—"

Shaking her head, Joy said, "No. I'm glad you didn't listen to her and called to let me know. Which hospital?" She ended the call and stood there, almost unable to breathe. "It's my aunt."

"Ruby?"

She pressed her phone against her chest. "They took her by ambulance to Bridgewater Regional Hospital in Crystal Falls."

"Is it serious?" Renee stepped closer.

"I didn't think so at first. She broke her ankle, but they're taking her straight to surgery. That's always serious, right? Especially for someone who's seventy." This day had pushed her emotions like a pendulum—from awful to amazing, and then princess to peril. If she were ever at a risk for a heart attack, today would most certainly have done her in.

"I can catch the Metro back to the office," Renee said, "and I'll give Margie an update. You'd better go."

Sweat dampened Joy's forehead, making her bangs feel heavy. "It's over a five-hour drive. I'll never make it back in time for the presentation at the off-site meeting tomorrow." Panic filled her, making the chorus of "Rudolph, the Red-Nosed Reindeer" playing in the store sound like white noise as she tried to process the news.

"I can cover that. Plus, it gives you the whole weekend to take care of your aunt and get back home."

"Right. Yeah. Oh my gosh." Joy swiped at the tear that slipped down her cheek.

Renee placed her hand on Joy's arm. "Are you sure you're okay to drive?"

Joy fumbled for her keys. "Yes. I'll be fine."

"Then don't just stand there. Go. Don't worry about a thing at the office." Renee hugged Joy and stepped back, urging her to leave.

Joy walked as fast as she could to the nearest elevator to the executive parking level, then ran all the way to her car with the dress bag billowing over her shoulder.

Chapter Four

Ben stooped to pick up an ornament that had fallen from the Christmas tree in the atrium of Bridgewater Regional Hospital. He'd worked at the hospital for ten years running—ten Christmases—and this had to be the prettiest tree yet.

He flipped the ornament in the air and caught it.

It had taken him three trips to find the perfect Fraser fir that would do the skylighted central court justice. He'd made careful calculations to determine just how tall the tree needed to be so that once it was in the stand with the tree topper, it would just clear the ceiling. All his effort had paid off too. Not an inch to spare. Decorating for the holidays hadn't been in the budget, but his staff had embraced the opportunity to get creative. Garlands made of plastic patient bracelets laced the branches in a twisting kaleidoscope of color. Recycling at its best. The staff had also volunteered to decorate everything themselves since there was also no budget to hire the team that usually came to do that work. The people in this town lived the holiday spirit every day.

Ben admired the ornament he'd just rescued, its shimmering fabric pinned into place with stacks of sequins in red, white, and green. Each ornament was tagged with the name of a patient, and the shiny length of ribbon on this one read SARA. Ben hung the ornament carefully on a limb near a bright blue twinkle light, hoping Sara would be back home by Christmas Day.

It was tradition at Bridgewater to have ornaments that represented each patient staying in the hospital over the holidays—a tradition his mother had started years ago as a candy striper. When a patient was released, they took their ornament home with them, or moved it out to the community tree located in the grassy area outside the emergency room.

Ben had always hoped that by Christmas Day, the only remaining ornaments on the tree inside would be the shiny red balls. That wasn't realistic, but it didn't stop him from believing that maybe one day that would be the case. Because every heart deserved to be filled with hope, no matter what seemed logical. After all, miracles happened at the most unexpected times.

Soft holiday music filled the corridor, and the scent of pine from the fresh boughs of greenery draping the hospital entrance hung in the air, masking the usual aroma of antiseptic and adhesive.

Only one family sat in the waiting area right now. Although it wasn't good for business, seeing a near empty waiting room had its pluses. Especially this time of year.

Ben shared a smile with the family waiting to be called to complete admission paperwork. He wondered which member of that family would have an ornament on the tree tomorrow. The mom, dad, or one of the children?

His phone rang as he walked down the hall toward his office. "Hello, Mom."

"Honey, your grandmother just called. Ruby took a fall, she just got out of surgery. If you have time, could you stop in and pay Ruby a little visit while your grandmother is there with her? It would make her day to show you off a little, and I thought maybe you could pull a few strings to make her stay a little more pleasant."

"Of course." Ben always had to laugh at how Mom called Bridgewater *his* hospital. He refrained from asking her what had happened to Ruby, or else he'd end up on the phone for a good thirty minutes.

"Thank you, son."

"It won't take but a few minutes. No problem."

"Thanks, Ben. Oh, and I wanted to talk to you about Christmas dinner. I heard from your brothers. Finally. Everyone will be here this year. Kendra and I have an idea. Can I run it past you? Do you have a few minutes?"

"Sorry, Mom, I don't." If he hung on the phone with her too long, he'd have to mention that they might have to drop out of the Extreme Gingerbread Bake-off this year. He'd rather find a replacement for Ashley than disappoint Mom. Either way, it was better to have that conversation in person. "Tell Kendra to hang around. I'll stop by the shop and catch up after work. Does that work for you?"

"Yes. It can wait. But don't forget to stop in on Ruby."

"Got it. I'll talk to you later." He pushed his phone into his pocket, turned, and headed for the elevator. Might as well knock that out now while he was thinking about it. He took the elevator to the top floor. The facility had only three floors, the first dedicated to the ER, gift shop, cafeteria, Outpatient Services, and Administration. What used to be the physical therapy wing was now rented out as doctors' offices to bring in more money for the facility.

When the doors of the elevator opened on the third floor, gone were the soothing holiday scents of pine from the first floor, and the holiday music was replaced by the sounds of nurses doing their jobs.

A first-year nurse glanced up from the beeping monitor

in the nurses' station. "Good evening, Ben. What brings you here?"

"Checking on a friend who was admitted earlier. Ruby Johnson."

"She came through surgery fine. She's still foggy as a Froot Loop, but you can visit her. She's a pistol, that one."

"That's an understatement. What happened? I hope it's not serious."

"She took a nasty fall, but she's going to be fine." She pointed down the hall behind her. "Hope I'm just like her when I'm her age. Room 326."

Ben exchanged hellos with a couple other nurses moving equipment down the hall. He knew most everyone who worked at the hospital, if not by face, then certainly by name, since he oversaw all the hospital's accounting, including payroll.

Easing open the partially closed door of room 326, he knocked as he entered Ruby's room. She was propped up against pillows with her leg elevated, her bruised toes sticking out of the end of the cast. "What have you gone and done to yourself, Miss Ruby?"

"Ben." Ruby dragged his name out like it was three syllables long. "Did Shirley call you to help spring me from this joint?"

His grandmother was seated in the chair next to the bed.

"Hardly." Ben's lip trembled with the need to smile at that. He placed his hand on his grandmother's shoulder. "But you and my grandmother better be behaving."

Ruby put her hand across her mouth. "Your grandmother and I always behave."

"I wish I believed that," he said, teasing her affectionately. "They treating you right, Ruby?" He squeezed his grandmother's shoulder. "How are you doing, Grandma Shirley? You keeping Ruby in line?"

Ruby raised her arm, sending the plastic tube of the IV flinging like a jump rope. "Keeping *me* in line? If she were a good friend, she'd be wheeling me out of this place!" She crossed her arms over her generous bosom and harrumphed. "I can't believe I broke that easy. I've had much worse falls. I just stepped in a hole this time. Funny thing is, it isn't even the ankle of the foot I stepped in the hole with that got broken. Figure that out, would ya?"

Shirley shook her blond curls and tsked. "I keep telling her she needs help around that place. If it hadn't been bridge day, no telling how long she'd have lain there until someone found her." Shirley tugged on Ben's sleeve. "She never misses bridge. When she didn't show up, I knew something was wrong."

"You were just missing my famous spinach artichoke dip." Ruby wasn't spitting out her words quickly or clearly. "I'm fine. Be a good boy, Ben, and fetch me some crutches so I can get on about my business."

"That's big talk for someone who just came out of surgery," Ben said. "I believe those pain meds have you feeling ten feet tall and bulletproof, but I don't think you'll be going anywhere anytime soon. What can I do to help make your stay more comfortable?"

"Get me home."

"Besides that."

"Not a thing. It was sweet of you to come by and check on me, though," she said with a crooked smile.

Shirley shook her head. "Actually, there *is* something he can do for you."

Ruby's eyebrows shot up. "What?"

"Have you forgotten how much work it is to get your place ready for the Crystal Christmas Cookie Crawl? It would be a shame for me to have to cancel your house as a stop. Oh goodness, we don't have much time to figure this out. They are printing tickets this week!"

Ruby glared at Shirley. "Cancel me? You will do no such thing. This is a temporary setback. I will have my house ready, like I always have for as many years as you've hosted that holiday home tour."

"Have you even started?"

"No, but I'll get it done, and Ben had already scheduled to come over next Thursday to start the outside lights."

"Then you'd better plan on letting Ben get moving along on decorating the inside too."

"I'm happy to do that," Ben said. "Don't worry about a thing."

Ruby's face sagged. "You know how much I appreciate you helping me out now and again, but you don't have to do that. I can still carry my own weight. I'm not some helpless old lady," she insisted. "No doctor is going to treat me that way either. I'll be up and out of here tomorrow. Take my word on that." Her lips pulled into a tight line. "I can decorate some trees and bake with a cast. It's not like my arms are broken. No big deal."

"Not so fast there, Ruby," Ben said, carefully choosing his words. "You need to follow doctor's orders, or your stay could end up even longer."

Pffft. Ruby's face contorted and dismissed the very thought.

"After seven years running, I know exactly where everything is stored and where it all needs to go. I'll take care of the decorations, Ruby."

Brushing her hair back from her face, Ruby sniffled and said, "You know how much I appreciate you being my handyman, but I will *not* ask you to do all of that by yourself. Besides, you've got your own place to worry about."

"You don't have to ask. I volunteered. Besides, my

house is not on the Cookie Crawl. It's as much for me as it is for you. I like winning." And there it was. One more thing on his top-heavy plate to juggle. "Besides, you know how much I enjoy those projects."

Her expression softened. "That's true. You can sure whistle a holiday tune like nobody's business too. You kinda break all those stuffy, boring accountant stereotypes."

"Thank you. I think?" He had to admit he hadn't had much in common with the other students majoring in accounting back at NC State. In fact, most of his buddies there had been in vet school or off campus, already working blue-collar jobs. And as much as those guys had bellyached about those jobs, Ben loved doing that kind of work. His position in administration at Bridgewater Regional Hospital had come with a nice salary, but there was something to be said for getting outside and seeing the sunshine now and again. "Your farm will be the best-looking stop on the Crystal Christmas Cookie Crawl again this year. I promise. I'll have it all ready for you in time for the event."

She shot straight up in her bed. "I better be home well before that!"

"I hope so, but don't push yourself, and don't give the nurses a hard time." Ruby was known for her fiery redhead behavior in this town.

"I won't be here long enough to give anyone a hard time."

Somehow Ben doubted that. In fact, if he had to guess, everyone already had their hands full with Ruby, and she hadn't even spent the night yet. "I'll check in on you to-morrow."

He checked his watch. It was going to be a late night in the office for him tonight, but he had errands to run too.

Maybe he'd zip out now, take care of a few things and grab dinner, then come back. Probably wouldn't hurt to check in on Ruby later either.

He hoped, for her sake, that she did get back on her feet soon, and home, else he might have to put a warning label on Ruby Johnson to protect the staff.

Chapter Five

Joy clung to the steering wheel so tightly that her arms ached. For the last hour she'd wrestled with her emotions, unsure which was winning—concern for her aunt or regret for letting so much time pass since her last visit to see her. Okay, and the guilty feeling that she should really have stayed at the office, but it had to have been over two years since Joy last made the trip to Crystal Falls, North Carolina.

Ruby had come to visit her in D.C. twice during that time.

Joy stretched tall in the seat, trying to ease the pain of sitting still for this long. *How could I have let a seventy-year-old make this trip?* Maybe because Ruby had always seemed rather invincible, but now Joy could kick herself for not having made a better effort. Joy stretched her back against the driver's seat. It was a long drive even for her.

Once she finally reached her exit from the interstate, the roads quickly became narrow and dark. Water ponded along the side of the road from a recent shower, splashing beneath the wheels of the car, sounding as if someone were saying "shhhhh." Joy wished the white noise would shut down the negative thoughts playing in her mind. *Mom would hate that I haven't kept in touch with Aunt Ruby.*

What if Ruby's injury is serious? I can't lose her. She's all I have. Ruby is so different from Mom, so why does it break my heart all over again when I'm with her?

Joy pulled in front of the small Bridgewater Regional Hospital just before nine o'clock.

She swung into a front parking spot and rushed inside. Her footsteps echoed in the atrium, empty except for the furniture and a huge Christmas tree. Across the way, a uniformed security guard, who had to be pushing seventy himself, sat behind the reception desk, flipping through a magazine.

"Ruby Johnson was admitted earlier. I'm her niece, Joy Holbrook. Can I see her?" She slid her driver's license across the desk, trying to speed up the process.

"That's not necessary, young lady." The old man tugged his glasses off and cleaned them on his shirt. "Visiting hours ended a little while ago, but let me see what I can find out for you."

She glanced around the familiar atrium, trying to remain calm. This place still held icy memories for her.

The last time she'd been to a hospital, it was to visit Renee after her daughter, Cassie, had her tonsils removed. There were still five minutes left before visiting hours that day, and they wouldn't let her up. Her worry had only increased during the five-hour drive when her attempts to call Ruby's friend back to get an update had gone unanswered. *Don't let it be bad news.*

The hospital lobby looked different decorated with fresh greenery for the holidays, adding cheer to the place in an odd way. Not how she remembered it all. So maybe it wasn't exactly like the last time Joy had been here, but those memories still haunted her.

The security guard made a phone call, then snapped his fingers to get her attention. "You can go right down this hall and take the elevator to the third floor. The desk nurse will help you."

The flood of relief that those words gave her made her want to leap across the desk and give that guy a hug. If she hadn't been able to see Ruby tonight, there was no way she'd get a wink of sleep. "Thank you so—" She spun and nearly collided with a gentleman walking by. "I'm sorry. I—"

The dark-haired man caught her by the arm, her keys just inches from his shoulder. "Whoa, there."

She shrank back to keep from stabbing him with her keys. Out of habit they had been laced through her fingers like little spears. City living kept a girl on her toes.

"Yeah. Sorry. I'm here to see a family member." She yanked her hand down to her side and shook the keys loose from her fingers.

His smile was easy. His grip firm. Even though he wasn't wearing a doctor's coat, he had that I-belong-here look about him. "Sorry to hear that. The elevators are that way." He pointed down the hall, although she already knew the way. Knew it all too well.

"Yes. Excuse me." Joy sidestepped him and forged ahead. She stabbed at the elevator button, then glanced back. The man walked with purposeful intent down the far end of the hall.

Those days she'd spent here with Mom suddenly felt like just yesterday. Fighting the frantic feeling washing over her, she searched her mind for something less personal. *Research studies proved that the traditional lighting in hospitals never gets bright enough to tell the brain it's time to be awake and alert, nor does it get dim enough to ease sleep, which could impact a patient's ability to heal.*

She knew more trivia about things she'd done market

research on, from agriculture to health care to zoo life, than one person should ever know. That trivia was usually her safety net, but right now it felt highly inappropriate. Hopefully, her aunt wouldn't be in here long enough for the lighting to make a difference. *Please be okay.*

Joy punched the elevator button again and waited. Then pressed it again. Finally the elevator arrived. The doors opened so slowly that she practically ran into them as she got on. After a painfully slow lift to the third floor, she stepped out, and the desk nurse, a ripe-bodied woman, smiled and motioned her over. "You must be Mrs. Johnson's niece."

"Yes, ma'am. I just got here from D.C. I've been so worried. Can I see her?" The last words barely made it out. She took in a deep breath and pressed her hands together. "Please?"

"Oh, honey, you better settle yourself down or you'll end up her roommate. I'm busy. I don't have time for any more patients on this floor tonight." A hearty laugh filled the air as the woman hoisted herself up from the chair. Her bright white shoes squeaked with every step as she rounded the nurses' station to Joy's side. "Your aunt is going to be just fine. Come with me."

For a moment, Joy froze. Unsure if she could walk down the hall. The beeping of machines and the chatter on the hospital floor competed with her ability to breathe and separate her memories from the present.

"Are you okay?" the nurse asked.

Joy glanced down the hall in the direction of room 304. She hadn't realized, until just now, that she even remembered her mom's room number. Her palm sweated against her keys.

"Come on. Let's get you down to see your aunt. You'll feel better once you see her," the nurse said.

Joy's lips felt numb as the scent of the hospital cleaner mixed with the cherry gelatin that seemed to always be on the food trays around here tugged at old wounds.

The nurse motioned. "She's down this end of the hall."

Joy fell in step next to the nurse, who walked as slow as the elevator ride had been. If Joy could get her mouth to work, she'd just ask the nurse to give her the room number so she could sprint down and see for herself that all was well.

"She came through surgery fine," the nurse said. "Broken ankle. Bad break." The nurse shook her head, bunching her lips. "Real bad. Took a few screws and a rod to put her back together, but she's awake and fussing. I usually take that to be a good sign."

A burst of laughter floated into the hallway. Aunt Ruby's laugh always made Joy smile. She could've found her without the room number or the escort. *Thank goodness.*

The nurse stopped short of the door. "They've been in there awhile. Make it quick. Visiting hours are over. We don't see any reason to rush folks too much, but your aunt does need her rest."

Joy hesitated at the door. Two women she didn't know stood next to Shirley, Ruby's best friend, practically blocking her view. But even from here, the outline of Ruby's body looked tiny lying there in bed. Then again, Ruby always looked small next to Shirley, who had to be at least five feet eight inches with wild Shirley Temple curls and the take-charge skills of a drill sergeant with a southern twist that left you unaware you'd been manipulated. Quite the opposite of Aunt Ruby, who, like Joy, was a fiery-tempered strawberry blonde just a smidge over five feet tall.

Ruby rattled off the details of her accident as if it had happened to someone in a Hallmark Channel movie. Her familiar voice reminded Joy of the many late nights Ruby had entertained her with her tall tales.

Joy listened, her worry falling away with each word. It wasn't until one of the women moved to get something out of her purse that she finally caught a full glimpse of her aunt. And had she not heard her aunt's voice already, she wasn't sure that she'd have recognized her.

Ruby must have switched hair stylists because her red hair was now closer to tomato red than strawberry blond. She'd aged significantly since their last visit. *Stop that. She just came out of surgery. Be grateful Ruby sounds like her old self . . . even if she doesn't look like it.* Joy's lips quivered as she forced a thankful smile.

". . . and I stepped in a hole. It hurt like the dickens when I fell, but that's not even the ankle I broke. I don't know how I managed to break the other ankle. I must have been a sight, toppling tail over teakettle. Anyway, with one foot in the hole, and the other all twisted backwards, I couldn't pull myself back up."

"How long did you lie there?" one woman asked.

"Most of the morning. Glad it wasn't raining. Now, that could've been miserable. As it was, I think my menagerie thought I was hanging out for a sleepover, because they all came over and just walked around me in circles like it was a game of Ring Around the Ruby. All they wanted was for me to get up and get them a treat."

"You're lucky," another lady said. "You could have died right there, lying in your yard."

"Seriously? It's a broken ankle, and it was almost sixty degrees. Don't be so dramatic!" Ruby snapped at the woman.

"Maybe you need one of those medical-alert necklaces. My son was telling me about those."

Ruby tugged the sheet up around her. "Stop it. It was just an accident. One teensy mishap. I'm fine."

Shirley cut in. "When Isabelle had that broken foot, she was in the hospital for days, and then had to go to the rehab center for physical therapy."

"Well, that's Isabelle. Not me. I told them I had things to do at the farm. Give me one of those walking casts and some crutches, and I can get some chores done."

"Now, Ruby, you heard Ben—"

"Don't you start—" Ruby's voice rose two octaves.

Even after being gone so long, Joy still recognized the tone Ruby took when she was ready to argue. "I came as soon as I heard," Joy said, hoping to head off a quarrel between her aunt and Shirley.

"Joy?"

The look on Ruby's face nearly caused Joy to choke on the tears that threatened to fall. "Yes, ma'am."

"You drove all that way? You didn't have to do that. How did you know? Who called you?" Ruby demanded.

Shirley bristled but didn't speak up, and there was no way Joy was going to throw her under the bus.

"I must be listed as your next of kin. Besides, I deserve to know these things. We're family." Joy knew that she hadn't treated Ruby like real family, though. While dodging her own painful past, she'd shoved Ruby aside too, always allowing work to take precedence unless Ruby showed up. And even then, Ruby had to resort to showing up with hardly any notice to keep Joy from worming her way out of the visit.

"Phooey. It's no big deal. Next of kin is for when you're going to die. I'm nowhere near dead. But you get on over here. It sure is good to lay eyes on you." Ruby flung her arms open wide, and her friends stepped back to let Joy get close to the bed.

"Girls. This is my niece, Joy," she said proudly.

"It's good to see you. I'm sorry it's been so long. It shouldn't have taken something like this to get me here." Joy leaned down to hug Ruby, whose grip hadn't suffered one bit.

"You're busy, sweetie. Don't you worry. I understand." Ruby's eyes glistened, and guilt stuck in Joy's throat like a pill too big to swallow. Lying in the hospital bed, her aunt didn't seem like the vibrant, unstoppable woman Joy had always known. Was it the surgery, or had she really paid so little attention?

A blond-haired nurse knocked on the door. "I hate to break up the party, but our patient needs her rest. She'll be up for visitors again tomorrow."

All Ruby's friends left, but Joy lagged behind. "I'll be back in the morning."

Ruby grabbed Joy's wrist. "Honey, I'm sorry they called and worried you, but thank you so much for being here. Seeing you has almost made it all worth it."

Those words stabbed like a knife to Joy's gut. "Don't say that." But her voice came out so quietly, she wasn't even sure Ruby heard her. Joy cleared her throat. "Please, don't you ever worry about worrying me. I'm here. Where I should be tonight." She rested her arms on the rail of Ruby's bed, and lowered herself into the bedside chair.

Ruby laid her hand against Joy's cheek. "You're staying at the farm, right?"

"I'd planned to."

"You look exhausted. Are you working too hard?" Ruby waved a bony hand. "Don't answer that. You always do. I know you better than you think, young lady."

Of course she did. She was Mom's sister, and had been there through the hardest times of Joy's life. "I can help you until you get on your feet."

"I'll be home tomorrow. They never keep anyone in the hospital long these days. Insurance runs that mess, not the doctors. But you can help me with one thing."

"Anything."

"Could you please feed the animals for me tonight? That would be a huge help. I know they're probably raising a ruckus. They're used to their six-o'clock feeding. I've taken in a few more since you were last here. I just can't bear the thought of animals going to slaughter, so I've kind of become the rescue lady. Oh, and Molly, that darn rabbit, is in a cage on the sunporch now. She just can't tolerate the cold these days since Mr. Bugs crossed the rainbow bridge. At least there won't be any more baby bunnies."

"Not a problem."

Ruby's face contorted into a frown; then she began pushing the sheets down and edging to the side of the bed. "It's too much to ask. I really need to get home. Help me get out of this bed and get dressed."

"Lie back down. You're just feeling good because of that cocktail they have in your IV." She placed her hand on Ruby's shoulder. "You relax. I'll make sure every single animal gets fed something tonight. No one will go hungry on my watch." She crossed her heart. "I promise."

Ruby deflated back into the pillows. "There's a list on the barn wall of everything that needs to be done. The goats, Nanny and Waddles, and the donkey, you remember Jack, right?"

That stubborn donkey had to be fifteen years old by now.

"They should have had a new bale of hay put out today. Don't worry about the cow. He belongs to Tommy, a 4-H'er in town who needed somewhere to keep her until showtime. Good little boy. He never misses a day, but check the gate. He doesn't always latch it right."

"Got it."

"The chickens have most certainly dumped their water over, they always do. Oh goodness, they are all probably starving."

"I've got it. Don't worry a—" Joy spun around at the sound of the door swinging open.

"Ladies. I'm sorry. I really need to ask you to wrap this up." The nurse who had escorted Joy down earlier cocked her head in that way that told Joy she meant business.

"I'm going." Joy stood, stepped away from Ruby's bed, and started for the door. "I'll be by tomorrow to visit."

"Molly!" Ruby called out, waving her hand frantically. "I almost forgot. You have to take care of Molly. She can't be alone in the morning."

"You girls can talk tomorrow," the nurse said.

Joy kept moving. "No problem. I've got it all under control. Go to sleep." Joy breezed through the doorway, and the nurse pulled the door closed behind them. "I'm sorry. I haven't seen her in—"

"I get it. She'll be here tomorrow." The nurse ducked into the room next door to reset a beeping monitor.

Loneliness hung over Joy as she made her way down the empty hallway. She had every intention of making up lost time to Ruby, no matter what it took.

Chapter Six

Joy got in her car and started the engine, feeling a huge relief that her visits to Bridgewater Regional Hospital would be short-lived this time and the outcome different than with Mom. Ruby's injuries were not life threatening. Thank goodness.

She leaned forward and glanced up to the third floor. Not toward Ruby's room on the east wing, but toward the room where Mom had spent those last weeks. Why did it still feel just as raw tonight as it had over twelve years ago? She took a napkin out of the console and dabbed at her tears.

Heartache steamrolled her. Back then, she'd had Ruby to lean on. Now everything was on Joy, and if she ever let these tears go, she wasn't sure they'd stop.

"It's going to be okay this time." She stuffed the napkin into the top of her purse and looked in the rearview mirror. "It's okay."

Feeling lonely, she picked up her phone. It was too late to call Renee. Her kids would already be in bed for the night. One tap on the callback button, that's all it would take to hear a friendly voice. She checked the call log. Todd's number hadn't come up in over three weeks.

She hadn't even realized it had been that long.

It wasn't like she and Todd had ever been exclusive or anything. She'd heard from a friend that he'd been seen out on the town with a couple different girls. Definitely not looking like he was searching for something long term. Fine by her, because she wasn't.

She didn't have anyone to call, so she dialed the office and left a message for Margie. Joy felt bad leaving Renee with the presentation tomorrow afternoon, but Joy knew even if she left now, she'd be so exhausted, she wouldn't make a good impression anyway.

Margie's voice mail picked up. "Margie, it's Joy. I wanted to update you about my family emergency. I'm down in North Carolina. I won't be back in time for the presentation. My team has been briefed, and they are prepared. Renee has all the files. You've got my number if you have any questions, and I'll have access to my e-mail if you need me. I should be back in the office on Monday."

In her heart, she knew she was doing the right thing, but doubt niggled at her brain with an endless loop of *Don't mess up your chance for the promotion now* and *I've worked so hard for this, will they hold it against me for being away?*

Those little voices nagged at her.

"Stop. It's only a day," she said out loud to calm herself, then dropped the shifter into reverse and pressed the accelerator.

No sooner had she tilted her chin to glance into her rearview mirror than the piercing screech of metal meeting metal sent a jolt right through her. She jammed her foot so hard on the brake pedal that her butt lifted from the seat, causing the seat belt to tug against her.

The car lurched to a stop. "No!" She put the car in park and jumped out, running to the back of her car to check the damage.

"This cannot be happening!" But it had, and it was no-body's fault but her own. She'd backed right into the open tailgate of a pickup truck. Her whole back quarter panel had been ripped open like a flimsy soda can. She reached out and touched the jagged edges.

"What is this thing made out of?" She closed her eyes and glanced back at her parking spot. There'd been plenty of room to pull out, but she hadn't noticed that the tailgate was down on the truck parked across the way. Even so, this wouldn't have happened if she'd been paying attention.

"No." She dropped her face to her hands. "Just no." This place was just bad luck.

She got back in the car and pulled forward slowly, but the car was locked metal-to-metal with the big blue truck. Her car wasn't moving an inch, and that high-pitched twisting sound wasn't reassuring at all.

"Could this day get any worse?" She laid her head against the steering wheel, then looked up at that third-floor window. Room 304. Knowing full well that it could have been much worse, and probably was for some family tonight.

Keep it in perspective.

Joy pushed the car door open and walked around to the back, hoping for a solution that wouldn't make things worse.

It looked even worse. She took out her phone and searched for a tow truck.

Approaching footsteps stopped her mid-search. A tall man walked through the parking lot in her direction.

"What happened? Are you okay?" The condensation of his breath wafted from his mouth as he spoke.

"I'm fine," she said. As he got closer, she recognized him from the lobby earlier. Of course it was. Just her luck. The same good-looking guy whom she'd nearly speared with her keys earlier. "Better than my car." She wished she could just disappear.

He raised a hand to his cheek and stroked the light scruff there.

She cringed when she heard his quick intake of air. It shouldn't have surprised her. That had been her response too.

"Whoa. You sure you're okay?" he asked, looking over at her. "That's quite some damage. What were you doing? Doughnuts in the parking lot?"

"No. I was just backing out. Thank goodness, the truck looks better than my car," Joy mumbled.

"Don't see any damage on the truck at all."

He had a great smile, but this was not the time for jokes. "It's not funny," she said. He could stand there and laugh as long as he wanted, but she had things to do. "I better go and see if I can find out who owns this truck."

"Take it easy. Once you get the car moved, I bet the truck isn't even scratched."

"I still have to tell the owner." She heaved a sigh that could've filled a balloon. "This is not my day. I should have known better than to come back to this place."

"It's not that bad."

"That's easy for you to say. You didn't just shish-kebab your car."

"True, but I was actually referring to *this place*. Crystal Falls." He shrugged. "It's not so bad. And frankly, the damage to your car could've been worse."

"Thanks for your concern, but I've got to go." She turned and headed for the building.

He trotted up next to her and caught her elbow. "Where are you going?"

She turned, ready to explode. "To find. The. Owner. Of that truck." She spat out the words. *How many times do I have to say it? Is the guy an idiot or what?* "I realize you're trying to be nice, but I'm tired and standing here talking to you is not going to make this any better." The lively twinkle in his eyes only made her madder. "You can leave now. Good night." She spun around and marched toward the front door of the hospital.

"Stop."

"What now?" She regretted her short-tempered tone immediately, but really, couldn't he take a hint?

He inclined his head toward the vehicles. "It's my truck."

Something about his nonchalant response hit her wrong. "Why didn't you say something before?"

"You were upset."

"Yeah, I'm upset. Why aren't you?"

"I was just trying to figure out what happened, and not make the situation worse for you."

"I just wasn't paying attention. That's what happened." *That sounded weak.* "My mind was on something else. What do you want me to say? All I know is I came up empty searching for a tow truck company in this town on my phone, and I tried to move my car, but it's stuck."

That smile quirked up at the edges, revealing a dimple. "Stuck?"

"Yes. Stuck. As in I tried to move my car and it just made noise. Didn't budge. Would you happen to have any suggestion on how I should get us unstuck?"

"Well, since my truck and your car have become so close, it only seems right that we should at least introduce ourselves." He extended his hand, and there was that smile again. "I'm Ben."

She reluctantly extended her hand. *He better not be thinking we're going to get as close as our cars.* "I'm Joy, although I'm clearly not spreading much of it today."

Her response seemed to amuse him. "Relax. It's a car." He shrugged out of his sport coat and put it around her shoulders. "Here, you're shivering."

She pulled the wool sport coat around her, the smooth, outdoorsy scent of his cologne teasing her. The coat engulfed her. Although the warmth was welcome, it was her nerves, not the weather, that had her shaking tonight.

"Give me a minute." He walked around to the passenger side of his truck and came back with a flashlight.

Now that he wasn't wearing his jacket, it was hard to ignore his well-toned biceps and the athletic taper to his slim hips. Probably the best-looking guy in the whole town. And a doctor? Although he hadn't said he was a doctor, and why would a doctor drive a pickup truck? He'd better not be lying about this being his truck.

"I *think* I can just pull my truck forward. That shouldn't do any more damage to your car than you've already done."

"It's worth a try. How can I help?"

"Stand right there and watch. Let me know if your car starts coming along for the ride when I move my truck forward. Wave your arms if the car moves, okay?"

"Got it." Joy positioned herself near the driver's side of his tailgate, relieved when he took a wad of keys out of his pocket and started the truck. At least he hadn't lied about it being his truck. Christmas carols blared from his speakers. He turned down the music and dropped the truck into gear.

The brake lights dimmed. As he inched forward, there was only a minimum amount of scraping, and then the tailgate cleared her car.

"That's good!" she yelled, waving her arms.

He got out of the truck, the sound of sleigh bells and a joyous chorus of "Jingle Bells" drifting from the cab as he walked to the back and slammed the tailgate shut. "Mine's fine. Unfortunately, your car looks even worse from this angle."

Angling the light beam to the back of her car, they stepped closer.

By her side, he seemed much taller than she'd first noticed. Over six feet tall, for sure. "I think mine's going to need life support."

He peered into the backseat of the car. "Nice dress."

The sequins on her dress danced in the ray of light. "Thank you. I . . . it doesn't matter. This looks bad. I'm probably going to wish I didn't just spend all that money on that dress when I get the estimate to fix this damage."

He draped his arm around her shoulder. "You should be able to drive it. There's nothing hitting the tires. A little cosmetic surgery will go a long way."

"Is that what you do? You're a plastic surgeon?" He had that overly put-together plastic surgeon look to him, with the drop-dead blue eyes and dark hair. Probably colored contacts. Not many people had eyes that blue.

He smirked. "No. I just rescue women who get into trouble."

"Like a superhero?"

"Yeah. Maybe."

Easy for him to laugh. His truck looked fine. "Let me get you my insurance information in case your truck is damaged when you see it in the daylight."

Ben shook his head. "No. It looks fine." He took a pad of paper from his pocket and scribbled on it. "Here's the information for the body guy up the street. Tell him Ben sent you. He'll take good care of you."

"Thanks. I'm so sorry about all of this." She gestured toward his truck. "About the wreck and for yelling at you."

"Forget about it." He got back in his truck and waved as he drove off.

Was he that easygoing in every bad situation? She'd been a maniac, and now her embarrassment was nearly as bad as the damage to her car. Sure, her car could be fixed, but the way she'd just acted was leaving her feeling in need of resuscitation. Only her luck it would be Mr. Blue-eyed Superhero who would show up to save her.

Chapter Seven

Joy had forgotten just how dark Crystal Falls could be in the winter. Beyond Main Street, there weren't many lights along the old twisting roads. There was a time when she'd have sped down the back roads to Ruby's at high speed without a worry in the world—except during hunting season, when she had to be careful of deer darting out in front of her. But that was a long time ago. She'd been reckless and angry then.

Tonight she carefully negotiated each turn with her bright lights flooding the way.

She drove up to the old farmstead where Ruby lived, and parked in the sandy gravel driveway near the side door. The white-columned porch had always made the house look like a mansion to Joy. The two-story structure wasn't fancy, though. Just an old cedar shake saltbox colonial, but Uncle George had added the amazing wraparound porch the summer Joy and Mom stayed there.

Joy got out of her car and climbed the porch stairs, her heels clicking against the decking boards. She leaned against one of the fat pillars, hugging it like an old friend, embracing the darkness that hung over the acreage. There were a lot of memories in this old house.

The animals whinnied and called out what sounded like

a welcome, but was more likely their high hopes for a meal tonight. If it weren't for the single light in the barn, it would be pitch-black out there.

Joy stood for a moment longer, enjoying the peace and fresh night air. She went inside, then realized that it hadn't even crossed her mind to ask for a key. Thinking back, though, she was pretty sure that door had never been locked the whole time she lived there. But then, that was a long time ago.

She ran her hand along the wall and flipped on the lights. Everything looked pretty much the same as it always had, except Uncle George's old recliner that used to be in front of the fireplace had been replaced by a new floral love seat. She meandered back to the kitchen and opened the refrigerator. Just like old times, the gold glass pitcher was filled with sweet tea. Joy poured a glass and sat down at the kitchen table.

The caffeine wouldn't be enough to keep her awake, as tired as she was tonight.

Nothing seemed to have changed here in the last ten years. The kitchen was still painted an outdated green, but it was sparkling clean. She rinsed out her glass and placed it on the counter, then headed back to Ruby's room. Since she hadn't taken the time to stop and grab a change of clothes before she left D.C., she'd have to find something to wear to go out and feed the animals. She certainly couldn't do it in high heels and her favorite pantsuit.

The hall leading back to Ruby's room was lined with family pictures. Joy's high school graduation picture still hung in the same place that it had over ten years ago. Pictures of people she'd never met, like her grandmother and grandfather, and pictures from Ruby and Mom's childhood, which had faded from years of being on display. Some of them she wasn't sure she'd ever seen before.

She lifted a picture of the three of them—Mom, Aunt Ruby, and herself—from a hook. Joy remembered the day the picture had been taken. It had been the fall before Mom told Joy she was sick. It still hurt that Mom had kept it to herself for so long, claiming that she thought there was no reason to worry her. Wasn't it her right to worry when someone she loved was sick?

They'd spent the afternoon selling pumpkins down at the local Ruritan Club to raise money for the holiday drive, then gone to the little diner on the corner of Main Street. Ruby had asked the waiter to take the picture as a keepsake. Joy couldn't for the life of her remember the name of the diner now. *I wonder if it's still there.*

Joy carried the framed five-by-seven with her to Ruby's room. She sprawled across the bed on the log-cabin-patterned quilt that had always been on Ruby's bed, the mattress soft beneath her. She studied the picture, gliding her fingers across the thin glass. Joy had never thought she looked like her mother, but now that she was closer to the age that Mom had been in this photo, she could see the resemblance between them. Joy swept her fingertip across her mother's smile, demure and serious—a contrast from her gregarious sister, Ruby.

Joy set the picture on the nightstand. She crossed the room to the tallboy dresser. The heavy top drawer groaned as she slid it open to rummage for something to wear.

Winter hadn't officially arrived on the calendar, but it was cold out tonight and she still needed to feed the animals. A pair of sweatpants and a hooded sweatshirt would do the trick. Thank goodness she and Ruby were about the same size.

She was lucky to find just such an outfit in the dresser drawers. After changing clothes, she slipped on the muck boots she'd seen next to the back door. Picking up the flashlight from the counter, Joy headed to the barn.

The building hadn't always been a barn. Ruby and Uncle George didn't need a barn when he was alive. Back then, this building had been Uncle George's garage and workshop. He'd always been out there, tinkering away on something. Many nights she'd fallen asleep to the sound of his saw humming, the scent of damp pine wafting through the window. That fresh-cut pine lumber from the local mill had always smelled so sweet.

There weren't any tools in the barn now. Gone were the old workbenches, replaced with four stalls that lined one whole side of the space. Just as Ruby had said, there was a list of chores hanging on a clipboard dangling from a nail next to the door. Not just any clipboard, but one that Ruby had Bedazzled somewhere along the way with the words FEED THE ANIMALS in beads next to a cow with googly eyes.

> AM daily. Throw handful of scratch for the chickens.
> AM daily. 1 carrot and ¼ cup of rabbit chow for the
>   bunny.
> Change water in the chicken coop and bunny cage.
> Check water in the pasture.
> PM daily. Hay.
> PM daily. Pelleted feed for livestock. Bins labeled.

Joy flipped to the second page of yellow ruled paper. There she found a detailed rendering of each of the animals' pens, their names, the type of food they ate, and their feeding schedules. The third page restated what was written on each of the feed bins.

"Easy enough." Joy followed the list, one chore at a time.

She fed the bunny, Molly, on the sunporch first to be sure she didn't forget about her, then the goats, the chickens, the horse, and the donkey. Tommy's cow kept walking over to the fence.

"Ruby said not to feed you," Joy said to the cow. "Sorry, buddy." When Joy reached over the fence and scratched her head, she was rewarded with a supersized lick that soaked her sweatshirt sleeve. "How am I supposed to resist those big brown eyes?" The cow lifted her nose. "I bet Tommy won't mind if I give you a snack, but just a little one."

Joy grabbed a scoop of livestock feed and carried it into the pen. "Don't tell on me." The cow lumbered along behind her. Just as Joy dumped the food in the feeder, the cow danced with excitement, and that made Joy nervous. She hurried toward the gate; then she stepped right smack-dab in the middle of a big pile of stinky poop. Her heel slipped forward about eight inches, nearly landing her on her behind. She caught herself, but not without a scare. She wrinkled her nose at the gross smell that had risen from the pile.

That'll teach me not to follow instructions.

She scraped her boot against the dirt, trying to remove some of the stench, then got right back to work. All the water buckets had been refilled except for the chickens'. She couldn't figure out how to open that red-and-white contraption and finally gave up, filling a bowl she found in the barn instead. That would do until morning.

Now on to the hay. The bales of hay stacked in the barn were much heavier than she'd expected. She reached for the lowest bale, but couldn't get a grip. How the heck did Ruby move them around?

Joy grabbed a nearby pitchfork and tried stabbing at the end, but the bale didn't budge. Unwilling to accept defeat, she climbed up to the third tier of bales, sat down, and pushed with her feet to send a bale tumbling to the ground. It bounced, rolled, and finally settled in the middle of the barn, about four feet away.

She climbed down and put her hands under the bright orange strings that secured the square bale and tugged.

A stream of light washed over the barn as a vehicle pulled into the driveway, sending the chickens squawking through their pen. The unexpected visitor had probably spotted the lights on in the barn and, knowing Ruby was in the hospital, was stopping by to check on things.

That's how neighbors were around here. Always had been.

Joy went about her business, trying to move the hay, but as she yanked, one of the strings gave way and she went reeling. The bale of hay unfolded in front of her like a deck of cards.

Shirley walked right past her and picked up one pad of hay. "It's easier to handle if you cut the strings while it's still up on the pile. That's how Ruby does it."

"Good to know. Those instructions weren't on the list. Thanks for calling to let me know that Ruby had hurt herself."

"Thanks for not outing me."

"I wouldn't do that, but I'm sure she suspects it was you. How've you been, Shirley?"

"Fine, dear. I'm glad you came. She can suspect all she wants to. We don't have to tell her. Besides, she was so happy to see you."

Joy stood and brushed the dirt off her pants. "I can't believe Ruby does this every single day."

Shirley pursed her lips and shook her head. "Me either. And some of these critters get fed twice a day. I tell you, that hardheaded aunt of yours is borderline cuckoo when it comes to this place. The animals are more work than a day care full of toddlers, and it's not cheap to feed this bunch."

"Yeah, she was worried to death about them, still shouting orders as I left her room tonight."

"That's how she is. She ought to be worrying about that broken ankle of hers. Girls our age don't mend as fast as we used to. Anyway, I wanted to stop by and let you know my grandson will be coming by. He's going to get all the holiday decorations down and start decorating for Ruby. Her house is the first stop on the Crystal Christmas Cookie Crawl map, so they need to get busy."

"I'm sure it can wait a day or two." *Or forever. Is decorating for the holiday really that important in the scheme of things? Maybe the focus should just be on getting Ruby well.*

Shirley blinked. "You don't really think she's coming home tomorrow, do you?"

"She said—"

"That's Ruby talking crazy. They are not going to let her come home. She's got screws and rods holding her ankle together. There's going to be rehab—weeks of it, probably."

Joy reached for the stall door and steadied herself, then stepped over a bale of straw sitting next to it and dropped to a seated position. "Are you sure?"

"Quite certain. The doctor said as much when he checked in on her after her surgery. She was still woozy from the anesthesia, so maybe she just didn't remember him saying that. On second thought, we're talking about Ruby here. At times, she has selective hearing."

Weeks of rehab? This couldn't be happening at a worse time. Joy had critical projects wrapping up soon, and one screwup could ruin her chance for that promotion. She hated being away from the office with so much on the line, but Ruby was all the family she had.

"She'll get more details tomorrow." Shirley's voice had softened. "I'll let y'all work that out, but if a tall dark stranger shows up, don't shoot him. He's just the help."

Joy had to laugh. She could easily picture Aunt Ruby

aiming a shotgun at an intruder. She stood and walked over to Shirley. "I'm quite capable. I don't need any help. You can tell your grandson I have things completely under control."

"Oh, Joy. There's so much to do. I don't really think you know what you're getting yourself into, and my grandson—"

"Probably has better things to do," Joy said, completing her sentence for her. "I promise I'll let you know if I run into any trouble. How about that?"

Shirley hugged Joy. "Yes, you are a lot like your aunt."

"Thank you."

"That wasn't exactly a compliment. I meant you're hardheaded when you set your mind to something."

"One of my finer traits." Joy picked up an armful of hay, and she and Shirley both walked over to the fence. Shirley threw hers over to the goats. Joy followed her lead and threw some over near the donkey too.

"Get some rest." Shirley waved as she headed for her car. "Oh, and you know about Molly?"

"Yes. Got it covered. Molly in the morning."

"Right," said Shirley.

Joy turned off the light in the barn and shoved her hands in the pockets of Ruby's hoodie. Shirley backed out of the driveway, and Joy watched until the red taillights disappeared around the curve in the road.

She'd worked up a sweat doing the chores, and was tempted to shrug out of the sweatshirt jacket, but the temperature outside was way too cool for just the T-shirt she had on under it.

She turned off the lights and flipped on the flashlight. Lighting a narrow walkway toward the house, she breathed in the fresh air once she sat on the stoop.

The stench of the poop on her boot wafted up, nearly

gagging her. She kicked off the boot and tossed it to the far side of the porch. This day had run the gamut from glamorous to god-awful in a hurry.

She pulled her feet underneath her and relaxed into the quiet. Not a still quiet, but a country quiet. Soft whimpers and thumps from the livestock played in tempo with the rustle of the bare tree limbs in the breeze.

Joy closed her eyes and wished on a star. She'd forgotten how much she loved looking up at the starry night sky. She'd prayed and made a million wishes and promises on those stars. You just couldn't get this view in the city.

Remembering her dress in the back of her car, she went over to rescue it. She carefully held the long dress bag in the air and took it inside. She twisted the lock behind her. Ruby might feel safe without locking up, but D.C. had made Joy a little less trusting. She carried the dress upstairs to the room she'd always stayed in as a little girl when she and Mom lived here. She hung the dress over the molding that framed the door in the hallway.

This morning seemed so long ago now.

She stepped over to the half-opened door. Joy flipped the light on, and the ceiling fan took a lazy loop above the light.

The room was exactly as she'd left it when she'd moved. Everything. Even the fountain pen that Uncle George had given her during her senior year. Even though she'd ruined the nib, she'd never been able to throw it away. Just being in this room made her feel like a teenager again.

It was still a pretty room. And the posters and memorabilia would lead any casual observer to think it was the room of any happy teen, but beneath that façade, she'd been in such a state after Mom died. Her whole world seemed to have gone black.

In the closet still hung her graduation cap and gown in

her high school colors, her prom dress, and other clothes she must've decided weren't fit for her big venture to the city. The flannel and long-sleeved T-shirts would come in handy, and she might even fit into a pair of those old blue jeans. At least she'd have something to wear while she was here. Hopefully at least one pair of those pants would still fit, or else she'd have to resort to wearing some of Ruby's stretchy old-lady pants.

She caught her reflection in the full-length mirror. The dress dazzled and sparkled just behind her. She sure didn't look like the same woman who had tried on the extravagant gown just this morning. It felt like days since she'd been standing in Wetherton's—the beadwork glistening under the fancy lighting in the lush dressing room. She took a moment and unzipped the fancy clear bag and removed it. The sequins shone extra bright, like they appreciated being freed. She lingered for a moment, imagining herself dancing at the gala in that gown.

With a flip of the switch, the room was dark. But the day reminded her very clearly just how quickly life could change.

Across the hall, the door to the room where Mom had slept was closed. *Did Ruby leave that room untouched too?* If she'd visited like she should have over the years, she'd probably know the answer to that question already.

She stood there for a moment, but couldn't bring herself to look. Maybe she'd sleep in the guest room tonight.

After closing her old bedroom door behind her, she went downstairs and out to the sunroom. The bunny scurried around in her cage, startling her. "Sorry, Molly. Didn't mean to frighten you."

Joy walked outside and sat down on the back stoop and tilted her chin to the sky. For a split second, it was as if her mom were sitting next to her. She could almost smell the perfumed powder she always wore.

Mom used to point out the Little Dipper and the North Star. It wasn't like Joy couldn't find them on her own, but she loved it when Mom held her hand and pointed out the stars. They'd done that hundreds of times. And wished on them. Together. So many times. Every night that Mom was able to come outside.

Tears fell to Joy's cheeks. She really missed Mom tonight. This feeling, the heaviness in her chest, was why she'd made such rare visits back here.

Her phone buzzed in her pocket. She didn't even have to look to know it was an alert from work. Seven days a week, that alert sounded to let her know the day's reporting had been completed and was available for review.

Joy clicked through the automated dashboard report. Everything had been updated today. Thank goodness for Renee. She hadn't missed a beat. The projects were all still in green status, and Joy trusted her team to make good decisions in her absence.

An e-mail from Renee was the last one that had come in. It read,

> I've got your back. I hope Ruby is fine, but take all the time you need. Everything happens for a reason. You're always telling me that. Maybe this was the only way of getting you to take a break before you get that promotion and everything gets even busier. Rumor has it the new director is not only going to get the whole Wetherton's account, but also the theme park we just landed. We're talking major travel and lots of work. Don't forget me!
>
> Best~ Renee

Joy shoved the phone back in her pocket. Maybe Renee was right. Even on the off chance that Ruby came home tomorrow, these little farm chores added up to hard work. Sticking around a few days was the least Joy could do for family.

After scanning the night sky for the brightest star, she squeezed her eyes shut, then clutched her hands together, pretending one belonged to her mother as she made her wish. She wanted that promotion to director so badly.

Wishing to the night sky, she quietly said, "Please let this be the right stepping-stone on my journey."

The next morning, Joy stood at the kitchen sink, sipping a cup of coffee. The house was chilly. An old hooded sweat-shirt jacket that had seen better days was draped on the back of one of the kitchen chairs. She slipped it on and pulled her braid free from the back. In so many ways, this place was exactly the same; it made her feel like a teen-ager again.

She stared out the window at the familiar property in the daylight. Ruby had always been an animal lover, but Uncle George would flip out if he knew that she'd adopted all these wayward animals.

She glanced at the worn edges of the oversized sweat-shirt jacket. Had it been one of Uncle George's? Maybe the animals were Ruby's way of filling the gap that Uncle George had once filled. Couldn't blame her for that. Had to get lonely out here by herself, but the place was beginning to look like a petting zoo. The smell was farm-y too. And at the moment, every single one of the motley crew was lined up side by side, like they'd rehearsed the formation all night long.

Seven o'clock wasn't early. Joy would normally be up, dressed, and out the door by now, but last night's farm duty had kicked her butt, and she had a little trouble getting a move on. Another twenty minutes of coffee time wasn't going to kill those animals.

She turned her back on them and held the warm mug between her hands.

Feeding the animals had sounded like a real cakewalk, but Joy was feeling it this morning. In fact, she was sorer this morning than the last time she got cocky and went for the ninety-minute hot yoga session with Renee.

The sound of the front door swinging open caused the hot coffee to catch in Joy's throat. The animals were definitely getting restless, but without thumbs, it wasn't likely to be one of them coming in to drag her outside. So what—or who—was it? But this was Crystal Falls. And she hadn't heard a car.

"Ruby-rooo-roooo."

Now, that was one sick rooster, or someone was messing with her. She relaxed a little, fairly certain that no one was ever murdered after a See 'n Say sound check.

A fast clippity-clomp came charging down the hall, getting closer to the kitchen.

The only image Joy's mind could muster, besides that giant Foghorn Leghorn from the cartoons, was that pesky goat, Waddles, kicking and galloping down the hall. Now, that could be a mess.

Rushing toward the ruckus to limit the damage, Joy stopped dead in her tracks at the sight of a little girl standing in the hallway, looking like she wasn't sure whether to scream or scram.

Only about six feet separated Joy from the blond-haired child. "Who are you?"

The little girl clutched a black lunch bag in one hand

against her blue jumper with a fancy *M* monogrammed on the front, and two chubby orange yarn hair ties hung from the other. The freckle-faced child looked so fragile standing there.

"What's your name?"

"I'm . . . I'm Molly."

"You're . . ." *Like the rabbit?* Joy noticed the hand-painted rabbit on the little girl's lunch bag that looked an awful lot like Molly the Bunny. *This can't be happening.*

Little-girl Molly's mouth hung wide and her eyes darted like a wild animal's. Cornered and desperate. "Wh-where's Ruby?"

"She's not here. She's in the hospital with a hurt ankle."

"But I come here every day. Ruby makes my lunch and we go to the bus." Tears welled in Molly's eyes.

Maybe the goat running down the hall would have been better than this.

Oh no, please don't cry. "Where's your momma?"

The little girl pointed toward the door, her hand shaking.

"It's okay. I'll straighten it out." Joy whipped around Molly and ran toward the front door just in time to see a blue compact car back out of the driveway. She waved her arms spastically as she took the porch steps two at a time. "Excuse me. Hello!" She raced out to the front yard, but the driver of the car seemed completely unaware of her yelling and hailing. As Joy ran to the end of the driveway, the car became a dot in the distance, then disappeared.

Out of breath, and out of her element, she turned and walked slowly back to the house.

What am I supposed to do with a little girl? There are certainly no instructions in the barn about that.

Chapter Eight

Ben couldn't remember the last time he'd lazed around in bed. Except on a Saturday. Or maybe he could, but he'd had a woman in his bed back then. No sense lolling around alone.

Then again, he wasn't complaining. Because alone suited him just fine. Not having to fight for mattress real estate was just one of the perks of bachelorhood.

Between the to-dos he had piling up and thinking about the girl from the hospital parking lot last night, he may have gotten a total of three hours' sleep—if he was lucky.

She was pretty. Her hair had shimmered under the moonlight, and her waist was so petite that he was certain he could've wrapped his hands around it easily. He wondered if her eyes sparkled like that even when she wasn't flustered. Green? Maybe blue. It was hard to tell, but the way her thick lashes lay against her cheeks when she was looking down had made him want to tip her chin up and pull her in close. Waking up to her this morning might not have been half bad either. But the sun streaming through his window was all the wake-up call he'd needed on this Friday morning.

He swept back the sheets, sending them into the air,

then landing in a soft parachute over the black Lab still snoring on the other side of the bed.

"I keep you up last night, P?"

Profit belly-crawled out from the covers and shook his ears. The nickname P suited him better once Ben had realized people thought he'd named the dog Prophet. Totally different thing. Profit had seemed like a cool dog name for an accountant, but maybe he was the only one who got the joke.

"Sorry about that." Ben showered, and P was still right where he'd left him, lying with his chin on top of his paws as if watching while Ben got dressed. Ben pulled his belt through the loops of his jeans, then reached over and gave the dog's head a scratch.

After a long lazy stretch, the dog bounded to the ground and padded behind Ben to the kitchen. Ben poured a cup of coffee and dropped three pieces of wheat bread into the toaster.

He checked his planner and sipped coffee until the toaster popped. Slathering crunchy peanut butter on all three slices, he stood at the sleek granite counter and munched, tearing pieces from the third slice of toast and tossing them into the air one at a time for his pal. P never missed a bite.

Ben popped the last morsel into his mouth. "Sorry, man. All gone."

P didn't look convinced.

"I didn't ask you to share your kibble with me." Ben held out his hands like a blackjack dealer proving himself. *Why am I having to prove anything to my dog? Who's really the boss here?* "It's tree day. You ready to go?"

P spun around in a delighted canter, and then leapt in the air, nipping at Ben's sleeve.

"Thought you'd forgive me."

The dog danced and pranced, matching Ben's gait all the way to the front door.

Ben grabbed his keys off the hall table and locked the door behind them. P dashed through the yard, kicking up crunchy dry leaves in his wake while Ben went around back to the shed.

By the time Ben made it to the truck, P was already waiting, stomping his feet impatiently by the driver's-side door. With the chain saw safely secured in the bed, Ben opened the truck door. P leapt into the front seat, hopped over the console, and settled in the passenger seat to ride shotgun. Ben started the truck, then lowered the passenger window for Profit.

With a twist of the knob, the radio speakers filled the cab with holiday tunes. Ben pulled out of his driveway and then took to the back roads toward Murfees Corner. He knew these roads well. He'd driven them for so many years that he knew where he could exceed the posted speed limit, and where not to dare go even five over. P's shiny black ears flew back as he chomped at the wind and squinted against the breeze.

By the time they made the hour drive west to pick out trees, P would be asleep from all the fresh air.

Ben whistled along with the Christmas carols on the radio, his thoughts wandering back to the first year he'd been married to Cecilia. She'd demanded that they have an artificial tree. His first ever. Damn thing was still in the attic. That should have been a red flag, warning him that things were going to go downhill from there, and they sure had. At the speed of an Olympic downhill ski race.

P was the best thing he got out of that relationship.

He reached over and gave P a pat on the back of the head. The girl from last night looked like a real-tree kind of gal, even if she did drive a hybrid. Washington, D.C., tags. That meant she was either visiting or new to town.

Hopefully new in town.

Where the heck had that random thought come from? He snagged his sunglasses from the visor and put them on. Maybe to shield the sun, but more likely to distract the thoughts of that girl who kept leaping to mind. After the debacle with Cecilia, the last thing he had interest in was a woman.

But then why had he noticed her ring finger was bare?

He always picked the wrong girls, and he'd pretty much decided alone was better. But a few dinners out with Joy wouldn't be a half-bad way to spend some time. Everyone needed friends, right?

He pushed that thought aside too, putting blame squarely on the fact that the holidays were closing in. No question that holidays were more fun when you had someone to share them with.

White's Christmas Tree Farm had been around since Ben's dad was a boy. Passed down through generations, with old cedar fence posts and rusty twisted barbwire still surrounding the vast acreage. Not that it was needed for Christmas trees, but the original Farmer White had been a cow farmer. Unfortunately, it seemed that every time he'd gone to town, those darn cows would find their way out of the fence, leaving his wife stuck with trying to round them up. After a while, enough was enough, and the little missus finally demanded they pick something else that would be less of a hassle. Since Mrs. White was a Christmas fanatic, always decorating several trees herself, they'd made the choice to grow trees.

Ben slowed as he neared the turnoff.

The sign, an engine-less shell of a red 1950s-era

Chevrolet step-side pickup flaunting straight block lettering along its soft curves, marked the entrance near the road. The truck bed held what looked to be at least twenty small four-foot trees—stacked one on top of the other. A stripped tree trunk rose from the center bearing a sign in the shape of a star nailed to the top, boasting a price of ten dollars each, payable on the honor system. Just toss your money in the slot cut in the glove compartment of the truck.

Ben wondered how many people took advantage of that convenience. Either way, it was a cool idea and a pretty awesome deal. He pulled his truck into the lane and idled through the open red gates, kicking up a rooster tail of dust as he cruised.

He passed two painted milk cans with the same color and lettering as the pickup truck, pointing the way to the parking area.

The old homestead had once stood where the tree attendants hung out. The brick two-story chimney and firebox was about all there was left of it. Sturdy and strong, it still served a purpose, stoking up a fire for whoever was working the cutting station that winter. They wouldn't need a fire today. The sky was as blue as the waters off the Caribbean coast, and it was more like football weather on a September afternoon than mere weeks from Christmas.

Ben and P got out of the truck.

Dave White met them halfway. "Good to see you again, Ben. The tree I sent over for the hospital worked out okay, didn't it?"

"It was perfect. Already have it decorated. Wait until you see it."

"Good. I measured it twice to be sure."

"Right to the top of the skylight."

"Good. Hey, you haven't met my grandson. This is his

first year out here with me. Mike, this is Ben Andrews. He gets his trees from me every year. He wasn't any bigger than you the first time his daddy brought him out."

"Put her there, Mike." Ben shook the young boy's hand. Kid couldn't be more than eleven or twelve, but he looked ready for business, standing proud next to his grandpa.

"Thought you wouldn't be here for your own trees until this weekend," Dave said.

"That was the plan, but things have gotten so busy, I thought I better work this trip in while I could. Besides, I figured it wouldn't be so busy here on a Friday."

"Got that right. The usual?"

"Yep. Tabletop size for Mom, three five-foot and two seven-foot trees for Miss Ruby, and a ceiling scraper for my place."

Dave's white Santalike beard bounced against his chest as he laughed. "Right. Twelve-foot ceiling. I remember." The huge man bent over and patted P on the head. "You gonna dehydrate trying to christen every tree we walk by again this year?"

Mike giggled at his granddad's comment.

P barked.

"It *is* tradition." Ben lifted his chain saw out of the truck bed and shoved a pair of gloves into his back pocket.

"It's quiet here this morning. Mike and I'll help you." Dave walked over to a John Deere Gator UTV. Mike sat in the front, and Ben and P slid into the backseat. They rode off through the trails between the precisely planted trees. "There are some awesome trees back here!" Dave hollered over his shoulder. "Haven't opened this lot up to anyone else this year."

"Thanks. Nothing better than selecting and cutting down my own trees. I look forward to this all year."

"Know what ya mean," Dave agreed. "Even after all

these years, I love the sound of the chain saw firing up. The mixture of the pine, gasoline, and sawdust. They make that into a man's cologne . . . then they'd have really done something."

Ben wasn't a small guy, but he always felt like a kid next to Dave. Not just because of the age difference either. Dave had to be every bit of six feet four inches or better with shoulders as wide as a linebacker's, only he didn't need any pads. And the acreage of trees and countryside quickly put into perspective how a person fit into the bigger scheme of nature. Just one tiny piece of a huge landscape.

Two and a half hours later, P's tongue was dragging and the Gator was stacked high with the trees Ben had picked out. Dave drove them back to the lot. One of the young guys hoisted the trees one by one from the Gator into the bed of Ben's truck while P lapped from a huge trough of water meant for the goats. Twelve goats bleated and climbed the fence for attention in a makeshift petting zoo for visitors, but the truth was, those goats were one of nature's fastest tree-trimming chipper solutions. A goat farmer from up the road switched out the small herd every few days, treating them to something green this time of year. The goats devoured the trimmed limbs and peeled the bark right down to the raw wood.

Ben pulled cash from his pocket and paid Dave. "Until next year." He turned to Mike, who was guzzling a cola next to the counter made out of old pallets painted in candy cane stripes. "Nice to meet you, Mike. Maybe I'll see you next year."

"Hope so, Mr. Andrews."

Ben tucked a five-dollar bill into the boy's hand as they shook.

Mike looked in his hand, his eyes popping wide. "Thanks, Mr. Andrews."

"You're welcome, Mike. Keep up the good work." Nice kid. Good manners. He hoped one day his kid would make him as proud, but damn did being called "mister" make him feel old all of a sudden. "See you next year, old man," he said to Dave, if for no other reason than to make himself feel a little better.

"Counting on it. Don't forget to send me a picture of the tree lighting for the website and Facebook."

"You got it." Ben opened the door to his truck, slapped his hand to his thigh, and P pounced in and took his position. Ben lowered his window, enjoying the fresh air and the occasional whiff of the pine when he slowed at the stop signs.

Ben's phone buzzed against the center console of his truck. Not recognizing the number, he pressed Speaker and answered with a quick hello as he rolled up the window so he could hear better.

"Mr. Andrews, my daughter, Ashley, works for you."

Ben's concern had him pulling to the side of the road. Ashley was eight months pregnant. He hoped everything was okay. She'd worked for him for almost five years now, and she'd been trying to have a baby the whole time he'd known her. *Please don't let anything be wrong.*

Ashley's mom continued, "You're not going to believe this, but not twenty minutes after Ashley got into town here last night, she went into labor."

He let out the breath he'd been holding. "Labor? She's okay, right? I mean this is really early."

"A month early. I thought for sure it was Braxton Hicks contractions, ya know, false labor, but she sure fooled me. Good thing I humored her and took her to the hospital. Wasn't an hour later she made me the proud grandmother of the most precious, beautiful, smoochalicious little hunk of a man. That'll teach her husband's mom to try to horn in on scheduling a visit at delivery time with my daughter. It's only proper for the mother of the mother to be there. Not the mother-in-law! Anyway, please spread the word, and I guess you'll need to put her maternity leave into effect immediately. They'll be staying here for the next few weeks. And, if I have it my way, maybe they'll spend Christmas here."

"Well, isn't this a surprise." And not a particularly good one if he had to consider just what this meant to his work-load, although he was excited for the young couple. "And she's doing okay?"

"Oh, she did great. They are both strong, even if she can't seem to make up her mind on the name for him. Anyway, they'll be here in the hospital. Doctor wants to keep them a couple days just to keep an eye on the little guy. He's not but barely five pounds. Just a little peanut, but no worries. They are both going to be just fine."

"Congratulations."

And there it was, the jinx his buddy Jason had warned him about. Now he'd have to find a backup person to co-ordinate the details of the annual Carolina's Best Flour Extreme Gingerbread Bake-off. He'd taken on that volunteer activity for the hospital, thinking that he could free up one of his staff, Ashley, to handle all of it. She wasn't supposed to go out on maternity leave until January, so the timing had been perfect for her to cover that for him. At least he'd thought so.

A month early? Who would've thought he'd need a backup plan for an early first baby? *Crash.*

Ben smiled in an attempt to mask the frustration he was feeling as he spoke. "You tell Ashley not to worry about a thing. Congratulations on the unexpected arrival. Thank you for the call."

"You are so welcome. Oh, and she said her files for the

Extreme Gingerbread Bake-off are in her top right drawer, and apologized she hadn't gotten farther along."

And burn. He doubted the smile would hide the tightness of his words now. "No worries." He had no right to be upset. Ashley was managing that project as a volunteer. And even worse, the contestants had been announced in last week's newspaper, and he was on his mother's team, so it would be a huge conflict of interest for him to manage and judge the event.

Good thing Christmas was his favorite holiday, because he was about to be armpit deep in lights, caroling, and gingerbread houses.

Chapter Nine

This morning TGIF had just gone to a whole new level, because if Joy had to take care of Molly two days in a row, she might lose her mind. Child care was one skill that was not on her résumé.

By the time she'd figured out what needed to be done for Molly, gotten her on the school bus, and waved good-bye at the curb, Joy had already lost an hour of her morning. And for the first time she had a little compassion for those mornings when Renee rolled in to work about thirty minutes late, frazzled and apologizing. It was a wonder Renee wasn't late a whole lot more often.

Joy's plan had been to be at the hospital, checking in on Ruby by now. She liked to think she was flexible, but if there was one thing that drove her nuts, it was a day that started off with unexpected hitches. Okay, fine, maybe she didn't like any kind of deviation from her plan at *any* time, but was that such a bad vice? It certainly had proved beneficial from a career perspective.

Every plan needed a mitigation plan, and she was usually completely prepared, but the unexpected chain of events this morning once Molly appeared had left Joy exhausted. That god-awful cock-a-doodle-doo, like a See 'n Say on its last legs, rang in her mind. For a fleeting moment, she considered crawling back into bed and just starting all over, but her sensible side wouldn't let her succumb to the aggravation in that way.

Plus, Ruby was sure-fired ready and waiting to come home.

The morning sun was warming things up. A soft billow of steam hung over the morning dew, and the chill that had greeted Joy early this morning had been chased away. She wouldn't need a sweatshirt jacket now. She shed it, hung it on the chair in the front hall, and marched through the kitchen, snagging one of the crusts that she'd been instructed to cut from the peanut butter and grape jelly sandwich she'd made for Molly. *And next time, can you cut it in squares?* she'd asked. *Really?*

Joy stuffed the morsel into her mouth. It had been a long time since Joy'd had a PBJ, and it was a lot tastier than she'd remembered. The whitewashed wooden screen door slapped the frame behind her as loud as a gunshot. The donkey kicked his feet in the air and ran around the pasture, snorting as if buckshot had just zoomed past him. She rounded up Ruby's muck boots and ran the hose over them to clean them up after last night's stinky mess. She buried her nose in the sleeve of her shirt to keep from gagging, but as she moved, she splashed the icy-cold hose water on her socks.

She slipped off her wet socks and sat on the stoop to wiggle her damp feet into the rubber boots. She gave Molly the Bunny a sneer. "You tricked me. I thought you were the Molly everyone was so worried about."

The fuzzy rabbit lifted itself to its hind feet and wiggled its nose.

"Yeah, you want me to feed you. I know." Joy filled the scoop with food and sprinkled it into the bowl, then cleaned the water dish. "I bet you don't want crusts either."

Feeding the menagerie seemed like a long and tedious task at night, but it was much more so in the daytime, when the animals were wide awake and begging for attention. The goats were under her feet the whole time she tried to pour the feed in their trough. If she wasn't careful, she'd be in a cast too.

"Stop that!" She swatted at the donkey. "Quit chewing my braid!" She wasn't sure if he was chewing her hair or the ribbon, but either way, she didn't like it one bit.

As she checked off the last item on the morning chore list, one look around told the story of how well she'd done.

Even graded on a curve, she'd probably get a D+ at best.

The barn looked a mess. Ruby hadn't been gone even twenty-four hours. Joy tromped to the back wall of the barn and rummaged through the tools until she found a rake. Finding a quick rhythm, she swept the wide tines along the dirt floor of the barn. The pinging sound of metal against dirt soothed her, and the tension of the morning started to subside. With slow, measured strokes, she made her way from one end to the other until the barn looked ready for a dance. Just as Ruby had left it. Joy scooped the hay that she'd gathered into her arms and dropped it into the empty stall. It wouldn't be good for food, all dirty, but it would still make good bedding.

She double-checked all the gates, and then went inside to get cleaned up so she could get to the hospital. Hopefully, Ruby would be ready to come home, and they'd figure out what needed to be done from there. She'd get her aunt settled in and be back home before the weekend was over. She'd even have time to go through her e-mail before jumping back into the welcoming fray at the office on Monday morning.

Joy swung into the same parking space at Bridgewater Regional Hospital that she'd been in last night. She gave the parking lot a quick scan as she got out of her car. There was no sign of the pickup truck that her car had gotten so intimate with. If only that had been a dream. Unfortunately, there was a constant reminder of how real that had been. She glanced back at the gouge on the side of her car.

How she hadn't broken the taillight, she'd never know, but at least the damage was only cosmetic. She had to be thankful for that. Being stuck with no car or, worse, having to drive Aunt Ruby's ancient gas-guzzling Lincoln would have been torture. That car was nearly as old as Joy.

Hopefully, she wouldn't run into Mr. Indestructible Pickup Truck again while she was in town, even if he was super-good-looking, had given her his jacket to keep her warm, and declined her insurance information. But she'd be leaving soon. No sense making friends with someone she'd probably never see again. She was busy, and this trip had not been scheduled.

She hurried inside the hospital. Ruby was probably raising holy heck, waiting on her. A woman walked by with flowers and a balloon. For a second, Joy hesitated, considered ducking into the gift shop to grab something, but knowing her aunt the way she did, she'd rather not have to wait even an extra five minutes.

"Time is precious," she'd always say.

Joy caught the elevator door before it closed, and stepped to the back wall. The woman with the balloon stood near the door. The balloon seemed to have a life of its own, bobbing that giant smiley face in her direction as it bounced against the door with a *thwump, thwump, thwump*. The doors opened and that doggone smiling Mylar balloon trailed behind the woman, taunting Joy with every step toward the hallway. *Nah-nah-nah, you didn't bring a present. And you're late.*

Some of the rooms had two beds. She was glad Ruby had scored private accommodations. It would be annoying to have a roommate who had guests running in and out all day. Of course, in this case, Ruby would probably be the one causing the commotion. She'd lived in Crystal Falls her whole life. There wasn't anyone in this town who didn't know her. And if last night was any indication, she had lots of friends.

Joy tapped on the door as she entered Ruby's room. "Good morning, Aunt Ruby." Joy hoped her aunt had slept in and hadn't been waiting too long on her. "How are you feeling?"

Ruby hugged the covers against her tiny frame. "Honestly, I had a pretty rough night. I guess you were right. Once the good stuff wore off, things started getting bad."

"Oh no. Are you in pain?" No wonder Ruby hadn't called in a tizzy because Joy took so long to show up.

"Some, but they've got me doped up again. I'll be fine, honey. Did you meet Molly?"

"I did." Joy put her hands on her hips. "I thought Molly was the bunny. She nearly scared me to death when she showed up this morning. Waltzed right in without so much as a knock."

"I must not have been clear. I'm sorry, dear. Those meds had me high as trash can punch. She's a sweet little angel. Her mother is going through some rough times. Thank you for taking care of her."

"I got her out the door."

"Molly isn't any trouble, and her mother, Ginny, counts on me. I can't let her down."

Joy could only imagine how important it was to feel

needed at Ruby's age. "Well, I think she'll be glad to have you back. She wasn't entirely pleased with the way I cut crusts from the sandwich I made for her."

"Crusts off and then in fours. Just like you used to like them." Ruby's face contorted in a way that seemed to say, *Is there any other way?*

"I did?"

"Oh yes. You'd never eat a crust. And only white bread. Been a while." Ruby tapped a finger to her head. "I might not remember what I said just last night. Might not even remember what I ate for breakfast, but I remember those kind of details. Special memories." A lazy grin spread across Ruby's face. Her pupils were dilated from the effects of the painkillers, making her look a little cross-eyed crazy.

"Anyway, I got her lunch packed, and got her on the bus."

"Bless you."

Enough about kids. That is behind me now. Joy sat down in the only chair in the room. A huge monstrosity of a thing covered in a plastic that could best be described as durable and god-awful ugly. "So what's the plan to get you out of here?"

Ruby raised a thin hand. "I'm waiting on the doctor. He hasn't been in yet. Not like we have a golf course for him to spend his morning on. I have no idea what's keeping him."

"Well, at least you weren't waiting on me. I was worried when I was running so far behind." Joy pulled the chair closer to the bedside. "I don't know how you get all that done every day. You need help."

"No. I don't need help. I've got a routine. A system."

"It's a lot to do."

"I enjoy it, and it's keeping me in good shape."

"Well, that leg has seen better days." The doctor ambled into the room. With his white coat, tablet, and a stethoscope around his neck, he looked like he'd never hurried a day in his life. He circled the bed to Ruby's side. "How're you feeling?"

"Anxious to get out of here," Ruby said. "That's how I'm feeling. What took you so long? You know I've got things to do."

"Don't we all," he said.

"You won't be getting your eggs if I don't get home and collect them. Those darn hens of mine would rather sit and hatch a pile of chicks if I'd leave them to."

The doctor reached across the bed to shake Joy's hand. "I'm Dr. Davis."

"Joy." She shook his hand. "I'm Ruby's niece."

"Emma's daughter. I see it now. Nice to see you again."

She hadn't even recognized him. He'd been old as dirt when she was a little girl.

The doctor pulled back the sheet at the bottom of the bed and touched Ruby's toes. "Feel that?"

"Of course I feel that. Your hands are ice-cold."

The doctor laughed. "The nurses keeping you comfortable?"

"Now, Doc, you know that I'm not going to be comfortable until I'm home in my own bed, so why don't you write me out of this place and let me get about my business."

"As long as you are stable when I come to see you in the morning, I don't see any reason that we won't be able to move you to Dixon County Rehab Center tomorrow."

"Rehab center? Look. I might take a little nip now and again, but I wasn't drunk when I fell. I don't need any rehab. Someone has misinformed you."

"Not that kind of rehab, Miss Ruby. This is for you to

get the physical therapy you'll need to get back on your feet, and to help you learn how to get around in that cast. This kind of break takes time to heal. Especially for a gal your age."

"I'll have you know that this gal seems to do just as much as, maybe more than, most of the gals half my age in this town."

Joy nodded. "I have to admit she must be in better shape than me. I could barely get the whole list of her chores done."

"Don't get yourself riled up. I know you're fit, and I have no doubt you'll make a strong recovery, that is, *if* you follow my orders. You really need to do the rehab."

"Why can't I do your silly exercise program at home?"

"Because we don't have the equipment to do that, and it's more than just exercise. Your insurance won't cover that type of care at home. Your recovery will be much faster if we let Dixon County Rehab do what they do best."

"It's all a scheme to get into our pockets."

"I can assure you that you'll be well taken care of there. Enjoy the break."

Ruby's face paled and her lips pulled into a tight line. "I've got animals on the farm that need tending to."

"I'm sure someone can help." Dr. Davis glanced in Joy's direction.

Shirley had been right all along. This was not going to go the way Ruby had predicted. Joy felt the pressure of Dr. Davis's gaze. "We'll find someone to help."

"I'm not letting just anyone pussyfoot through my stuff." Ruby grabbed the bars on the side of the bed, twisting and scooching herself to a seated position, her cast nearly pulling her off the side of the bed like an anchor.

Dr. Davis stepped back and let her squirm for a

moment. "You done fussing? The insurance will cover your stay. Do you have someone who can transport you to the facility?"

"I'll take her," Joy said.

"Joy, you've already missed work. You never miss work. I cannot ask you to do that."

"I'm already here. It's the weekend; I besides, it's where I want to be. You let me worry about what I can or can't do with my time."

Dr. Davis lifted Ruby's cast leg back up onto the bed, then adjusted his coat. "You just keep your focus on getting well so we can have you home by Christmas."

"Christmas? That's nearly three weeks away! I cannot be away from my house for that long. No, sir."

"You'll probably be home well before that. If things are going well, you could be home in just a couple of weeks."

"You promise that?" Ruby's eyebrow arched so high, it practically disappeared from view.

The doctor let out a breath. "You know I can't make that promise, but what I can promise is that if you take your role seriously at rehab and follow their instructions, things will go much faster."

Ruby shot a worried glance toward Joy. "But there's not just the animals. It's the decorating for the big Christmas event and Molly. Molly counts on me. I've made commitments. You can't do all of that. It's too much."

"Aunt Ruby, I am an experienced leader of million-dollar projects. I am sure that I can handle the things you've got scheduled."

"You'll miss work."

"I've got the time on the books to take. I'll just take it. No problem."

"It's too much."

"Give me some credit. You're my family." Joy rested her

hand on Ruby's. "I want to do this. Please let me. And if you're worried it's all too much, then I'll talk to Molly's mom. I'm sure she can make other arrangements until you're back on your feet. See, one less thing already."

"No!" Ruby shot straight up. "I can't make them feel like they're a burden. Of all the things on my plate, taking care of Molly is the one thing I can't let fall by the wayside. I cannot let them down. They count on me as much as you did back when your momma was going through troubled times. She needs the safe haven I can provide." Ruby's face flushed, her eyes flashing concern.

"Okay, okay. Calm down. I can do this. I'll figure it out."

Ruby collapsed back on the pillows. "You're finally going to take time off, and I won't even see you."

"There's just no making you happy today, is there? You know they do allow visitors at that kind of rehab, right? I'll come visit."

"You'll even make some new friends there if I know you, Ruby." Dr. Davis patted Ruby on the cast leg. "Let's get that leg elevated on that pillow. That'll help keep the swelling down."

As he helped Ruby get repositioned in bed, Ruby mumbled something about being helpless, but neither Dr. Davis or Joy acknowledged it. Sometimes it was just better that way.

"So, we have a plan, right?" Dr. Davis asked, looking for agreement.

Ruby's frown was so tight, her eyebrows almost touched. "We can't let Molly down, Joy. You have to promise me. That's the most important thing I do. Please don't let them know it's an inconvenience. It's important. Their story isn't mine to share, but trust me . . . they need my help. Our help. Please."

"I promise." But her mind was already sorting through the tasks. Surely she could run a farm for a couple of weeks, and decorating for the holidays might even turn out to be fun. Even though she hadn't done it since she was a teen living with Ruby, how hard could it be? But that little girl, Molly, was a whole other story.

Something in her gut told her that she may have bitten off more than she could chew, because entertaining children was something she had very little experience with except in the controlled environment of market research—with a staff to help.

Chapter Ten

It shouldn't have surprised Joy that when she arrived at the hospital, Ruby was sitting in a wheelchair, waiting. At least she wouldn't have to park and go inside, but even from the driver's seat, she could see that Ruby was in a mood. Even the young nurse was standing a good arm's distance away from her. Poor thing must've drawn the short straw.

Joy sucked in a breath and dashed from the car to help the fear-stricken woman with her aunt.

"Ready to roll?"

Ruby flashed her a look of disdain. "Been ready long enough to wonder if you were going to show up or not."

The nurse rolled her lips into a sharp line and shook her head. Not that Joy needed a warning.

The set of Ruby's chin was a sure sign, and every remark she made from the wheelchair to the front seat of Joy's car, which Ruby described as a Matchbox, was a grumble. Joy was determined not to argue or try to convince her otherwise. Wouldn't do any good anyway. She knew, because she had that same stubborn streak.

With Ruby situated, Joy got behind the wheel and pulled out of the parking lot. She pushed the buttons on the radio until she found a channel playing holiday music. At least if Ruby were singing, she'd have to wipe that frown off her face.

But even the joyous sounds of the music and familiar melodies weren't enough to soften Ruby's mood. That made for the longest hour's drive Joy'd ever had to make. D.C. traffic on a Friday afternoon was better than this.

Crystal Falls faded in her rearview mirror, and Joy had to admit the scenery was beautiful. The route traversed fields stripped of their latest crops, open and clear. The autumn leaves had abandoned the trees, leaving them bare and ready to brave the icy temperatures that winter promised would arrive soon.

Houses were few and far between down this stretch of road, but as the speed limit dropped from 55 to 35 mph, the next town vamped red and white candy canes from every lamppost. A cop sat at the edge of town, running radar. Pulling someone over would have somehow seemed wrong here at the holidays, but since he was sporting a wreath on the front of the patrol car, maybe that made up for it a little.

She didn't dare go even the unwritten five miles over the speed limit. She may have been gone from this area for a long time, but she still remembered the jokes about the tickets that funded small towns around here.

A slightly cocky feeling teased a smile on Joy's lips as she cruised past the policeman, and began to accelerate toward the increased speed limit sign ahead. *Falalala-lala-la-la*.

Finally the Dixon County Rehabilitation Center came into view. Set on acreage as lush and beautiful as an exclusive country club golf course, the building, all steel and blue glass, gleamed in the sunlight. "Wow. This place is swanky."

Ruby bunched her lips. "Pretty isn't everything. At least

our little hospital has heart. I would rather have been there. Close to home."

"I know, but if this will get you on your feet faster, it'll be worth it, and I'll visit or call every day."

"I'm a big girl. You don't have to make this drive every day. You're doing enough just holding down things at the house for me. I don't want to be a pain in your—"

"Don't be silly. I just wish I'd come to visit before you needed me." Joy felt the guilt catch in her throat, a sudden surge of sadness that caught her off guard. She'd been selfish, and she didn't like that about herself.

Joy pulled the car to a stop in the circle drive in front of a set of double doors. REGISTRATION had been chiseled into the stonelike structure. A high-end touch for a small town. The covered entry protected them from the wind and weather, and benches graced the extra-wide sidewalk.

A blue-haired team of three women swarmed out like a welcome committee. Each wore hot pink scrubs with fancy silver script embroidered across their left pocket tagging them as volunteers. Bright white sneakers on their feet, they scurried and scampered around the car like a NASCAR pit crew. One greeted Joy and asked for any luggage the patient might have while the other two opened Ruby's door and started urging her toward the wheelchair.

"I'm quite able," Ruby said in response to their fussing.

"Of course you are, but we have a job to do. Come on, just make us look good."

Joy respected their efforts. They acted as if Ruby were the sweetest little old woman they'd ever met. If the team of blue-haired volunteers were able to get Ruby out of the bitter mood she was in, Joy'd owe them more than a thank-you.

Ruby folded her hands in her lap and let the two women whisk her inside. The volunteer who'd taken Ruby's bag was already checking things off her clipboard and barking orders to the other two. "She's prechecked from Bridgewater Regional."

Ruby twisted in the chair, panic flickering in her eyes.

Joy couldn't help but feel sorry for her aunt. Joy double-stepped to keep up with the gray-haired welcome committee. "I'm right here," she said, hoping to reassure her.

Dixon County Rehabilitation Center was lovely, all right, but Ruby had a point. It wasn't as inviting as Bridgewater Regional. The Christmas tree in the lobby here wasn't real. No, it was one of those metal jobs with all the LED lights, and there were Kwanzaa ornaments, dreidels, and huge vertical boxcar-shaped ornaments representing Christmases around the world—FELIZ NAVIDAD, JOYEUX NOËL, FROHE WEIHNACHTEN, and in more than a dozen languages that she couldn't decipher.

The holiday tree fairly represented every religion and language Joy could think of, and a few she couldn't figure out. But at least they'd tried to be sure they'd included everyone. It was almost like a little history lesson in celebrations around the world.

The old blue-hairs stopped at the nurses' station and put another plastic bracelet on Ruby's left arm.

"What's your birth date?"

"The same as it was the other four times you asked." Ruby stirred uneasily in the chair. "July 26. For heaven's sake. Can you write it down? I'm tired of saying it." Ruby shook her wrist in the air. "And I'm quite dang sure it's on all three of these bracelets you insist on me wearing." She glanced at the most recent addition. A bright yellow one. "'Fall Risk'? I haven't fallen, and I don't plan to."

"Well, then, how'd you break your leg?" asked the tallest of the volunteers.

Oh, that woman had no idea the hornet's nest she

was poking. That volunteer had "pot-stirrer" written all over her.

Ruby settled her gaze on the woman, her eyes piercing and dark. "That was an accident, and *none* of your business."

But the crew wasn't to be waylaid. One woman lifted the brakes from the wheelchair and whisked Ruby toward the door as another punched in the code activating the automatic doors. They whisked her through the halls at the speed of a race car driver on his last lap.

Finally they parked Ruby in a private waiting room. The instigator wagged a finger toward Ruby. "As soon as you get in your room, you're going to want to get changed into your tennis shoes and sweats. Physical therapy starts at the top of the hour." The woman spun around and walked off before Ruby could respond.

Joy had to admire the woman's tenacity.

"Are you sure you haven't dumped me off at boot camp?" Ruby's head hung like she'd been put through the wringer, and they hadn't even been there fifteen minutes.

"It'll be fine. I packed your shoes and sweats. I'll help you get changed."

"This is really embarrassing. And how did you know to bring those things?"

"The nurse told me last night when I was leaving that you'd need those for rehab. I stopped at the store and bought you some."

"I'll pay you back."

"Don't be silly. It was nothing."

"Why do they want me to have a pair of shoes? I can't wear but one of them."

She had a point. But the sneakers were the least of their worries, because getting Ruby into the sweats with that cast was a bigger challenge than she'd considered.

"Everyone ready?" A petite brunette nurse came into the waiting room. "You must be Ruby Johnson. I'm Carolyn. I'll be your nurse while you're here with us. How are we doing?"

"*You* seem to be doing just fine," Ruby said.

"Can I call you Ruby?"

Ruby nodded, but didn't offer anything else in the way of niceties.

So, it was going to be that kind of day. "I'm her niece, Joy," she said, standing to shake the nurse's hand. "I thought we were doing okay, but I think we're going to need some scissors to cut the seam of the sweatpants I bought. I wasn't thinking about the cast when I bought them, and they have elastic at the ankles."

Carolyn laughed. "You'd think they'd make those casts smaller, wouldn't you? How much do you think that thing weighs, Miss Ruby?"

"A ton."

"I'm with you on that. Rather than tear up those new sweats, why don't I just let you wear a pair of these loose-fitting pants we have? They're gonna be a little long on you, but I'm an expert hem roller. You're a little gal like me. We short girls are always underestimated, aren't we?"

"You got that right," Ruby said.

"Hopefully we'll get you up and moving around in no time. Maybe they'll get you in a soft cast soon, so you can wear some of your own clothes. That always makes our patients feel better."

The deep lines in Ruby's face eased a bit. "I think I'm going to like you, Carolyn."

"Well, thank you, Miss Ruby." Carolyn gave a quick wink in Joy's direction. "I already do like you."

The nurse was so short that she looked about sixteen

years old, but Ruby had taken to the girl immediately. A good sign.

Carolyn pushed the wheelchair as Joy followed alongside. "Now, let's get you settled in to your room, Miss Ruby. We already have a physical therapy session set up for you this afternoon, and we don't want you to miss that."

"You make it sound like an afternoon tea."

Carolyn's soft laugh was reminiscent of wind chimes. Soft, but it grabbed your attention, and made you want to hear more of it. "Not exactly as pleasant as an afternoon tea, but if you give it one hundred percent, then I'll make you a cup of my favorite tea myself. From my private stash. Is that a deal?"

"Sounds delightful." Ruby reached her hand from her lap to her shoulder and patted the nurse's hand.

"Here we are. Room 142." Carolyn spun and backed the wheelchair into the room and in one half twirl had Ruby right next to the bed. "Home away from home."

"This is nice."

"It really is," Joy said. "Bright and cheerful. Look, they even have colored sheets."

"We do our best to make you comfortable while you're here. I'm going to let you girls get settled. I'll be right back with your palazzo pants, Miss Ruby." Carolyn moved quickly on polka-dotted clogs that probably added at least two inches to her height, yet she was still short.

Taking advantage of Ruby's mood shift, Joy tried to strike up a conversation before Ruby could grumble again. "I love that they have a Christmas tree up in the lobby. Very modern. Suits the building, don't you think? I bet it would be fun to do a modern tree like that."

"Don't you go getting any ideas like that for our trees. I have a whole plan for the holiday decor. I get five trees every year. Everything is mapped out. Just follow the plan, and it will be perfect."

"Sometimes something a little out of the box can be fun."

Ruby shot her a glare. "Don't make it more complicated than it is. You're doing enough already. Besides, my Handy Andy knows exactly where everything is and where it goes. Shirley is going to have him come and help you out."

"She mentioned something when she stopped by the first night I was here. I told her I don't need anyone's help."

"Well, don't you be stubborn."

Joy raised a brow. Who was Ruby to call her stubborn?

Thankfully, Carolyn came back in before Joy could say something she'd regret.

"Ready to suit up?" Carolyn had Ruby changed in record time.

"You actually look rather stylish," Carolyn said as she stepped back, admiring her handiwork.

"Thank you, dear."

A tall man with Italian good looks walked into the room, pushing a wheelchair. Joy couldn't help but notice that the man's arms were so thick that his short sleeves pinched at his biceps.

"Ready, young lady?"

"Me?" Ruby asked.

"Yes, ma'am. The cast is a giveaway. I think that makes you all mine."

"Flirty, aren't you?"

"And you're a feisty ol' gal. You put half that attitude into your workouts, and you'll be home by Christmas."

"Dang right, I'll be home by Christmas. I don't even want to be here now." She moved to the chair. "I'm no slacker. I'll be just fine. Don't even need this place, if you ask me."

"You're going to hurt Johnny's feelings," the behemoth of a nurse said with an exaggerated pout.

Ruby wagged a finger. "You always talk about yourself in third person? That's a little creepy, you know."

Johnny tossed his head back, looking ready for the challenge. "Oh yeah. We're gonna get along just fine."

"How old are you?" she asked.

"Too young for you."

She eyed him. "You single?"

"Why? You interested?"

Ruby's mood finally broke down. "No sir, but my wonderful niece here is single, and isn't she beautiful? Smart too. Big wheel at a big market research firm."

He cast his gaze in Joy's direction. "She's very beautiful. I believe I can see the resemblance."

"So maybe you two could do coffee."

"Aunt Ruby, let's just concentrate on you getting well."

"Well, doesn't hurt to do a little multitasking, and it's the holidays, after all. Who wants to be single over the holidays?"

"She has a point," Johnny offered.

"Let's get her well first." Joy turned her attention back to her aunt. "No matchmaking until you can walk."

"I bet you can get a discount on flowers in the gift shop to give Joy on y'all's first date."

Joy felt the flush fill her cheeks. "You better leave before she gives you a goat as a dowry to marry me."

"Always did want a goat," he teased.

"I'll be waiting right here for you, Aunt Ruby."

Ruby wiggled her fingers in a wave as Johnny spun her around in the wheelchair like a top.

Chapter Eleven

Joy walked down to the cafeteria to find a light snack and bottle of water to take back to Ruby's room. Visitors and nurses nodded politely and smiled as they passed. If she ever had to spend time in a rehabilitation center, she hoped she could come to one like this. It wasn't so unlike some of the nicer hotels she'd stayed in.

Once back in Ruby's room, she settled into the over-stuffed recliner next to the window and nibbled on a bag of raw almonds.

If Joy had realized that she'd have some quiet time, she would have brought her work computer with her. She could have worked on some of the year-end reviews that had to be done in the next few weeks. At least here she wouldn't have the constant interruptions of her staff and phone calls. Flipping through her iPhone, she deleted several messages she'd been copied on from the office that did not require any action on her part, and responded to one from Renee that was an update on the project plan. They were on schedule, but Margie had pulled one of their team to work on a project that had dropped in at the last minute. Renee said it wasn't impacting the schedule, but Joy could sense the frustration in Renee's rant. She'd never have mentioned it if it didn't bother her. On a brighter note, Renee had shared that the announcements for the promotions were going to be made at the gala.

There wasn't much Joy could or needed to do for work. And as happy as she was that she kept things so up to date on the project plan that anyone could pick it up and run with it, it also gave her a slight sense of dread. She liked feeling needed.

Ruby needed her right now, though, so it was a blessing that she could be here. "Yes. A blessing. Perfect timing, in fact," she said to no one as she grabbed a pad of paper from the bedside table and began a new list of all the things she needed to get done this week.

Before the page was even half full, Ruby's voice called from the doorway. Handsome Johnny wheeled her in, flashing an eye roll in Joy's direction.

Johnny seemed experienced, but was he ready for the likes of her aunt? "So, how'd you make out on your first physical therapy session?"

"About as good as you having a chance to find a husband in your thirties without my help," Ruby said. "We both need an accelerated plan. They had me sitting and standing about five million times. I mean, really, don't they know I've been sitting and standing for darn close to seventy years?"

"It's incremental, Miss Ruby. Trust me, you'll be begging for a break soon."

"Yes, well, overachieving does kind of run in our family," Joy said to Johnny.

Aunt Ruby raised her chin. "In everything except you getting married. I'd been married for years by the time I was your age. I did tell you she's single, didn't I, Johnny?"

"You might have mentioned it," he said, giving Joy a wink.

Joy bristled at the smooth gesture. Not her type. At all.

"I've got time. I will have you know that it is just an ugly rumor that women have less of a chance to marry once they pass thirty . . . which I have not. Market research shows that I'll have just as good a chance at love later, when I'm darned good and ready, as I do right now. So you can just stop worrying about me."

"I just want you to be happy."

"Who says I'm not?"

"You need more than just a job to enjoy life, honey. When your momma named you Joy, it was because she wanted for you all the things she hadn't been able to have. She wanted you to see the world, experience things, fall in love, have a family, dream dreams, and all that stuff. Not just work, work, work."

"I love my work."

"How do you know you won't love other things?"

Joy opened her mouth to argue, but Ruby actually had a point. How did she know? "I tell you what. I'll work on it."

"That's all I can ask."

"And you'll stop with the matchmaking?"

"Well, don't go half crazy. I'm your aunt. It's part of the job description."

"Great." Joy knew when she was beat.

Johnny laughed. "Let's get you into one of these chairs, Miss Ruby."

"Thank you, dear." Ruby raised a hand at him as he went to take her arm and help move her to the chair. "I can do it. I've mastered standing and sitting, remember." She swatted at him like a cat.

He backed off, and as soon as Ruby's bony butt hit the chair, he wheeled the empty wheelchair toward the door. "One of us from the physical therapy team will be back at seven o'clock tonight for just a quick little stretching session. We'll do it bedside. Won't take too long, but we want to keep you moving."

Poor guy didn't even wait for a response. Probably afraid he'd get an earful from Ruby.

"I could do this at home," Ruby argued.

"I heard that." He turned and looked over his shoulder. "You might even end up enjoying it if you give it half a chance. Don't knock it. You haven't even been here long enough to know."

She crossed her arms. "Oh, I know. Now, out with you!"

Aunt Ruby shook her head as Johnny wheeled out of sight. She bunched her lips like she had one more thing to say to him, then seemed to mentally push the thought aside and turned back to Joy. "Now, about those decorations. I've got some details for you. You might want to write these down."

Joy raised the list she'd already started, and Ruby rolled on with her dictation.

"I have some hardbound journals on the bookshelf in the living room. Middle right shelf. Red and green, of course. One might be silver. Anyway, all my notes from the past few years from the planning for the home tour are in there. Some of it is journaling, but you can just ignore that hogwash. At least it will give you a starting point."

"You were always so organized. I think I got those skills from living with you."

"Good. One of my best gifts to give. You are the closest thing I have to a daughter of my own. I'm so glad you're here. I really appreciate it, but are you sure you can take the time off with no problem?"

"Yes, ma'am. I've got it covered."

"Good—because, honey, there is a lot to do. You'll need to start making the cookie dough and freezing it so as we get closer to the date of the cookie crawl, we can bake them fresh. I usually spend the Thursday and Friday before baking all day long. I'm sure I'll be there to help you, but it's the only way to stay on schedule. I've usually got the freezer in the barn half-filled by now. Shame on me for not getting started last week. I sure hope you remember some of these recipes. I'm still using the ones that my mother made."

"That'll be fun. I haven't done any baking in . . . well, aside from a birthday cake for a girl at work, I may not have baked since we last baked holiday cookies together."

"That is far too long. Old family recipes and baking are good for the heart and soul."

"Hope I remember how."

"It's like riding a bike. You'll be fine, but we are behind."

"I'll catch up. You just tell me what to do."

"Oh goodness, so much to do." She tapped her finger to her lips. "All the recipes are in the wooden box on the shelf to the right of the sink next to the cookbooks. The ones that we can make the dough ahead and freeze have a blue highlighter line across the top. They'll be easy to find. Look through the notebooks and see what I've done before. I always switch things up each year so the locals feel like it's worth it to pay and come to the house again and again. It's how we raise money. It's important, and something I can do."

"Okay. Got it. Cookies. Journals."

"The ornaments are up in the attic."

"You put boxes in your attic?"

"No, silly. My Handy Andy does that for me. He's very helpful. Let him help. He loves it as much as I do."

Joy could just picture some old fart with tousled gray hair, a bushy mustache, and green Dickies hiked up under his armpits maneuvering up and down the attic stairs with dusty old boxes. That ought to be a real pleasure. Probably would move about as fast as a koala on eucalyptus leaves.

"And when you come back, will you bring my crochet basket? I've got to have something to do to keep me from going crazy in here."

"No problem."

"Have I told you how much I love you lately?"

"You have. I love you too."

"I'm sorry I've been so daggoned cranky, but I don't like being helpless. I worry I'm being such a pain in the fanny, you won't come back and spend time with me when we can have fun."

"I understand. Don't you worry. We'll have plenty of fun." But in the back of Joy's mind, as much as her heart meant it, she wondered if she could really make that promise. Good intentions were easy to promise, but actually taking time off for anything had not been in her master plan. Time off just seemed like time not well spent.

"That's good, because I can promise you, ignoring work-life balance will get you pretty much nothing except burnt out and probably always stuck with the assignments no one else wants. You do not want to be that person."

"Of course not." *Or maybe I already am?*

"You go on and run. Get home before dark. I love you, Joy."

Joy leaned over and kissed Ruby on the forehead. "Don't give them any trouble."

Ruby laughed, but didn't deny that she probably would. Which was good, because Joy wouldn't have believed it anyway.

Chapter Twelve

The ride back to Crystal Falls was quiet compared to the ride over with Ruby fussing the whole way. But over and over those words from Ruby about slaving away and getting the dregs of the project assignments nagged at her. Was that what she had done to herself? Missing the gala last year. Oh yeah, everyone was quick to pat her on the back for a job well done, but the truth was, no one else wanted that gig. Heck . . . she didn't even want it most days.

She checked her watch. There were still more than thirty minutes left of the drive back to Ruby's. The animals were probably already lined up against the fence, waiting for dinner. She twisted in the seat, her back feeling tight at just the thought of hulking those three-gallon buckets around to slop out scoops of food in each of the pens. She was using muscles she'd forgotten she even had.

As Joy passed through the last big town before Crystal Falls, she slowed to read the signs in each of the colorful storefronts. Maybe one day next week she'd stop in and pick up a gift for Renee for Christmas in one of these specialty shops. There wasn't time today. The forty miles still took nearly an hour since the speed limit dropped to

35 mph at least four times along the way. Of course, back in D.C., that forty miles would likely take her two hours on a good day, so she shouldn't complain. At least the scenery here was nice and there was no traffic slowing her down.

On the outskirts of Crystal Falls, a blue sign glowed in the distance. CRYSTAL FALLS LAZY CHOP. The new microbrewery. Well, maybe not that new. She remembered Ruby talking about it. Maybe that had been last year. Or the year before? Time sure did have a way of slipping away. The livestock at Ruby's would be screaming at her now anyway and she was hungry, so she might as well get something to eat now.

She signaled for the turn and slowed at the entrance. The parking lot was full, always a good sign, so she parked around back.

Inside, the restaurant was warm and inviting. The smell of malted lager and spicy barbecued meat mingled in the air. Her stomach growled.

She pulled off her coat and gloves as she waited to be seated. A sign boasted that Crystal Falls had the best food in the state. This town had no shame in amping up the value of their stuff. Maybe that had rubbed off on Joy when she'd lived here. It was the skill that had put her at the top of her career. Finding ways to showcase products and places in their best light so people would spend their money on them.

"Just one?" The woman, about her age, seemed surprised.

"Just me."

"Right this way," she said with a tone that probably included the unspoken "bless your heart," and led Joy to a table in the back corner. "Can I offer you one of our microbrews or a glass of wine tonight?"

"I'd love to try one of the local brews. Surprise me with your favorite."

"Perfect. I know just the one." The waitress went over the specials, then added, "but we're known for our smoked pork chops. Fall off the bone, melt in your mouth. You really can't go wrong with anything on this menu."

"I'll try the smoked pork chop dinner. Sounds perfect. Thank you."

"You won't be disappointed." She left to get Joy the beer.

Joy took out her phone and called Renee, who answered with an enthusiastic "I'm so glad to hear from you. How are things?"

The familiar voice was comforting. "Crazy. I just got Aunt Ruby settled in at the rehabilitation center."

"That sounds serious."

"She'll be fine. It's just going to take time."

"We miss you around here, but things are going fine. You doing okay?"

"Yes. There've been some challenges. I wrecked my car and then got sideswiped by a pint-sized seven-year-old. I'm not sure which was worse. How do you do that?"

"What?"

"The kid thing. I have a whole new appreciation for moms now. And for those mornings you're late. We might need to talk about adjusting your start time."

"After just one day?"

"One morning. An hour, tops."

"Then you have no idea."

"Please don't say that, because I just agreed to babysit and care for this kid until Ruby gets home from rehab. It could be weeks."

"Weeks? You're going to need wine."

"I'm in a local pub now. I might need more than that! Any mumbles about the promotions around there?"

"Not another word. It's been so quiet. I've never seen it so quiet when it comes to this kind of news before. I mean usually something leaks out about someone hearing they'd gotten the promotion. Not this time."

"That's weird." Joy had to agree that word was normally out by now.

"I was hoping you were calling to let me know they'd called and told you the good news."

"No. Haven't heard from anyone. I'm getting ready to call Margie to let her know that I'll be out until the end of the year. Are you going to be able to handle everything in my absence?"

"Of course."

"I sure hope this doesn't screw up my chances at the promotion."

"Don't be silly. You're the hardest-working associate here. Everyone knows you're next in line for that job. And things here are going great. In fact, Margie gave us the afternoon off yesterday so everyone could get some holiday shopping done."

Joy felt a pang of guilt. It was in her span of control to do those types of things, but she wouldn't have. There was always something that needed to be done in the office. Were her own priorities really that screwed up that she wouldn't have considered an afternoon off for her team? She pushed the worry aside. "I don't want to keep you, but I was thinking maybe you and the family could come down one weekend during the holidays. There's a big festival the Saturday before Christmas, including this big glittery Crystal Christmas Cookie Crawl, where folks come from all around to tour the houses, see the decorations, and snack on cookies. And, of course, Aunt Ruby's house is on it. Everyone is trying to outdo everyone else. I've got my work cut out for me."

"Christmas decorations? You'll rock that with no problem."

"I hope so. It seems to be a pretty big deal around here, and I'm out of practice. Heck, I haven't even put up a tree on my own before. Wish me luck," Joy said, feeling the tension in her neck. Decorating sounded fun, and easy, but she was feeling quite overwhelmed by it all. "You know, you ought to come. Your kids would love all the lights. It's not all that far, and I could use the support. I'd love it if you could come."

"Kevin would love it as much as the kids would. He hates that we live in a condo. I have to hear it every single year about how it's a disservice not to be able to have a real tree in the building. I mean, like, really? Who cares? They are so full of ornaments, you can barely see the tree itself anyway."

"I know what you mean." Although she really had never thought about it. A fake tree seemed to make much more sense from an investment perspective, and what a time-saver. Not that she'd bothered to put one up, real or otherwise, on her own . . . ever. "I'll e-mail you the details, and drop tickets in the mail to you. It's a fund-raiser, so it's my treat and if you can't come . . . it went to a good cause anyway. No pressure. There's plenty of room. You could stay right here on the farm. It would be great to see you."

"Thanks, but I'll see you before then. You'll be back for the gala, right?"

"Yeah, wouldn't miss that." Or would she? Getting someone to watch over things was a pretty big favor. Was there any chance Ruby would be back by the night of the gala? That was just eight days away. She glanced upstairs, thinking of the perfect dress hanging there. She'd think of something. "Yes. I'll see you then."

"Good. I can't wait."

"Right. Take care." Joy ended the call, feeling disconnected from everything she'd thought mattered. And the fact that Margie had let her team off work for the afternoon still nagged at her. Why did that bother her so much? She had a job to do. Was it so wrong to stay focused on the goals? To be ahead of the game when things weren't busy?

Joy's appetite had suddenly disappeared. She toyed with the phone in her lap. Nothing was going to change between now and Monday. She still had high hopes that she'd make the gala, but there was no way she'd be back in the office on Monday. At least she wouldn't have to go to Margie's kids' Christmas pageant. Now, that was a true Christmas gift!

She pressed the button to Margie's direct line. She'd readied herself to leave the message, but to her surprise, Margie had been in the office. *On a Saturday afternoon?* That had to be a first. The conversation was short and amicable, but why was it that Margie's overly enthusiastic support for Joy to take time off was unsettling?

Joy hung up the phone feeling a little off balance without the normal chaos of her schedule. And with things going so swimmingly without her at the office, it was hard not to take it a little personally.

A waitress walked by, carrying a stack of at least eight boxes in a tall, cakelike stack. She stopped at Joy's table and let the bottom box from the pile drop to the table.

"What's this?"

"Christmas ornaments. Tradition," she said. "Everyone joins in. Come on. It makes fast work of a huge project."

The tree stood in the corner of the restaurant, blocking the glass window that gave customers a view into the beer vats. Hundreds and hundreds of multicolored lights twinkled as couples and individuals made their way to the tree to do their part, starting to fill the green branches with pretty and colorful ornaments.

Joy watched as the others took their turn. It couldn't have been more well paced if they'd had a choreographer for the activity. She pulled the weathered-looking box of ornaments toward her. The cellophane was yellowed and torn from years of storage. Inside, six golden glass gingerbread men lay in wait for their chance to dance among the tree limbs.

With a shiver of vivid recollection, she could see herself standing at her mother's side, trying to decide where to place the next ornament. It had taken hours to decorate their tree. Something they'd always accomplished alone. Dad had never done anything but set up the tree and string the lights. That was a long time ago. She pushed the sad memories aside and carried the box to the tree. Her hands shook as she carefully hung the six merry gingerbread men around the tree, spreading them out among the colorful array of candy canes, mittens, and colored glass balls.

"Joy? Is that you?" someone called from near the front door.

She spun around to see Shirley with a basket over her arm.

"Hi. Good to see you," Joy said, stepping back from the tree.

"Are you here for dinner?"

"Yes, ma'am. I remembered Ruby talking about this place. I thought I'd give it a try on my way home."

"How's our gal doing? I've been so busy, I haven't caught up with her."

"Good. Settled in at the rehab center, although she's not too happy about it."

"Well, would you be? I certainly wouldn't be either. It's the holidays, for goodness' sake."

She wouldn't much like it any time of year. "Would you care to join me for dinner?"

"I'd love to, but can't. I'm just dropping off tickets. The restaurant is one of our sponsors of the Crystal Christmas Cookie Crawl. They sell tickets for us." Shirley fanned a handful of shiny foil tickets.

Joy plucked one from the middle and examined it closely. "This is beautiful. As pretty as a Christmas card."

"I spend months coming up with new ways to improve this event. I try my best to make this event better and better every single year so it remains a tradition that no family would dare skip."

What wasn't a tradition in Crystal Falls? They seemed to serve up tradition like they did sugar in their tea around here.

"Once I realized people were keeping their tickets as mementos, I started fancying them up. It didn't cost that much more, and sales have gone up every single year."

"Nice." Joy ran her finger over the raised ink. The front of a house filled the shiny cardstock. A red door in bright foil, the green wreath adorning the center raised.

"Is this—?"

"You noticed." Shirley smiled. "It's the door at the farmhouse. Ruby makes gorgeous wreaths every year, you know. People talk about them for months." Her face went still. "Oh dear, I wonder if she can do that from the rehab center? No way you could do that."

That comment rustled her feathers. "I'm crafty. I'm sure I could pull something lovely together."

"No offense, but I'm not sure you realize how import-ant this event is."

"I'm beginning to."

"Good. Because I count on Ruby's place as the premier stop every year."

"I won't let Aunt Ruby down."

"I would hope not, because this is very important to her. Well, to the whole town, really. We might be a small town, but this is a big deal to us. We earn a lot of money for good causes through this event."

"I'll keep that in mind."

"It's very tasteful. Not tacky."

Tacky? Do I look like I'd bring tacky to the table? This woman is beginning to annoy me. I know Ruby and Shirley are best friends, but I never noticed how pushy she was.

"We're very proud of it," Shirley said. "You have started getting Ruby's place ready, haven't you?"

"Yes." The lie didn't settle well on her lips. She'd never been a good liar, but she could sense the lecture if she'd answered with anything less.

Shirley looked like she'd prefer to scold Joy, but instead a motherly comment with that level of disappointment came out. "People will expect it to be spectacular. Please do let me know if I need to take this over."

She shuddered, but smiled. "I've got it all under control. Ruby and I were just talking about that this morning."

Shirley patted Joy on the shoulder. "I've got to get these tickets out. You check in with me this week, okay?"

"Wait a second." She dug into her purse and pulled out her wallet. "I need some of those."

"You don't need a ticket, dear."

"They're for a friend." She took her wallet out. "How much are they?"

"Twenty dollars each."

"That's perfect, and it's a good cause. You said so yourself." Joy handed Shirley a crisp one-hundred-dollar bill.

"Thank you so much. Everyone raves about this event. I'm sure your friends will enjoy it." She counted out the five tickets on the table in front of Joy.

Joy walked back over to her small corner table. The waitress had dropped off her meal at some point. She sat down and pushed her fork into a smoked pork chop, feeling even more pressure than before. The waitress had been right. They were so tender, she could cut them with her fork.

Even with the pressure of the decorations for the big event, Joy felt an unusual tingle of excitement about Christmas that she hadn't felt in years. That moment, that memory, of her and her mother at the tree had sparked something. For the first time in years, she'd pictured Mom in a happy moment rather than in the hospital.

She ate one of the pork chops, then pushed her plate to the center of the table. That was a lot of food. If she ate like this the whole time she was in Crystal Falls, she wouldn't fit into that perfectly altered gown on gala night.

She pulled a piece of paper from her purse. With the tickets in front of her for inspiration, she started a list of ideas.

Ruby's place was not only going to be the star of the Crystal Christmas Cookie Crawl this year . . . this would be the most memorable year of all years to come.

"I need a theme." She bounced the tip of her pen against the page.

Silver bells?

Frosty the snowman?

Something they wouldn't expect. Turquoise, purple, and pink. She quickly scratched through those ideas. No way would folks around here appreciate something like that. And Ruby would certainly not be a fan of it. No, it had to be more traditional . . . with a twist.

With the brainstorming list in her hand, she walked up

to the register and paid her tab. As she walked to her car, she realized she was smiling. For no reason. Somehow unfamiliar . . . and welcome.

The holiday tunes that she'd tried to soothe Ruby with earlier poured through the speakers with a realistic whinny of horses and galloping hooves in an old version of "Jingle Bells."

Horses. Horses. Horses.

And she suddenly felt like Meg Ryan, cruising the highway in *Sleepless in Seattle.* She moistened her lips and began whistling an almost recognizable version of the carol.

Chapter Thirteen

Joy drove straight back to the farmhouse. Seeing the place through a whole new lens, she put her key in the brass knob, noting the color of the red on the door. Shirley's comments about Ruby's magnificent wreaths echoed. Whatever Joy came up with for the wreath, it would have to accent that color. Really pop. So nothing too dark. Oh, and it needed to be absolutely awesome. Game on, Shirley!

Color palettes played in her mind as she pushed the door open. Just inside in the entry hall stood a table, a re-purposed old bank of card-catalog drawers that Ruby had gotten when the library upgraded its system. She'd white-washed them, but the yellowed Dewey decimal ranges still marked each drawer. Joy dropped her things on top of it and kicked off her shoes. Rummaging through the draw-ers, she found exactly what she was looking for. A pad of paper.

She had half a mind to write "buy some red paint" at the top of the list. That door could use a little fresh-en-up, but the last thing she wanted to do was further up-set things. Too much change could be uncomfortable for older people. She'd learned that during market research for a magazine a few years back.

The next morning, Joy got right down to work. After

feeding the animals she found the information she needed right where Ruby had said it'd be. The journals lined nearly the whole bottom right-hand shelf of the built-in bookcase in the living room. Uncle George had worked for weeks cutting, planning, sanding, and installing them for Aunt Ruby. She remembered him working tirelessly out in the workshop on them. Thinking back, she wondered if the project had been a way for him to get some peace and quiet away from Aunt Ruby, Mom, and herself that summer.

Joy stacked the notebooks into her arms and carried them to the couch. Ruby had already dictated a list of things to get started on, but she liked to have the full picture in front of her before she made a plan. That reduced the opportunity for rework, and she didn't have time for any do-overs. Besides, now she was curious to see what all the fuss was about with this decorating. Shirley had made it sound like an Olympic effort.

Her competitive nature was in overdrive. She was going to show Shirley that Ruby wasn't the only one in this family who could fashion up some holiday craft goodness. Besides, focusing on this would make being away from work easier.

With just over a week before the MacDonald-Webber gala, chances were good she'd have all this decorating done and Ruby might even be back home by then.

Joy began flipping through the journals. Faded Polaroids captured years gone by. Ruby dressed in holiday attire, wearing her hundred-watt smile in front of gorgeous Christmas trees. Old shopping lists for supplies to decorate the wreaths were stapled into each journal. Joy tugged at a paper clip that held a recipe for homemade ginger cookies. A rusty loop stained where the papers had been attached for so many years. It had been years since she'd had those cookies. She could almost taste them now.

Thumbing through journal after journal, Joy found it remarkable how Ruby came up with something different to highlight every single year. Sometimes the theme was whimsical . . . other years elegant . . . one year she made wreaths from peacock feathers and decorated one whole tree in birds and feathers. A snapshot of that Christmas tree boasted garlands with peacock feathers placed along a twisting ribbon like delicate angel wings.

Joy had forgotten about the albino peacock that lived here with Uncle George and Aunt Ruby. That bird would squawk—no, make that scream—in the middle of the night. Used to scare her to death. His calls were so loud and humanlike that they could wake the dead! He'd woken her out of a deep sleep so many times that she would have enjoyed being the one to pluck his feathers, although she was quite certain Ruby simply gathered the ones he chose to leave behind as he strutted around the yard. That wreath had to have been gorgeous, with the white-feathered fronds and silver bells tucked into the fresh greenery.

Funny. She couldn't remember a single thing about the last Christmas she spent in this house. Or the first one without Mom. Had Ruby decorated at all that year?

Somewhere in all these journals, there was an answer to that question. She was sure of that.

As Joy got lost in the details recorded in the journals, she noticed that Ruby's sketches had become less intricate over the past two years. Even her handwriting was a little less steady. Ruby had always had an artistic flair. Painting, sketching, any kind of craft. Joy's heart ached, knowing she'd missed these moments with Ruby. Moments she could never get back. Especially after Uncle George died.

Ruby had asked her to come for the holidays every year since, but Joy had opted to keep the holiday and Mom's memories at a safely comfortable distance.

Maybe Joy had kept everything at a distance, except for work.

She swept the books into a stack and picked them up.

It wasn't going to be easy topping the displays that Ruby had put together. Her heart was in every one of those designs. There were hundreds of tiny details. Not just decorations, but also the music, the food, the lights, and even the scents . . . peppermint, cocoa, pine, and cinnamon mixed with tangy orange. There was careful purpose put into each element that made it all work, and guaranteed that every sense would be touched. What guests couldn't see, they'd smell. What they couldn't touch, they'd hear. And the tastes would tease childhood memories.

"I can do this." She stood, clinging to the journals, hugging them like memories she wished were her own, and crossed the room. As she glanced upstairs, her dress, which still hung from the door at the top of the stairway, glimmered in the afternoon sun.

Chapter Fourteen

Ben was happy to wrap up his day at work. He'd experienced his share of bad Mondays, but now his grandmother, Shirley, was adding to it. She was convinced that her Crystal Christmas Cookie Crawl was going to be doomed unless he did some sort of intervention.

He'd been on his way out when she walked right in and plopped into the chair in his office. "Ruby's niece hasn't been here to visit her aunt even one single Christmas that I can remember, and now she thinks she can handle the whole house decoration by herself. My Crystal Christmas Cookie Crawl is doomed."

"It can't be that bad." Ben sat back down behind his desk. He wasn't going anywhere anytime soon, if his grandmother's mood was any indicator.

"That young woman insists she doesn't need any help. She has no idea how big a deal this is."

"Maybe she knows what she's doing. Ruby will give her some advice." It wouldn't be a bad thing if he didn't have to help out decorating Ruby's house this year. He enjoyed it, but it wasn't like he didn't have a hundred other things on his plate. He opened the folder on his desk. If he was going to be here, he may as well get more paperwork done. If there was one thing he'd learned over the years, it was if his grandmother stopped in to rant, she wasn't going to be quick about it. He signed an authorization and flipped to the next paper, listening as he multitasked through the backlog of paperwork that had come in over the weekend.

"Well, little Miss Joy Holbrook is just a little too big for her britches, if you ask me."

Joy? He slapped the folder closed and put his forearms on his desk. "Now, what would make you say that?"

"What kind of person refuses help from friends? Seriously. She might be a successful big-city somebody-or-other, but she has that big-city attitude to go along with it. A suit-wearing, hybrid-driving, city girl."

That didn't make it hard to put two and two together on who the drop-in niece was. There was only one Prius-driving girl named Joy in Crystal Falls that he knew of. And he had to admit something about that pistol of a girl had been taunting him since they'd met. He'd spent more than a minute or two hoping he might run into her again.

"Is she staying at Ruby's?" he asked.

"Supposed to be."

"I have to deliver her trees. I'll stop by there tonight and see how things are going."

"I was hoping you would say that," she said with an exaggerated sigh. "Thank you."

"Can't promise anything, but I can at least offer my help." It didn't surprise him that Joy had refused help. She hadn't been all that receptive to him helping her out in the parking lot the other night, and it wasn't like she'd had a lot of choices then. She seemed like the type that wanted to do everything her own way—even if it was the hard way.

Shirley got up and came around his desk, giving him a big red lipstick kiss on the cheek. "You are my favorite grandson."

"That's only because Jim and Bobby don't live in Crystal Falls anymore."

She smudged the lipstick off his cheek with her thumb. "Well, they don't really need to know, do they? Could you stop over there before dark tonight? I hate to lose another day."

"Of course."

He watched his grandmother scurry out the door, wishing his staff a cheerful day as she made it down the hall.

So at his grandmother's insistence, Ben had left work early to get home, load Ruby's Christmas trees in his truck, and deliver them. It was a cold day, so it was just as well to get the chore done early and get back home. When he drove up to Ruby's farmhouse, the bright red door looked naked for this time of year without a wreath. Well, as naked as bright barn red could look. Like Ruby, it was bold. Nothing subtle about it.

Usually by now, Ruby would have had the whole porch decked out in greenery and lights. He'd come to believe that Ruby used the wreath as a hint to tease whatever clever theme she'd come up with for the year. But tonight there wasn't the first hint of anything Christmassy in place. If this were a hint at a theme, the theme might be The Year Without a Christmas.

He knocked on the door and stepped back, trying to decide whether to act surprised to see Joy or cop immediately to the fact that he'd already figured out that she was the girl who'd skewered her car on the tailgate of his truck. Didn't take a rocket scientist. Especially with her car sitting in the driveway with the big can-opener-looking slice out of the back quarter panel.

Who was he fooling? It was clear as day that he wanted

to see her again. Otherwise, he'd just have put Ruby's trees next to the barn in a trough of water and left like he usually did. Then when she was ready to put them up, she'd call for help . . . or not.

He brought his hands to his mouth and blew into them. He smelled like a pine tree, but there were worse things to smell like, he guessed. After standing there an awkwardly long amount of time, he raised his hand and rapped three more times on the door, louder this time. But instead of footsteps, he heard the sound of something breaking on the other side.

He didn't even think twice, just tried the door handle, which turned easily in his hand, then ran inside.

"Joy? Are you okay?" He did a quick sidestep move he'd been known for back in his high school football days as quarterback for the Mustangs, only this time, instead of a football player, he was dodging cardboard boxes strewn from one side of the room to the other.

Did someone ransack the place?

He pivoted toward the kitchen, then noticed the pretty strawberry blonde sitting on the floor of the living room among opened boxes of holiday decorations.

She folded her empty hands to her lap and slumped. "You scared me."

"Me?"

She raised her gaze from the broken glass in front of her. "The pounding at the door. You startled me." She averted her gaze from his. Looking toward the ceiling. "Why is it whenever you're nearby, something goes wrong? You're bad luck in a good suit."

"I knocked."

"More like a battering ram."

"You didn't answer the first time. I thought something was wrong."

The bad luck she was experiencing wasn't his fault. But she did seem to be having a run of it. "Did you drag all these boxes out of the attic by yourself?"

"No, the tooth fairy and the Easter bunny stopped by to help out. You just missed them."

Nothing wrong with her sense of humor. "Sorry if I scared you when I barged in. I could have helped you with all these boxes. I put them in the attic for Ruby last year. Some of them are heavy." It had taken him the better part of a day to label and load all those boxes in the attic for Ruby last year. If he'd thought anyone else would have to manage them, he would have suggested smaller boxes.

"They were heavier than I thought, but look—" She gestured at the boxes around the room. "—I got them all down." She straightened her back and twisted. "I did take some Tylenol." Joy picked up a yellowed Christmas card and its red envelope from the floor beside her and began sweeping at the broken pieces of what was left of the glass ornament.

"Let me help you." Ben stooped next to her and swept the green glass shards into a pile with one of the box tops lying nearby.

"I've got it," she said quietly as she picked up a larger piece, then bumped her hand into his. "Ouch!" She squeezed at the prick to her finger. "Stop helping me, or I might end up dead!"

"I take it this ornament had special meaning."

"It was my mother's favorite." Her voice was fragile and shaking.

"I guess she'll be upset."

"Not likely. She passed away twelve years ago."

"Oh."

"It's fine. It's an ornament. Just one decoration." She sat back on her heels. "I'm sorry I overreacted."

"Not at all. Everyone has a favorite ornament. They bring back memories. Not a thing wrong with that."

"My mom and I hung that ornament together on the tree every year." She turned her hand to keep the blood from dripping to the floor. "We'd spend an hour just searching for that perfect spot where it could be seen from every angle, and the lights would shimmer and reflect the pretty color."

"You better go get that cleaned up. I've got this."

He watched her race-walk into the kitchen, her rear swishing as she negotiated the maze of boxes. She was even prettier in the daylight. Unsure of what exactly to do with the mess, he swept the thin broken glass into the yellowed envelope she'd dropped.

"There's a trash bag next to the chair," she called from the kitchen.

He started to toss the envelope into the trash, but something kept him from doing so. Instead he shoved it into his coat pocket.

"Can I help you with some of this other stuff?" he said, hoping she could hear him over the running water.

She stepped back into the living room with a paper towel wrapped around her fingers. "I overreacted. I'm sorry. Just leave it. I'll get it after I find a bandage."

But the tears in her eyes contradicted her words. His gut wrenched. He couldn't imagine what it would be like when he was faced with holidays without his mom, or any member of his family, for that matter. Family was the best part of the whole season.

This wasn't what he'd had in mind for his quick visit at all. Making her cry was not part of the plan.

"I already got it. Go on and finish tending to your hand."

Joy stepped back into the kitchen. The water running in the sink wasn't loud enough to camouflage her sniffles, though. He busied himself, stacking some of the boxes near the bookcases at the far end of the room, clearing a path.

Joy came back looking composed. "Is this about your truck?"

The envelope in his coat pocket taunted him. "No. Actually, I came by to lend a hand."

She gave an anxious little cough.

"Not starting off so well?"

"What would make you think I need a hand with anything?"

"My grandmother is Ruby's best friend. She runs the holiday home tour. You might have heard of it. The Crystal Christmas Cookie Crawl?"

"You're Shirley's grandson?"

"Yes."

"That event seems to be the talk of the town. I guess she didn't tell you that I said I had it under control when she tried to offer your services before."

No sense getting her all riled up again. Better to play stupid. "It's a pretty big deal around here. Everyone in town will show up. This place is the main attraction of the event. Ruby and I have been working together on it for the past seven years."

"Seven years?"

"Guess she hasn't mentioned that we've won all those years either."

"Must have slipped right by."

"Well, we have a system. In fact, I think that's why we're undefeated for the last seven years."

"Undefeated?"

"The Golden Wreath is up for grabs."

She looked hesitant.

"Um, yeah." He grabbed her good hand and walked her

into the dining room. "See. There in the china cabinet, on the top shelf, is a lovely gold and crystal trophy. That."

"I see. A coveted award, I take it."

"Yes, and my grandmother asked me to come get things started since Ruby isn't around. So here I am."

"Well, it's nice to meet you again, Ben. But I told her I didn't need any help with the Christmas stuff."

"I'm pretty handy."

The left edge of her mouth tugged into a half smile and her eyes narrowed. "You're Handy Andy?"

Ben lolled his head back. He hated it when Ruby called him that.

"I thought you said your name was Ben. That is what you told me, isn't it? The night I accidentally—"

"Plowed into my truck? Yeah. My name is Ben. Ben Andrews. You know how Ruby is. That whole Handy Andy thing is just her way of torturing me. She's like that."

"Yeah. She is." Joy folded her arms across the sweatshirt that had a faded high school Mustang mascot screened across the front. Bowing her head, she said, "Sounds like you know her better than I do—even though I'm her family."

He detected a note of guilt in her tone. "No. Of course not. I mean I've been helping her with holiday decorations and any little things she needs repaired throughout the years that she can't handle. Which I'm sure won't surprise you isn't all that much. But we're friends. Close."

"I see."

"Not family. But close. But you haven't ever been around at the holidays. I'd have remembered you for sure."

"Is that supposed to be a compliment?"

"Not really."

Joy's face tightened. "I have a pretty demanding career. In Washington, D.C."

"Ruby brags about you all the time. Market research, right?"

Her stance softened just a bit. "Yes."

"I'm not sure I even know what that means."

"Basically, we find out what people are buying, and what can be done to make them buy more of it. I spend most of my time crunching data and statistics to be able to do all of that."

"I bet that's interesting."

"I think so. What is it you do when you're not doing handyman work for my aunt?"

He pushed a hand into his pants pocket. "I work over at the hospital."

"Doctor?"

"I'm a numbers guy."

She didn't look convinced. "You sure work odd hours."

"I do what needs to be done, but it definitely increased our chances of meeting."

"Well, I'm sure my aunt appreciates your help. Me, on the other hand, I've got things under control. And I'm sure you are a busy man."

"Really, because it looks like kind of a mess." He glanced around the room. "No offense, but I'm a great organizer."

"As am I." She bunched her lips, her face still pretty with the scowl. "Well, usually." She glanced around the room, unable to contain a laugh. "I may have gotten carried away getting boxes down." She looked at him, their eyes holding. "Was there a reason you came by?"

"Okay, well, I brought Ruby's trees over." He tipped his head toward the barn. "I need to make a fresh cut and put them in the trough of water like we usually do. It'll help keep them fresh until it's time to put them up. There's a lot to do with the livestock, I could—"

"Them?"

"What?"

"You said you need to put 'them' in the trough. How many trees did you bring?"

"The usual. Three five-foot and two seven-foot trees. It's what we do every year. I mean a different theme, and sometimes she sets them up in different rooms, but always five. She mixes things up with the decorations so the people who come through here will be wowed. But we always do five trees."

"She's crazy to have so many." Her eyelashes batted as if she was taking in and considering the information. "I've got Ruby's list, and now I guess some of those notes make more sense if it's multiple trees. But is it really necessary?"

"It's a lot. Folks around here kind of expect that from her now. Which is why I'm here to help."

"It is a lot, but I'm sure I can take care of this and the animals just fine. Thank you, but no thank you. I will not be needing your help."

"Boy, you're more hardheaded than your aunt. It's just a helping hand."

"I'm quite capable of handling some Christmas decorating. Or even a lot of it. I've got nothing but time while I'm here. And pardon me if I'm taken aback by the offer, but I'm used to taking care of myself."

"This isn't a little decorating. To win the Golden Wreath takes a lot of effort. Time and effort, and planning."

"I'm an excellent planner."

"And patience."

"Well, I may bring new skills to the project."

She was not only hardheaded, she was just clueless. Shirley was right. A person didn't just march in and win this competition. "I really hate to lose our winning streak because some drop-in niece is too hardheaded to accept some help."

"Drop-in?" Her face flushed red, and her teeth clenched. "I'd appreciate it if you'd leave now."

"This is important to your aunt and my grandmother. At least let me give you a hand to keep my grandmother from coming unglued."

She paused, as if ready to argue. "I promise I'll make sure that everyone is blown away by just how lovely this place will look. Including your grandmother."

"You do know there's an open house that goes along with it, right? Baked goods, punch, singing. I mean, you've never taken the time to come. Don't deny it. If there's one thing I would have remembered, it would have been you. You might be hardheaded, but you *are* beautiful, and I don't forget a pretty face."

"Okay, that might be a bit more than I'd expected, but I think I can handle it."

Wasn't like he had the extra time to help her anyway. His plate was more than full already. And he sure didn't have the time for a pretty know-it-all girl either. He walked to the door, which still stood wide open. "Merry Christmas."

Chapter Fifteen

Joy peeked through the break in the curtains, watching until Ben cleared the driveway and was out of sight. Who did he think he was, just inserting himself into their business? And Shirley was relentless. Whom would she send next? If there was one thing Joy was more determined than ever about now, it was that she'd make this year's home tour look like fireworks compared to a candle. And she did know Ruby. She loved her and maybe she hadn't quite been around as much as she should've or could've, but her career was important too.

She glanced around the room. Ben was right. It was a mess, but she hadn't expected company. He had some nerve, stacking some of the boxes aside when she wasn't looking too. There were so many boxes of ornaments, she could have filled a Hobby Lobby and had a sidewalk sale and still had plenty of decorations to jazz up three houses.

Ruby had carefully kept the themes separated. Boxes by color. Boxes by types. And the years noted on some of them. It was the boxes labeled with her own name on them that had gotten her sideways, though. Some were things from her childhood, like the cheerleader ornament and the ornaments she'd made out of bread dough with Ruby one year, but others were things Ruby must've decided should fall into Joy's hands at some point. Things from Ruby's childhood with Joy's mom, and other heirloom-type ornaments.

So many memories had come rushing down on her. Memories she thought she'd tucked so far back in her mind that she'd never have to address them, but everything she touched in those boxes came with a price.

A tear.

A heartache.

A wish.

Her phone rang from somewhere in the mess. She leaned forward, looking and listening until she finally spotted her phone on top of a box labeled PEACOCK 2014. Renee's smiling face filled the screen. She pressed the button with a smile. "Hey, Renee. How's everything at the office?"

"Great, but I'm missing you! Things aren't nearly so fun without you around."

"I miss you too."

"You holding up out there in the country?"

"I'm settling into a routine. I think. Well, except for this guy who keeps popping up everywhere."

"Are you talking about Todd? Don't tell me he showed up there too."

"'Too'?"

"He came by the office first thing this morning, looking for you."

Joy searched for a plausible explanation, but the best she could offer was, "Maybe he was there to see someone else. I don't know, but no. I'm talking about the guy I wrecked into the other night. He keeps showing up everywhere."

"Wrecked? Oh yeah, that's right, I meant to ask you about that. You glossed right over it the other day when we were talking about that kid. I hung up thinking, did I hear what I think I heard?"

"Long story. I backed my car into his truck."

"You met by accident. Oh yeah, that's not cliché."

"I know. A regular Hollywood meet-cute. Right?"

"Destiny, maybe," Renee teased. "Is he good-looking?"

"Yes. No. Well, not exactly cute. More like super hot. Unfortunately, he's even more annoying than he is hot. Besides, long-distance relationships never work. So, who cares?"

"Not that anyone but you brought up anything about relationships, but actually, a lot of long-distance relationships work. They just take some creativity. But then again, you're not looking for a relationship. And even if you were, you're right, you'd never take that kind of a risk. You like things clean and neat. Simple."

"What's that supposed to mean?" The words came out way more defensive than she'd intended.

"Don't get all riled up. I just mean you lead a safe existence. No chance of being disappointed. No big risks."

"I do not." She felt her composure wavering. Was she being safe? Or just smart?

"Yes, you do play it safe, but don't sweat it. It's who you are. Nothing wrong with that."

But maybe there was something wrong with that. She'd considered herself a risk-taker all her life, but maybe she was fooling herself. She'd prided herself in thinking she was a bit fearless, living the perfect life and doing everything she wanted. Had the things she wanted changed, or had she never really let herself dream? Risk in business was a whole other thing from personal risk.

She hesitated, torn by conflicting emotions. "You really think I play it safe? I mean with my life?"

"Think? I know it. Anyway, you won't believe what I've got in my arms right this minute."

She couldn't begin to guess, because her mind was still doing inventory on the crushed reality of her not being a risk-taker. "One of Miss Jennings's famous fruitcakes? Hope you stretched first."

"No," Renee said with a chuckle. "I could pull a muscle heaving one of those suckers around. Plus, I would have left that in the office break room."

"Don't blame you."

"I happen to be hugging the biggest potted poinsettia I've ever seen."

"Oh great. You're going to murder another plant?"

"It's not mine."

"You've taken one hostage?"

"Funny. No, this was delivered to the office this afternoon."

"Someone sent you a plant? They don't know you very well."

"Actually, it was for you. I'm gracefully accepting this award in your absence. Well, not award, but gift . . . from Todd."

"Todd?" Maybe they weren't so off as she'd thought. "Haven't heard from him in weeks. He drops in, and then sends me a plant? Is there a card?"

"Sure is."

"Read it."

The sound of the envelope ripping was followed by Renee's "awwww." "It reads, 'You are the *Joy* of the season. Can't wait to spend time with you. We on for the gala this year? Call me.'"

"He just wants to go to the gala."

"Oh, don't be so skeptical. Maybe he really misses you."

"I doubt it. The gala is next week, and since he doesn't work for MacDonald-Webber anymore, he thinks I'm his ticket."

"Do you have a date?"

"I don't need one that badly."

"Maybe you can get car-crash guy to take you."

"It might be a better option." Todd was strictly a call for the obligatory armpiece kind of a guy. Convenient, handsome, and steady. Maybe she did need to take more risks.

"Whatever you say. I'm leaving your plant here at the office. I figured it would stand a better chance of living here."

"At least the cleaning service will keep it alive for a while. Thanks for the update."

"Give 'em hell down there," Renee said. "I'm holding down the fort here."

Joy hung up from the call. *Give 'em hell? Am I that hard to get along with?*

Ever since she'd put on that fancy gown at Wetherton's and made that wish that she was on the right path, it was like every flaw she had was being magnified.

Then again, everyone knew that things in a small town got around fast. That's probably why all the fuss about Ruby and her decorations.

Joy hoped word wasn't already zipping through Crystal Falls about her little hissy fit with Ben earlier. She'd overreacted, but darn if he hadn't pushed her buttons. And it did seem like every time something went wrong here in Crystal Falls since she hit town, he was there. Plus, there was something about his polished look, so out of place in this little town, that just sent up red flares and set her on edge. She couldn't even really put her finger on why. It just did, and her gut didn't usually steer her wrong.

Or maybe it was just the holidays getting to her. Wouldn't be the first time. Or the pressure of the promotion and not being in her usual routine. That was more likely.

She owed Ben an apology, but she probably needed to let Ruby know what happened first before someone else told her. Crystal Falls was a small town, and the last thing she wanted to do was embarrass or disappoint Ruby.

Joy called the private phone number for Ruby at Dixon County Rehab, but there was no answer in her room.

On the bright side, if she couldn't reach Ruby, no one else could either.

The next morning, she fed the animals and got Molly off to school in record time. On the way to visit Ruby, she stopped at the store, and as she shopped for things she'd need to decorate the farmhouse, she also picked up a burner smartphone for Ruby to keep nearby while she was in rehab. That way they could stay in touch. If she was going to get everything done, she wasn't going to have time to make an hour each way drive every day. Ruby had been right about that.

When Joy walked into the Dixon County Rehab Center, it was almost lunchtime. A group of school kids swayed in front of the Christmas tree in the lobby, singing "Jingle Bells." Onlookers of all ages were four and five deep, watching and enjoying the music. Joy scanned the crowd but didn't see Ruby's bright red hair among the crowd.

Once Joy made it through the first set of double doors, the halls were quiet. Probably because most everyone was down in the lobby, listening to the carols. Joy tapped on Ruby's door as she walked in.

"Hey. Why are you up here all alone? They are caroling downstairs. It sounds lovely."

Ruby shrugged. "Not in the Christmas spirit."

"What?" Joy sat on the edge of the bed. "You're always in the Christmas spirit. What's the matter?"

"I'd rather be home."

"I know, but I promise I'm taking care of things."

"I'm sure you are, and I appreciate it."

"Well"—Joy grimaced—"I do need to tell you something. I kind of jumped all over Ben last night. It's a long story. He was trying to be helpful, and something got broken. I got upset. I overreacted. It didn't end well."

"Joy! He's such a nice man. Why would you do that?"

"I'm sorry. He just made comments that made me feel like he knew you even better than me. I think I was a little jealous."

Ruby held out her arms. "Honey, no one will ever know me like you do. You are my precious angel."

She let Ruby pull her into a hug. "I love you, Aunt Ruby."

"I love you too. And time and distance don't break family bonds, dear."

"I'm going to stop over and apologize to him later."

"Good. Everything will be fine. Give him a chance. He really is good people."

Joy was relieved to have it all on the table. "So, let's get to work. I went through the journals. And I brought down the boxes of decorations. There are so many!"

"Yes, there are. But you won't need them all. Plenty to pick from, though."

"That's for sure. And I have a few ideas."

"Care to discuss them with me?"

"If it's okay, I'd like to surprise you."

Ruby's face spread into a wide smile. "I'd like that very much, dear. And I'll go along with that if you'll do a little something for me."

"Anything. Of course."

"I'd give my right arm for a chili cheese hot dog. I hear they have the best ones up the road at Tony's. Would you mind making a quick trip up there?"

"A chili cheese dog? Is that okay?"

Carolyn walked in pushing a blood pressure cart. "She's not on a special diet. She can have whatever you'd like to bring in."

Ruby grinned. "See? What she said."

"Well, then, I'm on my way to Tony's. Can I get you one too?"

Carolyn didn't even hesitate. "Yes, please. They are the best hot dogs around. Let me grab my wallet."

"No. I've got this. My treat."

"This *is* a treat. Thank you," Carolyn said. "Now, Ruby, let me get some quick vitals so I can finish my paperwork for the morning."

"Can you tell me how to get to Tony's from here?"

Carolyn cuffed Ruby's arm as she spoke. "It's just out the parking lot, turn right, and it's on the corner at the third stoplight. You can't miss it. Giant wiener the size of a minivan hanging off the top of the building wearing a bun like a jacket. I'll tell you it's not the branding that sells those hot dogs."

"Sounds a bit scary."

"Oh yeah. It is. But you won't miss the place."

And, boy, was Carolyn ever right. Sure enough, from a block away, Joy could see the outrageous giant hot dog hanging from the front of the brick building. It was faded and worn, like it had been there for years, but if the crowd was any indication of how good the hot dogs were going to be, she was the one in for a treat.

The line moved swiftly. Mostly because there were no choices. You wanted a chili cheese dog with or without onions. No other options.

Joy was in and out and back in Ruby's room in less than thirty minutes with a box of two dozen hot dogs, enough to share with the other nurses on the floor and whoever else happened by. Hopefully, it would help put Ruby back in the holiday mood and spread some cheer. Plus, it made her feel good to do a little something nice for the folks taking good care of her aunt.

After the hot dogs were gone and the nurses dispersed, the smell of chili still hung in the air. They should sell those things with a spritzer of air freshener.

Ruby crumpled the paper hot dog tray and her napkin together and tossed them across the room, making it right into the trash can. "Thank you, Joy. That really hit the spot."

"It was fun too." Joy pulled the bag out of her purse. "I almost forgot. I brought you something else."

"What's that?"

"I tried to call this morning, and I couldn't reach you."

"That's because I don't spend much time in this room. They always have me down in the gym, or walking the halls. It's not much of a relaxation type of place. I swear I've walked more the last twenty-four hours than I did last year, and I consider myself pretty active."

"Well, I wanted us to be able to talk whenever we needed to. So I got you a portable phone."

"Oh? How fun." Ruby took it but looked clueless.

"You don't know how to use one of those, do you?"

"I do not." She turned it over in her hand and pressed the button on the side. "But I can learn."

"Of course you can. It's so simple." Joy took the charger out of its package and then showed Ruby how to plug it into the phone. There was an outlet right next to the bed. "Here's the number in case you want anyone else, like Shirley maybe, to have it."

"I think just you is fine."

"Okay, well we can text, but I think just using it like a phone might be easier."

"I used to be quite a typist. When your uncle was in the military and I worked as a secretary, I could type over ninety words per minute, and that was on a manual typewriter."

"Wow. That's speedy."

"And I was accurate too."

Joy walked Ruby through the buttons and then set up her number in the contacts so that Ruby could call her with just the press of a couple of buttons.

"Okay, so now I'm going to call you." Joy pressed the keys on her phone and the one in Ruby's hand started playing a verse of "Jingle Bells."

"That's the ring?"

"Yes."

Ruby stared at the phone and then jabbed at the green phone icon. "Hello?"

"Hi."

Ruby grinned. "Easy! And how do I call you again?"

Joy walked her through the steps one more time. "I think you're ready for prime time," she teased.

"So I am. I'm just one hip old gal, aren't I?"

"For sure. Anything else I can do for you before I leave you today?"

"Promise me you'll make up with Ben," Ruby said.

"I can handle it."

"That's not the point. He's part of the tradition, and I'm sure you can handle it all by yourself, but why do that when you don't have to?"

Joy sucked in a breath. "Fine. I'll apologize and I'll work something out with him."

Ruby's eyebrow peaked in doubt.

"I will!" Joy insisted.

"Thank you. And promise me that you'll get a triple batch of each of those cookie dough recipes made and in the freezer. One each night is the way I usually do it. We have to have all fresh cookies on the cookie crawl day, and trust me, there is no way to make that deadline unless you make and freeze the dough ahead of time. That way we can just slice and bake them the night before and the morning of the crawl."

"I'm on it," Joy promised just as Johnny came strolling into the room.

"Well, if it's not Miss Ruby's beautiful, single, smart, very successful niece."

"And this is why you can never reach me when you call the room." Ruby pointed toward Johnny. "If I didn't know better, I'd think this guy had nothing better to do. Or a crush on me." She gave Johnny a flirty grin.

"Thought you said you wanted to be out of here by Christmas?" he challenged.

"That I do," she said with a wink, and started shifting herself around toward the edge of the bed. "See. I've aced moving around in bed already."

"I see. Good job."

Ruby waved her hand in Joy's direction. "You don't need to wait around. Go get busy on the house, and now that I have that fancy phone, you can send me pictures."

"Will you know how to look at them?"

"Johnny here will help me. Won't you, dear?"

Johnny grinned. "Absolutely. I'm great with gadgets."

"Don't you two be making prank phone calls." Joy felt better that Ruby's mood was higher when she'd left, but she worried about her being in rehab so close to the holiday. Maybe sending pictures of the progress would put her mind at ease and make her feel like a part of it. She wished she hadn't promised Ruby she'd let Ben help, although at this point, she was beginning to realize that having his help would make things a lot easier. And more important, calm down both Shirley and Ruby.

The thought of apologizing to Ben was bad enough, but groveling to ask him to help really sucked.

She'd accept Ben's help, only because she'd promised Ruby, but she'd be the one running the show.

Chapter Sixteen

Joy unloaded the basic supplies she'd bought this morning, glue sticks, floral wire, some scented oils, and spray paints. She'd marked several ideas with sticky notes as she'd gone through the journals, hoping that a cohesive theme would show up as she did. That had narrowed down her resources to three books with most of the ideas that she liked.

She changed into a pair of sweats and snuggled up with just those three books one more time. This time, intent to do more than just skim them. These weren't just scrapbooks. Ruby journaled nearly daily in them, sometimes not about the decorations at all.

The tiniest elements and details were all here. Not a formal project plan, but Ruby's random method of pulling something together. Precise plans written here that Ruby had used to give awe-inspiring memories to her neighbors. Even now, just reading about the fabulous displays and the love and time that Ruby had put into decorating, Joy felt it. Felt it all the way to her heart. Ruby didn't do this for the bragging rights. She did it for the community, and to share her special memories with others.

For a moment it was overwhelming to think that she'd been so sure she could duplicate what Ruby had done over the years. Unlike Joy, Ruby hadn't shoved Christmas under an icy snow blanket after Mom died. Not after Uncle George died either. No, instead she'd embraced the traditions more tightly. Clung to every little thing that reminded her of her family . . . of those departed and even of Joy . . . who may as well have been departed since she hadn't once made the time to spend Christmas with her aunt since she'd left. There wasn't a single year as Joy slowly absorbed the contents of the journals that she didn't connect to something. A recipe, a thought, a memory. She'd been in Ruby's thoughts every single year.

Her eyes stung, and the words seemed to swim as she read on through the tears. She raised her hands to her ears, wishing she could quiet the guilty negative speak that was running through her brain. She'd been so set on keeping herself safe from being hurt again that she never shared any of herself.

How could it have taken this many years for her to realize it?

When was the last time she'd sat and tried to really conjure up a best Christmas ever? What would that mean to her? She couldn't remember ever doing it. Certainly she must have. As a child, or as a teen, but nothing came to mind now. She closed her eyes.

If she opened her heart and her mind, what would be there?

She closed the cover of the leather journal and held it to her heart. She walked to the living room and sat down on the couch, looking out the window at the bright blue sky. Deceiving on the cold day. A cardinal flitted between limbs in the tree out front, its bright red catching her eye against the soft brown gray of the winter tree.

She lay back, letting the sun stream across her face. The

rays warmed her cheeks, and a bright glow like the warmth of a fire on a winter day danced on her eyelids.

What would her perfect Christmas look like?

Cinnamon, orange, peppermint, and pine mingle in the air as my husband hoists a live tree into the stand in our living room. Our dog, a black Lab, wears plush antlers with bells dangling from the ends, fetching Christmas decorations like it's a game. We've spent weeks making ornaments out of the pinecones and things we've found outside. Yes, we. Me, him, our children. A boy and a girl, giggling as they place their favorite ornaments in a cluster on the bottom half of the tree that we'll fix later—after they go to bed. We'll tell them Santa moved them.

Later that night, we sing carols along with the CD in the old player that doesn't get nearly enough use during the year and hang our homemade stockings from the mantel above the fireplace. Then, in those anxious last hours before bedtime, we place still-warm-from-the-oven cookies out for Santa. And, of course, a carrot and apple slices for his reindeer. After the children are tucked snug in their beds, me and my man carefully arrange presents under the tree. Then my husband stands. Reaching for my hand, he helps me from the floor. The scent of fresh pine in the air. I stand in front of him. His lips part in a smile that says "I love you," and he takes my hand. His hands are strong, and he pulls me close. Then he twirls me and slowly waltzes me around the living room. My green Christmas robe swirling around my ankles, until he stops and kisses me under the mistletoe.

She opened her eyes, feeling as if something magical had just shifted inside her. That robe was as green as the dress that hung upstairs. There wasn't anything flashy about what she'd just imagined. It was family. It was nature at its most basic.

And she knew exactly what the theme would be for Ruby's house on the Crystal Christmas Cookie Crawl this year. It had been right in front of her all along.

Nature's Bounty.

She'd repurpose the peacock feather decorations, bleached pinecones, and the Mason jars she'd found. Along with the scented candles, she'd capture all the senses in the most simple way. Less was more. She said that all the time to her team. Keep it simple, and she had a feeling this was going to simply be the best year ever.

There was no need for Ruby to worry about that Golden Wreath trophy.

First things first. Room to work. With the list of which boxes she needed to keep downstairs for supplies, Joy moved the rest of them out of the way. She'd get those back up in the attic as soon as possible.

As she put all the old journals back that she didn't plan to use, one of the pictures fluttered to the floor. Its invisible tape had yellowed and lost its adhesive over the years.

She picked it up and looked at the picture of her mother wearing a sweatshirt with birds and a snowy Christmas scene on it. Nature's Bounty. "Thanks, Mom." And this time she didn't cry. She felt a warmth where that cold heavy blackness usually held her hostage.

She grabbed her laptop and started moving all those lists she'd started into a cohesive project plan.

Time to get serious.

Chapter Seventeen

The next morning, Joy packed Ruby's crochet basket with her things to take to Ruby on her next visit. Hopefully, that would keep her occupied until Christmas, and make her stay a little more pleasant.

There was a quick triple-knock at the door. At just barely six in the morning, it was too early for Molly.

Joy opened the door. A young woman stood bouncing, trying to keep warm against the brisk morning breeze. Even in the heavy coat, she appeared slight in stature with skin so pale against her dark hair that she reminded Joy of Snow White.

"Hi," the young woman said. "I hate to intrude, and I'm sorry I haven't stopped in to talk to you sooner."

Joy glanced over the woman's shoulder, recognizing the car immediately. "You're Molly's mom?"

"Ginny," she said, wringing her hands. "I can't thank you enough for helping me with her, especially with Ruby hurt. Everyone at church is praying for her speedy recovery. You must think I'm so selfish for not stopping sooner. I—"

Joy placed her hand on Ginny's arm. "It's okay. Don't worry. You don't owe me an explanation. Come on in out of the cold." Joy held the door for her, gesturing her in-

side. "You and Molly are Ruby's top concern. It's my pleasure to help out."

"Molly can't stop talking about you. Again, I can't
thank you enough. Especially with Ruby hurt. I know you
have your hands full already."

"Don't worry about a thing. I don't know what's going
on with you, but I can tell you that Ruby thinks the world
of you and Molly. So it's nice to meet you."

"I need another favor." Ginny's eyes glossed over, and
her words tumbled out. "If there were any other option, I
promise I wouldn't bother you."

"Stop. Slow down. It's no bother. I'm here. What's
wrong? How can I help?"

The woman's chin quivered. "Can Molly stay with you
after school today and spend the night tonight?"

The thought of taking care of that little girl overnight
tossed panic into Joy's calm demeanor, but the look in
Ginny's eyes told her more than any words could. And Joy
was not about to add to whatever was going on in this
young woman's life. "I'm going to admit that I'm no Ruby
when it comes to handling children. In fact, I don't have
any experience at all, but I'll figure it out if you trust me
to. Molly will help me. Absolutely. You can count on me."

"Thank you. She's a good girl. I don't think she'll be
any bother."

"It'll be fine. Don't you worry. Do I need to pick her up
from school or—?"

Ginny shook her head. "No. The teacher can put her on
the bus that stops here at the end of the day, right around
three thirty. We've done it lots of times before with Ruby."

"Then we're all set. Don't worry. Everything will be
fine."

"I can't thank you enough." Ginny hugged Joy with
tears flowing down her face, and then turned and left.

Joy closed the door. *Don't worry?* Wish she could tell herself that.

An hour later, Molly came through the front door just like any other day, except today a holiday plaid jumper with white tights peeked out from her heavy coat.

"Hey, Molly. You look pretty. How are you doing today?"

"I'm good." She peeled out of her hat and mittens, then put her coat on the chair. "Is it really okay for me to come here after school and sleep over?"

"Yes! Are you excited?"

The little girl bobbed her head. "I am. It might snow."

"Really?" Joy hadn't even bothered to look at the weather forecast. "Well, then we might just have a real magical night, huh?"

"I love snow."

"Me too, but even if it doesn't snow, I have something fun planned."

Molly wiggled in excitement.

"Ruby makes her famous Christmas cookies every year, and she asked me to get started on them. Can you help me?"

"Yes!" She leapt in the air, her little suede boots softly bouncing on the kitchen tile floor.

"Great. So let's get you ready for school, and then we will have a fun night together."

Joy nibbled on the PBJ crusts as she watched Molly hop up the steps onto the big yellow school bus from the front door. When Mom had been sick, Joy could remember how afraid she'd been to get on that bus and go to school, afraid Mom would be gone when she came home. But somehow this farmhouse had been a sanctuary during those days.

The one place she'd felt safe. Funny that all these years later, it still was. Just this time, for Molly.

As she shut the door, she could almost smell the blend of sugar and spices from Ruby's baking all those years ago. Joy hadn't done a lick of baking since back then. In fact, even her cooking portfolio was rather limited. She opted to eat out more than anything, out of convenience. But she could follow directions, so hopefully it would be as easy as following the recipes that Ruby said were in the kitchen.

She meandered into the kitchen. The first thing in her project plan was to get all the supplies she'd need. At the top of the list were all the ingredients for the cookie dough that she needed to start freezing.

With the old recipe box in hand, Joy thumbed through the cards, retrieving every recipe on Ruby's list of annual favorites. It took almost an hour to do the math and write up the shopping list for all she'd need to prepare ahead of time. But tonight she'd focus on just one recipe.

Sand tarts.

They'd always been her favorite. And no amount of powdered sugar across the front of her clothes would keep her from sampling them if they were on the tray. She hoped Molly would love them too.

She grabbed her keys and headed for town. The market was bustling, and holiday tunes filled the air. Less than two weeks until Christmas. Endcaps were filled with the essentials for all the traditional recipes. Green bean casserole, candied yams, and candied fruit for those adventurous enough to try making fruitcake. The smell of country ham tickled her nose, teasing memories of Aunt Ruby's sweet potato biscuits with razor thin slices of salty ham, which were always the tradition on Christmas morning.

Marking items off her list one by one, she'd finally made

it nearly two-thirds through the store, and her grocery cart looked pretty impressive. Anyone passing by might think she actually knew what she was going to do with all these ingredients. Quite honestly, she still didn't have a clue what the difference was between baking soda and baking powder, but did anyone really know?

She picked up a bucket of chicken and a container of macaroni and cheese from the deli. She'd heard Renee say her kids could live on chicken and macaroni and cheese. It seemed like a hedged bet. Molly could always eat another PBJ in a pinch. She wouldn't starve in one night. *Oh Lord, what kind of mother would I be, thinking like that?*

That little Christmas daydream she'd had taunted her. A boy and a girl, huh? Highly unlikely. Especially seeing as how she was nearly thirty with no prospects.

Joy stood in the shortest checkout line, reading the headlines of the tabloids. Someone pregnant, a couple splitting up, another getting married, a man trying to prove he is the real Santa and over four hundred years old. Go figure. If he was, cookies and milk must be the key to the fountain of youth, because that guy didn't look a day over fifty.

She lined up all the baking goods on the conveyor and watched the clerk fill bag after bag. The groceries she'd just unloaded from this very basket didn't seem to want to fit back into the cart. Why was that?

One swipe of her debit card, and she was armed and ready for the next twenty-four hours. If she survived one sleepover with a seven-year-old, then she could make it through the week of cookie preparation.

Loaded as she was with plastic bags on each arm, it still took three trips to get everything into the kitchen. With all the ingredients spread across the kitchen counter, Joy took out her phone and snapped a picture, then shot it off to Ruby, who would be happy to see proof that she was getting busy on the baking.

Kind of made her day too.

She separated out all the items she'd need to make the sand tarts tonight, then put the rest of the ingredients away. She and Molly would make all the dough for the twelve dozen sand tarts as Ruby requested and then bake a couple dozen just for practice—and fun, of course.

A few minutes later, Joy received a text back from Ruby that simply read, *Bravo!*

Johnny was probably behind that.

She put the phone on the counter and started pulling out pans, bowls, and the mixer so they could get started as soon as Molly arrived.

She picked up her phone and Googled bedtimes for seven-year-olds. She hadn't even thought to ask Ginny about any of those details. She couldn't remember what her bedtime schedule had been at that age. There was no shortage of information on the Internet about the subject, but it looked like the majority seemed to settle on 7:30 or 8 P.M. That shortened the length of time to entertain the little munchkin by nearly twelve hours. That wasn't nearly so intimidating.

I can make it that long.

As soon as she set her phone down, it vibrated against the Formica countertop. She lifted the phone, expecting a text from Renee, but what she saw was a selfie of Ruby and Johnny.

She laughed out loud. Dixon County Rehab Center would never be the same.

Bellissimo, she texted back.

Joy climbed the stairs and made up the twin bed in her old bedroom with fresh sheets from the linen closet. The sheets with princess-like pink hearts had been among her favorites. Molly would sleep in here and Joy would sleep in the guest room. That way if Molly got scared or confused in the night, she'd be right across the hall. Besides, that room was still suited to a young girl, since Ruby hadn't changed it at all since Joy left.

Plus, she'd much rather sleep in the queen bed.

The hot pink and lime green quilt that Mom and Ruby had made for her was still in the closet. Joy took it out and spread it over the bed, just as she would have twelve years ago.

Joy carefully took her dress from where she'd hung it over the door molding. She held it to her body and swayed. She didn't have a date for the gala, but Todd never wanted to dance anyway, so he wouldn't make the evening more fun. She may as well go alone. Besides, he'd just be working angles all night with the MacDonald-Webber clients, and that was just wrong since he was working for another firm now. Not one they really considered competition, but still. It's the way Todd worked. Always on.

She twirled one more time and then carried the dress over to the guest room. She hung it from the hook on the back of the door and ran her fingers down the fine beading. She'd dreamed of this night for so long. She couldn't miss it, and things were in good shape here. No reason not to. She hoped the night at the gala would be as magical as this dress seemed to her.

The loud diesel engine of the school bus vibrated against the old wooden-framed windows. Joy looked out the window and saw Molly getting off the bus with her bunny lunch bag.

She ran downstairs to greet her at the door. "How was your day?"

Molly smiled. "I made you something."

"You did?"

Molly nodded. "It's a Christmas ornament." She held up a red circle of paper hanging from a piece of green rickrack. On the ornament in white paint, the letters J O Y stood out.

"It's beautiful."

"It's your name. And a sentiment."

"Yes, it is."

"It doesn't smell like sentiment." Molly sniffed at it.

"Do you mean 'cinnamon'?"

"Yeah. Is that different than sentiment?"

Her heart warmed at the thought of those tiny hands at work on a gift just for her. "It is, but just as nice. I love my present. Thank you, Molly." She hung the ornament over the hallway doorknob. "We'll hang it here until we have the Christmas trees up. Okay?" It took all she had to hold back the tears the sweet gesture brought forth.

"Yes." Molly peeled off her coat and earmuffs.

"Do you want to put those upstairs on your bed?" Joy started for the stairs. "Come on. I'll show you where you're going to sleep tonight."

Molly followed her without a word until they reached the landing. "I usually just sleep with Ruby. She snores."

"She does?"

"Really loud." Molly fell into a fit of giggles.

Joy couldn't help but catch them too. "You don't snore, do you?"

"No-o!"

"Good. I don't snore, but I thought you could sleep in my old room." Joy pushed open the door to her brightly colored bedroom. "I'll be just across the hall. Is that okay?"

Molly's eyes brightened. "This was your room?"

"Sure was." Until today, Joy had thought of this room as holding the saddest parts of her life, but seeing her room through Molly's eyes right now reminded her that there had been good times here once.

Mom kneeling at the side of the bed, reading her a story until she fell asleep. The times when she was sick and Mom had taken care of her. A cold washcloth on her head and the trash can by the bed just in case. Making the bed together. Parachuting the flat sheet in the air at least a dozen times just for fun.

"I love this room," Molly said. "Look at all those books. Can I sleep with that bear?"

The bear had been a gift from Mom and Dad on her sixth birthday. Joy still remembered clinging to that thing at bedtime as a little girl. It had been a long time since that bear had gotten any love.

"You sure can." Joy reached up and took the bear from the shelf. He was still just as soft as she'd remembered. That bear had brought her comfort for so long. He'd soaked up many tears and weathered a lot of washings. "I think he might like staying with you."

"Forever?"

"Sure. He gets lonely in here." She handed the bear to Molly. Even with all the memories that bear held for her, she knew it would be better for Molly to have it—and to inherit that sense of security Joy got from it during tough times.

"This is the happiest room ever." Molly tucked the bear under her arm. "I won't be afraid in here."

There were a lot of good memories in this room.

Chapter Eighteen

Molly put her things on the chair at the desk in front of the window, and then climbed onto the bed. Sitting cross-legged in the middle, she bounced with a smile. "This'll be fun."

"I hope so." She reached out for Molly's hand, and the little girl slid off the bed. She turned and tucked the bear under the quilt, then folded her hand into Joy's.

They took the stairs side by side. "I thought we'd get everything measured out and the cookie dough made before dinner. We'll bake some for dessert afterwards. The dough is easier to work with when it's chilled."

"Okay."

"I wasn't sure what you'd want for dinner. I got chicken and macaroni and cheese."

"I love macaroni and cheese."

Score one for the home team. So far, so good. She could do this.

Together they worked on the cookie dough. After making crushing blows to the pecans Ruby had been cracking for the last month in preparation for this, they measured the pecan pieces out and mixed them in with the butter, flour, confectioners' sugar, a little vanilla, and an egg, using Ruby's old Sunbeam mixer to do the hard part. If Joy had done the math right, it would take four of these batches to make enough for the twelve dozen Ruby wanted.

"Okay," Joy said, opening the pantry and lifting two aprons off the hook. Even after all these years, she knew that they'd be hanging there. She lifted the loop of an apron that was cantaloupe orange with cupcakes embroidered in turquoise and white along the bottom. Joy dropped the top loop over Molly's head and then gathered the middle section to make it shorter and tied it around Molly's waist. "Perfect."

Joy grabbed the green and white striped apron and crossed the long ribbons behind her back, tying them in a big bow in the front. "I think we're ready for business." She grabbed the box of wax paper and closed the pantry door. "I need you to cut a really long piece of this wax paper. Be careful of the sharp edge. Can you do that?"

"Yes." Molly took the box and gently pulled out about ten inches. "This big?"

"Bigger."

She pulled out another length and paused, waiting for confirmation from Joy.

"More," Joy said.

"Even more?" Molly looked like she was taking all the candy out of an unattended trick-or-treat bowl. With nearly two feet of wax paper scrolled across the counter, Joy finally gave her the *okay* sign.

"Careful," Joy reminded her.

Molly tilted the box and tugged.

"Perfect." Joy plopped the big mass of dough out of the mixing bowl and right down on the paper. "Help me squish. We're going to make one long skinny caterpillar."

She and Molly squeezed, stretched, and tugged the mound into one long cylinder that went from one end of the wax paper to the other.

"Now, lift your end and I'll lift mine. We'll position it right at the edge of the paper. Okay?"

Molly picked up her end, and they made the maneuver.

Then Joy rolled the paper around the dough like one giant slice-and-bake cookie roll.

"One down," Joy said.

"That was fun."

"Yep. Maybe you can come spend the night when we bake for the big Crystal Christmas Cookie Crawl." The words had just flowed right out of her mouth, surprising her as much as it had Molly, who looked absolutely delighted by the idea.

They made one more batch of cookie dough together and then took a break to eat dinner. Joy warmed up the fried chicken and macaroni and cheese while Molly set the table, singing quietly as she did,

> *Hey diddle, diddle, the plate is in the middle,*
> *the cow jumped over the moon.*
> *The fork is on the left,*
> *the knife is on the right,*
> *on the inside of the spoon.*

She repeated the melody as she arranged the other place setting, then turned with pride.

"It looks beautiful." Joy set the warmed food on the table and took a seat, gesturing to Molly to take the other. "Do you like the drumstick?"

"Yes, ma'am."

Joy's heart filled with love for this sweet little girl. What she'd give to be able to take a quick video of this behavior to send to Margie as an example of what her children should know. There was no comparison.

"How was your day at school today?" Joy asked.

"It was good. I love my school. Everyone is really nice and we learn a lot of stuff too. Plus, we got to make those ornaments today. That was the most fun."

"That's good."

"Sometimes we get to bring in snacks. Bobby's mom brought us cupcakes today. They were little ones, so we didn't even make a mess."

"That was nice of her."

"Yep." Molly took another bite of her chicken. "I like making stuff with you. You're nice."

"Thank you. I think you're nice too." Joy dragged her last bite of chicken through the cheese sauce on her plate. "You all done?"

"Yes."

Joy cleared the dishes, and Molly held open the dishwasher for Joy.

"We're a good team." Joy wiped her hands on the dish towel, and then started measuring out another batch of cookie dough. "You ready?"

Molly climbed up on the chair in front of the counter and held the measuring cup of flour over the mixing bowl. "Ready when you are!"

When Joy put the last cookie dough log in the freezer, she pulled out the first one they'd made and cut it in half. "Ready to make some cookies now? These are my very favorite kind."

Molly's eyes danced.

Joy set the preheat on the oven and got two cookie sheets out from the pantry.

"Okay, the trick to these cookies is that they shouldn't be too thick. So we're going to just take a little ball of dough and then kind of turn it into a log and flatten and curve it to look like the moon." Joy plucked a small ball of dough and worked it in her hands into the shape she'd always remembered Aunt Ruby making. "Think you can do it?"

"Let me try," Molly said.

Joy handed her a ball of dough. Molly worked it into a shape.

"Good, now just put it on the baking sheet. We want to leave some room around them, so not too close."

"Right there?" Molly asked as she dropped her cookie on the baking sheet.

"Perfect. We should be able to get twelve on this sheet. Want to count with me?"

"Sure." Molly counted out one and two for the ones they'd already put on the sheet, counting aloud as they each dropped their finished shapes onto the pan one by one.

"Twelve!" Molly said just as the buzzer went off on the oven.

They slid the first pan of cookies into the oven and Joy set the timer, then made the next twelve while she put Molly in charge of sifting confectioners' sugar to roll the warm cookies in.

Powdered sugar wafted into the air like fog. Joy pushed the sleeves of her blue sweater up. The warm oven had made the kitchen more comfortable, chasing the chill right out of there.

The timer buzzed. "They're ready."

Joy grabbed the cotton loom pot holders from the drawer and slid the pan out onto the top of the stove.

"They smell good," Molly said.

Joy inhaled the sugary smell. "Yes, they do." She slid the second tray into the oven. "Let's make another batch, and then those should be cool enough to put in the confectioners' sugar."

They balled and shaped the next twelve onto a sheet of parchment; then Joy held the warm baking sheet while

Molly negotiated the big spatula to carefully remove each cookie and set it into the pan of confectioners' sugar.

They'd moved only three cookies when the smoke alarm went off.

It was so loud that Molly dropped the spatula and put her hands over her ears.

Joy swung around and put the baking sheet on the table as she ran for the oven. Poking at the buttons on the oven, she turned it off, then tossed the hand towel from her shoulder to Molly. "Here. Fan this in the air near the smoke alarm."

Molly swung the towel like a seasoned Pittsburgh Steeler fan as Joy dived in to rescue the cookies, but there'd be no rescuing these. They were burnt to a way-too-dark-brown crisp. Smoke streamed from the twelve charred nuggets as Joy carried the baking sheet out the back door to the trash bin.

Molly the Bunny lifted up on her hind legs, sniffing the air.

"No feedback from the funny farm," Joy warned as she pushed through the screen door, opened the lid of the trash bin, and slammed the pan against it.

The bunny fell to all fours and hopped to the back corner of the cage.

"Everything okay?" Ben came running around the corner and slid to a stop when he saw her.

A flush raced up her cheeks. Why was it she always seemed to be telling this guy she could handle everything, and yet he was right there every time catastrophe struck? "I swear I am not always in trouble."

"I'm beginning to get a complex."

"Me too. I was joking when I said you were bad luck before, but now I'm really beginning to wonder. Were you supposed to come over tonight? Did I forget something?"

"No. I was checking the water for the trees. They take in a lot the first couple of days. I was over at the barn and heard the smoke alarm."

"Baking mishap. We might have been having too much fun. The first batch came out perfect."

"'We'? Is Ruby home?"

"No. I've got a little helper."

"Stove might run hot. Mom's does. To the tune of about twenty-five degrees. It's not all that uncommon."

"Really?"

"Yeah. I could check it for you."

"I—"

"I know. You can do it yourself, but if I do it, I have a reason to get one of the still-warm perfect cookies you just mentioned."

"Come on in."

He followed her inside, where Molly still stood in the middle of the kitchen, flagging that dish towel as she'd been told. "You can stop now," Joy said. "Thanks, Molly."

"Hi, Molly. I'm Ben." He leaned forward slightly, getting closer to her level. "I'm Ruby and Joy's friend."

"Me too," she said, brushing her sugared hands on her pants and then extending her hand to shake his.

Ben extended his hand and Molly shook it. He looked impressed. "How old are you?"

"I'm seven."

"I bet you're a big help in the kitchen." He leaned over and stage whispered, "Looks like she needs some help."

Joy pulled back, her brow arching. "Do I need to remind you the first batch was fine?"

Ben tapped Molly on the nose, causing her to giggle. "I'm going to check the oven so there won't be any excuses to burn the next batch."

"Good, because that was hard work, chasing the smoke out." Molly rubbed her arm dramatically.

"I don't think we have a thermometer," Joy admitted.

"No need for one. I have a little trick up my sleeve," Ben said.

"Of course you do. Else why would Ruby call you Handy Andy?"

Molly giggled, and Ben cut his eyes in Joy's direction.

"You can dish out some digs in fun too. I like that in a gal." He crossed the room. "Do you have any sugar?"

Molly and Joy burst into a fit of giggles. The entire kitchen was practically dusted in confectioners' sugar.

Ben followed their glances toward the kitchen counter and swept a finger through the mess. Then he slowly turned and smudged three dots across Molly's forehead and one right on the tip of her nose.

"Hey!" Molly said, raising her hands to her hips, then bursting into another fit of giggles.

"What?" Ben tried to look innocent, but Molly wasn't buying it.

"You put flour on me."

"No," Ben said. "That's not flour. That's Christmas cookie flour and when you dot that on your skin during the holidays, then it turns into magic snowflake wishes." He pointed to the dots. "See. All different. Just like snowflakes. But magic!"

Molly's eyes popped big and then narrowed. "Really?"

"Really. My mom always used to give us snowflake wishes when we made holiday cookies for the community tree."

"The tree at the hospital?" Molly balanced on tiptoes, eyes wide and looking very impressed.

Joy leaned against the counter. "What's the community tree?"

"My mom started it years ago. She started out as a candy striper and then worked at the hospital once she earned her nursing degree. One of the first years she was there a group of them planted a live Christmas tree in the island outside the emergency room entrance. Mom said it was a pitiful thing. The next year she had this idea to convince folks to decorate it with homemade ornaments to make it look more festive. It's become tradition. Families bake and decorate cookies with their family name on them and hang them on the tree. Some people make regular cookies, others make birdseed-and-suet-type concoctions in cookie shapes. Basically, it's a little nature buffet for the local birds, and it's fun, a place for neighbors to catch up."

"Sounds like a neat idea."

"Can we do that?" Molly asked.

"Sure. We could do that one morning before you go to school."

"We're a good team," Molly said to Ben.

"If you're going to be a team, then I think Joy could probably use some magic Christmas snowflake wishes too. What do you think, Molly?"

"Yes! Maybe we won't mess up any more cookies if we have extra snowflake wishes!"

He swept two fingers from each hand through the sugary mess and gave Joy a double line of sugar stripes on each cheek. "That should make for four magical wishes. Hopefully enough for every kind of cookie you're baking," he said.

"Here." Joy grabbed her phone and handed it to Ben. "Take our picture. We'll send it to Ruby. She'll be delighted to know we're making baking progress."

Molly and Joy struck a pose, and Ben clicked off a couple of pictures. "She'll love them. Now, about that sugar. I need plain granulated sugar."

"That I've got." Joy picked up a tall ceramic canister from the counter and set it in front of Ben.

"Great." Ben set the oven to 350 degrees. While the oven came back up to temperature, he placed a tablespoon of sugar in the middle of a cookie sheet.

"This is how you're going to test my oven? That sugar will burn and stink up the whole kitchen even worse."

"Trust me."

"That's what they all say."

The preheat tone sounded, and Ben slid the tray into the oven, then set the timer for fifteen minutes.

"So, while we wait, tell me about this baking you two are up to. This looks like a serious amount of work."

"Ruby asked me to prepare the dough for all the Crystal Christmas Cookie Crawl cookies, so I thought Molly and I would get started on some of that tonight. We decided to test my personal favorites."

"The burnt ones?"

She gave him a playful glare. "Sand tarts, funny man."

"My dad's mom used to make those. Haven't had those in years."

"Well, if I can keep from burning the next batch, maybe I can hook you up with a few."

The timer buzzed, and Ben opened the oven door. "Okay, see what we've got here?"

Joy and Molly peered into the oven.

"Melted sugar?" Joy said. "No surprise there."

"Oh, but it is. Sugar should not melt at three hundred fifty degrees. It should, however, melt at three seventy-five. That tells us that this oven is running at least twenty-five degrees hot. Something Ruby probably knows by heart."

"Thanks, Ben. That ought to save some more kitchen disasters, and that's good news for us, isn't it, Molly?"

"It sure is."

"Unfortunately, we're out of time tonight. I'll put this last batch in, but it's time for you to head to bed, young lady."

"Okay," she said without even an argument. "Will you tuck me in?"

"Sure."

Ben said, "I'll pop this tray of cookies in while y'all get ready for bed."

"Thanks. Should be eleven minutes if the temperature is right."

"Oh, it will be right on."

"I know, I know. Trust me."

He shrugged, and Joy and Molly headed upstairs.

Joy turned on the hall light and helped Molly get changed into her nightgown.

"I'm going to leave the hall light on for you." Joy pulled the sheet up around Molly's chin. "I hope you sleep good tonight."

"Thank you, Joy. I had so much fun. It was extra-super fun. Even with the fire."

"Me too, but it wasn't exactly a fire. Just a little well done. And our secret, right?"

Molly zipped her fingers to her lips and turned an invisible key, then bounced her head in agreement.

"Cool."

"I'll peek in before I go to sleep, but if you need anything, you just let me know."

As Joy left the room, Molly turned on her side away from the door and snuggled into the covers, pulling the bear into a hug.

A smile crept across Joy's face. One that seemed to come all the way from her heart as she watched the young figure curl under the covers. Joy had to agree. It was a pretty special night.

In the kitchen, Ben was just pulling the cookies out of the oven. "Perfect."

"They do look perfect. Thank you so much. How'd you even know to check that?"

"I told you that I like to fix things."

"You're good at it. I guess the nickname fits."

"I'd appreciate it if you wouldn't use it. I try to humor Ruby, but it drives me crazy."

"Probably why she calls you that. She has a weird sense of humor sometimes."

"She's a neat lady."

"The best."

"Molly's a good kid."

"She is. Thank goodness, because I really don't know anything about kids. I kind of inherited her after Ruby's fall."

"You were doing fine."

"Really?" That compliment meant more to her than she'd have expected. "Thank you. Molly's made it easy."

"She's sweet, but I can see it. You're a natural."

Todd had always gone on and on about how she wouldn't make a good mother because she worked so much, but until now, she'd never really considered it. "Thanks. Like you said, she's a good kid. Fun to be around."

"You're more fun than I expected you to be."

Joy readied herself to argue, then figured he kind of had a point. Every time they'd interacted, it was a disaster or a disagreement. Why would he think otherwise? "I could say the same about you."

"Since there's no damage here, this turned out to be a pretty nice way to end an otherwise problematic day. Even if you did move the largest Christmas tree too close to the goats' pen. Hate to have to be the one to tell you that they ate the whole back side of it."

"Funny."

He raised his hand, pledging. "Not kidding."

"They ate the tree? Like, bite-chew-swallow ate the thing?"

"Just like that. Right down to the white of the skeleton. Not a piece of pine bark left."

"I swear I'm a walking disaster these days." She ran her hand through her hair. "I can't believe this."

"We can make it work. In fact, I always tell Ruby that those fat trees are too big for the front room, but she insists. This might work in our favor. We can push it back another foot into the corner and really fill up the front with ornaments and lights."

"And this means you'll get your way."

"A small win."

"Hey, with Ruby, that's a big deal."

"I like the way you think." He leaned in so close, she could feel his warm breath on her cheek. And it felt nice. The scent of pine rose from his jacket. And mixed with the sugary cookies, it was sexier than the finest cologne.

She stepped back and sucked in one last breath of him. "Well, I know how that is." She kept her distance. "Um, thanks for your help tonight. With everything. With Molly too. I really felt in over my head, but when her mom stopped by and asked for my help, I couldn't say no."

"Looked like you knew what you were doing."

"That's just my boardroom cool showing. I was a mess underneath, but when you did that magical Christmas snowflake wish stuff, I felt like I finally let my guard down and enjoyed myself." *Did I just say that out loud? Shut up.* "So, you said you were having a problematic day. What's going on with you?"

"The volunteer who was supposed to handle all the planning for the annual Extreme Gingerbread Bake-off—"

"Oh no. Backed out on you? I hate that."

"Not exactly. Ashley would never just have backed out. It was Mother Nature interrupting."

"How so?"

"Ashley went home to visit her mom and went into labor. A month early, so I can't fault her for timing."

"Hardly."

"She and the baby are both doing fine, but they'll stay at her parents' through the holidays. Exciting for them, but I'm left to find someone else to finish up what she was going to be handling. I can't do it myself, because I helped my mom with her entry this year—disqualifying me from judging. Plus, I'm already up to my ears in things to do."

"Good thing you don't have to bother with the decorations here, then."

"Actually, I'd much rather work on these decorations. Event planning really isn't my strong suit. I'm a numbers guy. Detail oriented on money and such, and handy. I can fix anything. But when it comes to planning an event like that . . . not so much."

"Girl stuff."

"Parties? Yeah, pretty much."

The light twinkled in his eyes. Joy picked up a cookie and tossed it at him. He caught it midair and took a bite. At least she hadn't thrown like a girl. "I'd rather be planning," she said. "And by the way, I've got a project plan for the decorations. I'm all set, and starting to get excited."

His lips lifted into a smirk, and he leaned into her space. "Maybe I could help you and you could help me."

She laughed, letting him linger a little too close.

With a lift of the brow, he smiled. "I'm serious. What do you think?"

No was on her lips, but what came out was, "We could do that." Was it the manly mix of pine and sugar, or those eyes that were sucking the smarts out of her? She could not fall for this flirty numbers guy. She'd be heading back home in a couple of weeks, but what could it hurt to prove to him that she really did know how to organize a dazzling party?

"Great. Well, I guess I'd better leave." But he stood there for a moment too long, too much like he was hoping she'd ask him to stay.

And as she watched him leave, she wished she'd asked him to stay and finish baking cookies—she already had those extra snowflake wishes on her side.

He turned back to her from the door. "Let's work out the details. Tomorrow? You can stop by the hospital, or I can come by here after work."

And just like that, she took on a new project—or traded duties, really. Depending on how you looked at it.

She walked him out, standing at the door as he got into his truck.

The chilly night air wrapped around her as she waved. Replaying the day in her mind, she locked up. Back in the kitchen, she put away the remnants of the evening's project.

Tomorrow, after she sent Molly off to school, she'd prep the remaining cookie batches and mark that off her list.

Upstairs, Joy quietly peeked into her former bedroom. Molly hadn't moved since she tucked her in.

Every floorboard in the old house seemed to creak under her feet as she walked across the hall to change into her pajamas. Exhausted, she set her alarm to be sure she got up in plenty of time to get things going around here before it was time for Molly to wake up.

Chapter Nineteen

Joy hugged her robe around her as she tried to quietly traverse the squeaking stairs. It seemed like the more she tried, the louder she was. Her body was as tight as if she'd just done an hour of Pilates after the stealth trip down only a dozen steps. She relaxed once she took that final step into the living room and headed to the kitchen to make coffee.

And after all that careful maneuvering to keep from waking up Molly, the little girl was already sitting at the table, dressed for school.

"Hey, you're up early," Joy said. There was still a lot of time left to go before that school bus would come and pick her up. "Didn't you sleep well?"

"Yes. Mom says I'm an early bird."

Molly had already poured herself a cup of milk. "Well, we might have time to go to the community tree this morning if you'd like to do that."

"Can we?"

That little smile tugged at Joy's heart. "Sure. I can feed the animals after you go to school. I think Jack, Nanny, and Waddles will understand. It's just one morning." Besides, it wouldn't be completely awful if she happened to run into Ben again. "Should we make a fresh batch of cookies and decorate one to place on the community tree?"

"Yes!"

Joy pulled out a stick of the frozen cookie dough and sliced enough pieces for a baker's dozen of cookies and two larger slices to cut into shapes for the community tree ornaments.

"If you pull out that bottom drawer by the sink, there should be some cookie cutters in there. See if you can find us two extra-special Christmas shapes."

Molly ran across the kitchen, her shoes slapping across the tile, then plunked down on the floor and started pulling things out of the drawer.

Joy set the oven temperature and laid a clean cookie sheet on the counter. Their aprons from last night were draped over one of the chair backs.

"What do you think? Are our aprons too messy to wear again today?"

Molly laughed, showing a missing front bottom tooth. "We'd be messy before we started."

"True. That would not be good. Hang on." Joy walked down to Ruby's bedroom. Ruby had a stack of T-shirts from events going as far back as the nineties, probably older if Joy had taken the time to really peruse them. She took the top two from the stack and carried them back into the kitchen. She slipped the first one over Molly's head and then pulled one on herself. "There. We're ready."

Joy let Molly shape the thin slices into little crescent moons while Joy found the rolling pin, then carefully and neatly sifted confectioners' sugar into an eight-inch square baking dish for the finishing work.

"All done," Molly said, wiping her hands on her T-shirt.

"Perfect timing." Joy slid the tray of crescents into the oven, set the timer, and then joined Molly at the counter.

Joy picked up the rolling pin and said, "Okay, now we're going to sprinkle just a little of this confectioners' sugar on the rolling pin, then push down and roll the pin forward to flatten out our two big pieces of dough. I'll do one and you can do the other."

Molly watched intently as Joy rolled out a level four-inch round, then let Molly give it a try.

"Good job," Joy said. "It took me forever to learn how to do that."

Molly picked up the two metal forms, one in each hand. "Christmas star or stocking."

"Awesome. Which shape do you want for your cookie?"

"The stocking," Molly said.

"Okay, then I'll decorate a star." Molly handed Joy the stocking cookie cutter and they both pressed the metal forms into their dough at the same time. Without a word, Joy let Molly learn by following along. They swept away the extra dough, then carefully pushed the shapes from the cookie cutters.

"I'll put these on the cookie tray too," Molly said.

"Uh-oh. We forgot one thing."

Molly's head tilted. Joy could almost see the thought bubble full of question marks above the little girl's head.

"We need a hole in those cookies so we can put a ribbon through them to hang them from the Christmas tree."

"Oh yeah!" Molly frowned. "How do we do that?"

Joy held up a finger and gave Molly a wink. "I have an idea." She went to the pantry and got a straw. She cut the straw into two pieces and handed one to Molly. "I think we can just use these straws to twist a circle out. Let's see if it works."

"Taa-daa," Molly said, throwing her arms in the air. "It worked."

"Sure did." And just then, the timer went off. "Hope this batch came out. Cross your fingers."

Molly crossed her fingers and scrunched her face as Joy slid the cookies out of the oven. "They're perfect."

"Mr. Ben helped with the oven. Now all the cookies will be perfect all the time."

"I hope so."

Molly climbed down from the chair in front of the counter. "Can I put our special ones in the oven?"

"Sure, but let's be careful." Joy grabbed two red oven mitts. "Hold out your arms."

Molly held her hands out like she was ready to do a Frankenstein walk, and Joy slid the mitts over her hands, covering the little girl's arms clear up past her elbows.

"Okay," Joy said, holding the tray of cookies out and resting it in Molly's hands. "Got it?"

"Yes," she said with a nod.

Joy swung the oven door open and slid the middle rack out.

Molly pushed the tray of cookies into the warm oven, then stepped back and clapped her mitts together. "Eleven minutes," she said.

"Exactly." Joy set the timer and went to the pantry to see what kind of icing or holiday decorating goodies Ruby had stashed away. In a short time, she and Molly filled the kitchen table with sprinkles, icing, edible glitters and dots, and even fancy confetti and silver dragées.

They worked the first batch of cookies through the confectioners' sugar.

Once the two cookies were done, Joy set them on the cooling rack while she and Molly filled a plate with the sand tarts they'd just finished. Molly stretched red plastic wrap taut across the top.

They cleaned up their mess while the stocking and the star cookies cooled, and then put all their attention on decorating them with extra details for the community tree.

"We need our names on these," Molly said. "Will you help me? I don't write pretty."

"I bet you write beautifully, but I'll help. Which color?"

"Blue."

Joy took the top off the gel icing. "You hold it, and then I'll help."

Molly took the tube in her hand, and Joy wrapped hers around Molly's tiny fingers. She scrolled out the letters in a quick, even flow. Then she grabbed the red and wrote JOY across the star ornament she'd made.

"What do you think?" Joy nudged Molly. They looked beautiful.

"I love them."

"Let's take a picture. We'll send it to Ruby and your momma." Joy grabbed her phone, and Molly held the cookie ornaments and mugged for the camera.

Less than an hour later, they had thirteen cookies on a Christmas-patterned plate covered in red plastic wrap, along with their community tree ornaments on a separate plate. "We still have time to go to the hospital and put our ornaments on the tree if you want to."

"Yes, please."

"Great. Then get all your stuff. We'll take it with us, just in case we're running late."

"Okay." Molly ran out of the kitchen and then appeared back in the doorway. "Thank you."

"You're welcome, sweetie." Joy watched Molly race out of the room again, her footsteps pounding up the stairs to gather her things. *I should be thanking you.*

She and Molly loaded Molly's things in the backseat and then carefully set the plates of cookies on the floorboard to keep them from sliding around as they drove.

Joy swooped into the hospital parking lot, her heart doing a jig when she spotted Ben's truck, already parked in the same spot as the other night. And since Molly's bus wasn't due to arrive at Ruby's for almost an hour, Joy had plenty of time to stop in and deliver those cookies personally.

"Want to take our cookies to Ben to say thank you before we put our ornaments on the community tree?"

"Yes, and maybe he can come with us."

Wouldn't that be nice. She handed Molly the plate with the community tree ornaments on it and balanced the other in her hand with her keys. Molly grabbed for Joy's hand as they walked into the hospital.

"Excuse me," Joy said to the young lady at the reception desk. "I need to meet with Ben Andrews."

"He's expecting you?"

Not officially, but then she'd always found acting as if she belonged worked best, and he had said they'd connect today on a plan to swap out tasks. "Yes, he is."

"Down the hall, third door on the left. His secretary can help you."

"Thank you." Joy turned and headed down the hall with Molly at her hip, but when they entered the office space labeled ACCOUNTING, no one was at the secretary's desk. Joy could see the lights on in the office down the hall, so she wandered in.

"Knock, knock," Joy said as she poked her head into the office. Ben sat at his desk, reading something on his computer screen. "Your secretary wasn't at her desk. Hope you don't mind me coming on back."

"Joy? Sure. Come in." Ben stood from behind his desk, looking handsome in a single-breasted charcoal suit with a classic notched lapel. The initials on the cuff of his sleeve didn't go unnoticed as he reached forward to put his ink pen in the cup on his desk. "Hi, Molly."

The office wasn't fancy, but the furnishings were of

high quality. The desk and bookcase were both made of a deep-stained wood. Silver frames glimmered in carefully placed spots next to books and binders on the shelves showing relationships and vacations. Memories. An African violet with bright purple flowers brightened the spot on the table between the two chairs facing the desk. "We brought you a little present."

"Cookies!" Molly shouted. "And we're putting these pretty-shaped ones on the community tree." She teetered side to side as she extended her plate for Ben to see. Her little smile so wide that her lips practically disappeared.

Bringing him cookies had seemed like a nice gesture early this morning, but Joy was finding it a bit awkward now.

Ben took the covered plate from her. "If you'd brought these a couple of days ago, I'd have had them tested for poison before I ate them."

Joy felt a blush rise in her cheeks. "Sorry I pounced on you that first night. And then again over the ornament. Neither was your fault. You didn't deserve that."

"I like a girl who says what's on her mind."

"Then you just hit the jackpot." *Did I just say that out loud?* "The holidays always get me a little sideways, and you just happened to be in the wrong place at the wrong time. Honestly, if I had it my way, I'd just hibernate starting the week of Thanksgiving and wake up after the New Year's ball has dropped."

He sat on the edge of his desk. "Really?" His easy smile lifted to his eyes, and she could make out the well-muscled outline of his biceps under the high-collared white shirt and jacket. "I don't think I've ever known anyone who really wished they could miss Christmas." He smiled at Molly. "You don't want to miss Christmas, do you?"

"No way. Never. No sir," Molly said.

Joy pointed her thumbs toward her chest. "Now you have. But I'm one heckuva project manager, and my lack of enthusiasm for the holiday will not impact my ability to produce the best house on the infamous Cookie Crawl, or help you with your event."

"That's good, because I need your help. May I?" Ben pulled back the wrap from the plate. "These look great, but there's something missing." He grabbed Molly's hand and started for the door. "Got a minute?"

"Sure. Well, yeah. But where are we going?" Joy triple-stepped to catch up with them.

They'd already cleared the door to the hall. By the time she was at his side, Ben had pulled the badge from his belt and the door to the cafeteria, which appeared to be closed, opened. "We need ice-cold milk, and it just so happens we have the best cold milk around. After you, ladies."

Joy walked inside, and Ben stepped in front of her and pulled out two chairs at the nearest table, putting the plate of cookies right in the center. Rubbing his hands together, he glanced between the two and asked, "White or chocolate?"

"Chocolate?" Molly said, glancing hesitantly in Joy's direction.

"Me too," Ben said.

"Then make it three."

"I like smart girls," Ben said with a wink. He stepped away, but was back in jiff with three fogged glasses of chocolate milk forming a triangle in his grasp.

Molly took a sip of hers and then tugged on Ben's sleeve. "Can I go look at the decorations over there?"

Ben looked to Joy for an answer.

"Oh yeah, sure. That's fine, Molly. We'll be right here." Joy watched Molly skip across the room, and then turned back to Ben, who was practically staring at her. She ran her hand through her hair. Recognizing her own nervous habit, she put both hands around her glass to keep them still.

Ben raised his glass. "This is a divine current-year pasteurized milk. Perfect with home-baked treats. Cheers."

"A regular Food Network host." She took a sip. "Cheers."

"Well, my mom does happen to own the bakery in town. I'm a quick study."

"You are full of surprises, Ben Andrews. First, you impress me with the sugar test, and now with perfect food pairings. You know a little bit about everything, don't you? I guess you're more than just the average suit."

They clinked their glasses and dived in. Ben asked, "What do you have against suits?"

She opened her mouth and then shut it again. "I'm not sure. Maybe it's just because I work with them all day long. And accountants are normally kind of quiet guys. Aren't you?"

"Maybe I'll change your mind." He handed a cookie to her, and then took one for himself. "So tell me, how in the world does a girl named Joy dread the holidays?"

Biting her lip, she looked away. It was so much easier to just ignore the holidays and pretend the bad things had never happened. Dealing with them just brought more pain. She glanced back over to him. He sat. Patient. Quiet. Sincere. "My dad left us around Christmas one year. Christmases were never the same without him. That's when Mom and I moved here to live with Ruby and my uncle George. Then a couple years later, my mom died. At Christmastime. It's not a happy time for everyone." Her heart clenched, and she could see the sorrow in Ben's eyes. She didn't want him to feel sorry for her. Just to understand. And what she saw in his face right this minute made her feel vulnerable. She wished she could rewind those words. Trying to compensate, she said, "Besides, people waste time and money on gifts just for the gifts' sake. And more often than not, they can't even really afford it. How can that be good? Quite frankly, I don't want all that hanging over my head."

"That had to be hard. And you're right. Sometimes people get caught up in the what instead of the why." His voice was gentle. "I'm sorry about your mom."

"Thank you." His words were surprisingly comforting. "It was a long time ago. I was just a teenager." She closed her eyes and took in a breath. "She died right here, in fact. In room 304."

"Which explains why you were so distracted that first night we met. Probably brought back some feelings. I'm sorry for your loss."

"Yeah. After all these years, it's still hard. Maybe mostly because she died with a heart full of hope, and it didn't do her a bit of good. I miss her all the time."

"Do you still talk to your dad?"

"No." She stared into the glass of milk. "Funny. I was mad at my mom for a long time for making me switch schools. I blamed her for the separation from my dad. Only when she died, I tracked him down. I found out that he was the one who left us when he found out Mom was sick. She'd been sick for a long time, and I never even knew."

"She probably didn't want you to worry."

"She was so sick by the time I knew what was going on that we didn't even have much time. And I'd been angry with her for so long. And she never said a bad word about my dad. Not one. But then, I'm not sure I ever heard her say a bad word about anyone. Mom had had no choice but to pack me up and come here to live with her sister. My aunt Ruby. We were here for over a year before she finally told me she was sick."

"So you were here in Crystal Falls as a teenager?"

"I sure was."

"We must have crossed paths. It's a small town."

"You'd think, but I doubt it. I was an angry teenager. I kept to myself."

"That had to have been so hard for you."

"It still is." Why did she just tell him all of that? She never talked about her dad. "You know, we better get a move on if we're going to put our ornaments on the community tree. I have to get Molly back to catch the bus."

"I'll walk with you."

"I'd like that. Let me get Molly."

He stood and waited as she gathered Molly from the vivid holiday display. A Christmas village amid a fluffy pile of tufted sterile cotton.

"Follow me," he said. "I've got keys to the shortcut."

He led the way through the back halls of the hospital and outside. They crossed the asphalt parking lot to the grassy median just across from the ER entrance. A whimsical fence of two-foot candy canes outlined the perimeter, with the community tree stretching nearly thirty feet into the air from the center.

"It's a beautiful tree," Joy said, leaning back to see the whole thing. "The bark is almost a red, and the bluish green needles look so pretty."

"Carolina sapphire. My family has bought trees from the local farm that grows these for as many years as I can remember."

"This one is perfect."

"The hospital has the horticulture students from the university come out and prune and shape the tree every

year. It's good practice for them, and we get all the bene-
fits."

"So many people have already added their ornaments."

Molly made a beeline to the tree, still holding the plate
with their ornaments on it. Her mouth dropped wide as she
touched and cherished every ornament she could reach.
"So pretty."

Joy and Ben exchanged a gentle smile.

"I'm glad you're part of our community tree this year
too," he said.

"Do you have an ornament on the tree?"

"Of course."

"Which one?"

He took her hand and walked her around to the back of
the tree. "That one." He pointed to a letter *A* about four
inches tall, made of birdseed. *The Andrews* was written
in script on a glossy white card with holly leaves and
berries painted on it.

A tiny chickadee flitted from the tight branches of the
tree, sending Joy back a step with a yelp.

"You all right?"

"Yeah. It just startled me." She recovered quickly.
"Where do you want to hang your ornament, Molly?"

"Right here," Molly said.

They'd carefully strung pipe cleaners through the hole
in the top of each cookie so they could hang them on the
tree. "Here you go." She delicately held the stocking that
Molly had decorated with a row of red hot hearts and her
name in blue frosting along the top.

Joy had brushed a thin layer of watered-down confectioners' sugar atop her star-shaped cookie, then dusted
shiny sky blue sprinkles along the very edge of each point.
A row of rainbow jimmies etched a stitchlike look around

the whole cookie, and dragées in the shape of the letter *H* graced the center in shiny silver. The shiny silver pipe cleaner was curved into an S. She handed it to Molly to hang on the tree.

"Where should we put this one?"

"Wherever you'd like. When Ruby comes home, we'll bring her out here to show it to her."

"She will love it." Molly walked around the tree with a serious look. Finally she stopped and placed the star between a gingerbread-man-shaped birdseed ornament and a bright red Santa hat. "It looks pretty right here next to mine."

Ben said, "It sure does. Thanks, Molly."

"We better get going," Joy said. "Ben, it was good to see you again."

"I'll walk you to your car." He shoved his hands in his pockets as Molly reached for Joy's hand.

Ben finally cleared his throat. "How long are you going to be in town?"

"I don't know. I guess that depends on how long Ruby needs me."

"Do you have a boyfriend waiting on you back home?"

Joy almost stubbed the toe of her boot as she walked. That had come from left field. "Not really. No. I don't."

"Divorced?"

"Never been married."

The slight eyebrow raise didn't get past her. "What?" She hated that reaction from people. "What did that look mean? It's not like any woman never married by the age of thirty is going to be an old maid. Market research shows that women have just as good a chance of being married at thirty-five as at the age of thirty. And by the way, I am not yet thirty."

"Well, that explains it," he said.

"Explains what?"

"Why I didn't remember you from school. You're younger than me. Nothing wrong with never having been married."

She'd wondered the same thing. "What about you? Single?"

"Divorced."

"Oh. Sorry."

"Are you wondering why we split up?"

"It's really none of my business."

"Good. I don't really like to talk about it," he said. "We've got the obligatory Match.com questions out of the way and have agreed to work together. How about I stop by tonight around seven, unless you'd like to grab dinner?"

"I'll eat early. I've got a lot to do. Seven works fine, and that will leave me time to get some things done tonight before you get there."

"Okay. I'm looking forward to it." He opened the passenger door of Joy's wrecked Prius for Molly. "Have a good day at school, Molly."

"Thank you, Mr. Ben."

She should have offered to fix something for his dinner, but then that seemed a little forward, and why take a chance on sending him the wrong message?

"Oh, I almost forgot." Joy pushed her hand into her coat pocket and handed over a thumb drive. "I put my plan for Ruby's decorations on this. We can discuss it tonight when you come by."

"I'll take a look, and I'll bring the paperwork Ashley had on the Extreme Gingerbread Bake-off. It's really a matter of setting up the part for the community to vote. That's scheduled to take place this Sunday. We don't have much time. At least all the information from previous years is in the file too."

"Great. No need to re-create the wheel."

Joy had always thought she'd have a career instead of a family, because it was no secret that children required a lot of attention. Visions of Margie and her hellions popped into her head. But Molly had shown her a different side of the equation.

Had she been so focused on her work that she hadn't even taken the time to figure out what she wanted besides a career? She didn't have any hobbies. But then she didn't have the downtime to engage in them. And she couldn't remember the last time she'd turned on the television in her apartment. And she paid a pretty penny for the high-resolution curved screen, not to mention the cable bill each month.

She glanced over at Molly. Hard to believe that a child like Molly would do anything but add to your life.

Chapter Twenty

Joy was glad she'd thought to put Molly's things in the car just in case they were running late, because no sooner did she pull into the driveway and take the key from the ignition than the bus pulled up in front of Ruby's house.

Joy got out, waving to the bus driver as she helped Molly get her things out of the backseat. "Have a fun day."

Molly slipped her backpack over her shoulder and picked up her lunch bag. "I already did. Thank you for so much fun. I'll see you tomorrow morning."

"Yes, you will." And Joy felt something inside that she didn't expect as she watched Molly run for the bus with her bunny lunch bag swinging from her hand. She was looking forward to Molly's coming in the morning.

She looked so tiny as she stretched to climb the stairs, her knee practically touching her chest as she boarded.

Joy understood some of the comments Renee had made about watching her kids on their first day of school. They'd sounded so absurd at the time, but when Molly plopped into the fourth row of the bus and pressed her tiny face to the window and waved, Joy felt her chest tighten in a way it never had before.

"Bye, sweetie," she said quietly. The bus driver slapped

the door closed, and the gears ground before they finally took off with a jerk.

Joy went straight to the barn and fed the animals. Ben had moved the tree that the goats had eaten off to the side. How had she been so stupid? It wasn't like it was an unknown fact that goats would eat anything, but it hadn't even crossed her mind that the well-fed critters would bother the tree, since it had been placed on the other side of the fence. She grimaced at the sight of the naked quarter of the tree. At least they hadn't been able to reach the top.

Ben was right, they probably could camouflage the accident with a healthy dose of some big ornaments and extra garland. And since she'd already decided to do an updated take on paper garland this year for the tree in the living room, she'd have pretty good ammunition in hand.

Joy fed Molly the Bunny last. "Hey, Molly. Are you as sweet as your namesake?" The bunny stomped, nibbling from the bowl, and came to the front of the cage. Joy cautiously reached her finger through the chicken wire to scratch the bunny's ear, then bravely opened the door and lifted her out. The bunny nuzzled into Joy's arms. "You like that, don't you?" She paced the screened-in porch with Molly in her arms, then eased her back into her cage.

Joy went inside and showered. As she dried her hair, she noticed she'd missed a text earlier. Two hours ago, Ruby had texted her a picture of her breakfast with a note that said, *Please bring hot dogs! I need real food.*

She texted Ruby back with a smiley face. Since when were hot dogs considered real food? But who was Joy to argue? She made it to the rehab center by lunchtime with the hot dogs in hand.

As she strolled through the lobby, Joy eyed the decorations with new interest. Coming up with the theme for

Ruby's Christmas décor had turned the chore into more fun than she could have imagined. The only problem was figuring out how she could get it all done in the time she had left. Especially with the trip back to D.C. for the office gala just around the corner.

Ruby's nurse Carolyn was in the hall just outside Ruby's room. "Hot dogs again?"

"I got a text request this morning. Kind of hard to sneak anything with chili and onions in."

"Yeah, I could smell them from ten feet away. That aunt of yours is a pistol. She had Johnny bring doughnuts for her this morning."

"She sent me a pitiful picture of a breakfast. Not one single doughnut in sight."

"She's tricky. Loves her junk food, but she's healthy, so it's working for her."

"With all the preservatives she eats, she's liable to live to be two hundred!"

"Don't laugh. She's healthier than all of us put together. We should be so lucky as to be in her shoes at her age."

"Come have a hot dog with us. I bought extras."

Carolyn came around the desk. "I'll go grab a couple sodas from the fridge for us."

Joy could hear Ruby talking from her room. No surprise she had company. That woman made friends everywhere she went. Only when she walked into the room, it was just Ruby sitting in bed with her leg propped up, talking on her cell phone like she'd had one forever.

Ruby flipped her hand in the air in a wave and a just-a-minute gesture.

Joy rolled the table over to Ruby's bed, positioned it across her lap, and laid the box of hot dogs in the center of it. Carolyn came in with three pint-sized cans of ginger ale.

"My favorite," mouthed Ruby. "Shirley, I'm gonna have

to let you go, darling. I've got hot dogs and ginger ale here. You know I can't let those just sit." Ruby ended the call and placed the phone next to her hot dog tray.

"How's Shirley?" Joy asked, and bit into a chili dog.

"Not as good as me. Thank you so much. I was having such a craving."

"I brought dessert too. Although rumor has it, you may already have had your share of sweets first thing this morning."

Ruby glanced in Carolyn's direction. "There's no limit on sweets. Did you bring me cookies?"

"Yes, ma'am. Figured you better test them out and be sure I am holding up your tradition."

"You are the best niece ever."

She knew that was about as far from the truth as could be, but she hoped she could turn that around going forward. Not just for Ruby. But for Molly too. If some women could make time for career and children, certainly she could fit in a little family time and fun with people she cared about. Somehow.

After they ate lunch, Carolyn excused herself to do her afternoon rounds.

"I loved that picture of you and Molly last night," Ruby said. "You two looked like you were having so much fun."

"It was an evening of adventure, for sure. But yes. We did have fun."

"Thank you so much. That little angel deserves fun. Her mother—she's so young, bless her heart—is trying to keep Molly's life on an even keel, but she's been so sick. And Molly is a smart girl. She knows. I don't know how Ginny is keeping things going. I tried to get them to move in with me, but she wouldn't do it."

"Her mother is sick? Is it cancer?"

"She's had some complications. I haven't even asked

what all, because you know it really doesn't matter exactly what's wrong. Her husband ran off, and she came to this town with no one at her side. And she's sick. Just that they need help is enough. Right?"

Joy sucked in a breath. She hated the thought of Molly going through something so similar to her own tragic experience. And Molly was so much younger than Joy had been when her mom got sick. "She's a wonderful little girl."

"She is." Ruby sniffled and shook her head as if pushing the negative aside. "Let's talk about something happy. How are the decorations going?"

"I've sorted through the inventory of boxes. Goodness gracious, you have a ton of ornaments."

"I know. It's a little on the crazy side, but I always end up adding some new things every year. I feel like it keeps things fresh-looking, mixing the old and the new."

"You definitely have plenty of both, and I'm afraid I'm adding more to the collection this year, although I am reusing a lot of the stuff you already have. I was so excited when I suddenly figured out the theme."

"What's the theme?" Ruby's eyebrows sprang up.

Joy loved seeing that excitement in her aunt's eyes. "I want to surprise you."

"But—"

"Please? And if it makes you feel any better, Ben is going to help me."

"Shirley didn't mention that." Ruby looked relieved.

"She probably hasn't heard yet. We struck a deal last night." That quirky smile that Aunt Ruby got when she was up to something and the twinkle in her eye let Joy know the conclusions her dear aunt was already jumping to.

"Really?" said Aunt Ruby.

"You can get that sparkle out of your eye right now. This

is strictly out of necessity. His volunteer backed out of helping with the Extreme Gingerbread Bake-off, so we made a trade. I'm going to help him finish the final details on that event, since that's my strong suit, and in exchange he'll help with the decorating. We're just working smart."

"It sounds like a perfect swap to me. You'll make that event the best it's ever been."

"I can't believe you wouldn't have entered that. I've never even heard you mention it."

"It's not just cookies, it's actually building houses. Heck, last year someone built a whole village out of gingerbread and edibles. That's way more sit-in-one-place kind of work than this old girl has any interest in. You know me. I like being out and about."

"True." But even so, Joy thought it would be a fun project. Maybe next year. And maybe she and Ruby could partner with Molly and Ginny on the project.

Chapter Twenty-one

At seven o'clock on the dot, Ben stood at the front door of Ruby Johnson's house, feeling a little as he had when he was a teen picking up his prom date. Unsure of what the night would hold, but excited to figure it all out. He raised his hand and knocked.

When the door opened, Joy stood there looking more beautiful than ever, with her hair pulled up in a messy bun and wearing a long-sleeved T-shirt with the sleeves pushed up.

Disquieting thoughts danced through his mind, like what his hands would feel like running down her arms as he pulled her in for a hug, a kiss. Maybe even more than that.

He held back the involuntary reaction to gush over how pretty she looked.

The last thing he wanted to do was spook her, since he seemed to have a way of saying the wrong things around her. *Play it cool, Ben.*

Even with that neckline covering every bit of her, and not an ounce of makeup on her face, she was incredibly sexy to him.

"Come on in," Joy said.

Ben followed her into the living room and placed the

folders he'd been carrying on the pine plank coffee table in front of him. He tried not to stare at her as he sat on the love seat. "I printed copies of your plan. Didn't figure you'd have a printer here."

"Thanks. That's a huge help. Ruby doesn't even have a computer or Wi-Fi. Thank goodness I can use my phone as a hot spot, although even that has been iffy at times."

"I made some suggested adjustments to the plan on the paper copy. I figured I'd let you go through them and decide which you wanted to update in the file."

"Adjustments?" She looked surprised, and he hoped he hadn't just set her back on the defensive.

"Just a few minor things. Based on my experience."

He watched a tiny line crease in her forehead as she concentrated on the plan.

"Nothing major," he said. "Just a few tweaks on the order of things. Plus, lots of people start cruising the route the week before the Crystal Christmas Cookie Crawl in anticipation of the big event, so if we can do some of the outside decorating first, it gives them something to talk about."

"You don't think you're not making just a little bit too big a deal about all of this? I mean every single detail?"

"I'm just trying to help."

"Or take over."

He carefully chose his words. "I'm not." He braced himself; they were just getting on good footing here and he didn't want to ruin it. "But you seem to think you can do everything with no help or advice, and that is just silly when you don't have to. I get it. You're competitive and Ruby is your aunt and you want to do right by her, but it doesn't have to be me against you."

She let out a long breath and put the plan aside, offering a gentle smile. "You're right. I appreciate your input."

He let out the breath he'd been holding as well. He hadn't pushed her buttons. This time. "You're welcome. Now, let's get those boxes in the attic so you have room to move around here. Unless you were planning on building a box fort."

"I'll take a rain check on the fort."

"Don't knock it. It could be a good time."

She had a feeling he was right, but she wasn't going to go down that path. "I'll take a look at your suggested tweaks to my plan," she said, laying the paper down and changing the subject to something safe. "I've got all the ornaments sorted that I want to use for this year's design. I will take you up on that offer to get the rest in the attic."

"Sure. Happy to do it."

"Great. It's a lot easier with someone handing them up than one person climbing up and down."

"Not to mention a lot less risky. You don't want to end up Ruby's roommate at Dixon County Rehab Center."

Joy laughed. She took his breath away when she let her guard down.

"I'm not sure that place could take two of us griping about being immobile," she said.

"You said it. Not me. But I'll admit that neither of you seems to be very good at slowing down and taking it easy."

"Not in our DNA." She scanned the project plan for his changes.

He got up and walked over to where she'd stacked all the boxes. He picked up the one on top. "This one is light. You take this one." Then he stacked two and picked them up and followed her up the stairs.

She set down the box she was carrying and headed right down the stairs for another load.

He turned to flip the light switch in the hall, and a sparkle caught his eye. "This is a pretty fancy dress up here. Yours?" She'd look stunning in that dress. He walked downstairs, imagining her standing in the doorway wearing it.

Joy's cheeks reddened. "I'd just picked it up from getting alterations done when I got the call about Ruby's fall. There's this huge Christmas gala where I work. It's very formal."

"I remember that dress was in the back of your car the night we met. Must be some party."

They carried the rest of the boxes upstairs and Ben tugged the rope to the attic access panel, lowering the wooden ladder.

Joy picked up a box and held it over her head as Ben started to climb the ladder. "Did you know that there are over twenty million houses whose residents put up Christmas decorations in the U.S.?"

"That's a lot of decorations. Maybe slightly more than Ruby has here." He took the box and slid it up into the attic space.

"She definitely has more than the average home."

"It's for a good cause," Ben said. Only she seemed to be staring at him rather than listening.

"What kind of tree did you say that community tree was?"

"Carolina sapphire cypress," he said.

"Yeah. Almost the color of your shirt."

He looked down at the greenish-blue three-button Henley. "I guess so."

"And your eyes." She held his gaze for a long moment. And hers were Carolina blue.

She lifted another box and they continued to work in silence until all the boxes she wouldn't need were stored back in the attic.

His hand slowed as it touched hers, taking the last box.

He'd be lying if he didn't admit there was something in that touch. "Anything else for up here?" he asked.

Joy took a quick look around. "Nope. That's it. I figure we can just store the empty boxes in the spare room up here until it's time to take all the ornaments down."

"Sounds like a good plan to me." He climbed down the ladder and closed the attic access with a bang. The white rope swung gently above their heads, and with her standing so close, he was tempted to be playful. To hold her, kiss her. He wanted to hear her laugh. She had his attention tonight. Completely.

She cleared her throat and stepped away quickly, as if realizing that attic rope had some kind of holiday mistletoe magic to it.

"I figured we could get the lights untangled and tested tonight. Rain is supposed to move in this weekend, so I'd like to get the house lights started tomorrow while the weather is still in our favor."

"I can help you." Joy brushed dust from her shirt. "I've got all the boxes of lights down here."

"Great. That'll help." He cocked his head. "Have you eaten?"

"Not since lunchtime."

"Let's order a pizza from Max. Sausage and pepperoni work for you?"

"I can't believe that place is still around. I haven't had a Max's pizza in years." Joy sat in the rocking chair.

"He still has the best pizza around." He pulled out his phone.

"Do they deliver pizza out here now? Don't tell me they have an app."

"Better than an app." He tapped the keys and then pulled the phone to his ear. "Hey, man, it's Ben. Can you deliver a sausage and pepperoni pie over to Ruby Johnson's

place? I'm starting on the Christmas lights. I need rations."
He smiled. "Large. Great. I appreciate it." He tucked the
phone in his shirt pocket. "We've got forty-five minutes
to get some lights tested."

"They don't normally deliver, do they?"

"No, but no one minds going out of their way a little
once in a while."

Ben walked over and started dividing the boxes into two
stacks. One for indoor lights, and the other for the larger
outdoor bulb lights. "Let's test the outdoor ones first." He
pushed a red box in front of the rocking chair. "You can
start unrolling those."

"They look like they were packed pretty neatly."

"We always take the time to put them away neatly, but
I swear there are families of Grinch-gremlins that get into
the attic and twist them in a knot during the year, because
we always end up with some of them in a snarl when we
sit down to do this."

"Maybe we'll get lucky this year."

"If that happens, you will be required to come and
sprinkle fairy dust on lights every year." And maybe that
wouldn't be half bad. He could stand seeing a little more
of her around here.

"And magic snowflake wishes probably don't hurt
either."

Her smile was playful, and he liked picturing her with
cookie flour on her face, but then he saw her catch herself
and that wall went back up. He stepped closer, hoping to
calm her.

"Did you know that Christmas lights alone are a six-
billion-dollar industry?" she asked.

She was avoiding eye contact with him, and why was it
every time he went near her, she took two steps back?

He tested it. One step toward her. Yep, she stepped back.

"That's a lot of dollars. But maybe that's because half the strings of lights at any given house are too knotted up or don't work a second year."

"Not mine." She held up a long string of lights. Not one single snarl.

"Those must be the ones I put away." He held up his string. A knot right in the middle of what must have been a one-hundred-light strand.

"Are you blaming Ruby for that mess you've got there?"

"I'm not going to place blame, but I'll admit that I have two new strands in the truck that I bought at the end of last season. Just in case. If any of these are too much of a pain in the butt to untangle, I'm turning them into Christmas tumbleweeds and making them part of the decor." He pointed to the printout of her project plan. "In fact, add that as a contingency plan to your fancy list."

"Got it." She ran the thick green wire through her hands, draping another length of lights around her neck in a neat wide loop. "Be happy we don't still have to use candles. Can you imagine having to light dozens and dozens of candles every night? At least we can just flip one switch each day once we get them all in place."

"I think I'd have been highly motivated to invent electricity."

"When I was doing work for the Wetherton's account last year, I learned that even though the first electric Christmas lights were created in 1890, they were too expensive for most people. So they didn't actually become popular and replace candles until 1930."

"Interesting." Ben dragged wire across the room in an attempt to untangle the string of lights.

"And the average household in the U.S. will use a thousand lights on their Christmas tree."

He could push her into a cha-cha and she'd never know

it, the way she was dodging him. Why was she so nervous? "Do you specialize in Christmas trivia?"

"No. Not really, but I have been working on a Christmas account for a long time, so I do have a lot of it."

"I see." But darn if she didn't quit spouting trivia like some kind of Christmas *Trivial Pursuit* dictionary of lost facts, and start answering his questions, he was going to lose it. "Do you like white lights or colored lights on your trees?"

"One of the leading vendors out of Georgia has reported that, of the hundreds of thousands of strings of lights sold each year, seventy percent are white. So I guess white are the most popular."

Ben dropped the string of lights from his hands to the ground and stood there, blinking.

"What?"

"I'm not asking you for a free market research analysis. Not even what's popular. I'm asking what *you* like."

"Does it matter?"

"Yeah. Sure it does. I'm interested." *And you're beautiful when you quit sidestepping me.*

She fumbled with the lights, as if he'd said that out loud. "I don't know that I can answer the question. I haven't put up a tree by myself. Ever. So I don't know what I'd pick."

"Never?"

"No. I've never had a Christmas tree of my own. In fact, the last Christmas I celebrated was here with Ruby when I was a teenager, and there wasn't much celebrating going on that year."

"The year your mom died?"

She nodded.

"But that was, like, what—ten or fifteen years ago? What about all the Christmases since then?"

"I just stay busy. Head down. Work. Keep it all a safe distance from me."

"How's that working for you?"

"Until this very minute, it seemed to be working fine, but I'll be honest—" She stopped pulling the string of lights through her hands. "—I'm feeling a little nostalgic about it all now."

"Holidays will do that," he said.

"It's like I've missed out on making memories with Ruby because I was so afraid of reliving the painful ones with Mom."

He wanted to hold her. Tell her he understood and wished she weren't hurting. To be there for her. But she didn't seem ready to share her pain. He resisted the urge and simply offered, "I'm sorry."

"It's okay." Her words were soft. "I can't change the past. But I can definitely revisit the way I do things going forward."

Better to reroute this discussion to something safer, and anything that might lift the mood. "So you are a workaholic who has never been married. Have no children. Haven't celebrated Christmas since you lived here in Crystal Falls."

She plugged her string of lights into the wall. Nothing. "Sounds kind of pitiful, doesn't it?"

"Nothing pitiful about it." He dragged his strand over and plugged it into the other socket. His strand lit and began to blink. "I do think," he said as he laid his hand on her leg, "that maybe you're overdue for a very special Christmas."

She wrapped her fingers around the coiled rope of dark bulbs that hung around her neck. "I think I'm ready for that, but this—" She shook the lights, hoping they'd give her a glimmer of hope. "—doesn't look very promising."

He reached over and wrapped his hand around hers. Then he tugged the wreath of lights toward him and leaned in for a slow, gentle kiss.

She hitched a breath, but then leaned into him. Accepting him.

Her lips were soft. Her mouth warm and tempting.

His heart quickened. Brushing his lips across hers.

And as they slowed down and opened their eyes, the entire strand of lights around her neck was bright . . . flashing reds, greens, and blues.

"That was a surprise," he said, enjoying her smile, which seemed as bright as the lights around her neck.

"Must have been a loose wire." She swept her bangs back from her face.

"I meant the kiss."

He could tell by the look on her face that she'd felt it too. It hadn't just been him. But what was he supposed to do with that kiss? And why the heck had he started it?

"Let me get those from you." He lifted the lights over her head and laid them out next to the other working lights they'd unraveled.

An hour later, they had all the outside lights untangled and tested. Only one had been a complete dud. "Why don't you take the lightbulbs out of the bad string? You can never have too many extra bulbs. I'll move all the rest of these out to the front porch so I can get started on that tomorrow evening."

Joy jumped up and held the door as Ben pulled the long strands of lights to the porch and stretched them out from one end to the other.

She let the door close behind them.

He stood there on the porch for a long moment, wanting to kiss her again. But she seemed to be trying to keep her distance, and he knew better than to get mixed up with a girl like her, especially under the twinkle of magical Christmas lights.

Stepping over the lights, he went back inside. "I think we made great progress. I'll see you tomorrow night, okay?"

"Yeah. I'll look over the gingerbread bake-off file and make a list of questions for you."

He turned and opened the door to leave. "Let me know if you want me to take you over to see what's been set up."

"I might just go over there early, but I'll let you know." She didn't get up, but kept the safe distance between them. "Good night," she said. "And thank you for your help tonight."

"You're welcome," he said as he left.

Walking to his truck, he couldn't help but wonder what a Christmas with Joy in his home would be like.

That simple thought hung like mistletoe in a doorway, begging for a kiss.

Chapter Twenty-two

"He kissed you?" Renee sounded stunned.

"Yes. No warning, just leaned right in and kissed me." Joy twisted a bread tie between her fingers. She'd have to go grocery shopping to get more bread for Molly's lunch this week. It was hard to believe she'd already been here a whole week.

"Was it nice?"

Joy touched her lips and smiled. "Very." Ruby used to say that if a girl was really paying attention, all she'd need was one kiss to know if the man kissing her could actually make love to her soul for eternity.

Kissing Ben had seemed magical.

Until now, Joy really hadn't understood what Ruby meant by that. But this morning, she was pretty sure that Ben's kiss was the closest thing to that she'd ever experienced.

"So what's the problem? You sound like he did something wrong," Renee said.

"No. Nothing wrong. I mean, I don't even know him. Besides he's bad luck. Every time he's around, something bad happens. No need to set myself up for that."

"What bad happened last night?"

"The kiss!"

"I don't think you can consider that bad. I mean wrecking your car. Sure. Burning the cookies—well, maybe. Although, let's be honest. You don't do much cooking. But a kiss? A *very* nice kiss. Ummm, no."

"I can't have that kind of distraction. He's not even my kind of guy."

"So just have a good time. Why not? No one said you have to marry him or anything. If you're going to be in Crystal Falls, you might as well have fun. You said yourself you didn't want to go out with Todd. You should invite Bad Luck Ben to the gala."

"It's black tie."

"So? You don't think he has a tux? They rent tuxes in every town, don't they? I mean, the kids have to be able to rent tuxes for prom. Come on. That's a lame excuse."

"I don't know. I mean, he wears suits to work every day, but really? This is Crystal Falls, not Crystal City, and I don't think I want to take a chance like that at work. What if he shows up in something inappropriate? Or worse, what if he says something embarrassing? I don't know him. It could happen. That's an important party with our most important clients. I think I'd rather fly solo than risk a faux pas."

"Joy Holbrook. When did you become such a snob?"

"Well, I didn't mean it that way. I just . . ." What was her argument? It sounded a little lame even to her. "The truth is, Ben would be fine. I know he would. I shouldn't have said those things, but he scares me."

"How so?"

"He makes me feel . . . I don't know. Off balance. It was easy with Todd, since there were no strings. Plus, he had as much to lose as I did at work events. He was kind of the perfect convenient date. I knew what to expect with him."

"Well, clearly Todd's available for the gala if you want him."

"But I don't." And she didn't want him before she'd met Ben, but now, after that kiss with Ben, she was positive she didn't want to spend time with Todd. There'd been fireworks, or maybe it was the blinking Christmas lights, but either way, that kiss was different from any kiss she'd ever had before. "Besides, Todd works for the competition now. He'll be surfing our clients. That's not cool under any circumstances."

"I think you should give Ben a chance," Renee said. "What could it hurt? If you put as much enthusiasm into dating as you do into working, you might be surprised at just how much happiness you could find."

"Who says I'm not happy?"

"Joy, I know you don't need a man, but having one just makes everything that much better. You don't want to be alone forever."

Maybe she did. Or not? Loving someone that much meant that losing them would hurt. That was something she never wanted to feel again. "I don't even know that he's interested in me."

"He kissed you."

Joy looked down at what she was wearing this morning. "And you should see me. I'm a hot mess. Since I didn't have time to pack anything, I've been wearing old sweats and pull-on pants from Aunt Ruby's closet. I even used lipstick as rouge yesterday."

"So go shopping. They've got stores there."

She felt frumpy without her own clothes and makeup with her. And Ben would be back again tonight to start working on the lights. "Maybe you're right."

"You know I am. I'm surprised you hadn't already mail-ordered something in by now."

"Me too, now that you mention it, but who knew I'd be here a week already?" Time was moving quickly. "All right, I'm going to let you go. Thanks for holding down the fort there. I can't wait to see you at the gala."

"Keep me posted on Ben. I'll keep Todd at bay until I hear from you again."

Joy hung up the phone and, without hesitation, grabbed her keys and headed to town to stock up on a few necessities like makeup and a decent change of clothes, maybe even cute underwear.

In less than two hours, she was back at the house, showered, changed, and feeling like her old self again.

Then she sat down and started going through all the details in the folder for the Extreme Gingerbread Bakeoff. The rules were clearly stated from the previous year. A list of six contestants was attached to the back page along with their entry forms and a deposit slip from the entry fees.

Sponsors had been secured and recorded for the prizes, and all the entries were already on display in the theater at the botanical gardens. All that was really left was to make sure all the contracted advertising and sponsorship agreements were fulfilled, and to schedule the photographer. *Check.*

She made one quick phone call to the photographer on the list, and that was taken care of. Easy enough.

Then she followed up with the printer to make sure he had everything he needed for the signage to complete the contracted sponsorship advertising. They had the proofs waiting for approval. "I'll be there this afternoon." *Check.*

The only gap seemed to be a final decision on how the public would cast their votes on Sunday. The rules clearly indicated that the judges would cast their votes on the evening the gingerbread displays were set up. That information was in the folder; however, the public would cast votes for their favorites on Sunday up until six o'clock, when all the scores would be revealed and the winners announced.

She needed to figure out what that process would be and how to integrate that into the final judging numbers.

A rumble of thunder shook the farmhouse, and the lights flickered. The donkey brayed, followed by a loud bang. By the time Joy reached the window over the kitchen sink, the goats were running toward the barn. They'd stand right out in the middle of a blizzard, but, boy, they hated rain more than anything. Large drops splattered against the roof, and it wasn't long before it was raining so hard that she could hardly make out the animals in the barn, peering out, wishing they'd already eaten dinner.

"Sorry, guys, I'm not coming out in this weather to feed you. You're going to have to wait." But she did step out on the back patio and feed Molly the Bunny.

The spray from the rain was blowing against the screen. She ran back inside and dabbed at her face and arms with a paper towel. Her phone rang, buzzing across the table. Probably Ruby checking in. "Hello?"

"It's me, Ben. Looks like we'll have to postpone lights tonight."

"I know. It's a frog strangler here. I brought the lights back inside."

"Was thinking if you want to come by and go over the event plan, I could fix you spaghetti."

"You cook?"

"It's the only thing I cook, but I do make a pretty mean bowl of spaghetti."

"You're on. What's the address?"

She punched the address into her phone GPS as he gave it to her. "I just put it into my GPS. Looks easy enough."

"It is. Just off Main Street. You'll see my truck in the driveway."

"Great. Can I bring anything?"

"No. Just yourself, and your assessment of what still needs to be done on the Extreme Gingerbread Bake-off."

"Just so happens that I've got an update for you. On my way."

Joy stepped outside and opened the tiny travel umbrella that she kept in her purse. She ran to her car, but the rain was coming down so hard that she was still soaking wet by the time she jumped into the driver's seat. She closed the umbrella and tossed it into the passenger floorboard.

Why did I even bother doing my hair? She glanced into the rearview mirror, swept her fingers under her eyes to get rid of any smudges, and then ran her fingers through the top of her bangs. Going in and starting over would put her late, and probably leave her in the same position unless she took to wearing a trash bag over her head, but even still, she'd look a mess when she ran from the car to Ben's door. Not worth the hassle. Besides, she wasn't trying to impress anybody.

With the address punched into her navigation system, it was only a few turns to Ben's house.

Even in the rain, the house looked inviting. And huge. She wasn't sure exactly what she'd expected, but it wasn't this. The mailbox matched the house with amazing detail in color and design. The house had to have been built in the early 1900s.

The grand old home flaunted more architectural details than she'd ever noticed on a house. Old trees edged the property. The driveway curved from the street around to the side of the house. And a brick path led to both the side and front doors. She parked, wishing the rain would slow down, but as she gathered her purse, Ben's side door opened and he came jogging outside, carrying a huge black umbrella toward the car.

"Thank you!" she said as she ducked under the cover he offered.

"It's nasty out here." He held the umbrella and pulled her in close as they walked inside. "Thanks for coming out in this weather. You're soaked. Come on in."

When she stepped into the kitchen, the aroma of garlic and tomato filled the air. Water boiled in a tall red pot on the stove. And this wasn't your everyday bachelor kitchen. It wasn't your everyday any kind of kitchen. Bobby Flay and Scott Conant would cross culinary cutlery to battle over who got to cook in here. The dark granite only highlighted the high-end stainless steel appliances. "This place is beautiful."

"Thank you," he said just as a black Lab ran into the kitchen from the other room, tail wagging. With each step, the dog's blue bone-shaped tag made a tinkling sound against the metal clasp on his leather collar.

"Hey, buddy," she said, stooping to pet his head. "Ruby used to have a Lab. Actually, he was Uncle George's dog. A chocolate Lab named Brownie. Original, huh? What's his name?"

"Profit."

"Accounting joke?"

"Sort of." He sidestepped past her. "Hang tight. I'll be right back."

It had been years since she'd thought about old Brownie. That dog had slept at the end of her bed every night the whole time she and Mom lived with Aunt Ruby and Uncle George. She wondered what ever had happened to him.

Ben was back in just a moment with a red plaid flannel shirt in his hand. "Here. Why don't you slip this on, and we'll toss your shirt in the dryer."

"Thanks." She held the shirt to her cheek. It felt soft and warm. "Bathroom?"

"Down the hall on the right. There should be a blow dryer under the sink. I think my sister left one last time she was here."

"Thanks."

When she came back into the kitchen, Ben was pouring wine into two glasses. "Hope you like cabernet."

"Sure. That's fine." She lifted the glass and inhaled the fragrance. "Nice."

"Biltmore," he said, taking another sip. He swirled a long wooden spoon in the sauce, then dropped the pasta into the bubbling water on the front burner. The timer buzzer rang out. Ben hit the reset, then pulled a long loaf of crusty bread out of the oven.

"That smells so good. Anything I can do to help?"

"Yes. There's a cutting board over there. Will you slice the bread?"

"Sure." She cut four thick slices and placed them in the bread basket. "What else?"

"Cut one more thin slice."

"Okay," she said. Maybe she should have asked how thick to slice the bread. "That good?"

"Yeah. Tear it in half and bring it here."

She did as he asked and then stepped to his side at the fancy stove. He stirred the sauce and lifted a spoonful.

"It smells so good." Joy closed her eyes as she inhaled.

"Wait until you taste it." He held his hand under the spoon. "Dip the bread in the sauce and give it a taste."

She swept the warm bread into the sauce, then took a careful bite. "So good. You do make great spaghetti."

She dipped the other piece of bread into the sauce and held it to his mouth.

He bit into the bread and flipped the rest of the piece into the air, which Profit snapped up in an instant. "Tastes about ready to me. By the time the pasta is done, it should be perfect."

"Already tastes perfect to me."

Profit stared up at them, licking his chops.

Joy patted Profit's head. "I think Profit agrees with me."

"He's not picky. At all."

She laughed.

"We still have about seven minutes on the pasta, so let me give you the five-minute tour." He led her into the living room. "This room took twice as long to finish as I'd originally planned. The moldings had been discontinued decades ago, but I didn't want to compromise on the original craftsmanship."

"It's beautiful," she said, admiring the fact that he'd taken the time to do the job right, accenting the fine architectural features with color against the deeper hues of the wood. A warm and inviting result. "This place is amazing. The high ceilings make it feel so open, and the details of the craftsmanship in here are unbelievable. Is it all original?"

"I wish. This house was in such bad shape when I bought it, but I could see the potential. It's taken a lot of work to restore this place back to its original opulence, but it's coming together."

Over the past eighteen months, the house had finally started looking as beautiful as she had before she'd become worn and neglected. Now she was quite the painted lady, in rustic muted jewel tones of that era like Needlepoint Navy, Sheraton Sage, with Harvest Gold and Crabby Apple Red accents. He'd gone a little hog wild with the colors, but with so many architectural details to highlight, he could get away with it.

This house was the ultimate fixer-upper, but he was loving every minute of it, and sharing it with Joy today was bringing him an unexpected rush.

"It's lovely." Several family pictures were arranged on a bookshelf, along with some leather-bound copies of books. "Look at all these books. You must be an avid reader."

"Not exactly. When I had the housewarming gathering here, I didn't need anything. Mom told everyone to bring books to fill my bookshelves. These are the favorite books of all my friends. I haven't actually read them."

"That's really something." Just as in his office, there were personal smatterings of his life here. Not an egotistical display. No, this was more of a reflection of priceless moments. Passions. A picture of him sailing with three other guys holding beer and laughing. A family picture that looked like it was probably his parents in their early years of marriage. Ben had his dad's nose and strong jawline. A man in a military uniform. She lingered in front of the bookcase, taking in the pictures and snippets that told little details about this man.

"My brother and I built that bookcase."

"Some assembly required," she teased.

"Yeah, like every board and nail and joint."

"You mean you really built it? Like, from scratch?"

"Planed every board. Routed every edge, created every groove and corner."

It was hard to believe he could have made it. It looked like fine furniture. The finish was flawless. "Cherry?"

He gave her a slow nod.

And not cheap. She was impressed. The man in front of her was full of surprises, and now each of these pictures tempted her to ask even more questions, to get to know him a little bit better. One picture looked like Mayan ruins, another a tropical beach. She wondered when they'd been taken. A snapshot of Jet Skis in the water next to a dock was placed next to a picture of someone parasailing. She picked up a picture of Ben and Profit in a frame shaped like a bone. The puppy couldn't have been more than six weeks old. "He was so tiny."

"He still thinks that he's that tiny sometimes."

Profit came in and sat between them, his tail swishing left and right.

"You knew we were talking about you, didn't you, Profit?" Joy suddenly felt small and insignificant. Her condo was like a model home. At any time, someone could drop in, and nothing would be out of place and there wouldn't be one personal thing anywhere to identify who lived there unless they went into her desk, where she kept her bills and checkbook. All she had were air miles from all the travel she did; he had pictures and memories that were as alive today as the day he'd taken those trips.

She didn't even have a picture of her mother out on display in her apartment, except for the one in her bedroom on her nightstand. And even if pictures of Mom might still bring back too many raw memories, was there really a good reason that she didn't have a picture of Aunt Ruby in her home? Or a picture from a vacation? Well, aside from the fact that she really hadn't taken any in the past five years.

This house held not only its own history, but Ben's too. And suddenly she felt like she'd missed out on a lot more than just Christmases along the way.

Chapter Twenty-three

As far as Joy was concerned, that whole "everybody dreams" theory was up for debate. But darned if last night she hadn't woken up at least four times, each time remembering the last dream that had been playing in her mind. The same dream every time.

She lay there with her eyes closed to remember the dream. Christmas lights around her neck, and the lights blinking as she kissed a handsome stranger. Okay, fine, he wasn't a stranger. He seemed a lot like Ben, right down to the pine and sugar cookie smell of him. And then the two of them lying on the floor in front of the fireplace, where Christmas stockings hung from the mantel while carols played softly as they snuggled on a quilt on the floor, her head pillowed in the crook of his muscled arm.

She opened her eyes, a little disappointed to confirm it really had been just a dream.

This was all Renee's fault for planting those seeds.

She reached for Ruby's robe. The house was chilly this morning, the hardwood floors icy under her feet. She pulled on a pair of thick socks and went downstairs.

While the coffee dripped into the carafe, she toyed with ideas on how to integrate the popular vote with the judges' votes for the Extreme Gingerbread Bake-off. Ashley had planned to give each visitor a coin to put in a box positioned in front of each display.

The problem with that was that being able to see the voting status could influence the popular vote, introducing bias. Something she was careful about in her market research.

There would be some people who would vote for the underdog, just because they wouldn't want their feelings hurt. Honorable, especially with the amount of work that went into these edible creations.

There'd also be the majority voters. No, she needed to ensure the popular vote was based on the most appealing display.

How best to accomplish that?

She snapped her fingers.

"Got it!" She grabbed the magnetic shopping list notepad from the refrigerator and jotted down a step-by-step process flow.

She swept her pen in a swirly flourish under the last line.

The best part was that after she went outside and fed all the animals, when she read back through the plan, it still worked. And on top of that, it was one that she could put into motion and manage with little effort. Plus, she already had everything she needed to tweak the plan right here. Yes, a good plan all the way around.

"Good morning." Molly's voice rang out, followed by the front door slamming shut.

"In here," Joy called from the kitchen.

Molly came in and placed her empty lunch bag on the kitchen table.

"Happy Friday!"

"No school tomorrow," Molly said, and she didn't look too happy about it.

"I thought we'd do something different today," Joy said, taking her coffee over to the counter where she'd already laid out everything that would go into Molly's lunch. "How about we make your lunch together today?"

"I don't know how."

"I'm going to teach you," Joy said. Somewhere in her dream-filled night, she must've dreamed of Mom, because making lunch together used to be something she and her mother always did. She'd loved spending that extra time making her sandwich side by side with Mom every day. So rather than do it for Molly, as she had for over a week now, she thought they'd switch things up.

Molly dragged the kitchen stool over to the counter and stepped on top of it. "Can I still have peanut butter and jelly? That's my favorite."

"Absolutely. I just thought it would be fun to do it together. Kind of like making cookies. That was fun, right?"

"Yes. Lots of fun."

Joy laid the bread out on the counter. "You want to spread the peanut butter or the jelly?"

Molly bunched her lips, eyeing both. "Jelly!" She wrapped both hands around the fat generic grape jelly jar and pulled it toward her.

"Then I'll do the peanut butter."

They both smeared the toppings on their slice; then Joy reached over with her peanut butter knife and swept a smiley face onto Molly's jelly bread.

Molly clapped her hands and giggled. "I love smileys!"

"Our secret." Joy stacked the slices, then proceeded to cut the crusts and then the sandwich into the fours that Molly liked.

Joy placed a plastic bag of baby carrots and a cookie in the bottom of the lunch bag, then folded two napkins on top and added the sandwich.

"Thank you," Molly said. "I like doing stuff with you. I wish you could come to my Christmas pageant."

"Are you selling tickets?" The least she could do was support the cause. It had to be a better one than what Margie's kids were raising money for.

"No. We can invite two people. My mom can't go, though. And Aunt Ruby can't come either. I thought maybe you'd come."

"What about your dad? Any other family? I bet they'd love to see you in the Christmas pageant."

"We don't talk to my daddy anymore," Molly said quietly. Joy's chest tightened. She knew that feeling all too well.

Molly's eyes were wide, pleading. "Can you come? Please?" The little girl tugged Joy's heartstrings.

"When is it?"

"Next Tuesday at nine."

"That's late."

Molly laughed. "Nine in the morning, you silly. We don't go to school at night. Our grade is in the morning. The older kids do their program in the afternoon."

Her heart sank. "I wish I could go, but I can't. I'm sorry. I have to go back to D.C. for work, and I won't be back by then."

Molly's bottom lip pouted, and she looked as if someone had just walked by and maliciously popped her favorite helium balloon. Probably one with a smiley face.

"I'm sorry, Molly. I know you'll be wonderful in the pageant. Tell me about it. Is it a play?"

"No. It's music. I'm playing the bells. We've been practicing a lot. And I'm singing 'Rudolph, the Red-Nosed Reindeer' too."

"Do you know all the words?"

"By heart," Molly said.

"I love that song. Rudolph is my very favorite reindeer."

"I love them all."

Joy carried the lunch bag out to the living room and put it with Molly's notebook by the door. They'd found a routine and a comfortable friendship. Who would have thought she'd make friends with a seven-year-old? "We still have about fifteen minutes until the bus comes."

The little girl's eyes lit up. She rose onto her toes, those little freckles that speckled her nose appearing to dance as she grinned wide. "Ruby said she used to braid your hair just like mine when you were a little girl. Do you know how to do braids?"

Joy smiled at the memory of sitting on her aunt's bed. Ruby would pull that tight bristled brush through Joy's hair one hundred times. "So it will shine like the sun," she'd say. Then she'd braid two long pigtails. Ruby made the tightest braids. They always lasted all day long. It was still one of her fondest memories. That and playing jewelry box. She'd sit and fondle the jewelry from the many drawers, some even like secret compartments, carefully arranging them as if they were the queen's jewels.

Joy reached for the little girl's hand. "Come sit over here." To think she might make that kind of memory for someone. For Molly. Joy gloried in that brief moment. "We can use some of the red rickrack I found to tie the ends."

"Pretty! You really know how? Like Ruby?"

"Sure do. I learned from the best."

"Ruby is the best."

"Yes, she is." Joy turned Molly's back to her and ran her fingers through her hair. "Want one down the back?"

"Can you do one like yours? On the side?"

Joy raised her hand and touched her own braid. It had been a half-baked attempt to tame her hair this morning. "Sure. Your hair is long enough." She pulled Molly's hair

over her left shoulder and then swept her fingers through
the child's long tendrils, tightening each section of the
braid as she worked her way down to the end. Joy took the
short length of red rickrack and tied it in a double knot to
help keep it from slipping. "I don't have a hair band. I hope
it will stay without a rubber band."

"I'll be careful."

Molly jumped down and ran over to a mirror near the
door, tippy-toeing to see herself. "It's so pretty. Thank
you."

"You're welcome."

"We're like twins." Molly climbed up on the couch and
sat quietly.

She was so well behaved. It still amazed Joy how
different Molly was from the sugar-high kids she'd
been researching this past year, and even more so from
Margie's two.

"We still have a little bit of time. Why don't you practice your song for me?"

"I have to stand." Molly slid off the couch and stood in
the middle of the room. "That's how we practice." She
looked side to side and then slid over about three steps to
her left. "I stand over here."

Joy stifled a laugh at the invisible classroom of kids. It
must be wonderful to have the imagination of a child.

Molly bobbed her head as if imagining a one-two-three
countdown, and then her voice filled the room. "Rudolph,
the red-nosed reindeer . . ." Her little hands flung to the top
of her head like antlers. And then to her nose.

Joy pulled the pillow from beside her and held it to her
heart. She really may never have seen anything this darned
cute in her whole life. And just how did that little girl sing
that big?

Molly's voice carried loud and strong enough that Joy

imagined the animals were probably outside, queueing up to the fence line. Not for food this time, but a front-row seat to the performance. With each animated moment, Joy felt a ping of delight. Her eyes stung as Molly belted out the final "His-tor-*eeeeee*."

Joy leapt to her feet and gave the little girl a standing ovation. "That was perfect. Lovely. Bravo!"

Molly curtsied. "You liked it?"

"I *really* liked it." Joy held open her arms. Molly walked right into them. "That was fabulous."

Molly clung to Joy's neck, and then the sound of the diesel engine of the bus vibrated through the house.

"Time to go, sugar."

Molly dropped her arms and ran to the table next to the door to gather her things. Joy helped her with her coat and then opened the front door.

"You have an awesome day, Molly."

"See you Monday!"

Joy's phone rang as she watched Molly run for the bus. "Hello?"

"Hey, it's me," Renee said. "Hope your day is going better than mine. Everyone is about as festive as the Grinch around here."

"What's going on? Are those sirens I hear?"

"Sorry, yeah, I'm walking down to Starbucks for a fix."

"Oh, you had me scared there. I thought there was a fire or someone finally broke down and went nuts. You know everyone is so burned out by this time of year."

"There's something going on. People are starting to get worried since there still hasn't been word about the promotions. And now there's a rumor we won't even get Christmas bonuses."

"That rumor goes around every year. Just ignore it.

Things will be fine. I think some people just like to stir up drama."

"Someone said this morning that they heard we're losing one of our big accounts. But I haven't heard any details."

"In the scheme of things, does it even matter? Clients come and go. We are always picking up new ones."

"You're not even worried? Did I dial the right number? Is this Joy Holbrook?"

"Funny. Yes, it's me."

"Are you okay?"

"Yeah. Couldn't be better." And she wasn't worried, and it was strangely satisfying not to be worried about the promotion or what might or might not be happening at the office.

"You sound different. Melancholy. Is everything okay with Ruby?"

"She's doing great. Giving that rehab center a run for its money. And me too. I made the mistake of giving her a cell phone, and she's texting me constantly. It's kind of funny."

"Everything okay with the guy?"

"Ben? Stop. I told you there's nothing to that."

"I'm just asking. Something's up."

"No. I'm fine. Molly just left. She performed her Christmas pageant song for me in the living room a minute ago. She was so cute. I don't think I'm melancholy so much as I am . . . relaxed?"

"Relaxed? You?"

"I know. I can hardly believe it, but I'm actually kind of enjoying being here. And Molly singing 'Rudolph' has me in a pretty good mood."

"That's great. Oh, gosh. You haven't lived until you've seen an elementary school performance of the first Christmas. I swear I bawled like a baby when Hanna was a sheep in the manger scene one year. She didn't even have a speaking part. It was ridiculously adorable, though."

"Can I ask you something?"

"Of course."

"You really love being a mom, don't you?"

"More than anything. Are you softening on me? You've never liked kids."

"Technically, I just haven't liked Margie's kids. Okay, and a few during focus groups, but those are the bratty ones. Taking care of Molly has been kind of eye-opening."

Renee laughed. "They're all bratty at one time or another. It's just easier to take when they're your own."

"I guess that would be true." She thought about how Ruby must appear to other people. A crazy handful, but she loved her aunt for all her faults and shenanigans. "Everything else going okay with you?"

"The Wetherton's project has gone without a hitch. You're a star. Everyone knows it."

"We're a good team. What about you? Ready for the holidays? Your shopping done?"

Renee paused. "Yes. We're pretty much ready. The girls are excited."

"That's good. Things are shaping up here. Can't wait to see you at the gala."

"I had to tell you about the latest gossip, or maybe I was just looking for an excuse to call."

"Thanks. And you never need an excuse." She glanced at her watch. "Renee, I've got to run. I have to stop by the hospital and give the Extreme Gingerbread Bake-off plan to Ben, then go see Ruby at rehab."

"Gingerbread? Baking? You don't know a thing about bak—"

"Don't ask. I'll fill you in when I see you, but I promise I'm not in the competition, just helping plan the judging."

"Well, thank goodness, because you were starting to make me worry. Call me soon."

Joy dropped her phone in the top of her purse, pulled on her coat, and wrapped her infinity scarf around her neck.

After picking up a few things from the market, she walked down the block to the bakery. Each of the window displays was as nice as the next one. As magical as New York City shop windows, in a whimsical, down-home kind of way.

Angels, snowmen, reindeer, and ornaments the size of a VW Bug filled the storefronts. Every light pole had been wrapped with pine garland and red ribbon. Giant trios of LED snowflakes hung from every one of the streetlamps. At night, this street probably sparkled like a night sky full of stars.

Maybe she'd stop by tonight and make a wish on one.

In the bakery window, a snowy village made of edible treats included Christmas trees made of stacked cookies with colorful sparkles next to Santa's workshop and the barn where he kept his reindeer. Warm sugary smells tempted her taste buds as soon as Joy pushed the door open.

She stood in front of the glass case. Filled to the brim with every holiday treat imaginable, it was almost too many to choose from.

"What can I get you today?" a young dark-haired woman in a bright pink apron asked.

Joy hugged her coat tight. "I'm not sure. Everything looks so good. Do you have a specialty?"

"The tarts are amazing. The crust of the key lime tarts is made of graham and pistachios. A family recipe handed down from my mom's mom. They are my absolute favorite, but most people get an assortment box."

"An assortment sounds perfect. I'm taking them to Dixon County Rehabilitation Center."

"A dozen?"

"Make it two dozen."

"Family member in there?"

"My aunt."

"I know she'll be glad to see you. My granddaddy was in there last summer. Hip replacement. It's a long ride."

The girl boxed up a couple of each kind of cookie into a big candy-striped box and then stretched a length of tulle around the box, tying it in a big fluffy bow. Then she put two extra treats in a wax bag. "Here you go. All set. I tossed in a couple on the house . . . so you can snack on the drive. Merry Christmas."

Joy cradled the big box in her arms as she left the bakery, shifting it to one arm as she unlocked her car.

An arm cloaked in brown suede swept the box from her arms.

She turned, ready for a fight.

"Whoa, there. Your hands are full." Ben held the box between them.

With a half step back that nearly tossed her into one of the lampposts, she huffed, "Ben? You scared me."

"Sorry. I seem to do that a lot."

She regretted that comment she'd made before about him being bad luck in a good suit. That was just mean, and she hoped he'd forgotten it. With her hands free, she clicked the unlock button on her key fob. "Thank you."

"This is a lot of treats. Where you headed?"

"To see Ruby in rehab. I'm glad I ran into you, though. I was going to stop by and see you later. I worked out the judging of the Extreme Gingerbread Bake-off."

"I have a free morning, how about I ride with you? We can talk on the drive."

"You're not too busy?" *Stupid. He's going to think I don't want him to come along, and I do. I really do.* "I mean, it's just that it's almost an hour drive. It'll eat up the better part of your day."

"I have the day off. Taking some time before the holidays. I was across the street when I saw your car."

"I'd love to have your company. Jump in." Her stomach whirled like the spin cycle on a washer, and she hoped she could think clearly enough not to say something stupid.

He opened the passenger door and folded himself into the front seat. His knees were darn near his chin.

"Sorry. There are buttons on the side there somewhere. I don't think I've ever had anyone as tall as you in my car."

"Clearly." He finally got his hands on the buttons and positioned the seat as far back as it'd go. "That's better."

"Buckle up," she said, then floored the gas pedal in her little red Prius, tossing him back against the seat.

"I appreciate you volunteering to help with the gingerbread bake-off. The voting is a key element," he said.

"Is it still volunteering if I bartered for your help on Ruby's decorations?"

"Absolutely."

"Cool. Well, Ashley really had more done than you'd thought, but I did make a few tweaks to remove the bias from the voting process."

"Occupational hazard," he teased.

"Yes. For sure." She laughed. "In a good way. So we'll use the coins like Ashley had planned, but I'm having the acrylic boxes covered in shiny holiday wrapping paper so no one's vote will be influenced by the other votes."

Ben cocked his head slowly. "We've never even thought of that. But you're right. I can see how that would happen in a town where everyone knows everyone."

"Exactly."

"I'm glad you happened to town when you did," he said.

Her heart giddyupped, and when she turned, she met his gaze, and there was more than just appreciation in his eyes. "I'm glad I'm here too."

The hour's drive didn't feel nearly so long with someone to talk to, and Ben was excited about her plans on how to gather and tally the votes from the community on the Extreme Gingerbread Bake-off entries. When they got to the rehab center, Ruby was sitting in her room watching TV, surprisingly. "Knock, knock."

Ruby's face lit up. "Well, look who's here."

"Hi, Aunt Ruby." Joy leaned forward and kissed Ruby on the cheek. "How are you feeling?"

"Better now that I see the two of you together." That impish grin on Ruby's face made it clear that her wheels were already turning.

"We're not—" Joy started to explain.

Ruby waved off Joy's debate. "Ben, you get over here and give me an update. I knew the two of you would figure out how to work together. Are we going to win again this year?"

Ben nodded. "Yes, ma'am. I'd never let you down."

"Good, because the doctor said that I'm doing so well that I'm sure to be home for the holidays."

"That's great!" Joy took a stack of envelopes out of the leather tote she'd carried in. "I brought over all the Christmas cards you've received so far. I thought they'd brighten up your room."

"Thank you, dear. That was so thoughtful." Ruby thumbed through the stack of unopened cards. "You could have opened them."

"No, ma'am. That's a federal offense."

"Ha. Your uncle George used to say that."

"I know. I remember." As Ruby read through the cards, Joy took them from her and placed them in the window-sill one by one.

"And look. This one is from Ben." Ruby smiled.

Joy turned to Ben, whose cheeks flushed. "You send cards?" Every time she thought she was starting to figure this guy out, he threw another curve ball. She leaned over and picked up the envelope. The address had been hand-written in perfect block letters. Could anyone really be all these good things . . . and bad luck for her at every turn?

"Just to my special friends."

Ruby patted Joy's hand. "Maybe you'll make the list next year, dear."

"Maybe?" And why did that sound so appealing all of a sudden?

"What's in the box? Ben, did you bring those?" Ruby asked as she ripped open the last envelope.

"Not me. This was all Joy."

"I stopped and got some treats for you and all your friends," Joy said.

Ruby looked confused for a moment. "I just figured since they were from his mom's bakery—"

"That's your mother's bakery? I thought your mom was a nurse."

"She was," Ben said. "A long time ago. She opened the bakery about ten years ago. My sister works there with her."

"I don't think you would remember, Joy, but Ben's mom was one of your mother's nurses. Our favorite."

"What?" Ben and Joy both said at the same time.

Ruby smiled gently. "She was such a kind and thought-ful nurse. The best. When Emma died, it was hard on all of us, including your momma, Ben. I think she left nurs-ing not long after that."

Ben sat down on the edge of the bed. "I didn't know."

"Everyone over at Bridgewater Regional fawned over Emma. Her caring heart shone in everything she did. She could light up a room. Your momma, Ben, was about the same age as Emma. They grew so close that winter."

"I remember her," Joy whispered. "She arranged for a second bed so I could sleep right in the room with Mom, even though there was barely enough space for a second one." Those days had been so long. That nurse had been with them to the very end. She'd held Joy in her arms while Joy held her mother's hands those last few breaths. Ruby had been on the other side of the bed. Waiting.

The memories filled her, the weight of them dragging her down to an all-too-familiar place. "Excuse me." Joy turned and quickly left the room with tears in her eyes. This was exactly why she never let herself think about that time. It had always been too painful. Still was.

After wandering down the stairs, she slipped into the safety of the chapel and sat in the very back corner, tugging a handful of tissues out of the box in the back of the wooden pew. Just six rows filled the room. But the moment she stepped into the chapel, she felt as if someone had embraced her. Like a warm cloak had been wrapped around her that kept the sadness and worry that seemed to freeze her heart at just enough of a distance to let her breathe again.

Dabbing at her eyes and cheeks, sweeping her salty tears into the rough tissues, she looked at the beautiful stained glass at the front of the chapel. Soft lighting and quiet, except for the memories filling her mind. But in this place, the tears that flowed easily were cleansing tears. She let herself embrace the freedom of not holding back the fear and hurt. So many things had changed over the past week. Priorities seemed to be shifting, and her heart was opening to thoughts she hadn't even realized she'd care-fully stowed away to protect herself. A calming peace filled her as she quieted.

She sniffed back the tears and clutched the tissues in her hand. Joy stared into the backlit colorful scene that filled the entire front wall of the chapel room and was edged by an intricate wooden frame. That frame looked strong. And she felt like that fragile glass, wishing for a strong frame to hold her.

"I miss you, Mom." And that was the first time she'd uttered those words aloud in a long time. Warm tears stung her eyes and burned her cheeks. "So much. I don't know how to be happy without you. And I'm so afraid."

She'd been only seventeen that Christmas. Not even driving yet, and Ruby and George had tried to help her, letting her know she'd always be at home with them. They'd given her freedom that no girl her age should have had, but she'd been so sad that she never abused the priv-ilege. Somehow they'd known that would be the case. And she knew now how thankful she should have been to her aunt and uncle, and that hurt even worse, knowing that she hadn't appreciated them as she should have. That would have disappointed Mom.

Those high school years were quiet. She didn't partici-pate in anything. Went to school. Came home. Studied. Lost herself in books of all kinds. In fact, most of the books she'd bought still filled those bookshelves in Ruby's living room, and up in her own room. The library had been her best friend.

It wasn't until she landed in Northern Virginia that she'd made any friends, but even still, she kept them at arm's distance. Joy considered Renee her closest friend, and yet she'd never once gone to her home. Not because she hadn't been invited, but because she never made the time to accept an invitation. Never made it a priority.

Feeling calmer, she tried to slow her breathing. Gather her composure. And it struck her that the themes in this room were very much like what she'd gathered from the dusty boxes of Ruby's Christmas pasts. Nature's Bounty.

"This Christmas is for you, Mom." Joy lowered her head and clasped her hands.

Her heart felt lighter, but facing Ben and Ruby after she'd run out would be awkward.

Joy walked back down to her aunt's room. She heaved in a deep breath before walking in.

"You okay, darling?" Ruby looked worried, and Ben stood against the wall, looking like he wasn't sure what to do. "I didn't mean to upset you."

"Yes, ma'am. I'm fine. Thank you for sharing those memories. They were good to hear." Joy looked to Ben, who smiled gently.

"Give me a hug." Ruby extended her arms and scooted to the edge of the bed.

Joy vowed she wouldn't miss these hugs from Ruby in the future. The priorities in her life needed reexamining. She wasn't going to ignore that.

"Good. Ben and I were just talking about the decorations. No details. He wouldn't give away your surprises, but he assures me that all is on schedule and it will be the best year yet. I can't wait to see it all."

She smiled at Ben. "It's going to be beautiful. But we need to get back to work if we're going to get everything done on time."

"Before you go, they are having a holiday gathering next week. Bingo, and a holiday luncheon next Tuesday. Rumor has it, the nurses and doctors are going to do a little talent show for us. I'd love it if you'd come and spend the day. I can show you off to everyone. I've told them all about you."

No doubt. There'll probably be a lineup of possible suitors if I know Ruby. "I have the MacDonald-Webber gala on Monday night. I'm so sorry that I won't be back in time." How was it that everything seemed to happen at the same time? Molly's pageant and Ruby's rehab party on the two days she'd be out of town. She hated to disappoint them, but this was an important step in her career. She'd been working toward this for a long time. She couldn't miss it. "I was going to see if I could get that little 4-H'er to feed the critters for us while I'm gone. It's just two days."

Ruby looked noticeably upset. Joy should have had a plan in place before ever bringing up the subject today.

"You have to leave? Maybe I'll be home."

"You won't be, but don't worry, I'll get everything handled."

"I'm sure Tommy can feed the animals. That's fine. I have a little arrangement with him. He helps me when I need it, and I pay for the feed for his cow. But we'll need to figure something out for Molly."

"I'm going to make sure she gets on the bus," Ben said. "You didn't mention that part, Joy. You skipped right over it. We already talked it through. I'll be around doing things for the decorations anyway, and I met Molly a few times while we were baking cookies and putting ornaments on the community tree. It'll be fine. We have it covered. Right, Joy?"

Joy shot him a look of relief and thanks. How had she been so thoughtless?

Ruby let out an audible sigh. "Thank you both so much. I don't have many resources, but if it's one thing I can do, it's be there for others. That's why being stuck in this place is so upsetting."

Giving. It comes so naturally to Ruby. A simple but powerful gift, and yet I came in here without even considering that my leaving would worry Ruby. Thank you, Ben. For thinking on your feet. And for being there to help, even though I've fought you every step of the way.

Maybe that "drop-in niece" title fit her a little more than she'd like to admit. But there was time to change that.

Chapter Twenty-four

Ben stood on the sidewalk on Main Street next to his truck, where Joy had dropped him off. As on every Friday night, the sidewalks were buzzing with activity, but with every window on Main Street dressed for the holidays, the townsfolk meandered at a slower pace. People stopped to say hello and catch up.

But even though every window was lit up, and every snowflake danced in icy blue lights framing the picturesque street, he wasn't feeling the joy he normally did on a night like this. He was underdressed without a coat. He'd stopped in town this morning only to pick up a couple things when he'd run into Joy. Hadn't really expected to be out all afternoon. The air was crisp and cool, and the street dazzled, but it had been a quiet ride back from the rehab center in Dixon County with Joy. And what had started out as a nice time together ended with an appreciation of how serendipitous their meeting up was.

Realizing now that he and Joy had a connection that preceded their recent introduction had him wondering about destiny and fate. Paths meant to intersect. Maybe that's why the city girl had somehow tugged at his heart from the very first glance, even though she'd just crashed into his truck. Blamed him for causing her to break that ornament. And battled him at every turn, and yet he'd wanted to be around her even more.

His mother had been her mother's nurse. What were the odds? Probably not all that bad in a town the size of this. But then the two of them crossing paths nearly twelve years later, those were very different odds.

Was it always destiny that they would meet one day?

Seeing the pain in Joy's eyes had hurt him right down to the tender inside of his own heart, making it feel heavy and dark. He better understood why Joy tried to avoid that sorrow, but he also wanted to help her feel the joy she'd been missing.

And that broken ornament. It hadn't been his fault. He'd only knocked on the door after all, but her reaction made more sense now. It hadn't been about him at all.

He chased away a chill by shoving his hands in his pockets and lifting his shoulders against the chilly breeze until he reached the front of his mother's store. The familiar smells inside the bakery always made him feel like he was a kid again. Mom had always loved to bake. Even when she was busy raising him and his siblings, juggling a nursing career, and keeping Dad appeased with home-cooked meals, she somehow had managed it all, and she'd always seemed happy to do it.

"Mom here?" he asked his sister, Kendra.

"In the back. What's wrong with you?"

"Nothing." He shuffled to the back of the store, where his mother was putting finishing touches on a four-tier wedding cake. He could just barely see her behind the massive cake. His mom was still pretty, and how she stayed so clean and coiffed in the middle of the heat from the ovens and all the sugar and flour, he never had figured out. The cake was fancy. Gold gift boxes stacked perfectly one astride the next, adorned with ivory ribbon bows, diagonal

stripes, and polka dots. An elegant bow of ivory chocolate rose from the top layer with long ribbons that looked
as soft as real satin.

"That's beautiful."

"Thanks, son. I didn't expect to see you around tonight."
She carefully dotted the box on the third layer, filling in
the empty spots. Her hand was steady, and every fine
detail was uniform and precise.

"What flavor?"

"White cake with alternating hazelnut and chocolate
filling. A couple that can compromise from the first big
decision, the cake, is a couple that will last."

He should have remembered that when Cecilia hadn't
let him have any input into their wedding plans whatso-
ever. Wouldn't even let Mom bake the cake. So he'd been
the only one compromising when he asked Mom to make
his groom's cake. It was tastier and prettier than the wedding cake Cecilia had paid way too much money for and
had trucked in from Charlotte.

"Words to live by."

She smiled and then picked up another pastry bag with
a wide, flat tip and frosted ribbon-like rows in a criss-
crossed pattern on another layer, working her way around
the confection. "Simple. The right stuff is never that complex. You know that."

"I do." Only he wasn't so sure he'd ever say those words
again. "I was wondering, what made you change careers
when you did?"

"It was time. I loved being a nurse, but it was hard on
me too."

"How so? The hours?"

"No. Not that at all. I loved being a nurse, and I didn't
care about the long hours or shift work. But sometimes,
no matter what we did, it didn't matter. God's will. And

sometimes that seems so unfair." She leaned against the counter, looking as if she were drifting back in time. "I always thought that nursing was my calling. Some girls went to nursing school because their parents encouraged it as a career. Not me. I always wanted to be a nurse. To help people. But it took an emotional toll on me. When I realized I was carrying that home, and it was affecting my ability to be a good mom, I had to make a choice."

"Do you ever regret making the change? I mean, it had to feel like starting all over."

"No regrets. I like being a part of people's happiest moments."

He knew that feeling. It was the reason he liked staying active in the community, and going above the call of duty to set up extra volunteerism to do the things that were cut from the budget. Maybe holiday décor wasn't a necessity at the hospital, but it was important. It brought moments of hope and happiness to those who needed it. That was important. "I went over to see Ruby Johnson today at the rehab center."

"That was nice of you. How's she doing?"

"I went with her niece, Joy. She's here helping out while Ruby is on the mend."

"Your grandmother mentioned that."

"Ruby told me something today that I didn't know."

"Oh? What's that?" She piped another row of ribbon, and then reached for a small white prep bowl of gold glittery icing and a paintbrush to add a few highlights that made the ribbon look three-dimensional. Then she piped another ribbon.

"I never knew you were Ruby's sister's nurse."

"Emma?" She paused, a slight smile playing on her lips. She set her pastry bag down. "I was more than her nurse.

We'd become friends. She was such a beautiful person. She changed who I was, just by knowing her."

"She was special." *Like Joy.*

"So special. Why are you asking all these questions? That was a long time ago."

"I don't know. Because of meeting Joy, I guess."

"You like her?"

"I don't really know her."

She let out a soft laugh, and that face she made when she knew he wasn't telling the whole story.

"Fine. She's . . . intriguing."

"Intriguing. That's good. I'm not surprised. Her mom, Emma, was the same way. An unforgettable lady."

"Were you friends before she was in the hospital?"

"No. We met when she was sick. We bonded immediately."

"It must have been hard."

"Losing patients is part of the job, but it's never easy. If being a nurse taught me anything, it's that life is fragile. It doesn't matter how good a person you are, or how much money you have, or how well connected you are . . . life begins and ends based on something that is out of our hands. And sometimes it's unfairly short."

"Do you remember Joy?"

"Of course I do. The most beautiful strawberry blonde girl. So afraid. Rightly so." His mother's eyes were misty and wistful. "It was the year that Emma died that I started the community tree as a way for people to associate something good with the hospital. The first ornament I put on that tree was a heart that had the name *Emma* on it."

"Emma isn't the only one who is special. I'm proud to be your son. I love you, Mom."

"I know. All those things I just told you about—it was the only way I knew to bring some kind of spark of light to people who were going through hard times. The patients and their families. Some were going through things that would change their lives forever. We'd take patients to that end waiting room and let them look out the window when the nurses went out each night to sing. I wish they still did that, but I know people are busy."

"Too busy for the little things that mean the most. I hope I never get that busy."

"You're a good man, Ben. If any of my kids will always keep things in perspective, I think it will be you."

"Thanks, Mom."

"You really do like this girl. I don't think I've seen you this way in a long while. It's nice."

"Don't get your hopes up. It's not going anywhere."

"No?"

"No. I admit that I was attracted from the minute I saw her. Should've known she'd be a bigwig city girl with a big job. Don't I always fall for those? Always the wrong ones."

"You just haven't met the right one yet. I don't think where she's from has anything to do with it."

"Well, if it's not them, then it must be me that's the issue."

"Don't be silly, Ben. You're a catch. Any woman would be lucky to be with you."

"No offense, but that doesn't mean much, coming from my mother."

"Well, it's true." She picked up her pastry bag and went back to work.

"I'm not going to repeat my mistakes. I just wondered if you remembered the situation. When Ruby mentioned it today, it got me thinking that I didn't really know why you changed careers. I guess I always just thought that baking was your real passion. That maybe you'd done the nursing thing because it's what your dad had wanted."

"Oh, he did. For sure. But sometimes you have to let life take you where you're supposed to go. I don't have any regrets. Those experiences made me who I am. And I needed those field-dressing skills for as many times as you got banged up as a kid. You were always getting hurt."

"You make me sound like a klutz."

"No, furthest thing from it. You were fearless." She lifted her eyes and met his gaze. "Maybe you should consider being a little more fearless when it comes to love."

Chapter Twenty-five

After Joy dropped Ben off at his truck, she drove to the other side of town to pick up some feed for the livestock. She drove up to Hoff's Feed & Seed just before it closed. Thank goodness Ruby had an account and a standing order, so the boys knew exactly what she needed, because Joy had no idea there would be so many choices when it came to feeding farm animals.

With the back of her Prius loaded with chicken mash, rabbit pellets, goat chow, and horse feed, she was thankful she didn't have anything else to pick up, because the only room left was the passenger seat.

Now, if Ruby would just quit texting her more things to do, she'd already have completed everything on her list for the day. No sooner had she crossed off "grocery store" from her list, and enjoyed just a quick moment of satisfaction, than her cell phone signaled another text from Ruby.

She read the text as she got into her car. It simply read: *Call me.*

Joy stared at the text. Now, why in the world hadn't she just called? She pressed the button to dial Ruby. "Hi, Ruby. What's up? Everything okay?"

"Yes, dear. I forgot to tell you when you were here

earlier. I'd promised Molly she could wear my pearls at her Christmas pageant this year. Would you make sure to make that happen for me?"

"Of course." Joy didn't have to ask where the pearls were. She'd played jewelry box on Aunt Ruby's bed so many times, she could probably list off the contents by memory.

"Thank you. I kept forgetting to mention it. Also, I was thinking about this year's wreaths."

Joy slumped in the driver's seat. She hadn't discussed the details of all her ideas with Ruby, because she'd wanted to surprise her, but she was nearly done with the wreaths. Even gone the extra mile to buy supersized ribbon and decorations for the giant forty-two-inch-wide wreath she'd seen in the first stall in the barn, lodged between the feed barrels and a roll of fence wire. From everything she could find, it looked like Ruby usually hung just the greenery wreath over the barn door. This year it would match the others.

"You know," Ruby continued, "I usually do something unique for the front door. If you look for a box in the attic labeled SNOW CONES, you'll find some ornaments from a long, long time ago. It's not snow cones like the summer treat. You'll see. They were so pretty. I think you could reuse those. That would make it easy on you."

Relief flooded over her because she was already using those in her design. "Thank you, Ruby, that's so thoughtful." Joy had seen the contents of that box already. How did you not look inside a box from the attic that says SNOW CONES on it?

It was exciting that Ruby had fond memories of those. Joy had a feeling Ruby was going to love what she had done with the box of bleach and sparkly snow-dusted pinecones.

"And will you stop by the department store and pick up one of those giant buckets of individually wrapped peppermint puffs? Folks love those, and they'll look pretty next to the peppermint wreath in a big glass punch bowl next to the door when folks walk in. And a couple peppermint candles. Smell is just as important. Did I tell you that before?"

"Yes, ma'am. You've mentioned it." Joy tried not to sound impatient, but she was tired. All that talk about Mom today had made her feel a bit fragile—plus, every time she thought she was done, Ruby added one more thing to her never-ending list. She grabbed her pen and added the two new items to her list.

"Will you send me some pictures tomorrow?"

"I wanted to surprise you."

"I'm too old for surprises. I could have a heart attack and die!"

"You are not old. You're in better health than most of us."

"That's all a benefit of country living. You should try it."

She couldn't disagree, and she did feel better since she'd been here at the farm. Probably all the fresh air and exercise she was getting. And even now, exhausted and fragile as she faced the past she'd avoided for so long . . . this place made it seem doable.

Joy made what she hoped would be her last trip to a department store this season. The aisles were crowded with families. She found the peppermint puffs Ruby wanted and picked out candles to fit the theme. On an endcap there were stacks and stacks of wire ribbon on sale. She picked out a design in a satiny sheen that would offset the natural features in her designs, and loaded every single spool they had into her cart with the other items. This year's decorations were going to blow Ruby's socks off.

Socks!

She swerved the cart around and headed to the ladies' department to pick out some fun holiday socks for Ruby and herself. And some for Molly, Renee, and her girls too—a new tradition. And before she made it to the checkout, she grabbed a pair of velvety soft red pajamas. If that wouldn't put a girl in the mood to decorate and bake for the holidays, nothing would.

With one last check mark, every single to-do was officially a ta-da. Finally.

She pushed the start button on her car and headed to the farm. If she weren't so tired, she'd stay up late tonight so she could have everything staged to get the rest of the decorations up this weekend. But if she got up early, she should still be on schedule. That would leave next week when she got back from the gala to put the final tweaks on things and bake cookies.

Christmas music filled the car. Even though she was in the Christmas spirit tonight, Joy wasn't ready for the angelic glow of color that softened the darkness as she drove around the last curve before she got to the farmhouse.

She leaned forward over the steering wheel. "Ben." He'd been busy.

White lights edged every angle of the house, and the fence line twinkled a path all the way to the barn, where big red bulbs lit the outline of the peaked roof. The shrubbery around the house glowed bright green, but the other trees dazzled in multicolored strands from the tippity-top to the lowest limbs.

Ruby was right—Joy could never have been able to replicate this light display without Ben's help.

She sat at the edge of the driveway, her car running, still staring in awe. Her lips were dry from the wide smile that had spread across her face. She couldn't wait to see Molly's reaction to this. It was beautiful, and happy, and inspiring. Yes, definitely inspiring—because although she'd come home feeling tired and ready to crash, now she was eager to complete everything on her list and up her game to be sure that what she'd planned stood up to Ben's contribution. So maybe she was a little competitive. Was that so bad?

She pulled her car up to the house, then backed up to the barn to unload the bags of feed.

The guys at Hoff's Feed & Seed had lifted them and set them in the back of the car like they weighed nothing, but they weren't light. She pulled the top bag out of the car and put her foot under it, lifting with her arms and kicking the bag forward a step at a time into the barn close to the feed bins. The huge barrels were nearly empty, and filling them wasn't going to be quick. The animals bleated and nickered, begging her to feed them first. "I'll get to you as soon as I get these unloaded," she said.

The fifty-pound bag was too heavy and awkward for her to lift and pour into the barrel, so she grabbed a large feed scoop and five-gallon bucket and began moving the feed from bag to bucket to barrel, until the bag was light enough for her to lift.

She hoisted the dusty bag, balancing it on her hip, then tilted the contents until it spilled into the barrel.

"Let me help you with that."

Joy jerked around at the sound of Ben's voice. Her heart fluttered. He'd carried two of the other bags over at once. Making light work of it. His muscles flexed, and that made her want him to wrap them around her. She'd kissed this man, and that kiss still made her tingle.

He grabbed the sack and shook the last pellets out of it,

then folded the bag flat. "Ruby will get a rebate for each of these bags she takes back to the feed and seed to get refilled."

"They didn't even mention that."

"Guess they didn't mention they usually deliver her feed and put it away for her either."

"No. They did not."

"Lazy kids. I'll help you. Open the barrel for the chicken mash."

Joy lifted the top and held it as Ben let the powdery mix flow. "You want to be sure the goats never get into the laying mash. It'll bloat them right up."

"Is that bad?"

"It can kill them."

"Goodness. That's all I need." Ruby would probably never forgive her if that happened. She put the lid on the barrel and opened the next one.

Ben poured until the bag was about half empty. "Here, hold this bag steady, it's almost empty now, and I'll get the last bag."

She moved into position and finished, folding the empty sack just as he had, and stacked it with the others that were inside another bag by the door.

"Thanks for your help," she said as he walked up with the last bag. "Perfect timing."

"Happy to help."

"The place looks beautiful. When I drove up tonight, it was . . . really amazing."

His smile spread wider. "I'm glad you like it."

"I was shocked. I swear it took my breath away when I came around the corner. Every light is strung so perfectly, and I love the way you switched up the colors for different parts. Red for the barn. White on the house. It's all great."

"It's what I do," he said with a wink.

"What? Rescue women with your handiness?"

"I'll take that as a compliment."

And it was one. She'd never really known anyone quite like Ben before.

The goats climbed up on the fence and bleated.

"Have you fed them yet?" he asked.

"No. But they'd act that way whether I had or not."

"That's why I asked. Why don't I feed them while you get changed? I thought maybe we could get all the trees in their stands tonight."

It still hit her a little wrong when he seemed to know more about this place than she did, but it was her own fault she hadn't spent much time here over the years. But she could change that going forward. "Deal."

She turned before he could change his mind. She wouldn't miss that donkey nibbling and slobbering on her hair every time she walked by him. That was aggravating. And Nanny and Waddles jumped and pushed their faces in the food scoop. It was like being an offensive lineman for the Washington Redskins. Only she wasn't very good at it.

By the time Joy got changed into jeans and a sweatshirt and came down the stairs, Ben was wrangling the half tree into the living room.

Joy took the last few steps two at a time and ran over to hold the door open. "That tree looks pitiful."

"It'll be fine."

"I hope you're right." He slid past her.

She shut the door and followed him over to the corner of the room. "Let me get the stand. It's right over here." She disappeared through the kitchen and came back with the plastic stand. "These things are huge. Sure seems like overkill."

"I bought them for Ruby last year."

Of course you did. Suck-up.

"Ruby was having trouble stooping down to add water to the trees every day, and a dry tree is a recipe for disaster. Especially in an old place like this."

A hero. Again. Was there anything he didn't think of? "That was really thoughtful of you."

"You'd have done the same thing."

The unspoken *if you'd been around* poked at her.

She got down on her knees and slid the stand toward the corner.

Ben dropped the base of the tree into the stand, and Joy started twisting the screws to hold it in place.

"Not too far," he said. "Step back and see if we have the right side out to hide where the goats went wild. Then, we'll straighten it up."

She stood back toward the center of the room. "Twist just a smidgen to the left."

He turned the tree.

"Whoa. Perfect." Joy held her hands up. "You're right. No one will ever know. This is great."

"Is it straight?"

She cocked her head to the left and to the right. "A little more toward the kitchen?" After he made the adjustment, Joy clapped her hands. "Yes. That looks great. Let me tighten it up." With a few twists of the eyebolts, the tree stood sturdy and tall. "All set."

Ben let go and eased away, joining Joy in the center of the room. "Looks good. I'll help you with the lights. That's always easier with two people."

"Thank you."

"It's fun. I don't mind." He took his worn jean jacket off and placed it on the ottoman. "What kind of lights do you want to put on this one?"

"All gold. I found a whole box of tiny gold lights. I'm not sure they've ever even been opened."

"Not surprised," Ben said. "Ruby loves shopping the sales after the New Year. I think she forgets what she's bought by the time the next year comes around."

They unpacked the lights and made short business of lighting the tall tree. Every time she stretched her arms around the back and he caught her hand and took the string from her, a giggle swelled inside her.

When they finally reached the very bottom row of branches, Ben held her hand and pulled the branches back, smiling. "You ready?"

She was so ready, and not just for the lights. "Yes."

Ben plugged the lights into the foot switch plug that came with the tree stand, then tapped his foot on the button. There was a soft click and the tree lit. The gold cast was warm and soft. Even prettier than white or colored lights.

"Remember you asked me before if I liked white or colored lights?"

"I do. Sorry about the lecture."

"No. You were right. It's kind of an occupational hazard, I guess, or maybe it's a nervous habit, but I tend to spout facts when I get anxious. But I didn't have an opinion on my own."

"And you do now?"

"I do. I like gold lights the best."

He stepped next to her and pulled her close. "They really are beautiful."

"And I like lights that I've put up with you. Thank you for your help. This has been the best Christmas I've had since I was a kid."

"Christmas isn't even here yet." He playfully tapped his

finger on the tip of her nose. "Just wait. If you give Crystal Falls half a chance, you might make the best memories of all, and some new traditions."

"I'd like that."

He touched her cheek, and her phone sounded.

She lowered her gaze, grabbing her phone. "That's Ruby texting. I better get that."

"Just proves what I was going to say next is true."

"And what is that?"

"That Ruby will love you being here too." He grabbed her hand and tugged her toward the tree. "Come here. Let's send her a picture. It'll make her night."

Joy hesitated. She'd planned to surprise Ruby with the tree decorations, but being snuggled up to Ben seemed more important at the moment. What would one little picture spoil?

"Come on. It'll be fun." He waved her over, his phone already outstretched in front of him in selfie-mode.

She moved in next to him, and they scooched in closer so they both fit in the frame with the lit tree behind them. He clicked off three pictures, then turned his phone for her to look at them.

"That's funny. Send the second one."

"What's her number?" he asked as he pressed a few buttons.

"Here." She took the phone and typed in the phone number, then pressed Send. "She's going to love that."

Ben put his coat back on. "Grab your jacket. Come tell me where you want these trees. I'll show you where we usually put them."

"Okay. I have some ideas."

"Why doesn't that surprise me?"

She swatted the loop of her infinity scarf on his

coat sleeve as he led the way outside. The brisk air made her sniffle. "It's gotten cold out here."

"Always feels colder after you've been inside. It's not that bad. You'll get used to it."

"Feels like snow," she said.

"It's not even in the thirties. All right. So Ruby and I usually use one big tree and one small one in the house and the other three out here."

Joy shook her head. "Not this year. Instead of the small tree in the dining room this year, I'd like to put that one at the top of the stairwell so it will draw the visitors' eyes up. I have a mistletoe moment in store for them. And then one of the big trees in the dining room. That'll give us one big one and one small one out here."

Ben's lips bunched. He wanted to say something, she could tell, but he didn't. Instead, he gave her a simple nod.

"Hear me out," Joy said. "I went through all the pictures from the past few years. Of course, the photos don't do justice to the in-person effect. But I thought another tree in the house would make for a more brilliant experience as they make their way outside. We'll start them up the walk and funnel them through the house. But we're going to serve the cookies and cocoa out here in the barn. It'll give more room for mingling, and—" Joy felt her own excitement rise. She clapped her hands together. "—I'm going to rig up some music too."

"That's actually a really good idea."

"Thank you. And I'd like to make the animals a part of the display. We can move them to the front fenced area and do a nativity."

"A live nativity?" Ben said, raising a finger in the air. "In fact, I can get volunteers to play those parts. I'll take care of that."

"Really?" Her heart felt as bubbly as champagne. "This is so exciting."

"I can move that goat shelter over into the front yard, and rather than using strings of lights, we can use soft spotlights. I think that would be much more tasteful."

"It sounds perfect."

"Where do you want to put the trees?"

"The small one along the walkway between the house and the barn, and the big one on the walkway out. And here's where I think it will become even more fun. I'm going to put a bin of ornaments next to the tree. We have tons of them, and every person who comes through will get to hang a decoration before they leave. It'll be interactive and get prettier as the night goes on." Joy hugged her coat tighter against the cold. "I thought it was kind of like what your mom did at the hospital. And that is so special."

"Joy. That's nice. Thank you."

"Don't thank me. It's a lovely sentiment, and I want our Crystal Christmas Cookie Crawl stop to be the most memorable one they've ever had here."

"I think you're on the right track. Ruby is going to love it."

"Thank you. I really want it to be perfect for her." *And for you, Ben.*

"She will love this light display, but don't you know it's you being here that will make her the happiest?"

The chill in the air made her shiver, or maybe it was Ben's honesty getting to her.

"It's never about the lights, or the lavish displays. It's friends and family who make it."

A puff of frosty air floated between them as she let out a breath. "This feels so . . . I'm not even sure how to describe it."

"It's what you feel in here." He tapped her heart. "Interacting with the world, with people, in ways that leave joy along the path."

She swallowed hard. His mouth close to hers. She wanted so badly to feel his lips on hers again. His touch had given her a renewed belief that someone someday might just reopen her heart.

"You're cold. Go inside. Put the stands where you want the trees. I'll bring them inside for you after I take a few measurements so I can move those things around to the front yard and light them up later this week. Go on. I'll be up in a few minutes."

And right now, even just a few minutes felt longer than she wanted to be away from him, and that scared her more than anything.

Chapter Twenty-six

Joy had already put the tree stands in the dining room and at the top of the stairs, and filled the one in the living room with three pitchers of water. That tree stand had a huge reservoir. Ben was right, there shouldn't be any need to re-fill it for a while.

She sat on the floor in front of the ottoman with two stacks of foil strips, one silver and the other gold. She'd wanted to come up with a new twist on the glittery look of tinsel, and when she'd stumbled upon the old seven-inch rolls of embossed foil, she knew they'd be perfect. The original receipt had still been in the bag, showing that the short rolls had been purchased back in 1980. Who knew how old some of the other stuff was up in that attic?

The paper was the perfect natural medium to make the garland in her Nature's Bounty theme. Plus, hand-made garland would bring back memories for so many, while offering a nontoxic sparkle.

She rummaged through the old junk drawer in the side table next to Ruby's chair for a tape measure. Unfortu-nately, all she could find was a cloth tape measure like the kind that would normally be in Ruby's sewing box. Only sixty inches long, but it would have to do.

She ran the tape back and forth across the chair, summing the inches as she went to figure out exactly how many links she'd need to make enough garland for the entire tree. Having only half a tree to decorate made the task much easier.

Something banged against the door.

Joy ran over and opened the door. All she saw was pine needles. Ben had to be under there somewhere. He had somehow managed to carry both trees up at the same time.

"Please tell me you're on the other side of these trees, Ben."

"They didn't walk up," he said with a laugh.

"Well, thank goodness, because that's not the kind of Christmas magic I'm going for. Let me get the small one," she said.

Ben moved the mound of trees through the door. Joy grabbed the small one and, with only some minor teetering, managed to get it over next to the stairs. Ben carried the other one into the dining room.

Joy went to see how the other one in the dining room looked. "This tree is perfect. It's much skinnier than the fat one we put in the living room. You've already got it straight. Don't move. I'll tighten it up." She went to work on the bottom, and then stood. "Done. One more to go."

They climbed the stairs together. "I thought we could put this one up on the chest from the bedroom to give it a little height. Can you help me?"

"Sure."

They moved the chest, then Joy draped it in red velvet, holding the fabric while Ben lifted the tree and placed it on top. Ben asked, "Can you get the lights on these two okay?"

"Sure." He'd already spent half his evening here helping her. "I'm sure you've got things to do."

"I thought I'd run and get those supplies for the front

lawn that we talked about. If I leave now, I can still make it before they close."

"That would be great."

"I'm outta here, then." He headed down the steps.

"Hey, Ben," she called after him.

"Yeah?" He stopped at the bottom of the steps and turned around.

She didn't want him to leave. She liked working with him, but he'd be right back. Why had she called out to him? "Thanks for everything."

That cute dimple tempted her. "Told you I liked doing this stuff."

"Yes, you did. And you're good at it." And then there was an awkward silence.

"I'm just . . . going to go," he said, then let himself out.

Since the lights were already on the big tree, she decided to tackle decorating that one first. The theme for this one was the Twelve Days of Christmas. When she'd stumbled across the timeless set of ornaments, each hand-carved out of wood and decorated with beads made of acorns, it had been an easy decision. That box must not have been opened in years, because it had been in the very back of the attic. It hadn't even been marked as a Christmas box.

To set the mood, she turned the radio to a Christmas station. She changed into her new red pajamas and danced her way downstairs. How appropriate that "The Twelve Days of Christmas" should be playing as she walked back into the living room.

She set to work, placing the ornaments on the tree in twelve evenly spaced rows. Humming along with the music, the only words she sang out loud were the "five golden rings"—her favorite part.

Carefully hanging each of the delicate ornaments, she placed the partridge in the pear tree nestled at the very top and worked all the way down to the twelve drums hanging from the very bottom branches.

Each ornament was a detailed treasure, signed by the artist, although she couldn't make out the name.

Each of the twelve tiny drums had a different design and color scheme, with shiny silver and gold accents. Finally done, she stood back and then adjusted a couple of the ornaments until they were evenly aligned in a perfect pyramid formation. One last thing to do. She and Mom had always made it the final quality check. She squinted and stared at the tree to make sure the lights were in the perfect blurry alignment that looked like every spot was glowing. She exhaled a long sigh of contentment. *Spot on.*

Her mood was buoyant as she settled on the floor in front of the ottoman, where she'd stacked all those precisely cut three-inch-by-seven-inch strips of shiny paper and the other supplies to make her handmade garland. One by one, she looped the shiny foil, stapling their ends into a perfect circle. Once the twelve silver rings were daisy-chained, representing the Twelve Days of Christmas, she added five golden rings to the lightweight shiny garland. It didn't take long before she had the first fifty links put together. "It's going to be so pretty."

She was so tempted to send a picture to Ruby of the work in progress, but that would spoil the surprise.

A soft knock came at the front door.

She walked over and peeked out the sidelight window. Ben? "Hi," she said, opening the door. "I didn't hear you drive up over the Christmas music."

"I see you already have your pajamas on. I wasn't going to bother you, but I saw the lights on."

"Did you forget something?"

"No. I was just going to drop off some things I got at

the hardware store. Some of it is for the house, do you mind if I bring that stuff in?"

"Not at all. Do you need my help?"

"No." He jogged off the porch back toward his truck, then came in with two bags. "But I'll come back and get all this done this week."

"What is all of that?"

Ben toted the bags inside, tucking them in a corner of the dining room. "It'll help when Ruby gets home. Safety rails for the shower, that kind of stuff. My mom had me do this for my grandmother a couple years ago. Ruby and Shirley both scoffed at it then, but now it really is a necessity."

"Oh, well, you'd have thought they might have mentioned that at the rehab center so I could prepare."

"I'm sure they will. But if we take care of it now, you'll have less to do when Ruby comes home. It's a good thing to do at this point in her life anyway."

"That's probably true," she admitted.

"And I think we both know that if you wait for Ruby to admit that she needs the extra safety precautions, that'll never happen."

He was right.

He looked past her at the deep pile of foil links. "What are you doing? Making your own garland?"

"Yep. Found the foil in the attic."

"It's pretty." He walked over to the tree. "These ornaments are awesome." He lifted one of the four calling birds from the tree. "These are real feathers. And hand-carved. Nice workmanship. I've never seen Ruby use these before."

"They caught my eye immediately. I think the shimmery garland and gold lights will really set off the intricate details of the ornaments too. Don't you?" She held a stretch of the garland out against the tree. "Look. It's turning out even better than I'd imagined. Like jewels."

"You city girls sure dig all that glitz and glamour, don't you?"

"What's wrong with that?"

He shrugged. "Nothing."

"But?"

"My ex was into glitz and glamour too. Cecilia never could appreciate the little things. She couldn't get out of this town fast enough. Guess a lot of women are that way about swanky things and sparkles. Left me feeling a little bitter I guess."

"What's that got to do with me?"

"I've seen that dress. The company gala. You live in Washington, D.C. That's a pretty big difference from Crystal Falls. I'm sure as soon as Ruby gets home, you'll be gone."

Joy bit her tongue. She'd like to wipe that smirk right off his face. Was he insinuating that she was uppity in some sort of backhanded way? It wasn't all that long ago that he'd called her a drop-in niece. Clearly his opinion of her hadn't improved as much as she'd thought.

"Well, I'll let you get back to your silver and gold garland chain," he said. "I'll see you in the morning."

When the door clicked closed behind him, Joy sat there, steaming. He didn't know her at all.

Only that smile wasn't going to fool her.

She gave the stapler such a hard squeeze that it jammed up.

"And as usual, bad luck comes with Ben," she said as she tugged on the stapler, trying to reload it, only to have it spring wide open, sending the staples flying across the room.

"Great. Just great. And don't act like you know me so well, Ben Andrews."

Chapter Twenty-seven

Ben had been at Ruby's house for over an hour before Joy finally wandered outside to feed the animals. Of course, he'd already fed them all. If he hadn't, those goats would've woken her up earlier, for sure. They were pretty vocal when they had something to say. Besides, it had been a lot easier to get the animals moved with a bucket of feed from the back pasture to the front, where they were going to set up the live nativity.

"You've been busy," Joy said. Her words more clipped than complimentary as she eyed his progress.

"Good morning."

She walked by him, heading straight for the barn without so much as a hello or good morning.

"I already fed all the animals for you," he called out.

She spun around and just stood there. "Oh."

He wasn't the most astute when it came to women, but he could tell she wasn't herself. "Is something wrong?"

Her head bounced in one of those you're-daggone-right kind of nods that were never good news. "Yeah. In fact, there is something wrong. I've been thinking about it all night."

Why did I ask? I know better. But I always do it. Keep your mouth shut, Ben.

"Last night, when you said I was a high-maintenance uppity city girl . . . I really take exception to that." Her hands were balled into tight fists, and her jaw was so tight that her chin was actually quivering a little.

"That's not exactly what I said." And yet here he was, opening his mouth again.

"Close enough."

"I didn't mean anything by it. I wasn't talking about you. I was talking about my ex. Sorry if you took it personally."

"I did," she said. "Just because the way I choose to live my life might not be your way, doesn't mean it's not okay."

"I know you're right. But I can't help trying to not repeat past mistakes. I mean, it's not like she didn't know I was from a small town when we met. It was like she did this bait and switch on me to get me, only she didn't really want me all along. Maybe we should change the subject, but I promise you that those comments were not meant to be derogatory toward you." He put his finger under her chin and turned her to face him. "Really. And by the way, that glitzy dress of yours looks like a Christmas ornament. I like it."

A smile eased across her face. "That's exactly what I thought when I saw it."

"You'll look gorgeous in it. The green, with your green eyes and your red hair." He swallowed. And as pretty as she'd look all dolled up, he liked her just the way she was right now too. Beautiful in a jacket over a hooded sweatshirt, muck boots, and a red and gray wool cap tugged over her head, her bangs barely peeking out, with not a bit of makeup on.

"Thank you."

"You're welcome." He breathed a little easier as she relaxed. "When's the party? Or wait . . . the gala."

"'Gala' does sound kind of stodgy, doesn't it?"

He pulled his lips together, as if afraid to agree.

Joy said, "The gala. It's Monday night."

At the risk of being blasted again, he admitted it. "I'm sure it's nice to get dressed up and do something fancy now and then. I take my mom down to Charlotte a few times a year for some culture. It's not but about an hour away, and she loves getting all dressed up. I'll admit I enjoy the nice night out as much as she does."

"Really? I didn't really see you as that kind of guy."

Wasn't that just the pot calling the kettle black? She'd been making her own assumptions about him all along. "Stay tuned. There's more to me than meets the eye." Maybe there was a chance they might have something. He wasn't quite ready to discount that chance.

"I like what I see," she said.

"I like what I see in you too." He leaned forward and kissed her on her cheek, then brushed his lips against hers as she spoke.

"I—"

He pulled her close, her lips warm and sweet against his. "Joy, I know we've just met, but I like what I feel when I'm with you. I like you."

"Why?"

"I can't really put my finger on it. Independent. Thoughtful. Determined. Capable. Funny. Absolutely gorgeous. Do I need to go on?"

"I think you left out hardheaded and opinionated."

"There's that, but they are kind of cute on you."

She swatted his arm, and he caught her by the wrist, pulling her hand to his heart. He wondered if she could feel his heart beat faster. He'd never met someone who made him feel like this before. Like he needed to know her more. No matter what.

Nearly breathless, she said, "Thank you."

"For the kiss?"

"For reminding me what butterflies feel like."

He'd felt a swirl himself. "Thank you for letting me make them take flight." He took her hands into his own. "I like kissing you. Besides, we make a pretty good team."

"I never really thought of kissing as a team sport." Only she was kidding. He could tell by the way her eyes twinkled and that mischievous tug of her smile that made her eyelashes nearly touch her cheeks.

"Well, then, you haven't been doing it right, but I'm an excellent teacher."

"I bet you are."

And if he didn't stop right now, then there wouldn't be any stopping at all, and he knew he needed to take this slowly. "I have something for you."

"You do?"

He'd gone back and forth with himself about whether to give her the gift now or wait. But the timing felt right. "Wait right here."

She looked bewildered as he scooted past her and headed for his truck. His heart pounded. Not from the jog to the truck, but because he really hoped she'd like the gift.

He carried the white glossy box to the door. He hadn't wrapped it, just added a simple length of red ribbon tied in a bow. As he took each step closer to the barn, he started second-guessing the gesture, but it was too late now.

She was standing in the doorway of the barn, looking at him. Looking at the box.

She caught his gaze. "What is this?"

"You'll have to open it and see." He handed her the box.

Nervously, she moistened her lips. "I don't have anything for you."

"It just something I made. It wouldn't have the same meaning to anyone else."

She seemed to calm a bit, pulling the end of the ribbon, then sitting down and lifting the top off the box.

The heavy lashes that shadowed her cheeks flew up. "Ben?" She lifted the heart-shaped wooden ornament out of the box by the wire that he'd twisted and shaped himself. Hanging between her fingers, it looked so elegant. "You made this for me?"

The hours he'd spent turning and shaping that wood into a single heart, rounded like one full of love, had been almost therapeutic. It had been a while since he'd slowed down long enough to work on something so intricate, but this had been important. Inspired work. Something he'd wanted to do. Once he'd finished the heart and it was perfect, he'd been so nervous to take his cutting tools to the center of it. Especially after working so hard to get to that smooth finish. But he'd done it. Carved that smaller heart in the center, where he'd sprinkled those broken green glass ornament pieces and sealed them safely in acrylic.

Joy could drop this a hundred times and never do it harm.

"It's beautiful." She held the heart in her hands, running her fingers over the smooth surface. "The grain of the wood is so pretty."

"It's olive wood. I rubbed it with Danish oil. That's what brings out all the lovely dark grains."

Her lips parted slightly as if she was going to say something. "The heart in the middle? The green glass? It's just like—"

"I felt so bad about that ornament."

"Why?" She held the ornament to her chest. "It wasn't your fault. I overreacted."

"Didn't matter whose fault it was. It was important to you."

"How did you—?"

"When I realized how upset you were, I couldn't throw away those pieces. I wasn't sure what I was going to do with them, but somehow putting them in the trash seemed wrong. I woke up one night and knew I wanted to make that for you."

"I will treasure it. It's the nicest gift I've ever gotten." Her eyes glistened. "Ever." She motioned him to follow her to the house. Inside she took the ornament stand out of the box and set it on the end table, then hung the ornament. "It's perfect."

"As perfect as you."

"I don't know how I'll ever be able to thank you. This is so thoughtful."

"That smile is thanks enough." What he wouldn't give to see that smile every single day. "And maybe we could meet for coffee after the judging of the gingerbread bake-off tomorrow night?"

"That would be really nice." She cocked her head. "Does that invitation stand—win or lose? Because I wouldn't want to think you're trying to bribe me."

"The invitation definitely stands."

A smile trembled over her lips. "Then you're on. Coffee. Tomorrow night."

"Well, I'd better head home. I'll see you tomorrow."

"Yes. You will."

As Ben backed out of the driveway, he saw Joy sweep the curtain to one side, watching him leave. He wondered if she was having the same thoughts he was right now. That he wished this morning together could have lasted all day. One could hope.

Chapter Twenty-eight

A brightly colored banner strung above the entry of the botanical gardens announced the annual Carolina's Best Flour Extreme Gingerbread Bake-off. Today, Sunday, was the day the community got to cast their votes and the winner was announced.

Voting would commence at one o'clock, and wrap up at four o'clock. Then Joy'd be done with her commitment here and could start getting ready for her trip back to D.C. for tomorrow night's gala.

Dressed in a gingerbread-brown sweater she'd found in Ruby's closet, and the suit she'd been wearing when she came to town, Joy had actually pulled off a festive look by adding a glittery golden scarf pinned with an adorable gingerbread man ornament.

All the entries were set up in the theater, which wasn't really a theater at all, at least not to her. She'd always thought of a theater as having stadium seating and a screen; this was more like a ballroom that had been misnamed. Elegant in an understated way.

The flour company that employed nearly 40 percent of the community here was the main sponsor of the event, and its PR team was already on-site. "Hi, I'm Joy Holbrook. You must be the PR team from Carolina's Best Flour."

"We are. I'm Phil Finnegan," said a tall man in a sweater vest. "The guys are hanging the last banner now. Hope you don't mind that we got here early and got started. We've been doing this for so long that we kind of have a system."

"No problem." Could she get any luckier? "I'm going to finish getting everything set up. Let me know if you need anything."

"We're going to put the giant winner's check behind the podium."

"That'll work, and will you be the one I'll call up to present it?"

"I'm your guy."

"All right, then." Joy busied herself giving instructions to the girls who would collect the tickets and hand out the voting coins as the visitors came in; then she went to work gift-wrapping the acrylic boxes next to each of the six entries that were finalists.

At one o'clock sharp, there was a line clear out the building past the wedding gazebo and the koi pond.

People in the community were eager to get their chance to cast a vote for their favorite gingerbread creation. Each person traded a food item for a ticket or sprang for the two dollars per person to get their voting coin. The coins were wooden disks that had been stamped with the town logo.

Joy had arranged for a giant whiteboard on wheels to be brought in, and had already transferred all the judges' scores to it so the final calculations could be done live. It would make for a dramatic and exciting evening. Speaking to groups of people was one of her strong suits. She enjoyed doing it, and this would be a nice shift to something in her comfort zone for once since she'd hit Crystal Falls.

Throughout the afternoon, Joy took the microphone and announced each of the finalists, and encouraged visitors to cast their coin for their favorite entry.

An air horn blasted three times, and the contestants took their places next to their creations. The theater was packed with what looked like more people than could possibly live in Crystal Falls.

Joy smoothed the front of her suit, ready to make the final announcement for the day.

"Greetings, everyone. Merry Christmas. My name is Joy Holbrook, and I'm so happy to be your hostess this afternoon for the eighth annual Carolina's Best Flour Extreme Gingerbread Bake-off finalists. We have amazing entries today. You've had three hours to look at all of the entries closely and select your favorite. I know it's not going to be easy to cast your one vote, but if you haven't done so yet, I need you to do just that . . . right now. At four o'clock sharp we'll begin counting votes."

People rushed to drop their coins and vote for their favorites.

Joy went through the list of volunteers and sponsors, then at four o'clock on the dot officially closed the voting. "Okay. That's it. All voting is complete. Can I get my official helpers out to each station?" Three girls and three boys walked across the stage wearing Crystal Falls Botanical Garden T-shirts and made their way down to the voting boxes.

"Thank you. Okay. We have six very worthy teams here today. Some beginners, some professionals, but that's the beauty of this competition—it's anybody's to win. For anyone who is a first-timer, each entry was judged the day these amazing creations were set in place. A panel of judges that specialize in this type of baking, and representatives from our sponsors evaluated each entry on the following criteria: originality, execution, theme, and degree of difficulty."

The crowd clapped, and there were whistles from the back of the theater.

"Let me introduce you to each of them. First, from Crystal Falls Lazy Chop House we have Chef Daniel Wallersky. This is Chef Daniel's first time entering the competition in Crystal Falls. He's originally from Buffalo, New York, and now calls Crystal Falls his home."

The crowd clapped politely.

"At table number two, we have the mother-daughter team of Sandra and Connie Black. They have family here in Crystal Falls and drove all the way from Myrtle Beach to be a part of this competition. Connie is a recent graduate of Johnson and Wales University in Charlotte. Let's give them a round of applause."

Joy carried the cordless mic and descended the stage, smiling and excusing herself to people as she moved through the crowd.

"Next, we have the team of cheerleaders from Crystal Falls High School. They've used the theme of a sunny Christmas since they are hoping to win this competition today to help fund their trip south to compete in the National Cheerleading Championship Finals this spring. Good luck, ladies!"

Joy paused as she saw Ben slip into place next to his mother at the last minute. His mother was beautiful. He had her eyes and dark hair. His mom gave his hand a quick squeeze. "At table four, the baking team of Janice and Ben Andrews. You know Janice Andrews from the bakery right here in town, and their extreme design and automation bring something new to baking."

A round of applause went up. They were clearly a favorite.

"Now, for any of you that don't know these next two gals, you're obviously a first-timer because I have here in my notes that these two ladies, Rosie and Bella, are not only twins, but they've also won this competition for the last two years. Can they hold their winning streak with this year's entry?"

The two ladies stepped forward and curtsied as if they'd rehearsed that move a hundred times.

"And last but not least, a very innovative design from the staff at Funky Flowers, who have integrated edible flowers into their entry. A big hand for them."

Joy clapped and let the crowd gain momentum. The excitement in the room was building. The contestants looked nervous. "All right, one more round of applause for all of them."

She marched back up to the raised platform, where there was a long table already set with six teams of two in each spot, ready to do the final live count of the entries.

"Can I have my officials please bring their wrapped voting boxes up to the table?"

Joy felt a tingle of excitement as she watched the crowd, and Ben smiled and gave her a look of approval. The theater was filled, probably surpassing the fire code limit, and it was beginning to feel a little like a hothouse. She needed to speed this along, else those confection creations were likely to start melting.

"Now, the moment you've all been waiting for. Counters, let's reveal the votes."

The sound of the holiday wrapping paper being ripped from each of the voting boxes filled the room. Cheers filled the room as the level of coins in each of the boxes was revealed. There were only two clear competitors vying for the title, unless the external judges' scores varied wildly.

Folks began to speculate. Yelling out the name of the team they thought had won.

"Not so fast," Joy said. "We have the external judges' scores to factor in." She walked over to the wheeled white-board. "On the back of this board, we have all the judges' scores." She waved her hand, and one of the volunteers spun the board around to show the scores so far. Nothing was tallied, but it still caused gasps to rise across the crowd.

"While the teams count and tally your votes today, I'd like to bring Stephanie from the Community Center up here to share with you how much money we've raised through this event." Joy spotted Molly standing next to Ginny near the entrance. She was so glad they'd made it. She could see Molly's excitement all the way from here.

Stephanie, a tall, willowy brunette, came up the stairs and took the microphone. "We raised over two hundred dollars in cash, and an amazing sixteen boxes of nonperishable food for the Community Center. That translates into more meals than we've ever been able to offer in the past. Thank you for helping us help those in need this holiday season."

Joy recalled the moment Margie had asked her to pay two hundred dollars for just two tickets for her kids' fundraiser. She'd doled out that two hundred dollars just because she thought it might help her land a promotion. Not for the right reasons. Giving to this cause really meant something.

A balanced meal was important. Not that the way she ate was a good example.

The box of peanut butter crackers in Joy's desk drawer back at MacDonald-Webber was the closest thing to something personal in her office, and even those crackers were probably mocking her right now. They served as Joy's lunch at least once a week, but didn't every good southern girl know to keep a stash of Nabs for emergencies? Aunt Ruby had always said so, and she'd never steered Joy wrong.

Joy pictured those private-school kids in their designer duds, reviewing seasonal menus, then fancy-dressed waiters bringing silver-covered dishes and presenting the children with Nabs instead. They'd probably try to eat them with a fork, and that was just plain wrong.

But somehow a month's worth of PBJs for families in this town seemed like a pretty special thing. Without crusts and cut in fours, of course.

She stepped over to where she'd tucked her purse under the podium, pulled out her checkbook, and wrote a check for two hundred dollars.

The crowd clapped and Joy let them, but she stopped Stephanie before she left the stage.

"I'd like to add to your efforts."

"Thank you! This is so generous. Make that over four hundred dollars! You just doubled it."

"You're welcome," she said to Stephanie, then walked back over to the microphone. "Are my counters ready with the final numbers?" Joy scanned the team, getting a thumbs-up from each of them. "Go to it."

The team leader walked over and turned the giant wheeled whiteboard around so the crowd could no longer see it. As each team completed their count, they disappeared behind the whiteboard wall. The markers squeaked against the board as they filled in the missing scores and did the final tally.

Joy scanned the crowd. Molly and Ginny had made their way to the next gingerbread house, and Shirley was talking to a couple looking at Ben and his mom's entry. Joy's personal favorite.

Joy almost dropped her microphone when she saw Todd

standing in front of her. A prickly heat ran through her body, and not the good kind.

He smiled his movie-star smile, but it still didn't make her glad to see him. She wrapped her hand around the mic and held it to her stomach.

He looked so out of place in his tailored suit. Then again, she probably had too, the first day she showed up, but she felt more like part of the community now. She could imagine people flocked around Todd's fancy sports car parked out front. That car cost more than a lot of these people would make this year. He was flashy. That was one thing she could say about Todd, and the women in the crowd hadn't missed his entrance either. But she knew what was behind the glitz and polish—not much, and he didn't shine at all compared to Ben.

The team leader came up to her and handed her an envelope. Joy waved it above her head, taunting the crowd. "This is so exciting. Are you ready for me to announce the winners?"

Someone in the crowd let out a whistle, and the rest yelled and clapped.

"I thought so. Let me get the contestants up here, please."

When Ben walked up onto the stage, she felt those butterflies again. Once all the contestants lined up on the stage and the crowd settled down, Joy began the announcements.

"In third place, Chef Daniel Wallersky. Come on up here, Chef Daniel."

"In second place, we have Janice and Ben Andrews." Ben stood next to his mother as she graciously accepted their trophy and prize money. The photographer snapped two pictures and then moved them to the side next to Chef Daniel so they could get a group picture of all the winners.

"And winner of the eighth annual Extreme Gingerbread Bake-off, sponsored by Carolina's Best Flour . . . Rose and Bella. For the third straight year. Congratulations, ladies. Here to award them with the check from our sponsor, Carolina's Best Flour Company, is Mr. Phil Finnegan."

Phil walked out with the giant check. He shook the ladies' hands, and they were just as excited as if it had been their first win.

Joy spoke loudly to reach across the excited audience. "Along with the monetary award, you'll see these faces in advertising all year long. Congratulations to our winners, and a round of applause for yourselves because without you, we wouldn't be feeding our own community. Merry Christmas."

Phil and Joy posed for pictures with the winning team, and then the photographer whisked all the winners stage right to get a picture in front of the sponsor banner.

She wrapped up the final details, handing over the mic and doing the obligatory thank-yous with the sponsors as the crowd started to thin out.

Joy's attention wandered over to where Ben and his mother were talking to some people near their display. Meanwhile, Todd hadn't moved. She could still see him in her periphery . . . staring at her.

As much as she'd like to ignore him, it was highly unlikely he'd come all this way and give up that easily. Better to just get it over with. But not here in front of everyone.

She stepped down the exit from the stage, and Todd met her halfway. "You look great," he said.

"What are you doing here?"

"I wanted to see you," he said. "You haven't missed me?"

Disconcerted, she crossed her arms and pointedly looked away. "How did you find me?"

"That's not a very warm welcome. It was a five-hour drive. I thought you'd be happy to see me."

"Why would you think that? We haven't spoken in weeks." Maybe it wasn't a particularly polite way to respond to his surprise, but she'd never been one to like surprises, and this wasn't a good one. Todd didn't do anything without an agenda. That had been charming when she first met him, but over the past six months, he'd begun to claw his way to the top instead of working his way to it. She didn't want to be part of his agenda. No matter what it was. Especially here in Crystal Falls.

"I missed you. It's the holidays. I've been trying to get in touch with you for a week."

If she'd sent a polite thank-you for the flowers, would he have left her alone? She knew how he liked to win. Her ignoring him, intentionally or not, was probably a challenge. "Thank you for the flowers."

She recognized someone from the hospital watching them and decided it would be best to have this conversation privately. "Come with me." She weaved her way through the crowd and beyond the big double doors that led to the garden paths, which were closed this time of year.

As soon as the doors closed behind them, Todd laid both his hands on her shoulders, then let them glide down her arms, stepping in closer. "It's been too long since we've spent time together." He lowered his head to the crook of her neck and whispered, "I've missed you." Then kissed her on the neck.

"No, you haven't." She wiggled out of his grasp. "You could have called. I don't really like that you've tracked me down and shown up unannounced."

"Oh, come on. I left you several messages at the office." His easy smile wasn't going to work on her.

"You have my cell phone number. You could have called. You could even have e-mailed."

"I wanted to see you."

"You knew I'd say no."

"And I don't know why that is," he said. "I thought we understood each other."

"Because we are done, Todd. In fact, I believe it was you who said we'd always keep things simple. This doesn't feel simple anymore." She leveled her gaze. There really wasn't anything to discuss.

"Oh, come on. We always have a good time. The big gala is tomorrow night. I'd love to take you to the party."

"That's what all this is about. I told Renee when you sent those poinsettias that getting an invite to the gala was your angle." She took another step back, increasing the space between them. "It would be completely tacky for me to take you to the gala, since you work for the competition now."

"Half the people there wouldn't even realize I'd left."

"I'd know," she said, gazing off to the side, trying to decide her best course to make an exit and send him on his way.

"Come on, Joy." He took her hands into his. "Give me a chance." He stooped into her line of sight.

"No. And I'd appreciate it if you'd just leave."

He straightened. His smile faded. "Are you serious?"

"I sure am."

His nostrils flared as he shook his head. "I can't believe you. This was a grand gesture on my part."

"Don't do this, Todd. Let it go. I'm not important to you. We both know that what we had was never like that." She put her hand on the door. "I'd appreciate it if you'd just take me out of your contact list." Leaving him behind, she walked back inside, over to the stage, where her things were stored behind the podium. People were still milling about, looking at the displays. She stooped down to get her purse, lowering her head to mask the anxiety she was feeling right now.

A folded slip of paper with her name on it sat on top of her purse.

She stood up, hitched her purse over her shoulder, and draped her jacket over her arm. Scanning the room, she didn't see any sign of Todd. Thank goodness. Maybe he'd taken the back exit from where they'd been standing.

She watched for Ben. She was ready for a relaxing cup of coffee with him. While she waited, she unfolded the slip of paper.

> *Have to cancel coffee.*
> *I'll see Molly off to school in the morning.*
> *Enjoy the gala.*
> > *Take care,*
> > *Ben*

A twinge of disappointment swept through her. She'd been looking forward to spending more time with Ben before she had to leave town. Maybe he was disappointed he and his mom hadn't won. Their entry definitely won the creativity score. The carousel on the turntable was beyond amazing, and the LED lights shining through the sugar glass still seemed impossible. Ben had definitely won that category by a landslide, but it was tight competition and the scores in some of the other categories had just eked the winners ahead.

She walked out to her car and left, glancing in her rearview mirror and in the parking lots for a sign of his truck. It wasn't like she didn't have plenty to do to keep her busy tonight. Maybe he'd stop by in the morning.

Chapter Twenty-nine

Joy had never been so happy to be back at her condo in D.C. Her butt was numb from the long ride home, and in just two weeks, how could she have forgotten how crazy traffic was in that area? The five-hour drive had taken nearly seven hours. If she hadn't lollygagged around the house so long, she would've missed some of that traffic, but she'd been riding on the hopes of a quick hello between her and Ben, which just hadn't happened.

She'd planned to get in for a deluxe pedicure at her favorite spa downtown today, but there was no time for that now. A quick in-and-out with the salon next door was going to have to do.

She swiped her card key at the condo parking lot entrance and waited for the arm to lift. She parked in her assigned spot, then got the gown out of the back. Holding the hanger of the dress bag high above her head to keep it from dragging, she fumbled for her keys as she made her way to the lobby of her building. Not quite so convenient as front-door parking in Crystal Falls.

As she waited for the elevator, the lobby felt cold and stark. There were no holiday decorations. Probably in an effort to be politically correct. A lot of that went on around here. Not that she'd planned to do any decorating either.

But that was different. She had her own reasons, and they were not politically driven.

The elevator chime sounded and finally the doors opened. Three people stepped off, none of whom she knew. She smiled politely and stepped inside. When the doors opened on the fourth floor, she stepped into the hallway. Her condo was just to the right of the elevator.

She worked her key in the temperamental old lock and went inside. The décor was minimal, and neat. A showplace that she'd really been proud to share, only today it felt different. Somewhat impersonal. More like a rental unit. No family pictures. No memories tied to random items that needed to be explained.

She hung the dress in her closet and went to run a bath.

The long drive had left her feeling weary. She poured some Purple Water into the tub, a scent she'd fallen in love with while staying at the Ritz on a business trip. The splurge always made her feel better after a long day, and she was going to need a resurgence of energy if she was going to enjoy the long night ahead.

She slipped into the silky water. At Ruby's house, in her old cast iron tub, Joy'd been able to scooch down into the warm water all the way to her chin. Her modern tub wasn't nearly so deep. In fact, she'd never noticed before just how shallow it was. The water barely covered all of her.

When she got out of the tub, she was clean, but not relaxed.

She was still upset that Todd had shown up. What had he been thinking? Todd had never been one to make a grandiose effort. Their relationship had never been like that. And although part of her wondered why she hadn't been swept away by the romantic gesture, she had to believe it was because she was over him—or there hadn't really ever been anything there to begin with.

If she hadn't met Ben, would she have reacted the same way?

She closed her eyes, trying to imagine herself with Todd, but nothing came to mind.

They'd shared some good meals. Equally good business outings, but that time had come and gone. Time to move on.

She climbed out of the bathtub and wrapped herself in a thick, plush towel. Ruby's tub might be better than hers, but there was nothing like these thirsty towels she'd splurged on. Maybe that would be the perfect present for Ruby this Christmas. She'd certainly never treat herself to them. Besides, there probably weren't any high-end stores within a couple of hours that even carried them out there.

She could stop and get them on her way back to Crystal Falls. They'd even gift-wrap them.

Joy slathered on her favorite moisturizer, then did her makeup. She swept her hair up in a clip that Renee had given her last year for Christmas.

The gown was so beautiful. She'd been so excited about it, and it fit perfectly, but now it seemed like a silly extravagance. This one dress cost more than all the money Crystal Falls had raised for meals for those in need.

And two weeks ago, this dress . . . this party . . . the promotion had been the only things she had on her mind. Tonight none of that seemed nearly so exciting as getting back to Crystal Falls. Even though she knew she'd be there only a few more days until her leave was up.

Surprisingly, she was looking forward to celebrating the holidays. And not just anywhere, with anyone, but in Crystal Falls with Aunt Ruby and her new friends Molly and Ginny, and Ben too.

Her phone buzzed. A text message that the car the firm had sent to take her to the MacDonald-Webber gala was downstairs waiting. Just one more perk bestowed upon the employees to thank them for another grand year of service to their customers.

She grabbed her beaded evening clutch and took the elevator downstairs.

The doorman held the door, and the driver stood at the back of the limo, ready to help her in.

"Holbrook. To the National Archives Museum?"

"Yes." She accepted his hand as she slid into the backseat of the car. A bottle of champagne sat in the ice bucket. Already open. She poured champagne into one of the glasses and took a sip. The bubbles tickled her nose.

She watched out the window as they moved through traffic. The world looked different through tinted glass. A little boy waved from the backseat of a car in the next lane. He probably thought someone important was hidden behind the dark windows in the fancy limo. But it was just her. And right now she wasn't nearly so excited as she'd thought she'd be about the gala tonight.

They slowed to a stop. She peered outside.

The line of black cars was at least twenty deep by the time Joy's limo arrived at the party. She checked her watch twice as they slowly moved toward the entrance. MacDonald-Webber's own art department had set up their staff photographers to capture the arrival moment for each employee. Coworkers stepped out into the camera flashes smiling and mugging for the photographers. She felt awkwardly alone. Maybe blowing off Todd hadn't been the smartest move. She could have given him the boot next week. Or after the holidays.

Too late now. Her driver pulled to the front of the line, and a white-gloved man helped Joy out of the car.

She pasted on her confident smile and tilted her head

for the picture, barely slowing down as she headed to the Rotunda Galleries in search of a drink.

But she had to admit some of the discomfort she felt at being alone was swept quickly aside as she walked into the glamorously lit room. Taken with the beauty, she slowed to a stop. The vaulted ceiling, open to seventy-five feet, glowed in hues of red and green like a psychedelic heaven up to the coffered panels.

Her heels echoed against the slick, marble floor. A waiter stopped, offering her a flute of champagne. "Thank you."

Colleagues mingled, and Joy recognized several of the heavy hitters from other areas of the firm.

Brock Webber caught her elbow as she walked by. "Good to see you, Joy. I wanted to personally congratulate you on your work this year."

"Thank you, Mr. Webber."

"It's a fine night to celebrate." He lifted his glass in the air.

No champagne for him. He was drinking brown liquor. Bourbon straight up, if she had to guess. "Yes, sir, it is."

"More to come," he said with a wink, then turned back to the group he'd been speaking with.

She tried to maintain her composure, and searched for somewhere she could get herself together. "More to come," he'd said. They were most certainly announcing the promotions tonight. This was her night. The night she'd wished for. After ducking into one of the other rooms, she stood, pretending to enjoy one of the many pieces of art. But mostly so she could steady her excited pulse.

Someone leaned in and whispered in her ear. "I knew you'd be the best-looking thing here tonight."

Joy spun around to see Todd standing there with his date. "You?"

"Hello, again." Todd smiled a lazy smile. Joy recognized the lollipop hanging off his arm as one of the young interns they'd hired permanently over the summer. Figures Todd would go for the easy way in. She should've known he wouldn't give up.

"What are you doing here?" she asked, trying to keep her voice steady.

"Mingling. Making contacts," he said, never stopping his scan of the room. "Have you met Sandy?" He lifted a brow. "Sandy Booker. As promised, this is my *dear* friend, Joy Holbrook."

Great. So when Todd couldn't use her to *take* him to the gala, he'd stooped to using her as a way to get someone else to.

The young woman giggled and held out her hand. "It's so nice to meet you. I've heard so much about your projects. I'd love to work with you someday. I hope you'll keep me in mind. When Todd said y'all used to be a couple and were best friends now, I was so excited. I wanted to meet you."

Joy would best describe Sandy's handshake as a wish-there-were-a-prince-kissing-my-hand kind of gesture, and that dress was too low and too short for any work event. "Careful of this one, Sandy," Joy said, pointing to Todd. "He's in it for himself. It's always about Todd."

Sandy's lashes batted like she wasn't sure whether Joy was kidding.

"Excuse me," Joy said. "I see someone I need to speak with." Thank goodness Renee and her husband had walked in right at the moment she needed a rescue.

She quickly stepped into the tight space between Kevin and Renee, hooking her arms between theirs. "Hey."

"I was looking for you." Renee came to a halt, and hugged Joy. "The office is not the same without you."

"You two look like you should be on top of a wedding cake or something. The perfect couple."

"And you came alone?"

"I did, but you won't believe who I just saw."

"Who?"

"Todd, with one of those young girls."

"I told you he'd do anything to get accounts. I can't believe you used to go out with him."

"How was I so blind?" Joy shrugged it off and turned her attention to Kevin. "How've you been?"

"Great. Heard you had a little fender bender while you were down in Carolina."

"I did, but my friend Ben is hooking me up with a great body guy down there. I'll probably save a ton of money by not getting it fixed up here."

"Except if you'd been here, you probably wouldn't have wrecked in the first place," he teased.

"True." Joy sipped her champagne. "Isn't this place . . . this party . . . elegant? And the architecture is amazing."

"I love all the little details."

"Yeah. Ben has an old house that he's been renovating. You should see it. He even had to have some of the moldings recast in resin to be able to duplicate them. It's just breathtaking."

Kevin stopped a waiter and ordered a drink. "You girls want more champagne?"

"Yes, please," Renee said, and Joy swapped hers out for a fresh glass.

A string quartet played music at one end of the space. As the room filled, the conversations carried in the air like a melody. "It's really beautiful, and the candles and poinsettias on the tables look festive, but it seems odd to have a holiday gala with no Christmas tree," Joy admitted.

"Maybe that's why they don't call it a Christmas gala," Kevin said.

"Just seems weird since one of our biggest accounts is all about Christmas," Joy said.

Renee pointed through the crowd toward a woman in a lovely winter white suit. "And speaking of Christmas. There's Poppy Wetherton."

"She's not afraid to let people know she loves Christmas."

"Cheers to Poppy," Renee said, and clinked her champagne glass to Joy's, then tossed back the rest of the bubbly liquid in one gulp. "Keeping 'em coming, baby," she said to Kevin.

"Boy, both MacDonald and Webber are over there schmoozing Poppy," Renee said.

"She's an amazing businesswoman."

"Sure is." Renee sipped her champagne. "And I love working on the Wetherton's account."

Joy watched the art of negotiating go on across the room. It might be under the guise of a holiday gala, but there was no doubt this was 100 percent business.

Renee broke Joy's concentration. "Did you get everything at Ruby's all decorated?"

Joy nodded. "Yeah, just about. I have a few more things to do when I get back. Ben was a huge help. It really looks pretty. It was actually fun."

"You really like this guy, don't you?" Renee smiled wide.

"Ben?"

"Yes. Ben. The only person you've talked about all night, Ben."

"No. Of course not. I don't even know him. Besides, he's not my type."

"Then why are you talking about him nonstop?"

"I'm not."

"Yes, you are." Renee elbowed Kevin. "She is, isn't she?"

"She is," he said. "Have to say his name has been in about every other sentence."

Renee bobbed her head in agreement. "Yeah. And speaking of types. Was Todd your type? Because frankly, I think he's kind of an ass."

"Well, he wasn't always as bad as he seems now. I don't guess he was my type from the beginning either, though. Todd was . . . convenient. He was really nice when I first met him, and then he turned kind of cutthroat and one-track-minded about his career, not caring about anything or anyone he hurt along the way. But that doesn't mean Ben *is* my type." But was that the point? "I don't even know if I have a type."

"Ben's single, right?"

"Yes."

"You said he's good-looking."

"Very." His dark hair and blue eyes were a tempting combination, and he was more handsome than some of the guys who were paid big bucks to model in some of the ads in their research studies. And she'd be lying if she didn't admit, at least to herself, that her first impression of him was how good he'd looked in that suit.

"And he's nice. And handy. What's the problem?"

Yeah, what is the problem? I've never met anyone quite like Ben. He has it all. He's smart and rugged. Handsome and romantic. "He lives in Crystal Falls."

"Instead of Crystal City, like these folks?" Renee raised her hand in the air, gesturing toward the high-society accents that surrounded them. "Seems like a plus to me."

Kevin interjected. "What's wrong with Crystal Falls?"

"Nothing. It's nice. And actually, you should plan to

bring the family for the Crystal Christmas Cookie Crawl. I think the kids would love it. It's a lighted home tour the Saturday before Christmas. Please come."

"That sounds fun. I've been telling Renee that we need to find something different to do this year. What do you think, honey?"

"Works for me. But . . ." She turned back and glared at Joy. "You quit changing the subject, missy. What's the problem?"

"Accountants aren't my type. Is there a more boring career than accountant?"

"But your Ben sounds anything but boring. I bet when he looks at you, it's not a budget he's got on his mind."

Her insides tingled at the thought of the way Ben looked at her. There wasn't one thing boring about him. In fact, he kept her completely off balance. She kind of liked that. "I don't know."

"Yes, you do. That pause. Right there. Right then. That said it all."

"You're reading too much into that."

"Listen to your heart—you'll always find your way."

"But my job is here. The promotion I've been waiting for so long, and he is down in that little town, and happy to be there."

"Hard as we work, we don't have to settle. There are lots of jobs you're qualified to do. Besides, who says he won't make a change for you? Why are you assuming you are the one who would have to make the sacrifice?"

Kevin kissed Renee on the cheek. "My girl moved here for me."

"We'll just see, I guess."

Kevin winked at Renee and said, "Next thing you know, you'll be married with two kids. You should have seen the Christmas concert at the kids' school yesterday. Too stinking cute. Cassie totally forgot her one line, so Renee shouts it out like she's a ventriloquist."

"Shut up. I'm her mother. I was helping," Renee said, looking anything but apologetic.

"It was great. And as usual, you were the best part," Kevin said with a smile, kissing Renee on the cheek again and then the mouth. "I love this girl."

"I love you too, honey." Renee's eyes flashed. "Don't look now, Joy, but you'll never guess who is headed this way."

"It better not be Todd."

"Nope. Poppy Wetherton."

Poppy Wetherton worked her way through the crowd. Joy was tempted to wave, because it looked like Poppy was heading right toward her. But wouldn't that be one of those awkward moments when you waved only to find out the person was looking at someone else, beyond you? Joy smiled, and to her surprise, Poppy did approach her.

"How are you tonight, Joy? You look absolutely beautiful."

"Thank you."

Poppy turned her attention to Renee. "And Renee. It is Renee, right?"

"Yes, ma'am."

"I see you found an equally beautiful dress. Well done, ladies." Poppy leaned toward Joy. "Could I have just one quick teensy word with you, dear?"

"Of course," Joy said, flashing a what-the-heck look over her shoulder toward Renee as she turned her back on the couple.

Poppy pulled Joy close. "I just want to thank you again for doing such a wonderful job for Wetherton's. I appreciate that."

"Wh—?" But before Joy could get the question out of

her mouth, Poppy Wetherton had breezed away, leaving Joy standing there with her mouth half open. Joy pivoted around to Renee.

"What'd she say?"

"She—"

Someone tapped the side of a glass, and the conversation quieted from a swarming buzz to a soft hum. "Thank you," Jacob MacDonald said. "Webber and I have a couple quick announcements, and then we'll let you get back to enjoying your evening. This celebration is about you, after all."

Everyone clapped.

Renee leaned in. "What was it?"

"I'm not sure." She paused, looking around to see who was within earshot. "I don't think I'm getting this promotion."

Renee looked crushed, and Joy was sure her own expression wasn't hiding much. She swallowed hard and steadied her smile, hoping no one would notice that her lip was quivering. She'd worked so hard for that promotion.

MacDonald droned on, ticking off a list of thank-yous to the who's-who list of execs in the room. Joy was barely listening, wishing she could snag another glass of champagne.

Renee whispered, "This is it."

"We at MacDonald-Webber not only appreciate all of you—our clients, our staff, our partners—but we consider you part of our team too. Tonight I have two promotions I'd like to share with you. As many of you know, John Pinkerton is retiring. We are excited to promote Edward Rose into the position of Director of Market Research and Analytics."

Joy clapped. Ed was a great guy and a whiz with

analytics and all things technical. He'd take that department to new heights.

"And one more promotion. Join me in congratulating Joy Holbrook, as we welcome her to the director table as Director of Focus Groups. And our youngest director."

Joy gulped a mouthful of air. She'd gotten it. Todd stood just to her right. In her periphery, she could see him giving a slow, uninterested clap. He wasn't even happy for her. What a waste of time he'd been.

"Big things are on the horizon here MacDonald-Webber. Thank you, and happy holidays!"

MacDonald stepped down, shaking hands and accepting slaps on the back as he headed for the bar. Joy smiled and accepted the congratulatory remarks from those around her.

"I knew you had it," Renee said.

Then what did Poppy mean?

Renee hugged Joy. "I'm so proud of you."

"Thank you."

"The kids just texted us. It's snowing at our house," Renee said. "We're going to sneak out. We don't want to get stuck in the city if the snow heads this way, and we have a first snowy night tradition of making snow cream."

"Oh my gosh. Condensed milk, vanilla, and snow? My mom used to make that for me too."

Renee laughed. "Are you kidding me? We do chocolate peanut butter snow cream."

"Now, that's worth racing home for." Joy hugged Renee. "I could never have done all of this without you on the team. I can't wait to see what next year brings us."

"Me either."

"Have fun. It was so good seeing you. And think about coming to Crystal Falls for the cookie crawl. It'll be even better if you're there."

"We will. Kevin said he thinks it'll be fun, and he's the driver, so I think you can count on us."

Margie walked over and stood between them. "Am I interrupting?"

"No. Not at all," Renee oozed.

Margie turned her back to Renee, who promptly made a face behind her back and made her exit. "Congratulations, Joy. You deserve that promotion. I hope you don't mind me keeping it a surprise. They wanted me to call and tell you a week ago, but with all you had going on, I thought the surprise would be nice."

It would have been nice to know, but then, Margie's decisions never ceased to surprise her. "Thank you so much."

"We're working on a schedule for some kickoff meetings. I'll let you know as soon as we have the dates and location nailed down. We've got some clever scheduling to do. Turns out we've got quite a bit more work on the horizon. We'll likely be shifting some things around."

"I'm ready." Only honestly, she wasn't sure how she could squeeze out even one more hour in her workweek. She already spent all her time at the office as it was.

"I'm so sorry you missed Lola and Richard's Christmas performance."

Joy held her tongue. Refusing to pretend she'd been sorry to miss it.

Margie rambled on. "Especially sweet Lola. It was simply amazing. I swear it was Broadway caliber. Should have been. We had legitimate staff on board to train everyone for an outstanding performance. I mean we have to give the ticket holders their money's worth, even if it was a fund-raiser."

"I wish I'd thought to have you pick up my tickets. They went unused. Sitting right there on my desk."

"Well, next year. It was heartwarming as a parent to see my children so excited about something. These little shows are so important to a child. Not just fun, but also for growing their character and confidence. I took some pictures. I'll have to show them to you."

"That would be so nice."

Margie went all wide-eyed. "What am I thinking? I have some of them right here on my phone." She whipped out her phone as if it were a magic wand and started scrolling through the pictures.

Joy had to admit, if she hadn't been subjected to the brattiness of Lola and her wicked brother, Richard, she wouldn't believe they were capable of such behavior. Lola looked like a little princess in the costume with layers of tulle and a tiny rhinestone-studded crown. Her thoughts drifted to Molly. She'd looked so disappointed when Joy said she wouldn't be able to go to her Christmas pageant.

"She really looked lovely, Margie." And Joy surprised herself because she wasn't just being polite. "I can tell you're very proud of them."

"Oh, I am. I know I probably spoil them, but I love them so much. They are my whole world." And Margie's eyes glistened as she beamed with pride. "I wouldn't miss one of their shows for anything."

"I bet it means a lot to them that you're there too."

"You can't begin to imagine," Margie said. "I'm surprised that some of the parents don't make time for their children. A child grows up so quickly. Every one of these milestones means something that will affect how they think, act, and treat others later."

Those words held so much meaning.

"Will you excuse me, Margie?"

"Sure. Is—?"

"Everything's fine. There's just something I need to do."
Joy weaved through the crowd and went outside.

"Car, ma'am?"

"Yes, please." She shot a look over her shoulder. She
hoped everyone was so busy that no one would even notice that she'd slipped out.

The valet raised a white glove in the air, and a black
town car pulled in front of the building.

"Thank you," Joy said. She slid into the backseat. "Excuse me. Do you have a pen and a piece of paper?" she
asked the driver.

"Yes, ma'am." He ripped a sheet of paper from a spiral
notebook on the front seat and handed it back to her with
a pen.

"Thank you so much." She started listing all the things
she needed to do. Tonight a lot of things were finally beginning to make sense.

The car slowed to a stop in front of her condo. The
driver got out and came around to open her door.

"Thank you so much," Joy said. "And Merry Christmas."

For once, the elevator was waiting for her. She stepped
inside and pressed the button. It shouldn't take too long to
change into some decent travel clothes, pack up a few
things, and get on the road to Crystal Falls. And she could
make it in time to see Molly in her pageant.

She stepped out of her gown and draped it across the
chair in her bedroom. Once she was packed, she looked
back over at the dress, remembering Molly making a fuss
about how pretty it was. An idea popped into her mind.
Ruby was going to love it. Joy would have someone take a
picture of her in this dress with Molly in her fancy red
dress wearing Ruby's pearls at her side and decoupage it
onto a Christmas ornament. One to remember this year by.

Joy flung the dress over her arm and snagged the shoes

by their straps, then headed out the door with her bags over her shoulder.

She pushed through the door that led to the ground-level parking and got into her car.

If she drove straight through, with no stops, she'd be back in Crystal Falls by early morning and have time to catch a couple hours of sleep before Molly's pageant. Her gas gauge was down below a quarter of a tank, so her first stop needed to be to fill up with gasoline. She pulled into the station near the interstate ramp and got out to pump her gas. She swiped her credit card through the reader, but when she went to pick up the nozzle, a man who looked like he'd just stepped out of an old Western movie stepped in. "I've got this. Get back in your car. It's cold out here."

"Thank you," she said, hesitating only for a moment, because tiny snowflakes had just begun to fall.

The man had one hand pushed into the pocket of his heavy jacket as he filled her tank. A ponytail hung down his back, slightly curling in the damp snow. His mustache wiggled as he spoke, puffing steamy condensation with each breath in the cold night. He patted the back of her car when he was done, and she waved. Thankful for the good deed. *That was so nice.*

She watched him walk off, tall and straight and not looking like he was in much of a hurry. He climbed into a black GMC pickup truck with a livestock trailer behind it. How often did you see that kind of truck, or that kind of guy in this area?

She started her car and pulled away from the pump, just as the guy in the truck started his and all the lights down the side of his shiny aluminum trailer lit up and danced.

"It's Beginning to Look a Lot Like Christmas" played on the radio. Fitting now that the snowflakes were falling at a pretty good pace. She wasn't too worried, though.

She'd probably run out of it the farther south of the city she got.

Three hours later, the adrenaline that had pushed her on the first part of the ride was wearing off just as she crossed the Carolina border. And if she heard "Santa Claus Is Comin' to Town" one more time, she might request they add a toll to Main Street and let the jolly guy pay his way in and out of this town . . . she'd had just about too much of that song by now.

She'd beaten the snow, and even the drizzle through most of Virginia had finally given her a reprieve, but she wasn't sure if she could make the last stretch of the ride. She rolled down the window to get some fresh air, but when the next exit boasted a chain hotel, she gave in to stop and grab just a few hours of rest.

When she got to the counter, a bleary-eyed, gray-haired man greeted her.

"I need a room," she said.

"Got a reservation?"

"No." The parking lot had been practically empty. There was no way the place was full.

He punched a couple of buttons, then slapped a slip of paper up on the counter. "Initial for me. That'll be ninety dollars and twenty cents."

She pushed her credit card across the counter and signed the paper. He traded her for the room key in a pouch. "Free Internet, and breakfast starts at six."

"I'll be out of here before then. I just need a quick nap," she said. "Thank you."

"Sleep well, ma'am."

She'd much rather have been sleeping in the bed at Ruby's house, but there was no sense in risking an accident. The room was nice. Nicer than she'd expected for a random pick just off the interstate. She sprawled out on the bed fully dressed. Just one quick nap, and she'd be back on the road.

All those dreams she'd had of wearing that gown at the fancy gala hadn't proved to be like the night she'd had. And that promotion wasn't nearly so spectacular a moment either. All she wanted right now was to be back in Crystal Falls.

Her body eased a little as she let her attention fall away.

She sat up with a start. She'd almost forgotten to set her alarm. She grabbed for the phone on the nightstand and set her alarm for 5:15, just in case. Even if she slept that long, she should get there before Molly headed off for school. She could surprise her, and Ben too. She wasn't sure which one of them she was more excited to see.

Chapter Thirty

Joy rolled over and stretched. She usually had trouble sleeping away from home, but she'd fallen right to sleep and slept hard. She felt well rested, and that was good. It had to be early, because her alarm hadn't even gone off yet.

She sat up and turned on the light. There was a coffee-pot in the room. If she made a cup of coffee here, she could take it with her and get right on the road. She padded across the room and filled the carafe with water. As she waited, she noticed the reflection of the clock across the room.

No. She turned and got her phone. She'd overslept. How did that happen? She'd set the alarm on her phone.

She quickly poked at the buttons on her phone. The alarm was set. Only she'd set it for 5:15 P.M. instead of in the morning, and right now it was already 5:57. If she hit any traffic on the way back to Crystal Falls, she might not even make it back in time for Molly's pageant.

She left the carafe in the sink. She didn't even bother to wash her face or try to fix her hair. It didn't matter at this point.

Joy cursed herself all the way to the parking lot and back onto the interstate.

To be so close and blow this surprise was just unfair. How had she let this happen? She wanted to surprise Molly.

Traffic through the Raleigh area was heavy, but at least she was still moving. She must've recalculated her arrival time ten times during just the first hour of the drive, but once she got through Raleigh, the roads opened up. She tried to relax, and she set her cruise control to thwart the chance of a ticket. She didn't have time for that.

Molly's pageant was at nine, and when Joy pulled into Ruby's driveway, it was just two minutes after eight. Joy had forgotten to give Molly the pearls to wear today like Ruby had asked. She had time to get the pearls so she could make good on the promise, then quickly change into something appropriate for a school pageant. *Like I have any idea what that is.* She felt like the last runner on a relay as she dropped her bags, hung the dress on a hanger in her old room, then hopped into a pair of slacks.

A quick brush to her hair didn't render good results, so she tugged her hair into a quick side braid. Molly's delighted expression played in her memory with each twist of her hair. She'd been so excited to have her hair braided like Joy's that morning.

She ran out to her car, shoving Ruby's pearls into her coat pocket, and backed out of the driveway. At the only stoplight between here and the school, Joy swept lipstick over her lips.

The parking lot was completely full, so she parked on the street in front of the elementary school. Joy touched the delicate strand of Ruby's pearls in her coat pocket. They'd belonged to Ruby's mother. There were three strands in the set. Ruby wore them together most often, but Joy had carefully detached the long strands and brought just the short one for Molly.

"Excuse me," Joy said. "I'm wondering if you can help me. I have something for my . . . niece." Okay, so one little white lie wasn't that bad, was it? "Can I see her before they perform?"

The dark-haired woman looked like the last thing she wanted to do was be nice or helpful. "The children are nervous. You'll only disrupt things. Can you please just take a seat so we can get started?"

"I won't take but a moment. Please?" Joy hated to beg. "This is really important."

The woman shook her head, and Joy knew exactly where this was going.

The marching sound of little footsteps filled the hall.

Joy turned to see a stair-stepped row of children all wearing red and white coming right toward her. A blond woman with a brilliant smile led the way. She stopped and had the fleet of shiny faces line up down the hall against the lockers. There, third from the end, was Molly.

Joy didn't wait for a response from the grumpy woman. Instead, she bypassed her and went straight over to Molly. *Do the right thing, and ask for forgiveness later* rang through her memory. Someone had once told her that at her first job. And that teensy piece of advice had served her well over the years.

Molly caught sight of Joy, and the smile that danced all the way to that little girl's eyes made tears well in her own.

"Joy!"

"Hey, Molly. I hurried back so I could be here for you."

"I thought you couldn't come."

"I couldn't miss it. Plus, Ruby said she promised you could wear her pearls." Joy pulled the pearls from her pocket and held them between her fingers.

The blond teacher walked toward her. Joy hurried, hoping she wasn't about to get run off.

"Turn around, precious." Joy swallowed and held her focus on Molly, unwilling to let anyone stop her. She carefully slipped the hooked metal piece into the intricately filigreed box clasp, and then connected the safety chain. It was way easier to do on someone else than herself. "All set. Let me see."

Molly spun around, her hands at the neckline of her red velvety dress.

Joy took Molly's hands into her own. "You are going to sing as beautiful as that necklace today."

The teacher stooped down next to Joy. "You look so pretty, Molly."

"She does, doesn't she?" Joy stood and as she did, Molly wrapped her arms around Joy's waist.

"Thank you. I'm so glad you are here. I asked Santa to let you come. You're the best part of this Christmas."

A tear spilled down Joy's cheek, and then another as she stood, trying to collect herself. The teacher dug into her pocket and handed Joy a tissue. "Don't worry. None of us can get through one of these Christmas shows without tears. I think you just made someone's day extra special."

"Thank you," Joy said. "She just made mine. And thanks for not running me off. My aunt had promised Molly she could wear those pearls."

"It's a lovely gesture. We're going to be getting started here in a minute. You might want to grab a seat so you can get a good spot and take a few pictures. They are going to announce no flash photography, but between you and me, you can take a video with your phone and no one will ever know. I know Molly's mom would love that. Oh, and Molly will be at the right end of the stage."

"That's perfect. Thanks." Joy walked down the hall, sweeping her fingers under her eyes. For so many years now, she'd thought only of how hurt she'd been when Mom died. But now she imagined how Molly's mother must feel, missing these moments in her daughter's life and having to trust people in the community to help her through a difficult time. Ruby had been there for her. For Mom too. Now for Ginny and Molly.

Joy walked into the large auditorium and found an empty seat toward the right end of the third row. Funny how people always sat in little groups, leaving empty seats between them. Suited her just fine. She put her phone in airplane mode so she wouldn't be embarrassed by an incoming call, then held it up to test her angle to record Molly's performance.

Excitement sizzled in the air. She sat alone, but her newly awakened sense of life—of community—comforted her. She smiled politely at other parents as they filed into the auditorium. She recognized some of them from the Extreme Gingerbread Bake-off, and the girl from the bakery was seated just one row in front of her toward the middle.

Plink. Plink. Plink-plink. Plink. Plink. Plink-plink. Like horses' hooves, and the pianist got the crowd's attention.

Then, piano music filled the room and quieted the crowd. A tall woman stepped onstage wearing a red dress. "Good morning, friends, faculty, and family members. We are so delighted you've joined us for this year's Crystal Falls Elementary School pageant. We will have a short ten-minute intermission between each performance. This should make it easy for those of you coming to see your children to leave after their performance, and allow others to settle in. We hope you'll help us by always filling in the seats from the center of each row so those later arrivals can slip into the end seats with as little interruption as possible. That being said . . . are we ready to bring a little Christmas joy to our day?"

The parents clapped, and rousing whoops and yips came from the excited kids backstage.

"Our first performance is Miss Allen's first grade."

The curtain opened and about twenty children hobbled out onstage, each dressed in a box that had been decorated like a gift and wearing giant bows on their heads. They grabbed hands and swayed as they sang "Santa Claus Is Comin' to Town." Joy tried to keep her laugh quiet as she lifted her phone and recorded the happy song. It wasn't but a few hours ago that she was about to scream if she'd heard that song again, but somehow those tiny bodies hopping around and bouncing off each other as they reached for each other's hands across the cardboard boxes was too cute. The chorus was strong and loud, most of the rest of the words were a mumbled mess, but the smiles on those kids' faces were undeniably adorable.

Everyone clapped and the children beamed. Joy had to blink to chase the tears that seemed to be teasing her out of nowhere. Since when had she become so sentimental? She didn't even know any of these people.

Parents filed out, and as requested, people moved in toward the center of the aisles, like they'd done it a hundred times. It was a good system. No "excuse me, excuse me" butts in your face as people got up and down.

The piano lady did her thing again and everyone hurried to their seats. Joy had reluctantly followed along in the scoot-in procedure, but thankfully she still had a good spot for when Molly hit the stage.

Just as the curtain began to draw, Ben walked down the aisle and took the seat next to the young woman from the bakery in the row in front of her. Her heart did a giddyup.

The curtain opened and there was a row of tables lined up across the stage.

And then the row of children in all red took the stage behind the tables. Each placed the hand bell they carried in front of them.

Their teacher sat on the floor in front of them and

raised her hands in the air. All eyes were on her. And then the tallest boy in the middle picked up his hand bell and started them off. It took a little while for Joy to finally ascertain that the tune they were playing was "Angels We Have Heard on High."

Before she recognized the song, it was still lovely to listen to, even with the occasional pause as one kid missed his cue and another waited or grunted at them to take action, which of course had sparked rousing giggles from the crowd. But Molly had hit every cue. And she looked adorable.

As the audience applauded, the kids marched around the tables and stood in front of them. Just as Molly had indicated in her little practice session at Ruby's, she was at the right end of the stage. She looked precious in her bright red dress.

Joy hitched a breath as she watched Molly raise her hand to her neck, toying with the pearls. *What a special moment.* Joy took out her phone to record.

She'd been so enthralled that she'd forgotten to take even one picture during the bell performance.

The choreography kept the kids on tempo and cue as they belted out the words to "Rudolph, the Red-Nosed Reindeer."

At the end of the song, someone in a reindeer suit with a red flashing nose ran across the stage. It must have been a surprise to the kids onstage because they were all jumping like they'd really seen Santa's favorite helper.

It was right then that she had the best idea yet for Ruby's house during the Crystal Christmas Cookie Crawl.

Joy got up and started edging her way to the end of the row to see if she could catch Molly on her walk back down the hall to tell her how wonderful she was. She kept her eye on Ben. She didn't think he'd seen her. It was going to be fun to surprise him. This morning, there were no shadows across her heart. She was excited to see him. To see where things might actually lead, even if just for a short while.

When she got to the end of her aisle, she politely let the next three people by, then reached her hand out to touch Ben's arm. "Hey, there." Her smile was so wide that she probably looked as excited as the kids onstage had.

"Joy?"

"I made it back. I left early." She sidled up next to him and let the slow crowd push them out toward the hall. "Wasn't Molly amazing? That was so cute. I didn't know you were coming today."

"Yeah, well, when she told me about it, I thought it would be nice."

"Thank you so much for seeing her off to school. Isn't she sweet?" Joy caught the movement of the red-outfitted group coming down the hall. "There she is." She rushed over to the side and waved to Molly. Several parents were hugging and talking to their kids. Joy moved in. "I'm so proud of you. You were perfect."

"Thank you! I'm so glad you came."

"I'm so glad I could be here. Ben's here too."

Ben waved from across the way.

Molly waved, and then the teacher was herding her little kittens into a line to get them back to their class. "No more school until after the holidays."

She'd miss her little morning time with Molly. She'd even begun to look forward to those PBJ crusts for breakfast.

Joy walked back over to where Ben stood watching. "What an amazing day," she said. "I think I'm going to stick around and record a couple of the other classes' performances. Ruby might enjoy seeing these."

"Good idea."

"I'm so sad we missed coffee Sunday night."

"Really?"

"Yes, really. Of course, really." She laughed, but there was something in his look that didn't seem right. "Is something the matter?"

He rubbed his hand over the scruff on his chin. "I don't know if this is the place for this conversation."

The piano sounded from inside the hall. "I'm going to record the next one. You gonna stay?"

"I need to get back to work."

"Oh, well, okay. I'll see you at Ruby's tonight, then?"

"Yeah. We still have a few things to get done." Ben hitched his thumb toward the door. "I'm going to get going."

Joy waved and went back inside the auditorium to grab an open seat as close to the front as she could. She not only recorded the next one, but also ended up staying until the last performance of the day. It had been so much fun that she'd completely lost track of time, and she couldn't wait to share the videos.

She stopped and picked up a large pizza from Max's so she and Ben would have something to munch on while they worked tonight. It was hard to believe that the Crystal Christmas Cookie Crawl was just three days away.

When she got back to Ruby's, Ben's truck was in the driveway. She pulled in behind him and carried the pizza over to where she'd planned to serve the hot chocolate on Saturday. "You've almost gotten everything done without me. I thought you might save it for us to work on together when I got back."

He climbed down the ladder. The huge wreath on the barn looked prettier than she'd hoped. You could see the details so nicely even from down here. "Didn't know what kind of time you'd have."

"Is something wrong? You don't seem like yourself."

"Maybe we don't know each other as well as we thought."

What does that even mean? "I don't understand."

"I met your fiancé."

She hesitated, blinking, baffled at the accusation. "My who?" What was he talking about? She searched her mind for what in the world he could possibly mean, and then Todd's face popped into her mind. "I am not engaged. Have *never* been engaged."

"Well, that's not what the pretty boy in the souped-up car seems to think. And y'all looked right cozy after the awards."

"There is nothing between us," she said.

"I saw the kiss. That wasn't nothing."

"It's not what you think."

"No?"

"He just showed up. I didn't know he was coming. I didn't kiss him. And I can promise you that we're not engaged."

"Engaged or not, I know what I saw. It was pretty clear you two are involved." He turned and walked away, carrying the ladder.

But explaining the shallow relationship wasn't going to earn her any points either. She felt ashamed and disappointed, and at a loss for how to fix it. She watched Ben as he went back into the barn and hung the ladder on the wall.

He wouldn't look at her as he walked back toward her. "By the way, Ruby called me today. They're letting her out of rehab tomorrow."

"I wonder why she didn't call me?" She pulled her phone out of her purse. "My phone is still in airplane mode. I totally forgot." She had six missed calls, but none of them were from her aunt.

"She knew you had gone back home," he said. The word "home" catching as he said it. "I don't think she knew when you were coming back."

"Well, I was coming back." Did he really think she wasn't ever coming back?

"Todd said he was in town to whisk you away to the company gala, and I believe he called it a 'ridiculously expensive romantic getaway from the catastrophe people call Christmas.'"

"Sounds like something he'd say."

"Not my place to judge," he said, but clearly he was judging. "I'll pick up Ruby tomorrow."

Joy didn't like where any of this was going. "I can pick up my aunt."

He looked at her, and she could see that he was hurt. "I like to be true to my word."

"Ben. I have been true to my word with you. I am not seeing Todd. We have had casual dates over the past couple of years; I'm not even sure I'd call them dates. He was a coworker. Two people with nothing more in common than work. We hadn't even spoken in weeks. He just wanted to go to the gala, and since he left our company, he thought he could worm his way in on my coattails."

"I saw the way he was looking at you while you were up there on the stage."

"There's nothing there. He's a player. He's like that with everyone."

"All it takes is a mere whisper to spark a flame. Sometimes old flames run hot."

"He was never a flame. Never any whispers. We were never engaged. I don't know what you think you saw, but it was nothing. What you saw was not a kiss. He tried to kiss me. But I didn't kiss him back. There's nothing there. It's not what you think."

"It's not my business."

"Maybe I want it to be." Only she hadn't meant to say that out loud. But there. She'd said it.

He turned and looked at her. His expression softening, then a cloud passed over his eyes. "Don't."

She shrugged. She wasn't even sure what she was feeling right now. Her emotions were cluttered with kindness, and kids, and Ben. So full of Ben. Everything she'd fought so hard for over the past ten years suddenly seemed to be turned on its ear. She glanced up at the starry night sky.

"Don't make promises you can't keep," he said. "I really like you. I don't play games of the heart. So, don't." He headed to his truck.

"Ben."

He stopped, but didn't turn around.

She gathered all the courage she had. "I like you. I don't know what I can promise. My job is back in D.C. I don't even know what it is you want from me."

"I don't know either. I was intrigued. Interested. I am incredibly attracted to you. You are smart and funny, and Lord knows you're beautiful to look at." He turned and took a step toward her. "I just wanted something honest. I liked spending time with you and Molly the other night. That felt real to me."

But she wasn't cut out to be a mom. She wasn't a small-town, stay-at-home, cookie-baking kind of woman. Or at least she thought she wasn't. She was confused. So she stood there. Without a word. Because the last thing she wanted to do was say something she'd regret.

He lifted his hand in the air and waved.

"I'll pick up Ruby tomorrow," she called out.

"Fine."

"Will you please be here Saturday with us?"

He opened the door of his truck and stepped up on the running board. "I promised Ruby. So, I'll be here this weekend."

Because you'd never let anyone down. How can I ever live up to that?

Chapter Thirty-one

Joy's Prius had done more hauling in the last couple of weeks since she'd been in Crystal Falls than any one Prius should in its lifetime. And Ruby's one bag of belongings had turned into a cart of flowers and gifts from the community that had accumulated into quite a haul. The backseat of Joy's car was filled, and balloons blocked the entire rear window. Joy got behind the wheel and waited for the last of the rehab team as they each took their turn hugging her aunt and exchanging Merry Christmases.

Do they treat every patient like this?

Somehow she doubted it. Her aunt always left a happy wake behind her.

Finally Johnny helped Ruby into the front seat and gave her a peck on the cheek. "You're my favorite patient from the whole year, Miss Ruby."

"If I were just fifty years younger," Ruby said with a giggle. Johnny slammed the door shut, and Ruby gave one last wiggly-fingered wave to the staff at Dixon County Rehab Center. "That was exhausting."

Joy pulled slowly away from the curb. "What? The good-byes?"

"That too, but I was talking about all that physical therapy. I feel like I'm ready for the Senior Olympics."

"I'm sure we could work something out. Knowing you, you'd land a major sponsorship. But let's just be happy with you being in good enough shape to get around at home first. You ready for that?"

Ruby patted Joy's hand. "Yes. I'm more than sure. I've been a good patient. I'm getting around fine, but a gal my age needs her routine." She leaned over and whispered, "And I really miss my naps!"

"It'll be so nice to spend time with you at home."

"The pictures look good, and I promise I trust what you and Ben have done, but I'm dying to see the place. Do you think we're ready?"

"You're going to love it, and I can't wait for you to see it at night all lit up. I almost wish I could keep you away until you could see it all lit up first."

"Don't you dare lollygag. I'm ready to be home. Trust me, I'll be able to tell. Besides, Ben is amazing. He would never let us down."

Might never let you *down. Me? Another story.*

But Joy kept that thought to herself. No sense stirring the pot.

As they got closer to home, Joy's palms began to sweat. Nervous over whether she'd make Ruby proud with the decorations, her mind suddenly came up with at least four more ideas for things she could've done to make it even more spectacular. But the truth was, there really hadn't been time. She hoped Ruby would like what she'd done.

"Close your eyes," Joy said.

Ruby squeezed her eyes shut, then placed her wrinkly hands over them.

Joy turned into the driveway. "Hope you're ready."

Ruby dropped her hands and looked around. Twisting from the front to the side and back again. "Oh my word!

You've moved things around." Ruby slapped at Joy's arm. "Slow down. I want to see every little thing."

Joy stopped the car.

"Look what you've done." Ruby pointed to the tree with the PICK AN ORNAMENT—HANG AN ORNAMENT sign next to it. The clear cube she'd made from just four pieces of Plexiglas she'd picked up at the hardware store and siliconed together sat under that sign, and those old ornaments that filled it to the brim really sparkled in the sunlight. It didn't even matter that some of them were so scratched, they'd probably never make it on a tree inside again, they'd just found a new purpose.

She kind of felt like those ornaments this year. Like she'd been damaged and scuffed, but was finding a new purpose. Finally.

"Everything is amazing. It's like Mother Nature came and decorated herself."

Joy smiled all the way from her heart. "That's exactly what I was going for. And we're going to serve the hot chocolate out here in the barn. And there's a big surprise for that. And I'm keeping that to myself until the official night. But it's pretty, isn't it? Nature's Bounty. That was my theme."

"You've nailed it. Now, park and get me inside. I can't wait to see the rest."

Joy pulled her car right up to the front door so she could limit the number of steps Ruby had to take. She got out and went around to help her aunt out of the car, and tears were streaming down Ruby's face.

"Aunt Ruby? What's the matter?"

"Honey, you've done such a great job here. All of this for me. It's so beautiful." She could barely choke out the words.

"I've enjoyed every minute of it. Really. It's been so

good for me. Inspiring in so many ways. I cannot even begin to explain what being here has done for me."

Ruby swept at the tears and got out of the car. She hugged Joy, clinging to her for a long minute, then steadied herself until Joy set out the walker they'd sent home with her.

"I hate that old-lady gadget."

"It's just until you get steady."

Ruby grabbed the sides of the walker as if she were getting ready to toss a steer to the ground and hog-tie it, then moved toward the door. "Won't be for long, then I'll donate it to the old-folks' home." She made her way up the sidewalk, and Joy helped her up the stairs. Ruby steadied herself against the porch wall as she reached out to touch the wreath. "I love what you've done, Joy. It's the prettiest wreath I've ever had."

Satisfaction rolled through Joy. She'd wanted so badly to please Ruby. "Thank you. It's made from stuff you already had. So in a way, we did it together. When I saw the white peacock wreath and tree you'd done that one year, I was so inspired. So I decided everything would be natural . . . except the lights, of course. The bleached pinecones looked so pretty in contrast to the soft feathers."

"You're right. The textures are perfect."

"I was so excited when I found the paper ribbon in the attic. It was like it was meant to go together."

Joy pushed the front door open. She'd left all the tree lights on so Ruby could get the full effect.

Ruby glanced at Joy with a quirky lift at the corner of her mouth that let Joy know she was happy. She raised her hands to her mouth and then laughed. "It's magical. Wonderful. Beautiful."

"I wanted it to be."

She peeked into the dining room at the tree there and

then walked up to the tree in the living room. "It's funny you picked out these ornaments."

"They're perfect. They look hand-carved."

"They are. Each a real piece of art," Ruby said. "You don't know the story behind these ornaments."

Ruby always had a story. Joy sat on the stair to listen.

"These were your mother's ornaments."

Joy sat up straight. "They were?"

"Yes. Her first true love gave them to her. He'd made each ornament, and each day the box seemed that much more meaningful as the entire Twelve Days of Christmas story came to life through them."

"Not my dad."

"Heavens no. I knew he was a mistake all along." Ruby lifted one of the ornaments from the tree and turned it over to the signature. "See here," she said. "Well, you can't really read it, but it says J. O. Young. She never admitted it, but I know that was why she named you Joy. After her first real love. She'd been so happy with Joe. He got a scholarship because of his art. And while he was away, your mom met your dad. I don't know that they ever saw each other again. But these ornaments were precious to her."

"They're beautiful. I don't remember them, but no wonder I was drawn to them."

Ruby hung the ornament back on the tree. "You and Ben must've really worked well together too." Ruby nodded her head again, with a knowing arch of the brow. "I kind of knew you two would hit it off."

"He was very helpful," Joy admitted.

"Ben can do anything. He's a lot like George was in that way." Ruby got through the doorway and settled into the chair in the living room, propping her cast up on the ottoman. "Maybe Ben is your one true love. Like George was for me."

"I don't think that's ever going to happen for me."

"Don't say that. Of course it will. You are a beautiful, brilliant young woman. You could have your pick of men. And Ben *is* handsome."

Joy had to admit Ruby had good taste in men. "He is handsome. No doubt about that." And understanding. What other man wouldn't have had a fit when she crashed into his truck?

"And kind," Ruby added.

"Very."

"And he likes you. I know him. I could tell the day you two came to the rehab center together."

"Ruby, he wants a hometown girl who wants a family. That's not me."

"It could be."

The thought scared her, although she could almost picture standing next to Ben on a Sunday morning at church with a child standing between them. But that was just silly. The night baking with Ben and Molly had been fun, but that was just a fleeting moment. And Molly wasn't her child. With her luck, she'd get one of those bratty nonreturnable ones. "I don't know if I want children. And it wouldn't be fair to Ben. I'm not sure I could ever love the way you loved Uncle George."

"Why? What would even make you think that?"

"Because love can hurt. Even perfect love like yours was with Uncle George. It comes to an end, and that hurts. I don't ever want to hurt like I did when Mom died."

"Honey, you can't live your life afraid of loss. True love outweighs the hurt. I promise you that."

"I wouldn't even know where to begin."

"Just relax. Let it happen." Ruby scooted over in the oversized chair. "Honey, here's the thing." She patted the seat next to her. "Come sit down."

Joy squeezed next to her in the chair.

"By protecting yourself, you may be lucky and never feel that kind of hurt again, but it's doubtful. You can't hide from it. Unfortunately, life is full of loss and hurt. It's a never-ending cycle, and we can't stop that. But by protecting yourself, you are shortchanging your own chances at true happiness. The 'joy' your mother wanted for you. And cheating yourself out of true love. You can't have true love if you never let anyone get close."

"I can't help it. My guard automatically goes up."

"Then manually break it down. Open your heart. Friendships and love require risk, but nothing is more precious. It's worth it. I promise."

"Maybe I was just meant to succeed in my career, not in personal relationships."

"Maybe. Who am I to say what your destiny is. Only one person knows that. But I've seen some differences in you over the past couple of weeks. Your mother would be happy to see you soften. I think it's been good for you to be back home."

"It's been nice."

"Then it was worth me taking a little fall."

Joy leaned back in the chair and reached for Ruby's hand. "I'm going to miss this place."

"Then don't go."

Joy laughed. "My whole life is up in D.C. My job. My condo. I can't stay. But I will visit more often. I promise."

"You can do whatever you really want to do. There are always choices. And other career options. Keep that in mind. Know what's in your heart."

"How am I supposed to know what's in my heart?"

"Where does your mind wander? When you really relax and let everything fall away, what's left?"

"I don't know if I've ever relaxed long enough to know."

"Maybe it's time you tried." Ruby pulled an afghan over her legs. "Think about it."

"My mind always goes straight to work." Joy closed her eyes. "But now there are other things that are getting my attention as well."

"Like what?"

"You. Molly. Ben." Joy's eyes popped open. "That darn Ben. He is in every other one of my thoughts, and not all of them are even good. He makes me a little crazy with his kick-back attitude. Nothing is ever a problem. He never gets riled up."

"But?"

"He's a good man," Joy said. "He cooked me dinner while you were in the hospital."

Ruby sat quietly.

"We had fun decorating this place."

"You didn't make it easy on him, but he kept trying. He really does enjoy helping people. It's just who he is."

"I'm used to doing things alone. I'm not used to collaborating with a stranger."

"Wasn't so bad, was it?"

"No. But, Ruby, Ben and I are so different."

"Not so different as you might think."

"It seems as if he thinks I'm someone I'm not. He sees me as the girl baking cookies with a seven-year-old, and decorating for Christmas. That's not me. I'm the girl who hasn't celebrated Christmas since I lived here with you. I'm the girl who bought a dress that cost more than my mortgage for an office party. That's frivolous. I've never wanted children. I'm not the partner he wants. Or deserves."

"You did great with Molly."

"She's different."

"No. She's a lot like you were when you were a little

girl. There's something you might not know about me. About the reason George and I didn't have children."

"I just assumed you couldn't."

"No. I never wanted children, and George and I self-ishly loved our time together. I always thought that I was happy with that decision, but my little sister had you. Honey, you changed my world. And I wouldn't trade my relationship with Ginny and Molly for anything. They've brought such meaning to this old lady's life. So maybe you won't have your own children, but you can still touch others' lives."

Maybe that was true. Or maybe someday she would have children of her own, but there'd been so much to take in lately that she suddenly felt unsure of things that she'd once thought she had all figured out. Joy got up. "Well, you probably need one of those power naps you've been miss-ing. And if we keep talking about this heavy subject, I'm liable to need one too."

Ruby stood and walked slowly through the room.

"You are getting around really well."

"Thank you, dear. Johnny would be so happy to hear that."

"Ruby, I thought I'd invite Ginny and Molly to help us with the baking over the next couple of days. Do you think Ginny would be up to it?"

"That's a wonderful idea. And Molly's on school break."

"What's wrong with Ginny? Is she—?"

The look on Ruby's face let Joy know that she'd just realized what Joy had been thinking all along. "Oh, honey, Ginny's not dying. It's a rough patch, and a jerk of an ex-husband, and a lot for a single mother to handle, but she's going to be just fine. She and Molly both will be fine."

"Thank goodness. I was worried."

"She's got a chronic kidney disease. It flares up once in a while, but she's got great doctors. It's not life threatening. Sometimes she just has to get a lot of treatments, and whenever those times happen to come around . . . I'll be here to help her."

"She's so lucky to have you."

"I'm lucky to have them too." Ruby headed for her bedroom. "Will you bring me my phone and my purse?"

"Sure." Joy collected Ruby's things and set them on her dresser, then went out to the car and started relocating all the gifts, flowers, and balloons. While Ruby rested, Joy started to work on cookies. They had only tonight and the next two days to get all the baking done. On paper that looked doable, but to actually consider getting it all done felt a bit overwhelming.

She pulled out the frozen sticks of chocolate chip cookie dough. She'd start with the quick ones that didn't require a garnish or decorating of any kind. At least she'd feel like she'd accomplished something.

The evening rushed by, and she had nibbled on enough cookie dough that she didn't care for any dinner, and Ruby had slept right on past it anyway.

At close to midnight, Joy had baked all twelve dozen cookies, and cooled and packed them away. The kitchen was spotless and ready for production tomorrow.

She peeked in on Ruby, who seemed to be sleeping comfortably, so she turned off the Christmas tree lights and then climbed the stairs to go to bed. The tree at the top of the stairs made the tiny beads on her dress sparkle from across the hall. She turned off those tree lights and went to bed, wishing her happiness were as easy as turning those lights off and on.

The next morning Joy woke to the smell of cookies coming from the kitchen. She should've known Ruby wouldn't take it easy. She turned over to get out of bed and was greeted with a joyous, "Surprise!"

"Molly?"

"Hi! Ruby invited me and Mom to help bake cookies."

Joy grabbed Molly and tugged her onto the bed. "And you are the best cookie helper around," she said as she tickled a squealing, wiggling Molly.

Breathless, Molly jumped off the bed. "Come on. You're missing out."

Joy got up and changed into a pair of jeans and T-shirt. With her hair pulled into a ponytail, she followed Molly downstairs. Ginny and Ruby were talking and working side by side at the kitchen table.

"Joy Holbrook reporting to duty, Mrs. Claus."

Ruby playfully shook a finger at her. "About time. Thought Santa was going to have to put you on the naughty list for being a sleepyhead."

Molly's lips bunched. "We're here. No naughty lists!"

"I'll put in a good word for her if you say so," Ruby whispered to Molly.

"Yes, please!"

And for two days, it was a well-paced bake-off in the Ruby Johnson house with Ruby, Joy, Ginny, and Molly working together.

On Friday night, all the cookies had been transferred into assorted trays that could be easily unwrapped and re-freshed throughout the Crystal Christmas Cookie Crawl.

Molly tapped on Ruby's elbow. "I'm going to wear my Christmas pageant dress tomorrow, Ruby. Would it be okay if I wear the pearls one more time?"

"Of course, dear. I'd love to see you in your official outfit. It's a very special occasion."

Molly turned and looked at Joy. "Are you going to wear your princess gown?"

"I'd love to see you both all dressed up," Ruby said.

"Please?" Molly pressed her hands together into a praying position. "It's so pretty."

"She's talking about the gown I bought for the gala," she explained to Ruby and Ginny. "Tell you what, Molly. If we can get our picture taken together, I'll wear it."

Ginny smiled gently as her daughter jumped with excitement.

"Molly has talked about the green princess dress nonstop. We have to see it."

"Can I go get it?" Molly asked. "Pleeeaaaase?"

"Go on." Joy wondered if Molly would even be able to reach it, but just a moment later, Molly was standing in the doorway holding the gown draped over her two arms like she was afraid she might wrinkle or, worse, drop it.

"Beautiful," Ginny said.

"Stunning. Hold it up," Ruby ordered.

Joy took the dress from Molly and held the bodice up to her. It still made her feel elegant today just holding it up.

"You have to wear it. No question about it," Ruby said.

Ginny said, "I agree. You have to. It's as pretty as the decorations. What a treat."

"Thank you." That fancy gown was a little over the top for the Christmas lighting, but it would be fun to dress up one more time. It wasn't like she got the chance to do that very often.

Molly jumped in excitement. "We'll be the prettiest girls around."

Chapter Thirty-two

On Saturday afternoon, by two o'clock, the entire farm was ready. Every decoration was in its precise place. The hot chocolate stand was stocked with volunteers scheduled to serve during the Crystal Christmas Cookie Crawl. The cookies were stacked high, ready to serve, and Joy was as excited as a kid on Christmas morning.

Shirley had already stopped by, and Joy was afraid for a moment she might have to revive the woman because she was so excited. She must've really been sweating it that Joy wouldn't come through.

Joy helped Ruby get ready first. Getting her in and out of the shower wasn't the easiest thing to maneuver, but they'd managed to do it. The outfit Ruby had bought to wear this year wasn't going to work. The pants, even though they were wide-legged and flowing, wouldn't fit over her boot. Instead, they'd found a pretty Christmas dress in the back of Ruby's closet that would be perfect for the night's event.

Showered and ready to get dressed, Joy twisted a wisp of hair that had escaped her braid into a soft spiral. She applied her makeup with a light hand. Nature's Bounty was the theme of the decorations, and that should go for her too. Her gown was the color of the forest in the summer. It kind of worked.

She stood in her childhood bedroom, feeling more at peace than she ever had. She stepped into the dress and pulled up the zipper. *I wish you were here with me today, Mom.*

"But you are. Aren't you?" she said to her reflection. "Please help me be the person you wanted me to be."

She finished getting dressed and then picked up her phone to go downstairs. She paused, and placed her phone back on the nightstand. *I don't need my phone on a night like this.*

She traversed the steps with a feeling of freedom from leaving the phone behind. Tonight it would be all about family and friends.

The doorbell rang.

"I'll get it." Joy stepped on the button for the tree lights as she walked by and then opened the door. "Renee?"

Renee and Kevin stood there. Between them, their daughters, who were pint-sized replicas of Renee, wore dresses in red and green.

"I can't believe you're really here."

"You said we couldn't miss it," Kevin said.

The girls looked excited. Renee said, "We've had the best day. It was a beautiful day for a drive. Kevin surprised us with reservations at the inn in town. We got here about two hours ago."

"And he packed all our pretty clothes," one of Renee's daughters explained.

"You look beautiful," Joy said. "Come in!"

"Crystal Falls is amazing," Renee said.

"It's like Santa's Village," Cassie said. Hanna nodded in agreement. "It's sparkly."

Kevin looked so proud of his girls. "We've got tickets for the whole thing, but we wanted to see you first. We'll stop by here at the end of the night."

"Perfect. I'm so glad to see you."

Cassie and Hanna stood in front of the tree in the living room. "It's the Twelve Days of Christmas, Mom."

"These are beautiful," Renee said about the handmade ornaments. "I've never seen anything like them."

"They were a gift to my mother a long time ago."

Ruby came into the room.

"This is my best friend, Renee," Joy said to her aunt. "And her family. Kevin, Cassie, and Hanna."

"You've come to Crystal Falls at the right time. Everyone looks forward to this event."

"We're so glad you told us about this."

Joy watched the happy family jog back out to their SUV. She'd never seen Renee in total mom mode. They made a beautiful family. Joy was surprised that she felt a little twinge of jealousy.

It wasn't long before guests lined the entire walkway up to Ruby's house. It was official: the Crystal Christmas Cookie Crawl had begun. The first group was always reserved for VIP ticket holders and sponsor families.

Joy's nerves were as tight as the lights strung across the fence line as she stood at her place in the dining room. Ruby was happy, and although that was her goal, she also knew how important this was to her best friend, Shirley. Suddenly that mattered to Joy too.

Next to Joy, Molly held Ginny's hand as they stood at the chocolate cookie station. Joy had decided to move all the decorated and fun-shaped cookies out to the barn with the hot chocolate, and the more decadent chocolate treats in here for casual adult conversation near the trees.

Someone raised a handheld set of jingle bells overhead and shook them. It sounded a lot like Joy imagined Santa's reindeer would sound as they flew in for a landing on the roof. Kids bounced with excitement, couples hung close, and families bunched together.

As Joy stood near the window, she heard remarks from the people waiting outside.

"The bright red door has never looked prettier."

"Look how the trio of wreaths glisten under the porch lights."

"Are those white pinecones and peacock feathers? So pretty."

Ruby swung open the front door, welcoming the crowd into her home.

Buckets of pinecones and cinnamon graced each side of the front door, adding a "scent-sation" as visitors entered.

Ben pulled off his tie, threw it in the glovebox, and unbuttoned his top button. Why the heck was he so worried about how he looked tonight? He wasn't that kind of guy, but maybe it was less about how he looked and more about stalling.

He'd been in a push-and-pull all day with himself about seeing Joy tonight. The joke would be on him if he spent all this time freaking out and when he got there, she'd already hauled her little eco-friendly car back to the big city. He drove over to the train depot, where the Crystal Christmas Cookie Crawl would kick off. Most of the people would start at this spot on the route. It's where all the booklets were distributed and shuttle buses made the route for those not in good enough shape to enjoy the festivities on foot. Ruby's place was the farthest out. Most people would use the bus or one of the tractor-driven hayrides between the depot and Ruby's house tonight.

His grandmother was zipping around like someone had

wound her up, giving last-minute orders and placing final touches on the snack table that the women's club had put together for this stop.

"Ben. You are a lifesaver." Shirley left a big lipstick kiss on his cheek.

Ben looked suspicious. "What do you need?"

"Not a thing. I went over to Ruby's this afternoon. You saved me. The place looks better than it ever has before. You've outdone yourself."

"I helped, but most of the credit goes to Joy. The theme, the plan . . . that was all Joy."

Shirley looked surprised.

"Really," Ben said. "She ran this project. Came up with the theme. Had a very specific project plan for the whole thing. I was just the muscle."

"Even the live nativity?" Shirley asked.

"Even that. I helped with the people, and we used the costumes we had in storage at the hospital, but that was entirely her idea."

Shirley's expression grew openly amused. "I may have misjudged her."

You and me both.

He watched as his grandmother kicked off the annual event. It was the highlight of her year, and she took it very seriously. Once the first three sets of visitors made their way down the tour path, lit by garland-strung sawhorses and red and green flashing lights, Ben decided he'd pay his visit to Ruby and get it over with.

When he got there, people were already lined up down the sidewalk.

A huge sheet had been hung on the side of the barn to form a makeshift projection screen, and the elementary school performances of Christmas songs were playing on a loop, bigger than life-size. Parents stood in awe, and kids pointed at their friends. What a great idea. Joy had really outdone herself on that one.

He walked inside, falling into step with the others, seeing the decorations through their eyes, and trying to forget some of his interactions with Joy. Some of them good, some not so much. At the very top of the tree in the living room that was supposed to hold only the Twelve Days of Christmas ornaments, something caught his eye.

The tree told a story. And only one thing was different. At the very top, the ornament he'd made for Joy hung from the highest limb. A place of honor. His heart pulsed.

When he turned around, Joy stood nearby in the dining room, next to Molly. Joy was dressed in the fancy green gown, and his heart forgot every doubt he'd had about her as he watched her standing next to Molly, looking so beautiful. Joy's hair hung in a soft side braid. He longed to touch it, and Molly's hair was styled the same way, only there was tinsel woven in the little girl's braid.

Joy moved with ease through the room, talking to neighbors and laughing. She was even prettier when she was relaxed. This woman, the one he could see his whole life with, would be gone soon. And there wasn't anything he could do about that.

"My Handy Andy!"

Ben turned and met Ruby's bright lipsticked smile. Her arms were raised above her head. "Gimme a hug, sugar. You always come through for me."

"You didn't need me. Joy had everything under control."

"I know it was a team effort. And as beautiful as everything looks, I'll tell you what makes me even happier tonight."

"What's that?"

"Seeing my niece take joy in something—and maybe someone—aside from work."

Someone? Had Todd worked his way back into the picture over the last two days? Do I even want to know? "I love what she did with the videos from the school pageant."

Ruby's head cocked to one side. "I'm not sure I know what you're talking about."

"I can't believe she hasn't shown you yet." Ben led Ruby outside, holding her at the elbow to steady her gait, but she was getting around well.

"Ben?"

Ruby and Ben turned around. Joy stood there, looking beautiful and nervous.

"Hi. I was just showing Ruby the pièce de résistance— the videos of the elementary school pageant."

Joy gestured toward the barn. "It was so much fun. I taped Molly's performance so you and Ginny could see it, then I had the idea of using it here so there'd be live caroling."

"Bravo!" Ruby raised her hands in the air. "I love it. The whole town will love it!"

"I hope they'll sing along."

Ruby took Joy's hand. "Well, let's get them started. Shall we?"

Thank goodness he knew all the words to this one. "Frosty the snowman was a jolly happy soul."

And when he turned to look at Joy, she was staring at him.

"You've made me so happy these last few days," she said. "When I left, Ben, I missed you."

He took her hand into his and joined back in with the carol.

Words weren't necessary.

And before they knew it, the crowd was joining in.

Chapter Thirty-three

Renee came up to Joy and pulled her aside. "Did you get that text?"

Joy patted her hip, not that she ever kept her phone there, but it was always nearby . . . except for tonight. "What text? My phone is upstairs. Why?"

"I hate to spoil a perfect night, but our friends at MacDonald-Webber have decided that we need to start kickoff meetings next week. Monday and Tuesday before Christmas and then follow up all day Monday and Tuesday before New Year's."

"What? But most everyone is scheduled out."

"Not anymore."

"But . . ." She'd probably have been the one suggesting that schedule in the past, but this year she wanted to spend time with Ruby. Maybe even through the entire holiday. She wasn't even sure what she felt. Angry? Disappointed? Conflicted?

"We lost the Wetherton's account," Renee said. "I think they're freaking out a little."

"Really? I hadn't heard about the Wetherton's account." Joy's thoughts went to what Poppy had said the night of the gala. She was relieved that the loss of the contract was not a reflection of her work on it, but who knew how MacDonald-

Webber would seé it? She wondered how this might impact her promotion. Clearly there'd be a shift in responsibilities, without Wetherton's filling a good portion of her plate.

"I can't believe they're going to make you work. That's ridiculous. Like things couldn't wait one more week?"

"I'm sure they have their reasons." She'd have agreed with them just a few weeks ago.

Renee squeezed Joy's hand. "When I saw that text, I thought you might be upset. I've got to run. Kevin is going to take us around to the other houses. I'll see you at the end of the night, okay?"

"Sure," Joy said, her smile fading. She walked around through the barn and stepped outside through the back sliding doors to the pasture. The darkest part of the yard.

She was happy here. Happy to be with Ruby. Enjoying the small-town camaraderie. Things were changing for her. Molly and Ben had profoundly changed who she was, or who she thought she was.

What do you think about all of this, Mom?

Joy closed her hand as if she were holding Mom's again. She closed her eyes. *Help me be the person you always wanted me to be, Mom. Let me bring joy to others. I want a richer life—full of family, community, and maybe even love—things that money can't buy. I just want to matter to someone. I want to find my one true love like Ruby did with Uncle George. The other half that completes me.*

Suddenly Joy heard Ben's voice. "I have something to say."

She opened her eyes and turned to him. "Oh, Ben. No. You don't—"

He placed a finger on her lips. "Stop arguing with me."

She closed her mouth, the corners of her lips turning slightly upward. "Sorry."

"You matter to me. Spending time with you isn't easy

at all sometimes, but it holds my attention. And I like it. I like you. A lot."

She tilted her head, taking in the many facets of this handsome man in front of her. He certainly was handy, great with numbers, and thoughtful. Who knew you really could get all those things in one package?

His smile was gentle. "I'm going to miss you when you go back to the city for that big promotion."

She ran her hands down her gown. "I'm not."

"Not what? Not getting the promotion? I thought it was kind of a sure thing."

"It was. It is." She shrugged. "But I don't think it's what I really want anymore."

"You okay?" Ben placed his hand on her cheek. Looking into her eyes for the truth.

She nodded her head slowly. "Surprisingly, I am. I thought I wanted that so badly, but today, tonight, right now, it doesn't seem quite so important."

He pulled her into his arms. "It was your Christmas wish."

"My priorities are changing. There are more stars. I can make a new wish."

"Can I take some credit for that?"

"Well, you're an accountant. It is all in the numbers, right?"

"Yeah. Something like that. If you were to make that wish over again . . . tonight . . ." He pulled her into his arms. "Right now. What would it be?" He tipped her chin up with his fingers and kissed her. Slowly. Tenderly. Then ran his thumb across her lips. "Wish on a star."

She glanced up. "You pick the one." Her voice shook.

"Doesn't matter which one you pick. If not in the sky, then in our hearts, in our memories." He brushed his fingers over her eyes.

She closed them, relaxing with the moment.

"Tell me." His soothing voice probed further.

"I wish how I feel right this minute would never end."

Then his mouth claimed hers. "I want that wish to come true for you."

"I'm afraid."

He took her hands into his. "Don't be. I'll never hurt you on purpose. We can do this. We'll take it slowly."

"You're right. I take huge risks in business, but I don't take risks with my heart. I can't deny that, but I've fallen in love with you. And I'm afraid. Not afraid in a bad way, more nervous and excited in a really good way. Eager?"

"Excuse me? Did you say—?"

"Oh, what? I say you're right, and you just quit listening."

"No. I don't need to be right. My brain couldn't process that last part because what I thought I heard you say was you love me."

"I did," she said quietly, her lips quivering.

"I never thought I'd hear those words from those lips, and they sound so sweet. Say it again."

"I'm falling in love with you."

"You're my perfect match. You are my joy. I was afraid to believe it could happen so fast, but something my mom said the other day really hit me. She said I used to be fearless as a little boy. Fearless."

"You're not going to try to fly off the second story with a towel for a cape, are you?"

"No." He laughed. "Not today, anyway."

"Good. Because that could be dangerous."

"And if I broke my leg, I couldn't take walks with you. I want to take lots of walks with you. And runs. In the rain. Or the snow. All the time!" he exclaimed with intense pleasure.

A warning voice whispered in her head. Licking her

lips nervously, she said, "Long-distance relationships can be difficult."

"Yeah, but if it's as real as this . . . we'll figure something out."

Relief filled her. "You've touched me in a special way, about so many things. Things I thought I never wanted to feel again. Thank you for that."

He held up a hand to silence her. "Do you hear that?"

Unsure of where the sound was coming from. "The bells?"

"The bells on Christmas Eve."

Joy bit her lip to stifle a laugh. "But it's not Christmas Eve."

"Not technically, but here in Crystal Falls, we ring them in celebration of Christmas during the Crystal Christmas Cookie Crawl too. At ten. So, it's not quite midnight. On almost Christmas Eve."

The warmth of his smile echoed in his voice. "I'm trying to be romantic here. Roll with it. And you are the best part about it." Ben kissed her softly.

"And you are the reason I will love every Christmas from now on. Including the real one next week." She touched her lips to his. "Thank you for that gift."

"Excuse us," Renee said. "Sorry, someone said they saw you come back here. Is this a bad time?"

"No. I want you to meet Ben."

"Ben." Renee looked at Joy. "*The* Ben?"

Joy giggled, and Ben took her hand.

"I've heard a lot about you, Ben," Renee said.

Kevin reached out to shake Ben's hand. "Nice to meet you, man."

"Well, this looks cozy, and the girls are pooped out. We're going to head back to the inn, but I had to ask you about something before I left."

"What's that?"

"Did you ever open the envelope from Poppy?"

"No. It said wait until Christmas."

"Feels like Christmas in Crystal Falls," Renee reasoned. "Go get it."

"Okay, I'll be right back."

Joy went inside and pulled the silver envelope from her purse, where it had been ever since the day Poppy gave it to her. She carried it back downstairs and outside, where Renee and Ben were waiting. "Kevin took the girls on back to the car. They were getting cold."

"Okay, well, let's make this quick, then." She slid her finger under the flap and lifted the embossed foil sticker that held it closed. "It's not a Christmas card."

> *Dear Joy,*
>
> *Just a personal little something from me to you. Changes are abounding at Wetherton's, and we will be conducting business a bit differently than in the past. You have been an important part of our external support. A real part of the Wetherton's family and values.*
>
> *The world could use more shining stars like you in it. You sparkle from the inside and are destined for great things. I'm bringing our market research in-house. I would love you to be on my leadership team.*
>
> *I'll be announcing a new store and corporate offices opening near Charlotte, NC, on January 1. If you're up to a new challenge in your career, I hope you'll call me directly the first week of January to discuss.*
>
> *Wishing you a brilliantly shiny new year,*
> *Poppy Wetherton*

Renee squealed and grabbed both Joy's arms. "This is great! More than great. Amazing! Oh my gosh. I can't believe you have a chance to work at Poppy's side. She'd be the most amazing mentor!"

"It doesn't exactly say that." But her heart was pounding. It wasn't a sure thing, but it sure was a compliment. That meant something.

"In Charlotte? That's commuting distance," Ben added.

"Well, it's implied," Renee said. "A new opportunity. She's handpicking her winning team. And you're on it. And she trusted you with top-secret news."

Renee had a point. The leaders at MacDonald-Webber would die if they knew that she'd been walking around with this news in her purse all this time.

"We can't breathe a word of this," Joy said. "Promise me. We have to keep her secret. You can't even tell Kevin. Promise me."

"I promise. No question about it, but you have to admit this is exciting. Ruby would be happy to have you nearby. Your condo will sell in a heartbeat. Or you could rent it out. No-brainer. I'll miss you like crazy, but we can still visit."

"Or I could steal you from MacDonald-Webber."

"Now you're talking. Yes! Steal me. Do that! We make such a great team. It would be amazing. And there's another plus too."

"What's that?"

"You'd be closer to Ben." Renee nudged Ben. "Is that what you were thinking?"

"You read my mind." Ben smiled. "I might be getting exactly what I dreamed of for Christmas."

"And every Christmas to come."

Read on for an excerpt from Nancy Naigle's

HOPE AT CHRISTMAS—

now available in trade paperback
from St. Martin's Griffin!

Sydney Ragsdale pulled her car along the curb in front of the elementary school and faced her daughter with a go-get-'em-kiddo smile. "Have a wonderful day, RayAnne."

"It's school, Mom."

The eye rolling was new, starting once they'd moved here last week, and she hoped it would leave as quickly as it had arrived. As aggravating as that was, her daughter's heavy sigh tugged at Sydney's heart. The divorce had been hard on them both.

Sydney's grandparents had left her the old Hopewell farmhouse when they passed away. It was a place full of happy memories, and with the move, it felt like a life raft in a rocky sea. A fresh start for her and RayAnne.

Unfortunately, to her daughter the idea of moving from Atlanta to tiny Hopewell, North Carolina, in November, after the school year had already started, had been worse than the divorce itself.

The move had been a necessary step in Sydney's self-preservation. It wasn't easy rebuilding your life when you'd been married for most of it. She'd prayed that moving to Hopewell might turn into a great mother-daughter adventure for them, but so far that hadn't been the case.

Managing a ten-year-old with an attitude was turning

out to be harder than finding a decent job. She'd almost given up hope of finding a job at all when the call came from Peabody's a whole three months after her interview. It had been a long shot to begin with, but it was near the old farmhouse, so she'd given it her best effort. The job offer was a blessing indeed, though the timing couldn't have been worse. School had already started, and the holidays were upon them.

Sydney watched her daughter schlep up the walkway to Hopewell Elementary School. Back in Atlanta, RayAnne had been so happy that she'd practically skipped from the car to class.

Her gut twisting, Sydney wished her marriage to Jon hadn't fallen apart and that the three of them were still one big, happy family. But then that had been a big lie. Tears puddled against the frame of Sydney's sunglasses, and she was too darned tired to even sweep them away. She sucked in a long slow breath to keep her composure.

Was moving to Hopewell a mistake?

Had it been a necessary step to regain her independence, or was it just a disguise for running away?

A car honked behind her. She waved an apology as she moved forward in the drop-off lane.

As she pulled out of the parking lot, her mind clicked through happy mother-and-daughter moments she'd pictured in this quiet little town. Laughs. Love. Lasting memories.

She eased out onto the street and glanced in her rearview mirror, barely recognizing herself in the reflection. Fluffing her bangs, she tugged the rubber band from her hair to release the messy bun. "Why am I letting Jon get to me like this?" she said aloud. She stared at herself. The answer was simple. Divorce hurts. She was broken. Wounded. His infidelity had torn her in a way she wasn't sure would ever heal. And some days this was the best she could do.

She drove up to the next block and swerved into the parking lot of the Piggly Wiggly, declaring, "I'm better than this." She shut down the car and shuffled through the console for a piece of paper and a pen.

"This has to stop." So did talking to herself, but right now that was about all she had. Tomorrow. She'd stop talking to herself tomorrow.

Rather than go back to the house and feel sorry for herself, she'd make a plan. It's what she'd always done to make sure she and Jon met *his* goals. Why was she treating her life any differently?

She tapped the pen against the steering wheel, then leaned forward and started writing.

> Step One: Get a job. *Check.*
> Step Two: Get out of Dodge. *Fine. So she made it out of Atlanta. Check!!*

It never hurt to start a plan with a few easy, achievable, or *already done* tasks to get things rolling. It's why she usually had "make the bed" at the top of her chore list.

> Step Three: Get involved locally to meet some people.
> Step Four: Regain my confidence.
> Step Five: Get into the holiday spirit.
> And the Finale: Get this divorce from Jon finalized and behind me, and never put all my eggs in one man's basket again.

After months of Jon still controlling her through his purse strings even though they had separated, the generous job offer from Peabody's had enabled her to move to Hopewell and stand on her own two feet. Free of Jon's hold.

Uprooting RayAnne had been such a hard decision, but she needed to set an example for her daughter, to show her that even when dealt a cruddy hand in life, one can respond with grace, strength, and independence.

Determined to make this a day that would change her path, she made the short drive to Main Street and parked.

She got out of the car and breathed in the fresh air. It was quiet as she walked down Main Street. The retail area was only two short blocks, unless you counted the mansion that sat across the way. Well, it hadn't been a residence for as far back as she could remember. Back then it had been a bookstore called The Book Bea. Her very favorite place in town when she was a little girl.

She smiled at a memory of The Book Bea. For the longest time she'd thought the word *bee* had been misspelled on the sign in front of the bookstore. It wasn't until she'd told her grandmother she wanted to help fix the sign that she'd learned that it was a play on words. The bookstore had been named after its owner, Bea Marion.

Sydney looked both ways, which was barely necessary with the light traffic, then crossed the street.

The thick wooden sign had been sandblasted, similar to those signs on fancy beach houses on the Outer Banks. The background of the perfect oval was bright cobalt blue, just the way she remembered it. The shop name, THE BOOK BEA, stood out in 3D next to a stack of colorful books with little yellow-and-black bumblebees circling above them, looking as cheerful today as it had twenty years ago.

She took a picture of the sign with her phone. An OPEN sign hung in the window of the front door.

It's still here! she thought excitedly.

She tucked her phone back into her purse as she walked

between the perfectly shaped box hedges that flanked the sidewalk leading to The Book Bea's front door, giving it a dignified air. Winter was beginning to fade the landscape, but the grass on the other side was still thick and green, making her want to kick off her clogs and walk barefoot through it on the unseasonably warm day.

She was tempted to buy a paperback and lie in the grass and read the day away, only she needed to be frugal until her job started after the first of the year. Couldn't hurt to browse, though.

Fond memories of trips with her grandparents to the bookstore rushed back. Hours spent scouring the shelves, getting lost in those stories, and trying to make a decision on which book to buy had been both agonizing and exciting.

She climbed the stairs to the huge old turn-of-the-century house. The wide front porch was painted a playful basil green against the glossy white wooden railing, giving it a soft southern air. Rockers in various colors popped like wildflowers swaying in a gentle breeze, making it hard to believe Christmas was just around the corner.

She'd so hoped that she'd be able to share a white Christmas with RayAnne this year. It would have been her daughter's first, but it didn't look too likely. Sydney left her snow dreams behind as she pushed open the screen door and was met with a blast of cool air conditioning as she walked inside.

Her footsteps echoed against the age-old wooden floors as she headed for the bookshelves. She'd found comfort here as a young girl. Books had always rescued her, and she'd never stopped trusting a good book to bring her joy, erase her fears, and give her strength. That same excitement swirled inside her. The place even still smelled of warm cookies. Like nothing had changed.

"Good morning," a shaky voice carried across the room.

Sydney swiveled to her right. The tall wooden counter still stood in front of the bay window. A bony hand waved in the air, looking almost detached from its body, like some leftover Halloween prop.

Could Miss Bea still be working here? Sydney marveled. *She'd always sat behind that counter, where you could barely see her unless you were really looking.*

"Hi." Sydney walked toward the counter to satisfy her curiosity. "How are you today?"

"Fabulous, Darling. Always fabulous. The only way to be."

Sydney's cheeks tugged as she smiled. *Miss Bea had always said that.*

The woman stood and stepped around the counter.

There was no mistaking the tall red-haired woman. Yes, she was older, and much thinner than Sydney recalled, but the signature hair and artistic attire were one hundred percent Miss Bea. Bright lime-green reading glasses hung from a colorful strand of beads around her neck. Her long black jacket, like a duster a cowboy might have worn back in the day, swung gracefully from her shoulders to her knees.

"Welcome, dear. Are you looking for something special today?"

Memories? A safe place to get my footing back? she thought.

But Sydney could hardly answer Bea's question with either of those responses. "I need a good book to take me away for a little while."

"Ah, then you've come to the right place. The Book Bea has been doing that for years. I have all the best sellers, and some of the best-kept secrets, too." Bea raised her glasses and put them on, giving Sydney the once-over. "I was going to ask if you were passing through, but you look so familiar."

Sydney laughed. "People have always said that I favor my grandmother. I'm Carmen and Bret Rockford's granddaughter."

"Yes. That's it." Bea snapped her fingers and then pulled her hands to her hips. "I remember you. Braids and bruised knees."

"I was so clumsy back then. I grew out of that."

"Thank goodness. Used to think we should maybe bubble-wrap you."

Sydney remembered Miss Bea saying that the summer Sydney had fallen off her bike and skinned both knees.

"Bless her soul," Bea said, studying Sydney's face. "You do favor Carmen. Such a lovely woman. Your grandparents really are missed around here."

"Sydney Ragsdale now." She reached to shake Bea's hand. "I moved into their old place over on Green Needles Lane."

"I'd heard that someone was moving in there. So happy to hear that it's you. That house has been empty too long."

"I know. I had great intentions of using it as a vacation getaway after they passed, but my husband never seemed to know how to take a break."

"Well, that's not good for anyone. What changed his mind?"

"There was no changing his mind."

"He's out of the picture now, I take it." Bea *tsked*, peering over her glasses, then letting them fall to her hefty bosom.

"Yes, ma'am. Totally out of the picture."

"Well, then we'll file that history on one of the bookshelves in the back," Bea teased.

"We'd have to find a spot in the children's section for him based on the age of his new love interest."

"Ouch. Don't know what gets into men sometimes. I swear they just go crazy." Bea swept a hand in the air. "Good riddance."

Sydney wished it were that easy.

"Take a look around. Let me know if I can help you find anything." Bea walked back around the counter and sat in a plush green armchair. "And stay out of the children's section, nothing good there for you anymore. If you know what I mean."

She meant Jon, Sydney realized. *Funny.*

The rest of this town seemed smaller than she remembered, but The Book Bea still felt as big and magical as ever. The big antique cash register that had looked old when she was ten still lorded over the ornate counter and was every bit as awe-inspiring today. The intricate brass casing had to be from the early 1900s but was still polished to a glimmering shine. The glossy circular buttons on the metal-keyed arms, like an old typewriter, probably took full force to press down. But the heft of the old machine looked so sturdy and strong. Secure. And there was beauty in that.

The smell of books, knowledge, and old ink may have been in her imagination, but it all worked like some kind of happiness pheromone. Suddenly, being replaced by a young model didn't feel like an insult as much as plain idiocy on Jon's part. The next time she had a pity party over that, she'd try to remember how amazing all these aged things still were. She could be special and unique, and age with a purpose too. Thirty-something wasn't that old, but he'd made her regret it.

She wandered back toward the bookcases. Thick carpets lay in the high-traffic areas, plush beneath her feet in some places and worn to the hardwood flooring below in others from years of customers.

"I'm just going to look around a bit, if that's okay," Sydney said.

"Help yourself. No hurries in The Book Bea."

After meandering through the stacks Sydney couldn't resist picking up a few books. Finally, she headed toward the cash register, setting her selections in a neat stack there. "I remember coming to town with Gram. It took hours to run errands, but she always made time to let me pick out a book. It was the best part of the day."

"Such a nice memory."

"It is." Feeling a little dizzy from the trip down memory lane, she leaned against the counter to steady herself. "She'd hold my hand as we walked down the street. Back then Hopewell seemed like a big bustling place to me. Gram parked in the same spot right in front of Lucky's Diner. I noticed it's not there any longer."

"That old diner has been gone for years. Lucky died and seems he took his luck with him, because nothing else that's gone into that space has made a nickel."

"Too bad. I remember his fried green tomato sandwiches."

"They were delicious, but there are still good eats around here. That hasn't changed."

Sydney could use one of those yummy sandwiches about now, too. "I remembered Hopewell seeming so much bigger. Now, I think I could walk the whole town twice and still be done before lunch time."

"Hopewell is pretty much the same unless you count the new gas station and fast-food restaurant at the interstate exit. Then again, what were you? Ten or twelve years old?"

"I guess everything seems bigger when you're ten years old."

"Probably, but if it makes you feel any better, Hopewell does seem bigger in the summertime, when people are back outside and the sidewalks are busy." She smiled and with a tilt of her head, she said, "But you hold on to those childhood memories."

"I will. They're great ones." The Nancy Drew hardbacks with the yellow-gold spines were still lined up on the long shelf in her old room. She could almost feel the excitement that used to swirl inside her when Gram and Pop would bring her here to buy a new book—sometimes two—and the way she'd clung to her precious purchase on the ride home, hardly able to resist the urge to read in the car even if that always made her carsick.

"So, what besides that rat of a husband helped you land back here in Hopewell?"

"I need to make my own life, and since I had the house here it just made sense. Jon was still controlling me while he built a whole new life for himself. It was time for that to stop." Saying it out loud was a bit empowering. "I just hope my ten-year-old daughter adjusts."

"She will. You loved this town at that age. She'll see what's special about it, too. And she'll make friends."

"Sure hope so. She's not very happy with me right now."

"You'll have to bring her in. We have a children's book club on Saturday mornings. If she's half the reader you were, she'll enjoy that."

"RayAnne loves to read. Thanks, Miss Bea. I'll do that," she said, sliding her books across the counter.

"You can just call me Bea, dear." She rang up the purchase. "If there's anything I can do to help you settle in, just ask. I know everyone in this town."

Sydney rested her elbows on the tall counter. "I need to keep myself busy until I start my job after the first of the year."

"Really? What is it exactly that you do?"

Jon had never wanted her to work, so her résumé was lean.

"Well," Sydney faltered for words. "All I've ever been is a mom and a wife, but I have a business degree. I did graphic arts for my ex, but that was all freelance stuff. My work won him a couple of his biggest contracts, so I think I have something to offer there."

"Being a mother and a wife is underrated. Budgets, schedules, creativity, project planning, and patience. I'd say any good CEO should have all of that." Bea's expression was sincere.

Sydney worried that even with more than ten years in that role, raising RayAnne through all of this change and working full-time was going to be more than she was ready for, but she couldn't slip into that worrisome dark place again.

"It takes all kinds of skills to accomplish the demands on a mother. So, you must be the new hire over at Peabody's."

"I am. How did you know?"

Bea's soft grin turned up on the corners in a bit of a smirk. "Nice thing about owning The Book Bea is I get all of the scoops. The folks who own Peabody's shop here. Nice family. I heard they are doing the marketing for a new movie studio, and a boot company. Things are going really well for them. That's big news in a town like this. They're good people. You're going to love working with them."

"Thank you. Now if I can stay busy through the holidays without going crazy until I start working, then I'll be fine. My daughter is leaving as soon as school gets out to spend Christmas with her dad. It's going to be really quiet without her around."

"You know . . ." Bea pressed a finger to her lips. "I could use a little help around here."

Sydney knew that her face probably lit up like a jack-o-lantern. Hopefully not a totally goofy one, but a pleasant, smiling one.

"Don't get too excited. The pay is lousy, and the job is a little of this and that, and only through the holidays. I can add the bonus of free books, though. If you're interested."

"Really?" Sydney could really use some extra cash. She wasn't on a super-tight budget, but she needed to be careful. No matter what, there was no way she'd ask Jon for money, even if they had to resort to eating cereal for breakfast, lunch, and dinner.

"Yes. It would be a huge help."

"I'll do it," Sydney said. "Of course I will."

She felt like dancing a jig. Heck, swinging Bea in a do-si-do seemed appropriate, but she held her feet firmly to the ground. "Thank you so much. I won't let you down."

The rows and rows of bookcases held a feeling of order that was welcoming in the chaos of her life these days. And how those bookshelves seemed orderly amid the varying sizes, thicknesses, and colors of the spines was interesting. Yes, this place might just be the ticket to getting a little order in her own house.

"When can you start?" Bea asked.

"How about now? I don't have to pick up RayAnne until school lets out at three."

"Excellent." Bea pointed to the left side of the checkout counter. There was a stack of boxes labeled CHRISTMAS piled next to an artificial tree that had dust clinging to its limbs. "I've got to start decorating the store, but the arthritis has really been giving me a holy terror lately. Maybe we could start there."

"I can definitely do that," Sydney said, and then a sinking feeling settled over her as she recalled that she'd never hung a single Christmas light in her life. Not because she couldn't, but because as a kid her daddy had had that honor, and once she'd married Jon he'd always handled it. Oh well, time to step up.

Bea leaned forward and whispered. "At least I was smart enough to leave all the outside lights up at the end of the season last year. One flip of the switch and folks passing by will think we've been busy as bees in here." Bea gave Sydney a playful wink. "Bees. Bea. Get it?"

"Yes. I get it." Sydney laughed. A little too hearty as it conjured up a very unladylike snort, but it was freeing to laugh over something silly.

Yes, working here, even for just a few weeks, would be a good thing. Plus, she hadn't planned to decorate, since RayAnne would be leaving soon to stay the whole Christmas vacation with her dad.

"I'm so excited to help you out over the holidays," Sydney said.

Bea's smile spread wide, little lipstick lines dancing in the wrinkles around her lips. She clapped her hands, and then held them to her heart. "Thank you, dear. You already know the layout of the store, it's never changed since I opened it. There is a washroom and storage area just under the staircase. And a small office back there." She reached into the register and pulled out a key on a keychain with a metal enamel bee on it. "Here's a key in case you need it. This is going to be a really good way to end the year."

Sydney set her purse on the counter. Step five on Sydney's list was to get into the holiday spirit, and this seemed to be the perfect way to begin. "I should be able to make some good progress before I have to pick up RayAnne. Shall we get started?"

Bea came around the counter and pulled her into a hug. "I had a feeling today was going to be extra special. So good to see you again, Sydney."

Her mood lifted, and the tight worry was replaced with peaceful relief from her accomplishments today. And Bea's hug helped more than she'd ever know. The old woman smelled of peppermint Life Savers and sugar cookies, and her hug held the kindness that Sydney hadn't felt since the last time she'd seen Gram. "I'm glad we crossed paths today. I needed this," she said to Bea.

Bea stepped back and took Sydney's hand into hers. "I think we may have needed each other today." She led Sydney toward the front of the store. "I usually decorate this window for the holiday, but I can't crawl around like I used to. Could you come up with a display for it? The townsfolk kind of count on our decorations as part of the caroling tour."

"The caroling tour?"

"Oh yes. Each of the merchants sponsors a song. It's quite popular. Even folks from neighboring counties join in. The carolers start in front of any shop. Each storefront gives away a different song page, and we provide the music on a loop. By the end of the night each participant has a whole Christmas songbook as a keepsake."

"That sounds like fun."

"It is."

"How do you pick a song?"

"We don't pick them out ourselves. The mayor assigns them randomly the day after Thanksgiving. The town makes the song sheets up for us. They'll deliver them to us closer to the event. Mine is 'O Christmas Tree' this year."

Sydney tried to maintain a pleasant smile, but that dusty old Christmas tree she'd seen next to the counter wasn't going to cut it. Certainly not as the main feature of the window to represent the song. She was going to have to think fast. She hoped the smile she pasted over her grimace looked confident. "I'll come up with something innovative and eye-catching for the window to go with that carol."

Bea's smile softened. "We'll have to use what we've got here. I'm afraid I don't have a budget for decorations this year."

"Don't you worry about that. I have just the thing." She glanced around the room with absolutely no idea what she could do, but she wasn't about to admit defeat on hour one of her new job. "And I believe we have everything we need right here. With one exception."

"What's that?"

"I'll bring RayAnne over after school to give me a hand."

"Have her pick out a couple of books for helping."

"She'll love that. Thank you."

A set of wind chimes sent a rich, muted sound through the room. Sydney followed the sound to a set of brass tubes hanging from a wooden dragonfly sculpture above the cash register. Thin fishing line ran from the chimes just below the coffered ceiling all the way to the doorway. Clever. And way more pleasant than those door alarms so many people used in their shops.

The UPS man wheeled in a cart with two boxes on it. "Good morning, Miss Bea. Got two for you. It's been a while. Thought maybe you were cheating on me with another delivery man."

Bea giggled like a flirty teenager. "You know that would never happen. Just haven't been ordering much, but can't get through the holidays without one last shipment of Christmas books."

"You know I'll be back to pick up the missus a couple

of those Christmas novels. She counts on those in her stocking."

"And I've got the wrapping paper and ribbon just waiting on you." She gave him a playful wink.

He dropped the boxes next to the counter. "You have a good day now."

Sydney reached for the pair of scissors on the counter. "How about I go ahead and unpack these and put them on display so the customers can have at them? I'll work on the decorations after hours. Less clutter for your customers."

"You don't mind?"

"Not at all. And the decorations will be a fun mother-daughter project." Sydney unpacked the boxes, stacking the books along the edge of the counter. A small table holding ink pens and other impulse-buy items caught her eye. Those things could fit on the counter right near the register.

It didn't take long to create a nice little arrangement at the checkout, and then she got right down to work on the Christmas book display. The shiny foil covers looked pretty enough without additional decoration, but maybe she could come up with something festive once she and RayAnne figured out what they'd do for the window display.

She checked her watch. How had that much time already swept by? "Bea, I need to run and pick up RayAnne. We'll be back in a while to work on the decorations."

"Thanks, Sydney. Take your key. No need to rush. If I'm not here just make yourself at home."

Sydney suddenly fought back tears. So much had shifted since this morning. "Thank you so much, Bea, for trusting me and giving me a chance to get my feet under me before I start my new job. This is exactly what I needed. How can I ever thank you enough?"

"Don't be silly. You were meant to come in here today. Trust your journey, dear. It will take you where you're supposed to go."

"I sure hope so, because I'll tell you that the journey I've been on for the past year has not been a pleasant one."

Bea nodded. "I can tell. There's trouble in your eyes. We'll sit and talk about it one day when you're ready. But I'll say this much: Your troubles will pass and you will see that something better is ahead of you. Some*one* better, if I were to say what was really on my mind."

And hadn't she done just that? Said what she wanted to say? At least she hadn't spouted that "one door closes another opens" hogwash. Sydney didn't plan to walk through anyone's door any time soon, if ever, anyway. "I'll be glad to have the troubles pass, but I'm not looking for anyone. I've decided solo is the way to go. No heartbreak. No lies. No problem."

Bea just grinned. "Sure, dear."

So Bea was a hopeless romantic. She could believe what she wanted, but what Sydney believed was that it wouldn't hurt RayAnne one bit to see that a woman didn't need a man and that you had to work for the things you wanted.

"Tomorrow you will walk into a Christmas wonderland." Sydney picked up her purse and headed out the door feeling about three inches taller. She smiled at every tree along the path and every puffy white cloud in the sky. Wrapping her fingers around the strap of her shoulder bag, she waited at the stoplight to cross over.

As she walked to her car, she took a closer look at the other shop windows along Main Street. Her competitive nature was already shifting into high gear.

She took in a deep breath and then blew out all the negative energy, letting it seal up like a bubble and float away, just like she'd read to do in one of the books that she'd downloaded about surviving the stress of divorce.

That deep breath was the first one that felt like it might actually work. Thank goodness, because she'd tried just about everything.

Sydney walked past the bike shop, cleverly named Wheelies. The shiny bike in the window caught her eye. It would be a splurge. Probably not a smart one in their situation, but one shiny gift was all she could do, so she wanted it to be a good one. Ten minutes later she walked out of Wheelie's as the owner hung a SOLD card from the handlebars of RayAnne's Christmas present. She'd told RayAnne they'd celebrate Christmas when she got back from being with her dad. That seemed a long ways off.

Sydney wondered if the splurge would look more like a pet rock following Jon's fancy getaway. Expensive gifts were Jon's love language. Always had been, and she had no doubt he'd go overboard more than usual this year with all that was going on.

Next door, Cookie Doe, a bakery with its glass case filled with all kinds of desserts, had her mouth watering. She walked inside, and the scent of sugar and frosting and something slightly peanutty wrapped around her. She knew exactly what she was going to buy the instant she laid eyes on it.

"Three peanut butter cookies, please."

"Just took them out of the oven a little while ago. Probably still warm," said the man behind the counter.

"Doesn't get much better than that." As she waited for them to be packaged up, she turned and looked at his window display. A three-story gingerbread house filled most of it, and cookies in the shape of snowflakes hung from a wide white satin ribbon, each with shiny frosty white icing and those little BB-looking silver dragées. The window was simple and elegant.

Less is more, Sydney thought.

The man behind the counter thrust a white wax paper bag her way. She paid for the cookies then stepped outside, stopping only to snap a quick picture for inspiration before heading to her car.

On the way to the school, Sydney hoped the cookies might allow for a momentary return of her daughter's sweet attitude. Her little daddy's girl blamed her for Jon leaving them. RayAnne was mad. And hurt. And some days Sydney couldn't help but wonder how much of it *was* her own fault. If she'd only done . . .

She stopped herself. There'd be no more of that. She had been a good wife, doggone it. The divorce was not her fault, which was all the more reason for her to move on.

Trying to ease the heavy burden of worry, she shoved her hand into the bag of cookies.

At the stoplight she took a bite.

There really wasn't much a homemade peanut butter cookie couldn't make better. At least for a minute.